THE NEW BREED

THE
NEW
BREED

Book VII of *Brotherhood of War*

W. E. B. Griffin

G. P. PUTNAM'S SONS   NEW YORK

G. P. Putnam's Sons
Publishers Since 1838
200 Madison Avenue
New York, NY 10016

The New Breed was written on a Sperry PC/IT Computer using
Perfect Writer Version 2.0 and Sidekick software and
printed on a QMS, Inc. "KISS" Laser Printer.

Library of Congress Cataloging-in-Publication Data

Griffin, W. E. B.
  The new breed.

  (Brotherhood of war ; Bd. 7)
    1. Zaire—History—Civil War, 1960-1965—Fiction.
I. Title.   II Series: Griffin, W. E. B. Brotherhood
of war ; Bd. 7.
PS3557.R489137B7 Bd. 7   813′.54 s   87-10570
ISBN 0-399-13305-4   [813′.54]

Typeset by Fisher Composition, Inc.

Printed in the United States of America
1   2   3   4   5   6   7   8   9   10

For Uncle Charley and The Bull
RIP October 1979

And for Donn
Who would have ever believed *four* stars?

And for Sp4 J.S.B. II
Alabama Army National Guard

I

[ONE]
The White House
Washington, D.C.
12 December 1963

L YNDON BAINES JOHNSON, the President of the United States, was sitting on a small couch in the Oval Office. Following the assassination of John Fitzgerald Kennedy twenty days before, Johnson had acceded to the presidency. This was enough time for Johnson to grow to like what he was doing.

The President was holding a squat glass dark with Kentucky sour mash bourbon whiskey. He had removed his jacket, revealing that he held up his trousers with suspenders. And he had draped his arm on the back of the couch and his right leg on the cushion.

Walter Cronkite, reporting the "Evening News," spoke of events that caused the President of the United States to shake his head and mutter an obscenity. And then the CBS Broadcasting System paused for the delivery of a commercial message.

As the President raised his bourbon to his mouth, the door to the Oval Office opened.

"Colonel Felter, Sir," the President's secretary announced.

She had been watching the CBS news on a small television in her office, not so much in order to pay attention to the news but to watch for a commercial. The President would prefer not to be interrupted while the news was on the screen.

The President looked over his shoulder at the open door.

An Army officer stood there almost but not quite at attention. He wore a green uniform, and his leather-brimmed cap was under his left arm. Silver colonel's eagles were on his epaulets; a Combat Infantry Badge was over his breast pocket; beneath that were the wings of a parachutist; and below those were four rows of colored ribbons, three ribbons to a row. There was another set of parachutist's wings (which the President correctly guessed to be French) on the other breast pocket, together with the American and Korean Presidential Unit Citations. Below the pocket was the insignia which indicated the wearer had completed a tour of duty with the General Staff Corps of the United States Army.

The Colonel stood five feet seven inches tall, was in an advanced stage of male pattern baldness, and weighed 148 pounds.

He was carrying an attaché case. It was obviously well traveled, and in several places the leather had been gouged and torn, exposing the aluminum under the leather.

It was the first time the President had ever seen Colonel Sanford T. Felter in uniform. When Kennedy became President, Johnson had noticed Felter now and again around the White House, but had then dismissed him as just one more baggy-suited intellectual, a specialist of some kind on the outer edges of Jack Kennedy's staff. But he had soon sensed there was more to Felter than what showed. Felter was more even than just another soldier "loaned" to the White House by the Defense Department. For one thing, Bobby Kennedy hated Felter's ass—as only Bobby Kennedy could hate anyone's ass; and that meant that Felter had to have Jack Kennedy's protection. Otherwise he would have been long gone.

When Johnson finally had a chance to ask Jack Kennedy what Felter did, the President had smiled and said he "runs errands for me," which was the same thing as saying, "None of your fucking business, Lyndon." This had not been the first question asked by the Vice President of the United States that the President had chosen not to answer.

It was only after Dallas and the funeral that Johnson had learned what kind of errands Colonel Felter had run for the President of the United States.

"I'll be damned," the President said when Felter's presence had sunk in. Then he raised his voice: "Come in, Felter. Help yourself to a drink."

"Good evening, Mr. President," Colonel Felter said and came into the room.

"Help yourself," the President repeated. "It's over there. You'll remember where."

Felter filled a glass with ice cubes and then poured it half full of vodka.

"What is that, a martini?" the President asked, a hint of disapproval in his Texas-accented voice.

"No, Sir," Colonel Felter said. "Vodka over ice."

"A drink ought to have color in it," the President said, shaking his massive head. "But go ahead. Sit," he ordered, indicating the matching chair beside his couch.

"Thank you, Sir," Colonel Felter said.

A quartet of men in service station uniforms finished their vocal entreaty to CBS's viewers to trust their cars to the men who wore Texaco Stars. Then Walter Cronkite's face reappeared on the screen.

Finally he announced, "And that's the way it is. . . ."

The President picked up a remote-control device and aimed it at the television screen as if it were a pistol intended to shoot the head off a rattlesnake. The screen went blank.

The President stood up, and Felter started to do the same.

"Keep your seat," the President said. "I can pour my own drink."

"Yes, Sir," Colonel Felter said.

"The reason I'm alone in here, Felter," the President said, "is that most people feel they have to say something whenever Cronkite pauses for breath. And if I watch it upstairs, Mrs. Johnson feels she has to say something to keep me from getting bored."

"Yes, Sir," Colonel Felter said.

"Unless you want another drink," the President said as an afterthought.

"Thank you, Sir," Felter said, and got up and walked to the bar and poured more vodka over his ice.

"You like the way that tastes?" the President asked dubiously.

"I don't like the way any of it tastes, Sir," Felter said.

The President laughed.

"You just want a little liquid courage, is that it?"

"Yes, Sir. More or less."

"I scare you, do I?"

"No, Sir."

"Does the Attorney General scare you, Felter?"

"No, Sir."

"I suppose you've suspected he doesn't like you?"

"I have that feeling, yes, Sir," Felter said.

"Story going around is that President Kennedy, with just the three of you there, told L'il Bobby that the reason he had it in for you was that you were smarter than him, and that the both of you knew it. True story?"

"Essentially, Sir," Felter said. "Secretary Rusk was also present, Sir."

"Why did you wait until now to come home, Felter? Why didn't you hop on the next plane out of Saigon when the thing in Dallas happened?"

"I hadn't completed my mission, Sir," Felter said.

"That's it? It wasn't that you didn't want to get splattered when the shit hit the fan around here?"

"I presumed, Sir, in the absence of orders from you to the contrary, that I was to complete the mission that President Kennedy had given me."

"And I guess you have? You're back."

"Yes, Mr. President."

"Everybody around here is—or pretends to be—a little vague about what you were doing over there, Felter."

"I have my reports, Sir," Felter said. He laid the attaché case on the coffee table, worked its two combination locks, and opened it. He took two envelopes from it, one letter size and the other a large manila envelope. He handed the smaller envelope to the President.

"That's what I was able to find out about the death of President Ngo Dinh Diem, Sir," Felter said. "I thought you would prefer to see that first."

The President ripped open the envelope, put half glasses on the edge of his nose and read the first couple of lines.

Then he raised his eyes to Felter. "I thought maybe that was it," the President said, "that he sent you over there to see who really shot who and why."

Felter nodded but said nothing.

"So what have you got to tell me about the can of worms in Vietnam?" the President said, making a "come-on" gesture with his left hand.

"On 1 November 1963, Mr. President," Felter said, "the Presidential Palace in Saigon was surrounded by troops unfriendly to President Ngo Dinh Diem. After the President discovered he was unable to contact Colonel Nomg, the commander of the troops charged with his protection, he realized that he was in substantial danger of being deposed in a military coup. He and his brother, Ngo Dinh Nhu, then escaped from the palace by secret tunnel. I believe it was their intention to reach a parachute regiment, whose commander he believed to be loyal to him; but he was unable to do so. He and his brother then took refuge in a private villa. The next day, 2 November, Colonel Nomg, accompanied by a body of troops, came to the villa and offered the Diems protective custody until such time as either the coup could be controlled or that there was no question that it had succeeded. In the latter case, Nomg guaranteed Diem safe passage out of the country. He offered an APC—"

"A what?"

"An M-113 armored personnel carrier. It is a tracked vehicle that looks much like a tank—"

"Go on," the President interrupted again impatiently.

"Colonel Nomg offered the President and his brother the APC and a detachment of troops to take them to the barracks of the parachute regiment," Felter went on. "They accepted. Shortly after leaving the villa, the rear door of the APC was opened, and the President and his brother were assassinated. They were shot to death."

"This Colonel Whatsisname betrayed them, in other words?"

"Colonel Nomg was acting under orders, Mr. President," Felter said. "My report offers several possible scenarios as to who issued those orders, and for what reasons. There is, of course, no proof."

The President dropped his eyes to Felter's report and read it through. Twice, his bushy eyebrows rose in obvious surprise. Finally, he looked at Felter again, over the half glasses.

"So, according to this, we don't know who the fuck is in charge over there in 'Nam. But whoever it is, it's not our guy."

"No, Sir."

"Goddamn. Where I came from, when we buy some politician he stays bought."

"Things are a bit different in Saigon, Sir."

"And you're also telling me Bobby Kennedy didn't know why Jack Kennedy sent you over there?"

"There have been missions about which I believe President Kennedy kept his own confidence, Mr. President," Felter replied. "Very possibly this is one of them."

"What about you, Felter? Who do you share your knowledge with? Who has seen this?" He waved the report.

"There is one copy, Sir," Felter said. "You have it. No one else has seen it."

The President folded the four sheets of paper and put them back into the envelope.

"No one else will, Felter," the President said. "This report doesn't exist. You read me loud and clear?"

"Yes, Sir."

"Who typed this?" the President said, suddenly suspicious.

"I did, Sir. And the ribbon has been burned."

"OK. I heard you were very good at what you do. I guess you are."

"Thank you, Mr. President," Felter said.

The President chuckled.

"I'm almost afraid to ask," he said, nodding at the thick manila envelope, "but what's that?"

"My report on the situation in Southwest Africa, Sir. I was there before I went to South Vietnam."

"You do get around, don't you, Colonel?" the President said, and gestured for the envelope. When Felter handed it to him, he tore it open and took out a nearly inch-thick stack of paper, bound together with a metal fastener.

"Don't tell me you typed all this by yourself?"

"No, Sir," Felter said. "I have a very good secretary."

"Then I can presume this isn't as dangerous as the other one?" Johnson said and started to flip through it. "Christ, I'm not going to read all this tonight!"

Felter started to speak, then changed his mind. The President's eyes flashed at him. "Go ahead," he said.

"Sir, it is my judgment that the situation in the Congo is potentially as dangerous to the United States as is the situation in Vietnam."

"I doubt that," the President said.

"May I speak freely, Sir?"

"As long as you're quick," the President said with a smile, holding up the thick and heavy report.

Felter thought a moment before speaking.

"General MacArthur's belief that we should not get involved in a war on the Asian Land Mass is being frequently quoted these days," Felter said. "I believe he would say the same thing about Southern Africa or, for that matter, specifically about the Congo, and for much the same reasons."

"Well, so what? I don't think anyone is thinking about our getting into a war in Africa."

Felter did not reply.

"Speak your mind, damn it!"

"I believe there is a very real possibility, Mr. President, that the well-intentioned granting of independence to the African nations, especially to the Congo, may result in a chaotic situation which our adversaries, especially the Chinese communists, are prepared to exploit. I believe, Sir, that the Chinese are in fact very actively engaged in creating that chaos, and that their efforts will intensify as they come to believe they can succeed. I believe their first major effort will be directed against the ex–Belgian Congo."

"Like how?"

"An army of liberation," Felter said. "Supplied and controlled by them, and directed against a government almost pathetically unprepared to cope with such a threat. And the last of the United Nations troops, as ineffective as they are, will leave the Congo 30 June."

"Pathetically?"

"There were thirty college graduates in all of the Congo before independence, Mr. President," Felter said. "The previous military experience of Colonel Mobutu, who heads their military, was as a corporal in the Force Publique, a paramilitary Belgian officered police force."

"That's not what I hear from State and the CIA," the President said sharply. He looked at Felter, coldly thoughtful, for a long moment. "You sound like Senator Goldwater, I suppose you know?"

"I don't know what you mean, Sir."

"He gave a speech where he said the first thing he would do if he were President—and he's going to get the nomination, you can bet your ass on that—he said the first order he would give as President would be to our people in the Congo: 'Change sides.' You didn't pick up on that?"

"I've been out of the country, Sir."

"Yeah, sure. Well, nobody ever accused Barry Goldwater of being stupid. I guess I'm just going to have to find out for myself what the hell is going on over there."

He went to the whiskey and half filled his glass.

"You know, *Colonel*," the President said, turning to Felter, "this is the first time I've ever seen you in your uniform. Not that I'm not impressed with all your decorations, but you could have saved the effort. Yours was one of the first dossiers I told Mr. Hoover to fetch for me."

"I presumed, Sir, that on President Kennedy's death, or certainly on my return from Saigon—"

"That you'd go back to the Army?" the President interrupted. "You want to go? Is that what the uniform and all your medals is all about?"

"I had hoped that I might be given a command, Mr. President," Colonel Felter said. "I'm eligible for one."

"You're supposed to be smart. That doesn't sound like it. There's a lot of people in the Army—hell, all over the Pentagon—who hate your ass. They're not going to give you a command, Felter. They'd send you to some forgotten fort in Arkansas and bury you until you got the message and retired."

"I was gathering my courage, Mr. President, to ask you for a recommendation," Colonel Felter said.

"With the vodka?" the President chuckled.

"I've never asked for a favor before, Sir."

"Then you're the only sonofabitch around here who hasn't. What kind of a favor?"

"Mr. President, there is a program in the Army, because of a shortage of senior officers, where officers of my grade are being sent to flight school."

"What makes you think they'd have you? That they don't hate your ass?"

"Sir, Major General Bellmon commands the Aviation Center at Fort Rucker. He and I are old friends."

"How can he afford you as a friend? General Taylor, when I asked him about you, said they hate your ass so much in the Pentagon that the President had to send your name to the Senate for promotion to colonel by himself; they weren't going to do it."

"Sir, during War Two General Bellmon was a POW. I was privileged to be with the unit which liberated him."

"According to Max Taylor, it was the Russians you liberated him from, not the Germans. Taylor told me you found where the Russians had him," the President said, "and then led the rescue column that went after him. If it wasn't for you, Bellmon would be in Siberia someplace cutting trees down with a dull ax."

Felter didn't reply.

"Is there something personal in this, Felter? You don't want to work for me?"

"Sir, I'm a soldier."

"And you want to go get shot at? You've been shot at before. And hit. How many clusters is that on your Purple Heart?"

"Four, Sir."

"You didn't answer my question. Is there some reason you don't want to work for me?"

"If I don't get a command in the near future, Mr. President, I'll never get one."

"The Army's not short of colonels qualified to lead regiments, or fly airplanes," the President said. "Your Commander-in-Chief is short of people with your qualifications. It's as simple as that."

"Yes, Sir," Colonel Felter said.

"OK," the President said. He leaned over and pressed one of the buttons on the telephone on the low table beside the couch.

His secretary appeared a moment later in the doorway.

"Honey," the President said, extending the smaller of Felter's envelopes to her, "without reading this, put it in an envelope, stamp it 'Presidential—Eyes Only' and then put it in my personal file."

"Yes, Mr. President," she said.

"Next, did you find what I told you to look for—about Colonel Felter?"

"Yes, Mr. President. The Attorney General had it. It was with President Kennedy's personal papers."

"You want to get it, please?"

She came in the office a moment later with a small sheet of paper in her hands and handed it to the President. He put his half glasses on and read it.

"I never saw this before," he said. "I heard about it. But I never saw it. I wonder why that was?" He handed the sheet of paper to Felter.

THE WHITE HOUSE
Washington

April 24, 1961

Colonel Sanford T. Felter, GSC, USA, is appointed my personal representative to the Intelligence Community, with rank as Counselor to the President. He will be presumed to have The Need To Know insofar as any classified information is concerned. No public announcement of this appointment will be made.

John F. Kennedy

"That wording all right, Felter? If you want it changed, now's the time to speak up."

"The wording is fine, Mr. President," Felter said.

"Who had copies of it?"

"The Secretaries of State, Defense, Treasury," the President's secretary began, "all the services, plus the Directors of CIA, FBI, DIA . . ." She stopped when the President's raised hand shut her off.

"Anybody not on that list that should be?" the President asked.

"No, Sir," Felter said.

"Do it again over my signature," he ordered. "Is there somebody around who can do it right now?"

"Yes, of course, Mr. President," his secretary said.

"Well, then, have it done. And see that they're delivered tonight. What did that guy say, *'the medium is the message'*? Make sure the Attorney General gets his personally. Take it out to his house, if necessary."

"Yes, Mr. President," his secretary said. She went to Felter and retrieved the letter and left the office.

The President picked up the thick report. He looked at Felter. "We understand each other, Colonel?"

"Sir?"

"I'm going to read this thing tonight. Or as soon as I can. I'll call you back in when I have. But—presuming when I read it, I don't decide you're crazy—Africa, the Congo, that's your assignment. I don't want to be surprised by what might happen over there."

"Yes, Sir."

"I did understand you to say you were there before you went to Vietnam?"

"Yes, Sir."

"Then, considering what happened in Dallas, I think you better go back and see how that's changed things."

"Yes, Sir."

"Very quietly, you understand, Felter? I don't want McCone or Rusk coming in here and wringing their hands about you."

"I understand, Mr. President," Felter said.

"Is there some way you could sneak in? Visit the Military Attaché or something?"

"I'm sure there is, Sir."

[TWO]
Langley, Virginia
14 December 1963

THE DEPUTY DIRECTOR for Liaison, who was the man who handled the CIA's dealings with other governmental agencies, disliked but grudgingly admired Sanford T. Felter. Felter neither liked nor admired the Deputy Director for Liaison. He thought the man was nothing but a clerk who had made it to his Deputy Director's job by doing nothing wrong, and who had done nothing wrong because he had taken no chances. In Felter's personal mental file of brief assessments of his professional associates, J. Edward Winton was a "fucking bureaucrat."

"Sandy," J. Edward Winton said, coming around from behind his large wooden desk with a smile on his face and his hand extended, "Good to see you!"

Physically, Winton was an impressive man. He was large but trim. He had all his teeth and an attractive display of silver-streaked curly hair. His suit was well cut, his tasseled loafers brilliantly shined, and his shirt collar immaculately cut and laundered.

Felter was wearing a baggy gray suit. His shoes were scuffed, and there were white marks near the soles where they had been soaked in salty slush and then dried. His tie was visibly not new, and his shirt collar had started to fray.

"Ed, how are you?" Felter said. Winton tried to crush Felter's hand and failed. There was not much to Sanford T. Felter, but what there was was hard.

"Actually, I was thinking of calling you," Winton said.

"Oh?"

"You ever consider coming out here? There's a lot of places where you could easily fit in."

Felter tried to see behind the question. When he could not, he asked, "What brought that up?"

"Well, what are you going to do now?" Winton asked.

The question was now explained. Felter wondered why he hadn't understood immediately.

"Now that what?" he asked innocently.

"For Christ's sake, Stan!"

"Oh, you mean Kennedy," Felter said. "I've been hearing that you guys terminated him. Anything to that?"

"Goddamn it, Felter, that's not even remotely amusing!"

"I take it that's a no?"

"What can I do for you, Felter?"

"I want a look at all the files, including the personnel files, on everything you've got going in the Congo."

"Which Congo?"

"I was about to say ex–Congo Belge," Felter said. "But I suppose I had better look at both ex-Belge and ex-French. Plus everything you've developed on the Chicoms in Rwanda and Burundi."

Winton smiled and nodded his understanding. Then he asked, "On what authority?"

"The usual," Felter said.

"Didn't that authority end when—"

"Kennedy was shot?" Felter interrupted. "Possibly, but I'm now working for Johnson. Same job."

"Stan, I don't have anything on that," Winton said. "Nothing's come down to me."

His face and tone of voice indicated general regret that he couldn't be helpful, but Felter suspected that Winton was really enjoying himself. Felter believed that bureaucrats took great satisfaction in being able to use their authority to say no.

"Call him," Felter said.

There was no question in Winton's mind that Felter meant the Director of the Central Intelligence Agency. His smile vanished for a moment, returned, and then he picked up a white telephone, one of three phones on his desk. One of the others was a multibutton affair, standard issue for CIA bureaucrats of a certain level. The other was red. It was one of perhaps a hundred telephones in the Washington area on what was called the White House net. When the President wanted to talk to someone, he used the White House net. Having one of the red telephones was a matter of great bureaucratic prestige, even if it never rang. Felter had two red telephones on the White House net, one in his small office high in the Old State-War-and-Navy Building adjacent to the White House and another beside his bed in his "townhouse" in Alexandria. Under Presidents Eisenhower and Kennedy both had rung frequently, and the one by his bed had already rung under President Johnson.

The President had called him the night before to tell him that he had spoken to the Secretary of State and explained the problem of Felter's cover to him, and the Secretary had agreed to include Felter on a group of State Department functionaries about to leave for the ex–Congo Belge on some administrative mission.

"You can take the missus with you, Felter," the President said. "Give her a little VIP vacation on the taxpayers. And it'll make you look legitimate."

Felter was beginning to suspect that the President was interested in the world of intelligence, and that he was going to be "helpful" in the future. It could be a problem.

"Is the Director in? J. Edward Winton here," Winton said to the white telephone, which was on the CIA version of the White House net. Felter had a white telephone on his desk in the old State-War-and-Navy Building, too. But when he used it, he got the Director on the line. Not his secretary.

Winton listened to the reply, said "thank you," politely, and hung up. "The Director's at the White House," he said.

"Well, I've got to go over to State, too," Felter said. "So that's not an overwhelming problem. When he gets back, Ed, I'd be grateful if you'd check with him and get this authority business straight in your mind once and for all, and then send someone over to my office with the files."

"Of course," J. Edward Winton said. "I'm sure you understand my position, Stan. You know how the Director is."

"Yes, I certainly do," Felter said. "But if there's any problem about this, Ed—I need this stuff today—call me so I can get it straightened out, will you?"

"Absolutely."

They shook hands and smiled at each other. Then Felter left the Deputy Director for Liaison's office and got in his battered and wheezing Volkswagen and headed back for the District of Columbia.

There was no doubt in his mind that the moment he'd walked out of the office, J. Edward Winton had called his counterpart at the State Department and warned him that Felter was en route; and more important that Felter had just been in his office and announced that he had been reappointed under President Johnson to the job he'd held under Kennedy. J. Edward Winton's counterpart at State was another fucking bureaucrat, and fucking bureaucrats had remarkably similar—and predictable—behavior patterns, one of which was that they took care to scratch each other's backs.

Felter drove to the FBI, not to the State Department. He knew there would be no trouble at the FBI about his access to whatever he wanted to see. And when he didn't show up at State when he was supposed to, J. Edward Winton's credibility would be lessened.

And he was sure that when he got to his office in the Old State-War-and-Navy Building, there would be a neatly dressed man from the Company sitting there waiting for him, with a briefcase stuffed with the material he had asked for.

II

[ONE]
Albertville, Democratic Republic of the Congo
14 December 1963

AIR SIMBA FLIGHT Number 104, Captain Jacques Emile Portet at the controls, made its approach to the Albertville airfield over Lake Tanganyika. The descent was shallow, as was the bank when Air Simba 104 turned on final. Low and slow, in pilot's cant.

Air Simba Flight Number 104 was a Curtiss Commando, a twin-engine, propeller-driven transport aircraft that was as at least as old as its captain, who was four months shy of twenty-two years.

Indeed, the pilot's father, Captain Jean-Philippe Portet, who owned Air Simba, harbored a strong suspicion that he had flown the very same aircraft over the Himalayas—"Over the Hump"—in 1943, when he had been a captain in the U.S. Army Air Corps.

There was a suspicious crease in the aluminum of the Commando's wing root, a groove about an inch deep and five feet long. Jean-Philippe Portet remembered a similar crease from long ago. After he'd landed a C-46 Commando loaded with fifty-five-gallon drums of aviation gasoline in the rain at Chunking, the plane had been backed into by a truck driven by an enthusiastic but not too skillful Chinese ally. The wing root had been creased, but it had been determined that the damage was superficial, so the skin had not been replaced.

It was certainly possible that the creased wing root had been examined by others in the ensuing twenty years and that they had all reached the same conclusion: that the crease posed no hazard to flight. So, following the hoary adage, "If it ain't broke, don't fix it," they all let the crease stay the way it was. Captain Jean-Philippe Portet had seen a number of interesting coincidences in his life, and he believed this was another one of them.

In the current Air Simba incarnation of the Curtiss, a stylized lion, leaping, was painted on the fuselage. Above that was the legend AIR SIMBA. This logotype was repeated on the vertical stabilizer. The aluminum skin of the airplane gleamed where the insignia and identification numbers had been painted, but elsewhere the skin was dull, and there were remnants of previous paint jobs and other identification numbers.

Air Simba itself was a new airline. And it had only recently come into possession of the airplane, so there had not yet been time to do much more to it than to see that the aircraft was safe for flight and to add the logotype and Democratic Republic of the Congo identification number. Whenever the Commando landed at Leopoldville for an overnight stop—and there was time left after all the necessary maintenance—service stands were rolled against the fuselage, and barefooted Congolese attacked the grime and old paint with Brillo pads. Eventually the whole aircraft would gleam. Now it was more important to put the plane to work.

The pilot of Air Simba Flight 104, Captain Jacques Emile Portet, had made a low and slow approach to Albertville both because, like his father Jean-Phillipe Portet, he was by nature a cautious pilot, and also because he had a 1963 MGB and a couple of heavy crates (as well as lighter cargo) lashed to the floor of the cabin. He did not place a good deal of faith in the structural integrity of the fuselage floor. And there had not been time since Air Simba acquired the aircraft to really have the cabin floor properly inspected and if necessary replaced. There were no facilities in the ex–Congo Belge to magnaflux large pieces of aluminum. Or for that matter, small pieces of aluminum.

Captain Jacques Emile Portet was blond headed, fair skinned, and large boned. He was wearing a light-blue sleeveless sweater over a white, button-down-collar shirt. His tie was pulled down and his feet on the rudder pedals were clad in scuffed loafers.

First Officer Enrico de la Santiago was black haired, swarthy skinned, and slight of build. He was wearing a khaki shirt and trousers. The shirt had once borne the insignia of a captain in the pre-Castro Cuban Air Force.

Captain Portet and First Officer de la Santiago comprised the entire flight crew of Air Simba Flight 104. There was supposed to be a third man, a flight engineer, but that would have meant another paycheck for Air Simba, and in the opinion of Captain Jean-Philippe Portet, who had often done so himself, the aircraft could be safely flown without one.

Captain Portet *fils* set the Curtiss smoothly on the ground, and then engaged the brakes very judiciously, using up almost all of the runway before he came to a stop, turned, and then started back to the Albertville Terminal. He didn't want the forces of deceleration to rip the heavy crates, or the shiny new 1963 MGB, loose from the cabin floor.

When, with an effort, Portet and de la Santiago had shoved the large cargo door on the left rear of the fuselage open and dropped the aluminum stairs out, a tall, tanned, heavyset man in a Stetson (of the kind favored by Lyndon B. Johnson) walked from a Jeep station wagon to the airplane and waited for them to climb down. The man's name was K. N. Swayer.

There was a representation of an oil well drilling rig on the Jeep's door, and the legend UNIT RIG TULSA. K. N. Swayer was Unit Rig's boss in Albertville.

"How they hanging, Jack?" K. N. Swayer said, enthusiastically shaking Captain Portet's hand.

"One lower than the other," Captain Portet replied. "Say hello to Enrico de la Santiago."

"Pleased to meet you," K. N. Swayer said, pumping the Cuban's hand. And then nodding toward the airplane, he asked, "Jack, you bring it?"

"It and the Christmas trees," Captain Portet said. "I feel like Santa Claus."

Captain Jacques Emile Portet's English was American accented: He was a Belgian-American. He had passports from both countries, both of which said that he had been born in St. Louis, Missouri, USA, on June 6, 1942, which meant that he was some five months shy of his twenty-second birthday. His Belgian passport further identified him as an *aviateur*, a pilot. The Belgian passport was nearly new, and when he'd had it renewed, he'd shown the clerks his pilot's license (Commercial; Instrument; Multiengine Land; and Helicopter, Commercial) and had them put *aviateur* in the "Profession" block. Previously it had said *"étudiant."* His American passport, not yet due for renewal, still read "student," but that was no longer true. The faculty of the Free University of Brussels had the previous June bestowed upon him a degree in history.

"The Christmas trees?" K. N. Swayer asked incredulously. "Already? What the fuck am I supposed to do with them?"

"How big is your freezer?" Captain Portet asked dryly.

Unit Rig Corporation of Tulsa, Oklahoma, had sold Union Minière, the Belgian conglomerate which operated most of the tin and copper mining operations in the ex–Congo Belge, well over a hundred million dollars' worth of outsized earth-moving trucks. Final payment was to be made only when the trucks were delivered and running in various locations in the Congo, including Albertville.

Moving the trucks by road from the port of Matadi, on the Atlantic Coast, to where they would be used was impossible for a number of reasons, and the assembled trucks were too large to be carried on what rail lines were available. It had thus been decided to build and test the trucks in Tulsa, then to break them down into manageable pieces and fly them to the Congo for reassembly. K. N. Swayer was the Supervising Engineer.

Despite the high pay and generous company benefits it offered its employees on the Congo Job, Unit Rig was having a morale problem. Some of this problem was based on the brutal Congolese climate and some of it on the isolation. Air-freighting a ton of Christmas trees from the State of Washington to various sites in the Congo was one of many gestures of company concern and goodwill toward its employees, and so was the air-freighting in of the 1963 MGB for Supervising Engineer K. N. Swayer.

With Jack Portet on his heels, Swayer climbed the aluminum ladder into the cabin of the Curtiss and walked to the glistening red sports car.

"Jesus, isn't that the cutest little fucker you ever saw?" Swayer said to Jack Portet.

"Adorable," Jack said. "All the Maniema maidens will be competing for a ride." The maidens of the Maniema tribe, the predominant tribe in the area, were not noted for their beauty.

"Fuck you, Jack," Swayer said amiably. "How are we going to get it off of here?"

"I put it on with a forklift," Jack Portet said.

"You didn't scratch it?" Swayer asked with concern, and bent over to look.

"I wrapped the whatchamacallits with rope," Jack replied, miming the forks with his index fingers.

"The forks," Swayer said tolerantly. "That's why they call them forklifts."

"*Fork*lifts," Jack said. "*Fork*lifts. I thought it was spelled F.U."

Swayer laughed. "Who's the Mexican?" he said.

"Cuban," Jack said. "He used to be in the Cuban Air Force. My father hired him in Brussels. His family couldn't get out."

"Jesus!" Swayer said. "What we should have done was drop the 82nd Airborne in on Havana and then we should have shoved a Garand bayonet up that bearded spic's ass. Goddamn Kennedy anyhow."

"Which Kennedy?"

"All of them," Swayer said. And then he looked around the cabin and walked to a bundle of wire and canvas wrapped Christmas trees.

"There's ten in a bundle," Jack Portet said. "I figured that one bundle would be enough for here."

"Where's the others?"

"In the meat reefer in Leopoldville."

"You think they'll keep in a reefer?"

"I don't think it will do them any harm."

Swayer walked to the door of the airplane and made a gesture to the station wagon. A tall, slim Congolese walked to the airplane and climbed aboard. He was wearing a white shirt and a necktie, which were symbols that he had gone to school and had non-physical-labor employment.

He exchanged a few words in French with Jack Portet, and they shook hands.

Swayer pointed to the bundled Christmas trees.

"You think they'll fit in the station wagon?"

"Yes, Sir," he said.

"Well, get a couple of boys and load them up and take them to the hotel and tell Whatsisname . . ."

"M'sieu Gorrain?"

"Right," Swayer said. "Gorrain. Tell him I would consider it a personal favor if he could keep the trees in his reefer until it's time to pass them out."

"Yes, Sir."

A half dozen Congolese climbed into the plane. They were barefoot and barechested, and there were far more of them than was necessary. Chattering animatedly, they manhandled the bundled Christmas trees off and into the hands of half a dozen more Congolese.

Jack Portet laughed delightedly and said, "Noel, Noel."

"What's so funny?" Swayer asked as he dropped to his knees to inspect the webbing holding the MGB in place.

"Your interpreter told them what they were going to do with the 'scrawny little trees.' They at first wouldn't believe him. Even granting that the Americans are crazier than the Belgians, the head boy said no one would really store firewood in a refrigerator."

Swayer was more interested in his MGB.

"What did you do with the rope?"

"Just wrapped it around the *forks*," Jack said.

"That it over there?" Swayer asked, pointing to a coil of rope.

"Air Simba strives to please." Jack picked up the coil of rope and stepped to the door. He ordered, with gestures and in fluent Swahili, that it be wrapped around the prongs of a forklift.

"Christ, I wish I could speak it," Swayer said. "I don't understand two goddamned words of it. I been all over the world, and this is the first time I haven't been able to learn any of it."

"You got to be raised here," Jack Portet said. "I got mine from my nurse and the houseboys."

"I suppose."

"Before you loosen the tie-downs," Jack Portet ordered, "make sure the parking brake is on."

Five minutes later the MGB was gently lowered to ground by the forklift, with K. N. Swayer at its controls.

And five minutes after that the three heavy wooden crates that had made up the difference between what the MGB and the Christmas trees weighed and the maximum lift capacity for Curtiss Commando aircraft had been off-loaded.

"Stick around, Jack," Swayer said. "Not only will I buy you dinner, but I'll take you for a ride in my new car."

"No," Jack replied, "thanks, but I want to see if I can't at least make Bukavu before the rain starts."

"Fuck it—stay over and leave early in the morning."

"Somebody I want to see in Bukavu if I can."

"Give her my regards."

"I will."

"You horny little bastard you," Swayer said admiringly.

"I have the strength of ten, because in my heart I'm pure," Jack Portet said piously. He looked at First Officer de la Santiago. "You want to fly the next leg, Enrico? You think you can get this bucket of bolts off the ground?"

"I'll check the weather," de la Santiago said quickly and started for the terminal building. Swayer started to say something, but saw the look on Jack Portet's face and stopped.

When de la Santiago was out of sight, Jack Portet said, "One of several things is going to happen. Either the *chef d'aérodrome* is not going to be there. Or he will be there and be drunk. Or he will be there and be sober and not have the foggiest idea of the weather, the telephones being 'temporarily' out of service again. I think he should learn that himself."

Ten minutes later Air Simba Flight 104, with First Officer de la Santiago at the controls, took off from Albertville, bound for Bukavu.

"Not really for Bukavu, Enrico," Jack Portet explained. "There's no airport in Bukavu. The airport's called Kamembe, and it's in Rwanda, which is on the east side of the Ruzizi River."

De la Santiago smiled at the strange names.

"But it does have an ADF?" he asked, referring to an automatic direction finder, a radio transmitter constantly broadcasting a three-letter Morse Code identification on which aircraft home in.

"It does," Portet replied. "KAM. But it's usually temporarily out of service."

De la Santiago examined the aerial navigation chart in his lap.

"In other words just fly up the lake?"

"Keeping well to the left of the center," Portet said. "The border runs right down the center of the lake."

"Between what countries?"

"Between the Congo and Tanganyika, then between the Congo and Rwanda, and finally between the Congo and Burundi."

"But if we're going to land in"—de la Santiago hesitated and then managed to come up with a Spanish-flavored approximation of Burundi—"what's the difference?"

"The difference is that this is Africa," Jack Portet explained. "And we would not want to give the Burundi Minister of Air the idea that we are the vanguard of an aerial invasion force."

De la Santiago looked at him and saw he was serious.

"Not that I would bet that all the parts are in the fighter aircraft of the Burundi Air Force, and that they could actually get one in the air, but this is Africa, and strange things happen here."

De la Santiago smiled and shook his head.

"There's something else I have to discuss with you," Portet said. "Something of a delicate nature."

"What's that?"

"Presuming we can find Kamembe, and that there's somebody there to meet us, and that we can get across the border back into the Congo, you will be spending the night at the Hôtel du Lac—"

"*I* will?" de la Santiago asked.

"If I'm lucky," Jack said, "which is to say if her husband is out of town, I will spend the night with a friend."

De la Santiago smiled and shook his head.

"There will be women in the bar and restaurant of the Hôtel du Lac," Jack went on, "which is the subject of this little man-to-man conversation. Congolese and European. One does not diddle with the natives unless one is suicidal, in a venereal disease sense. That leaves the Europeans, mostly Belge, but some French, German, and even the odd American. Most of them are married. The problem is with the Belgian women. If they are married to a Belgian, no problem. But some of them have found marital bliss with the Congolese officialdom. Their husbands are jealous. Phrased simply, don't fuck around with—don't even give any hints that you would like to fuck around with—some Belgian woman married to a Congolese."

"How do you know which is which?"

"That's the problem," Jack said. "It's a matter of experience. If the guy who owns the hotel's wife—Madame Fameir—is around, I'll introduce you, and you can ask her. But don't guess wrong. There's no second chance. You could easily wind up dead."

De la Santiago looked at him and saw that he was absolutely serious. "Then the thing to do is behave."

"This is the Congo," Jack said. "With the exception of my father, nobody behaves, at least for long, in the Congo."

[TWO]
Stanleyville, Democratic Republic of the Congo
14 December 1963

AIR SIMBA FLIGHT 104 landed without incident at Kamembe, Rwanda, just over an hour after taking off from Albertville.

The skies were already full of furious-looking stratocumulus clouds, their tops boiling. This happened every afternoon this time of year in this part of the Congo, Captain Jacques Portet told First Officer de la Santiago that no weather report was necessary. You just planned your flights to get back on the ground before three P.M. and if you could arrange it, before two.

A GMC carryall, painted white and with the Air Simba logo on its doors, met them at the airport. The carryall was driven by a squat, very black Congolese wearing a white shirt and a necktie. He spoke French, but not too well, and he and Jacques Portet carried on their conversation in Swahili. De la Santiago saw that Portet was as fluent in Swahili as he was in French and English, and this impressed him almost as much as the skill, the *professionalism,* with which the young pilot flew.

There were customs posts at both ends of the iron bridge over the fast-flowing Ruzizi River. The Air Simba Bukavu *chef de station* gave a little gift—money and a carton of Camel cigarettes—to the Rwanda customs officials to facilitate their passage, and a smaller gift—less money and two packages of Camels—to the Congolese customs officials.

The Congolese customs officials required lesser gifts only because of the special relation then in effect between Jacques Portet's father, Jean-Philippe, and certain very high placed and powerful members of the Congolese government.

When Air Simba had been formed not long ago, the brother-in-law of Colonel Joseph-Désiré Mobutu, head of the Armed Forces of the Democratic Republic of the Congo, had been asked to serve on the Board of Directors, and for his services had been given 10 percent of the outstanding stock. This was far less—half—than the usual arrangement, but Jean-Philippe Portet had known Colonel Mobutu since the Colonel had been a corporal in the Force Publique, and they were friends.

Jean-Philippe Portet (whom Santiago thought of alternately as The Old Captain Portet and Jacques' father) had two jobs. He was Managing Director of Air Simba, which had been in business for five months and had had aircraft for three, and he was Chief Pilot of Air Congo, the international airline of the Democratic Republic of the Congo.

As Air Congo's Chief Pilot, it naturally fell to him to fly the aircraft on which senior Congolese officialdom, including Colonel Mobutu, elected to travel. He had proposed the formation of Air Simba to Colonel Mobutu one day en route to Dar Es Salaam, while the Colonel was sitting in the copilot's seat and had seemed to be in a very good mood.

Since it was known to the Governor of the province that Air Simba had friends in high places, it would not have been necessary to give the customs officials any gift at all. It just made sense to be friendly.

Once across the bridge, the Air Simba carryall deposited Portet and de la Santiago at the Hôtel du Lac, a five-story building whose rear windows overlooked Lake Kivu. Congolese in immaculate white jackets (some of them even wore shoes; the Hôtel du Lac was a class establishment) opened the door of the GMC, greeted Captain Portet with warmth, took care of the luggage, and rushed to push open the gleaming, brass-framed glass door for them.

The hotel was small but well furnished, and obviously spotless. Jack Portet stopped at the desk only long enough to ask for messages and to introduce de la Santiago to the desk clerk as someone who would be regularly staying in the Air Simba rooms. Then he led de la Santiago into the bar.

Two bottles of beer and glasses were immediately brought, without orders, to the table by a very large, and very black, white-jacketed waiter. As de la Santiago waited for his beer to be poured, Jack Portet took a healthy swig from the neck of his bottle, and then he burped.

"I've been thinking of that for an hour," he announced. "The first sip is always the best."

A plump woman in her late forties came to the table and kissed Portet on the cheek when he stood up to greet her. Portet introduced Madame Fameir to de la Santiago as his sweetheart.

As they were shaking hands, a European couple walked up to the table. The man was in his early fifties, gray-haired, suntanned, and dignified. He wore a summer-weight gray suit and tie. The woman was in a light summer dress, with black lingerie visible at the neckline. And she was somewhere under forty, de la Santiago decided, older than she at first looked.

"I thought that was you flying over, Jacques," the man said to Portet as he offered his hand.

"I thought you were in the bush," Portet said, as he kissed the woman's offered cheek. And then he made the introductions. M'sieu et Madame Nininger, who were not only charming and witty, but new customers of Air Simba.

"I'll go tomorrow," Nininger said as he sat down. "You'll come for dinner?"

"Thank you, but no. We have a little business tonight."

At that moment Enrico de la Santiago realized that Jack Portet was going to be unlucky. His friend's husband was not going to be out of town. He had just invited them to dinner.

The Niningers had a drink—Orange Blossoms—and then left. Enrico de la Santiago, wondering if his ego and/or his imagination had run wild, had the idea that Madame Nininger had more in mind than simple courtesy when she asked him to call whenever he returned to Bukavu.

They sat drinking the beer (which like the airline was also called Simba and which was astonishingly good) until it was time to eat. In the bar, and later in the restaurant (where at Portet's suggestion they both had the broiled filet of a fish that Portet said was found only in Lake Kivu), Portet pointed out which European women were available and which were forbidden.

They went to bed early, leaving a call for half past four in the morning. The call was delivered by a Congolese carrying a tray with a coffeepot, orange juice, and a croissant.

They left the hotel a few minutes after five, and at 5:25 were at the airport. Nininger was there, leaning on the fender of a Mercedes, and so was a Mercedes truck with a refrigerated body. Its air-conditioning diesel engine was idling, but it roared into action when cooling was needed.

The previous evening Portet had explained why there would be a refrigerated truck here: Nininger had a cattle operation in the hills above Bukavu. What he was trying to do now with Air Simba was deliver fresh meat to Stanleyville and (most importantly) to Leopoldville cheaper than it could be obtained elsewhere. Most of the fresh meat—all of the quality fresh meat—now obtainable in Leopoldville came from South Africa. Some of the meat was flown in and some was sent by train; but all of it came to the capital alive, where it was then butchered. It was a seller's market, and the South Africans took full advantage of it.

Nininger's idea now was to butcher and chill his beef, lamb, and swine at his own plantation, and then air-freight it to Stanleyville, Leopoldville, and ultimately elsewhere. The problem was refrigeration, which was to say the temperature of the Congo, which lay on the Equator.

The meat could not be frozen because there was already an adequate supply of South African, European, and even Argentinian frozen meat in Leopoldville. Nor could it be iced down or shipped in insulated containers by air, because of the weight.

The solution they had found was to chill the meat to several degrees above freezing, transport it to the Kamembe airport in a refrigerated truck, and quickly load it aboard an Air Simba Curtiss cargo plane. For the past three weeks this solution had worked. The plane would quickly take off, and then climb quickly to an altitude which would keep the meat chilled en route.

If there was a delay, the meat would of course be ruined. And a close watch had to be maintained on outside temperature to make sure the meat didn't become frozen en route, either.

Before Nininger's workmen loaded the airplane with the contents of the truck, Jack and Enrico made very sure to check that the airplane was ready to go. They even fired up the engines and put the needles in the green, then shut down only the port engine. The cheesecloth-wrapped meat, some of it roughly butchered into loins and large parts and some of it in sides, was quickly laid on a sheet of plastic on the cabin floor, then strapped in place.

As soon as the door was closed, even before the port engine had been restarted, the plane moved to the threshold of the runway. It paused at the end of the runway only long enough to start the engine and check the mags; and then it roared off, heading northwest toward Stanleyville in a steep climb.

Stanleyville (estimated 1963 population 150,000) is 350 miles from Bukavu at the head of navigation for the middle portion of the Congo River. It is also very close to the exact center of Africa, equidistant from the Indian and Atlantic oceans, and from Cairo, Egypt, and Cape Town, South Africa.

The city sits surrounded by hundreds of miles of jungle—an island of apartment houses on wide boulevards, office buildings, hotels, warehouses, large villas, and shops. In Stanleyville in 1964, it was possible to buy Buick automobiles; Swiss watches; couturier clothing from Paris; and oysters, lamb chops, and newspapers (including the *Times* of London and the Paris edition of the *New York Herald Tribune*) flown in daily from Brussels. When arriving passengers descended from Sabena or KLM or UTA jets at Stanleyville, they were greeted with a multicolored neon sign urging them to FUMEZ LUCKY STRIKE!

The United States of America maintained a consulate general in Stanleyville, a large, white, red-roofed villa with a lovely swimming pool, as well as a splendid view of the white-water rapids of Stanley Falls (named, like the town itself, after the intrepid "Doctor Livingstone, I presume" journalist-explorer Henry Morton Stanley).

Stanleyville proved to have what Enrico de la Santiago thought of as a real airport. For one thing, the moment he tuned in the ADF, there was a strong STN signal. And when Portet called the Stanleyville tower an hour and fifteen minutes into the flight, there was an immediate response, in English, from a tower operator who left no question that he knew what he was doing—

"Simba One Oh Four, Stanleyville. We have you on radar. You are cleared to descend to two thousand five hundred on your present heading. The winds are five to ten from the north. The altimeter is two niner niner four. You are cleared as number one to land on runway zero five. There is no commercial traffic in the area, but please be on the lookout for light aircraft operating under visual flight rules. Report at flight level two five hundred and when over the outer marker."

And a minute later he was back.

"Simba One Oh Four, Stanleyville."

Portet, who was flying, nodded at Enrico to work the radio.

"Stanleyville, Simba One Oh Four—go ahead."

"Simba One Oh Four, Stanleyville, in flight advisory. You will be met by a refrigerated truck and a fuel truck."

"Roger, Stanleyville, thank you very much," Enrico replied.

"I have to figure out some way to RON here," Portet said: Remain Over Night. "Nice town. And we rented an apartment in the Immoquateur that's just going to waste."

"In the what?"

"The Immoquateur," Jack Portet explained. "It's a new apartment building, ten, twelve stories, on the river. Very classy."

"And you have friends here, no doubt?" de la Santiago asked.

"Two. Neither of whose husbands can be called stay-at-homes."

The radio came to life.

"Stanleyville, Sabena Six Oh Five, sixty miles north of your station for approach and landing."

Stanleyville gave Sabena 605 essentially the same information he had given Air Simba 104, except of course that he told them that "Air Simba, a Curtiss C-46 aircraft is number one to land."

Sabena 605, a Douglas DC-8, swooped in to land as Jack and Enrico were being driven to the terminal in a Peugeot station wagon. They picked up coffee and jelly doughnuts in the coffee shop, carried them to Weather for a briefing on en route and destination conditions to Leopoldville, filed their flight plan, visited the gentleman's rest facility, and started back across the terminal to where the Peugeot waited for them.

As they passed the newsstand, stacks of newspapers and magazines fresh from the belly of the morning Sabena flight from Brussels were dropped on it and cut open. Jack Portet stopped and bought the Paris Edition of the *New York Herald Tribune* and *Playboy*.

And then a woman rushed up to him, kissed him on both cheeks, and in an accent Enrico de la Santiago found enchanting called him *"Jacques, mon amour."* After that she expressed apparently genuine delight to find Jacques in Stanleyville, especially since her husband had been delayed in Brussels.

This woman was younger than the blonde in Bukavu, and French, Enrico decided, rather than Belgian.

And she seemed disconsolate when Portet told her he had a planeload of fresh meat he had to get back in the air in the next five minutes. And so, vicariously, was Enrico disconsolate for Jack Portet. It was not at all hard to imagine what pleasures with the French blonde the planeload of fresh meat would cause him to miss.

After they were in the air again and approaching twelve thousand, when it would become necessary to go on oxygen, Enrico asked the question that had quite naturally come to him.

"What's the secret of your success?"

"Seriously?"

"Yeah, sure, seriously. If it's some kind of cologne, I want to know what kind."

"Aside from my charm, good looks, and all-around overwhelming masculinity," Jack said, joking, and then grew serious, "the greatest risk a woman having an affair here runs is that the guy will get serious. There's a great shortage of European women here, of course, especially in the bush—the deeper in the bush, the greater the shortage of women—and after they diddle some guy and then go home, the guy sits around alone in his house, or his apartment, and decides that his quick piece of ass is the greatest love affair since Romeo and Juliet, and that he has to have her permanently. People go crazy here anyway, and it gets messy. They know that I'm safe, that I'm not going to appear wide-eyed at their door and tell their husband I can't live without them. If you play your cards right . . ."

"I'm married," Enrico said. "My wife and my kids are still in Cuba."

"My father told me," Jack said.

"I'm working on getting them out."

"You a Catholic, Enrico?"

"Yeah, sure."

"When Catholic priests come to work down here, they are relieved of their vow of celibacy."

Enrico looked at him in astonishment. He saw that Portet was again quite serious. He was unable to accept that a priest would be allowed to have sex—with the approval of the Church, but it was evident that Jack Portet believed what he was saying.

"A piece a day keeps the madman away," Jack Portet said solemnly, and then tapping the altimeter, which showed they were still climbing at 13,000 feet, he pulled a black rubber oxygen mask over his mouth.

It was almost eight hundred miles from Stanleyville to Leopoldville. The flight took a little more than three hours and fifteen minutes. Frequently there was no sign of civilization beneath them at all, not even the trace of a road. Even at 25,000 feet, Enrico reasoned, there should be some sign of civilization down there, but there wasn't, just green, broken every once in a while by a river.

A refrigerated truck pulled up to the airplane as soon as they landed. Jack felt the meat through the cheesecloth. It was cold but not frozen. Air Simba had done it again, which meant a profit and not the loss they would have had if the meat had been spoiled or frozen.

He got in his Volkswagen Bug and drove home.

He parked his car in the garage and entered the house via the kitchen. His stepmother, a statuesque blonde, was checking the bill from the grocery store against the groceries themselves. She suspected the grocery store of charging her for imaginary goods.

"You have a letter from the government in St. Louis," Hanni Portet said. She spoke in English with a strong but not unpleasant German accent.

"Oh, shit!"

"Cursing won't change anything," Hanni said, and went to him and kissed his cheek. "Your father's out by the pool. I think he would like to play tennis."

Jack looked out the kitchen window. His father was sitting at one of three umbrella-shaded tables by the side of the pool. On the table beside him were two tennis racquets and two cans of balls.

When the Second World War had broken out, Jean-Philippe Portet had been the age Jacques was now and had been in America with his father. *His* father, Jacques' grandfather, an official of the Société Anonyme Belge d'Exploitation de Navigation Aériènne (Sabena, the Belgian State Airline), had been sent to the United States on a purchasing mission. Sabena wanted to replace its Lockheed transports with Douglas

DC-3s, and to issue orders for the not-yet-in-production four-engine Douglas DC-4.

When Belgium fell to the Germans, Grandfather Portet made himself available to the Belgian government-in-exile in England. He was ordered to stay where he was and to continue doing what he was doing. Which he did. But Jean-Philippe Portet announced he was going to join the Royal Canadian Air Force and become a fighter pilot.

Grandfather Portet, who believed that most of the young fighter pilots being raised in Canada would soon be dead, reasoned with him to join the U.S. Army Air Corps. So did Patricia Ellen Detwiler, the eighteen-year-old daughter of a Douglas engineer who had decided to marry Jean-Philippe Portet the moment she laid eyes on him. If Jean-Philippe went off to the RCAF, God only knew when she would see him again. If ever.

Jean-Philippe Portet saw her—though not his father's—reasoning, and he was graduated from the U.S. Army Air Corps Flight Training School at Randolph Field, Texas, on August 1, 1941, and married Patricia Ellen Detwiler the next day. Their first child was born ten months later, by which time Lieutenant Portet was flying C-46 Commandos Over the Hump in the China-Burma-India Theater of Operations.

In early 1944 Captain Portet was discharged from the U.S. Army Air Corps to accept a commission in the armed forces of a friendly foreign power. The Royal Belgian Air Force commissioned him a commandant (major) and he was given command of a group (two squadrons) of C-47 aircraft in time to participate in the Normandy Invasion.

He ended the war a lieutenant colonel and afterward found immediate employment with Sabena. His wife and child remained in the United States until 1947 because of conditions in Europe. They rented a small house in Burnt Mills, New Jersey, and Captain Portet got to see them three or four times a month when he was laying over between flights between Brussels and New York.

In November 1947, shortly after she had joined her husband in Brussels, Mme. Portet, née Detwiler, was struck by a truck while crossing the Boulevard de Waterloo en route to the 11:00 A.M. service at the Eglise Américaine on the Rue Cap Crespel. She died the next afternoon without regaining consciousness.

It was decided—it was the only thing to do—that Jacques/Jack Portet would be raised in St. Louis by his maternal grandparents, with the understanding that as soon as he was old enough, he would come to live with his father in Europe and be educated there.

In March of 1951, Jean-Philippe Portet flew to California to accept delivery of the first Lockheed 1049D Constellation in the Sabena fleet. Developed largely through the efforts of Howard Hughes, the four-engine, triple-tailed transport had a range of approximately 5000 miles at a speed of about 360mph and was ideal for Sabena's African routes.

On the way over from Europe—for no other reason than convenience—he took a Lufthansa flight from Frankfurt am Main. When the Lufthansa DC-4 was forced by weather to remain overnight at Gander, Newfoundland, as a matter of professional courtesy he was asked to dine with the Lufthansa crew, and met Fräulein Hannelore "Hanni" Gruster-berg, a Lufthansa stewardess.

No one at Sabena said anything when Captain Portet married, in August 1951, the tall blond *Hamburgerin*, but the German occupation of Belgium had been brutal, and Belgians have long memories. Rocks were thrown through the windows of the Portet apartment and Hanni was once spat on while shopping.

It was arranged for Captain Portet to remove his bride from an unpleasant situation. He was taken off the Atlantic routes and assigned to the African, where he flew Lockheeds on the routes Sabena operated within Africa and between Africa and Europe. The Portets moved into a roomy apartment on a high floor of a new building in Johannesburg, South Africa.

Their daughter, Jeanine, was born in Johannesburg in February 1953. The next month Captain Portet was offered the position of Chief Pilot of Air Congo, a joint venture then of Belgian and Congo Belge investors (including Sabena). He was offered a substantial increase in salary, transfer of his retirement and seniority credits, and a written guarantee that if things didn't work out, he could return to Sabena.

As an inducement the job offer carried with it the offer of a mortgage loan at very attractive terms. Jean-Philippe had used it to buy a large villa on three hectares overlooking the Stanley Basin of the Congo River in Leopoldville. Jacques/Jack Portet, then ten years old, first saw his new half sister in June 1953, when he flew to Leopoldville to spend the summer with his father.

Hanni Portet promptly fell in love with him, and the first serious argument she had with her husband was over his refusal to insist that the boy be allowed to live with them. It would not, he said, be fair to his grandparents, for one thing, and for another he would rather have his son grow up as an American and not as an overprivileged colonialist. There would be time for his "Europification" later.

Hanni got her way the next year, though not as she would have wished. Jack's Grandmother Detwiler died suddenly. Thus it was either turn the boy over to his uncle (whom Jack despised) or his aunt (whom his father thought had the brains of a gnat) or bring him home to the Belgian Congo.

Jack finished the equivalent of elementary school in Leopoldville, attended Culver Military School in the United States for two years, and then finished his secondary education at the lycée in Brussels from which his father had graduated. After that he had gone on to the Free University in Brussels.

One of Captain Portet's responsibilities as Chief Pilot of Air Congo was the establishment of new service. In other words, he located places in the Congo Belge which Air Congo could service profitably and saw to it that they had the necessary navigation aids and ground-service equipment, and that they were adequately staffed.

Air Congo added three light, twin-engine Beechcraft airplanes to its fleet. Although Captain Portet was careful to remain current in the long-range passenger and cargo aircraft, he spent most of his time in the air in one of the little Twin-Beeches. He took a father's natural pride when his eleven-year-old son, sitting on a pillow, could keep it straight and level. By the time he was twelve, the boy could take it off and land it.

And then he discovered an interesting omission in the Rules of the Ministry for Air of the Belgian Government, which governed air operations in the Congo Belge. No minimum age for a pilot's license was specified, presumably because it had never occurred to anyone that a fourteen-year-old would present himself for the written and flight examination for a private pilot's license.

Jack Portet's private pilot license was his reward for a 3.6 grade average during his two years at Culver. As a legally licensed pilot, he could go on the flight manifest as pilot-in-command. And he did, whenever he went anywhere with his father in the Twin-Beech. Captain Portet was long past the point where he was concerned with building hours, especially in Twin-Beech, and no one at Air Congo was going to question his authority, or his wisdom, in letting the kid fly.

Before he was sixteen, Jack Portet earned his commercial pilot's license, with twin-engine and instrument indorsements. It was his intention to become the youngest airline pilot in the world, and he studied hard and long for the written examination, only to find out that the Belgian Airline Pilot's Rating (ATR) was governed by the International Airline Agreement, and the IAA said that you had to be twenty-one to get your ATR.

He took and passed the examination the week he graduated from college. He didn't need the rating to fly Air Simba's Curtiss aircraft, because they would not be flying passengers on a scheduled basis. But if they couldn't make a go of Air Simba, he would have to get a job elsewhere, most likely with Air Congo, and that would require the ATR.

Jack Portet went to his room, actually a three-room suite, opened the letter from the government in St. Louis, read it, and then changed into tennis clothes and walked down the wide stairs to the pool.

His father raised his eyebrows at him quizzically. Jack handed him the letter.

It said that his friends and neighbors had selected him for induction into the Armed Forces of the United States of America, and that he was to present himself at the Armed Forces Induction Center, St. Louis, Missouri, on Thursday, January 2, 1964, at 9:00 A.M., bringing with him such personal items as he would need for three days.

"You knew it was coming," his father said.

"Shit," Jack said. "If I had the courage, I would put mascara on my eyelashes, swish in, and kiss the doctor."

His father chuckled.

"Then the Belgians would get you," his father said. "They don't care about fairies. One way or another, you're going in uniform."

III

"DON'T ARGUE with me, Porter," Lieutenant Colonel Craig W. Lowell said to Porter Craig, Chairman of the Board of Craig, Powell, Kenyon & Dawes, Investment Bankers, "I'm a Norwich University graduate now, and don't you forget it."

"Oh, Jesus," Porter Craig said. He stopped himself just in time from demanding what the hell being a college graduate had to do with the question of where to set up a just delivered folding table (intended for use as a bar) in the living room of the house.

Lieutenant Colonel Lowell, who was a tall, muscular, handsome man with a mustache, and Porter Craig, who was shorter, a bit overweight, and balding, were cousins. Between them they owned just about equally 84 percent of the stock in the investment banking firm. Porter Craig did the actual running of it, although for tax purposes Lowell was carried on the books as Vice Chairman of the Board. Lowell was a career Army officer.

He was now in civilian clothing: a tweed sports coat, a red cashmere sleeveless sweater, gray flannel slacks, loafers. In civilian clothing, Porter Craig often thought, Craig Lowell looked like a model in one of the ads for twenty-four-year old Scotch whiskey in *Town & Country* magazine. In uniform, Porter thought, especially when he elected to wear his decorations, Craig Lowell looked like every maiden's dream: handsome, heroic, dashing, and just a bit wicked.

Craig Lowell had been expelled from Harvard as an eighteen-year-old and then drafted. He had won a commission (a battlefield promotion which for political reasons couldn't be called that), while serving with the U.S. Military Advisory Group in Greece. Then he had been released into the reserve. The Wharton School of Business at the University of Pennsylvania had been happy to have the heir apparent to half of Craig, Powell, Kenyon & Dawes in their student body, whether or not he had been granted the usually prerequisite undergraduate degree; and he had graduated from Wharton summa cum laude. But before he could move into the office reserved for him at the firm, the Korean War had broken out, and he had been among the first reserve officers called up to fight it.

He had never again taken off his uniform.

Porter Craig had at first believed that there was a sort of joining-the-Foreign-Legion element to Craig Lowell's Army career. His wife had been killed in an automobile accident in Germany—by a perverse coincidence on the same day Lowell had been decorated with the Distinguished Service Cross and won a battlefield promotion to major in Korea. Later he had come to understand that Lowell would probably have not stayed long with the firm under any circumstances; he far preferred soldiering to banking.

But Colonel Lowell had now become, as he had said, a college graduate. And this, Porter Craig thought, was both another example of the idiocy of the military mind and of the military's eager willingness to throw the taxpayers' money down the toilet.

Apparently a routine review of his records had uncovered the fact that Lieutenant Colonel Lowell was not possessed of a baccalaureate degree, a requisite for a regular Army officer. The summa cum laude from Wharton apparently didn't count, because that was a master's degree, and the regulation clearly specified baccalaureate. Nor did Craig Lowell's career (he was already a lieutenant colonel when The Great Discovery was made) seem to count, nor his awesome display of medals for valor.

The regulation required him to have a baccalaureate degree. And that, incontrovertibly and indisputably, was that. And further, in keeping with the Army's tradition of having a contingency plan for every contingency and to hell with what it costs the hardworking taxpayer, there was a program to deal with the requirement.

The program was called Bootstrap. Under it, the Army had sent Lieutenant Colonel Lowell back to college, not only paying his tuition, but keeping him on full pay and allowances while he spent just under a year picking up the necessary credit hours.

While Porter Craig did not exactly approve of his cousin's Army career, he wasn't exactly unhappy to have the firm mostly to himself either. But Craig Lowell was not the only member of the family who seemed to have succumbed to the siren call of the military. For Porter Craig was now worried about the parallels between Craig Lowell and his only son, Geoffrey. Geoff had also been drafted when he had flunked out of college. And then after Craig had gotten him out of a mess in basic training (Geoff had beaten up his sergeant), he had gone to Vietnam as a Green Beret buck sergeant; and he had returned the previous August with a Silver Star, two Bronze Stars, more Purple Hearts than his father liked to think about, and the silver bar of a first lieutenant. He had also, as Mrs. Porter Craig frequently observed, married a German girl—as Craig himself had done as a young man.

Lieutenant Geoffrey Craig, his wife, and Mr. and Mrs. Porter Craig, were now all pretending that Geoff still remained in the Army because the Army was not permitting officers to resign at this time—even those who had survived Vietnam. But Porter Craig thought the odds were seventy-thirty that Geoff would stay in the Army, period. He was in flight school; and the life of an officer flying airplanes has a great deal more appeal for a twenty-three-year-old like Geoff than going back to school for four years in order to prepare himself to sit behind a desk.

Porter Craig understandably wanted his son in the bank, but he was not a fool. He understood that this was not the time to discuss the issue. So he looked on the bright side of things, starting with the all-important fact that Geoff had come home from Vietnam alive. And he had come home not only an officer, but as a responsible and unusually mature young man.

And then there was Ursula, whom Porter Craig credited with having had a very great deal to do with placing and keeping Geoff on the straight and narrow. Porter saw in Ursula a potentially invaluable ally in his campaign to move Geoff out of the Army and into the bank. He had thus been very carefully sowing "I Want You Out of the Army" seeds in her mind, seeds he was confident would be fertilized when nature took its course and she got in the family way.

Lieutenant Colonel Lowell and Mr. and Mrs. Porter Craig were at the moment the Christmas holiday guests of Lieutenant and Mrs. Geoffrey

Craig. A most unusual occurrence, as both Porter Craig and his wife were well aware: Craig Lowell had last participated in a family Christmas gathering when he was seventeen. And yet when Geoff asked him to come, Lowell decided to fly in from Florida (where he was assigned to something called STRICOM) for this gathering without hesitation. And he'd flown in early, and with the obvious intention of staying long.

Porter thought he knew why Craig was doing that.

Craig Lowell had a child, a boy, who had been born in Fort Knox, Kentucky, in 1947. But now Peter-Paul Lowell lived with his maternal grandfather in Germany. Lowell had talked to him on the telephone earlier in the day. And the conversation had been stiff, brief, and awkward—a disaster. It was not hard therefore for Porter Craig to conclude that since for all practical purposes he had no son of his own (or a son who at sixteen took offense at being called an American), Craig Lowell had transferred his parental emotions to Geoff Craig.

Porter Craig recognized the symptoms of jealousy both in himself and in his wife; and perceiving them, he suppressed them. For one thing, short of causing a scene, which was the last thing he wanted, per se, and because it might force Geoff to make a decision he didn't want him to make, there was nothing he could do to make Craig stop playing visiting father-in-law.

If Craig Lowell wanted to put the goddamned bar in the middle of the living room and cover it with a tent, so what?

The important thing to keep in mind was that Geoff was home alive from Vietnam, that he was married to a really very nice girl, that it was Christmas, and that he and his wife were spending it in their son's home.

The reason for the bar was that Lowell was going to entertain. He was going to have what he called "some people call." The Commanding General of Fort Rucker, for instance, Major General Robert F. Bellmon, had quickly accepted the invitation, or rather his wife had. And other local big shots were also scheduled to appear.

Porter Craig soon realized that Craig Lowell was at least as interested in having Geoff and his wife meet the local big shots as he was in entertaining them, and Porter understood that as a gesture of affection and concern for Geoff.

Geoff came in as Ursula was spreading a sheet over the folding table. He had a case of whiskey in his arms, and he was leading a red-jacketed bartender, who was also carrying a case of whiskey. When the bartender set his case down, he immediately went out for another.

Porter forced from his mind the unkind thought that if there was one thing you could say about soldiers, it was that they drank like goddamned fish, and then he started for the table to help Geoff with the whiskey.

Craig Lowell made no such move. He sat in the most comfortable chair in the room, drinking champagne from a stemmed glass and puffing on one of his enormous black goddamned cigars.

And when the telephone beside him rang, he answered it on the first ring.

As if he owned the goddamned place, Porter Craig thought. And then immediately reminded himself that Craig Lowell did in fact own 227 Melody Lane. He had bought it when he had been stationed at Rucker.

"Ursula," Lowell called out, *"dein Bruder."*

Ursula, a blonde who looked as solid and wholesome as a girl on a dairy poster, went to the telephone. Porter was surprised and concerned to see the worried look on her face.

He couldn't hear the conversation, and of course it was doubtful he would have understood it if he could have heard it, for his German wasn't that good. But it was obvious that she didn't like what she was hearing. And just as obvious to Craig Lowell, who took the phone from her.

"Hier ist Oberst Lowell," he said. *"Was ist los?"*

Porter Craig understood that much.

Whatever was *los,* it triggered in Lowell a series of orders, delivered in staccato German. And then he hung the phone up.

"I don't believe he missed his plane," Ursula said to Craig Lowell, softly, and in English.

"Neither did I," Lowell said. "That's why I'm going for him."

Now Geoff picked up that something was going on, and the last half of Lowell's sentence.

"Going for who?"

"Your Kraut brother-in-law," Craig Lowell announced. "He called up and said he had missed his plane and couldn't get another reservation. You can't bullshit a bullshitter. He thought he would be in the way here, the damned fool. I told him I'd be there in two hours."

"Where is he?" Porter Craig asked.

"Fort Bragg. Actually, Fayetteville. Now, because he said he was calling from the airport, he'll actually have to go to Fayetteville. Serves the bastard right. You want to ride along, Porter?"

"No, thank you," Porter said.

"I do," Geoff said. When Craig Lowell looked at him asking for an explanation, he gave one: "For one thing, you've been at the bubbly—"

"Half of one lousy glass," Lowell interrupted.

"And I would like the time," Geoff added.

Craig Lowell owned a private aircraft, a Cessna 310H, which was a "light twin." So far as the Internal Revenue Service was concerned, the Cessna belonged to the bank, where it was used for the transportation of bank executives. The first time any executive of Craig, Powell, Kenyon & Dawes (other than Craig Lowell) had actually seen it was the day before, when Craig had picked up the Porters in Atlanta and flown them to Ozark.

"I thought you were still in the 'this-is-the-cyclic-and-that's-the-skid' portion of your training," Lowell countered.

"I've been taking commercial lessons," Geoff said, and added, "I've got three hours in a 310."

"The party . . ." Ursula protested.

"We'll be back in four hours," Lowell said. "I know your brother will be waiting for us. I could tell by the way he said, *'Jawohl, Herr Oberst!'* I could even hear him click his heels."

"Keep the party going, honey," Geoff Craig said and went for his coat.

"Thank you, Craig," Ursula Craig said softly to Craig Lowell.

[TWO]
Fayetteville (N.C.) Municipal Airport
1520 Hours 24 December 1963

URSULA CRAIG'S BROTHER, First Lieutenant Karl-Heinz Wagner, Infantry, United States Army, sat drinking a cup of coffee at a table in the coffee shop of the terminal. He was in uniform. He wore a green beret, but had taken it off and neatly folded it and then laid it on top of his overcoat on a chair.

The coffee shop was crowded with soldiers, most of them paratroopers from the 82nd Airborne Division, XVIII Airborne Corps, and their supporting units. There were also some Special Forces men. And two tables away from his were six noncoms wearing green berets, but without the flash certifying that they were fully qualified. They had smiled nervously at Lieutenant Wagner when they had come in, but they hadn't asked to join him, even though they knew him.

At Camp Mackall, behind his back of course, Lieutenant Wagner was known as "Otto"—as in Major Otto Skorzeny, the legendary, scarred-face Austro-German parachutist who had, among other spectacular exploits, planned and executed the brilliant rescue of Benito Mussolini from a well-guarded mountaintop prison. For this he had received the Knight's Cross of the Iron Cross from Hitler himself. When Skorzeny was brought before a war crimes tribunal after World War II, a number of Americans, including many senior officers, rushed to testify in his behalf. He was exonerated.

There was a scar on Lieutenant Wagner's face, too, and he spoke with a German accent, and, presumably like Skorzeny, he was a real hard-ass.

Referring to him as Otto, in other words, was by no means deprecatory. He was looked on with considerable admiration, but he was not the sort with whom one presumed to violate *his* concept of military courtesy.

Lieutenant Karl-Heinz Wagner was a tall, rugged man who wore his blond hair closely cropped. His uniform blouse was decorated with the Combat Infantry Badge, parachutist's wings, and ribbons indicating that he had been awarded the Silver Star, two Bronze Stars, two Purple Hearts, and had served in the Republic of Vietnam. There were also several ribbons indicating that he had been decorated by the Vietnamese, including the Medal for Gallantry.

In a locked metal box in his room in the BOQ (Bachelor Officers' Quarters) at Fort Bragg there were three colored ribbons representing military decorations Karl-Heinz Wagner did not think it appropriate to wear. On the other hand, for some perverse reason, he could not bring himself to throw them away, although he had come close on several occasions.

They had been awarded to him by the government of the German Democratic Republic (Communist East Germany) when he had been Oberleutnant Wagner of the Corps of Pioneers. Before he had deserted and crashed through the Berlin Wall in a Skoda truck—with his sister in the back protected from the expected hail of 9mm submachine fire by stacks of cement bags.

At the Refugee Center he gave his reason for coming through the wall as his desire to make a better life, in freedom, for himself and his sister. But it had been more than that. He hated communism, and communists. And later in America, when the recruiter had asked him why he wanted to enlist in the U.S. Army as a private, he'd given the same reason he had given the West Berliners at the Refugee Center. But the real reason was that he wanted to kill communists. He knew if he said that, they would probably not understand. You had to have lived under a communist regime to understand why someone would hate it enough to want to kill those responsible for it.

Karl-Heinz Wagner had been the honor graduate of his basic training company, and this carried with it a promotion to PFC. And he had met Private Geoffrey Craig in the airport at Atlanta, where they were both on the same plane to Fort Bragg to undergo Special Forces training. More importantly, Private Geoffrey Craig had met Ursula Wagner at the same time.

By the time PFC Wagner and Private Craig had gone through the Parachute School at Fort Benning, a prerequisite for Special Forces training at Bragg, Ursula and Geoff were looking at each other *that way*. Karl-Heinz Wagner had not really been displeased. Geoff was a nice young boy, though by no means yet a soldier, of course, and by no means prepared as yet to assume any serious responsibilities, such as marriage. And Ursula was a good girl, and levelheaded, and wasn't going to do anything she shouldn't.

When they were almost through the Special Forces basic course at Camp Mackall (a World War II military reservation near Fort Bragg, used as a training base for Special Forces), PFC Wagner was called back to Bragg for an interview with Lieutenant Colonel Sanford T. Felter, a slight and unassuming-looking man on whose uniform PFC Wagner had been surprised to see both U.S. Army parachute wings and those of the Troisième Régiment de la Légion Etrangère, the French Foreign Legion parachute regiment wiped out when the Indochinese communists had finally overrun Dien Bien Phu.

PFC Wagner was even more surprised to learn that Colonel Felter knew far more about him than he should; far more than he had told anyone in any of the half dozen "interviews" he had been given in West Berlin, in West Germany, and in the United States.

And Colonel Felter had then dangled a stick and a carrot before PFC Wagner's nose.

It was the Army's intention, Colonel Felter told PFC Wagner, to promote him to sergeant when he completed his basic Special Forces training and then send him to Vietnam as the Armorer of a Special Forces A-Team. This would mean, even for such an experienced soldier such as Wagner clearly was, probably more than six months before he could expect to be promoted.

And that meant that Ursula would be left alone in the United States, living on what allotment she would get from her brother and on what she could make from whatever job she could find.

There were "people" in West Berlin very anxious to share ex-Oberleutnant Wagner's knowledge of construction details of the Berlin Wall and of the East German military and civilian agencies charged with its maintenance.

If PFC Wagner were willing to go to West Berlin and share his knowledge with the "people" interested in it, for a period of three or four months, the Army would graduate PFC Wagner now from Special Forces. And as a staff sergeant rather than a sergeant. As a staff sergeant, Wagner would be authorized on-post quarters for his dependent. Quarters would be immediately made available; and since his West Berlin duty would be as TDY (Temporary Duty), his dependent would be authorized to occupy the quarters during the absence of her sponsor. Finally, Lieutenant Colonel Felter said, he would have a word with the PX, and Ursula would be given a job while he was gone.

Private Geoffrey Craig assured Staff Sergeant Wagner that he would look after Ursula as long as he could. Karl-Heinz Wagner believed him, of course, but he didn't quite understand what Geoff Craig had in mind.

Staff Sergeant Wagner had been in West Berlin not quite three weeks when there was a radio message from the United States:

CIA LANGLEY 1915ZULU 8MAR62
ROUTINE ENCRYPTED
STATION COMMANDER FOXTROT
DIRECTION DEPUTY DIRECTOR DELIVER FOLLOWING
SOONEST S/SGT KARL-HEINZ WAGNER, USA
SERGEANT GEOFFREY CRAIG AND URSULA MARRIED THIRTY MINUTES AGO NEW YORK CITY PROTESTANT EPISCOPAL SERVICE VESTRY SAINT BARTHOLOMEW'S CHURCH. DEPARTED IMMEDIATELY FOR STUDENT DETACHMENT USA ENGINEER SCHOOL FT BELVOIR VIRGINIA. THEY WILL ATTEMPT TELEPHONE TOMORROW. NICE WEDDING.
REGARDS.
S.T. FELTER LTCOL INF

When Geoff and Ursula telephoned afterward, Karl-Heinz Wagner, realizing that he was facing a fait accompli, did not upbraid Geoff for the marriage. At least he'd married her, and in a church. Instead, he told them that until they got their feet on the ground, he'd be happy to help a little financially. When Geoff turned him down, Karl-Heinz thought that was simply (stupid) pride speaking, and that he would arrange to help them tactfully.

By the time he came home from Berlin, Geoff had been sent to Vietnam. Ursula was staying with Geoff's mother and father in New York, and Karl-Heinz thought it was nice of the parents to take her in. He had actually wondered if it would be a financial burden for them.

Ursula and her mother-in-law had met his plane from Berlin. With a chauffeured limousine. And taken them to the Craig apartment, fourteen rooms on two floors on Fifth Avenue, overlooking Central Park. As they drove up Park Avenue and turned onto Fiftieth Street, Mrs. Porter Craig touched Karl-Heinz Wagner's arm with a hand bearing at least a hundred thousand dollars' worth of diamonds on it and pointed out Saint Bartholomew's Church.

"That's where they married," she explained. "My husband is on the vestry. When Geoff was a little boy, he sang in the choir there."

The Craigs were nice, but they made Karl-Heinz uncomfortable. Though raised in a communist state, he had acquired a strong sense of class differences. He was a peasant and the Craigs were aristocrats.

Seven months after Geoff had gone over to Vietnam, Karl-Heinz had followed him. By that time, Geoff had won a battlefield commission and had been an A-Team commander. Karl-Heinz had won a commission in Vietnam, too, but directly, rather than as a result of anything he had done specifically. One day they had called him into Group and told him there had been a TWX (Teletype Message) from the States saying that he was qualified, under some obscure provision of Army Regulations providing for the direct commissioning of linguists, and that he might as well take it.

He was commissioned as a first lieutenant, assigned to Headquarters, Military Assistance Command, Vietnam (MACV), and then immediately reassigned back to Special Forces. He was sure that Lieutenant Colonel Felter's hand was involved somehow.

First Lieutenant Wagner, newly returned to the United States from Vietnam, where he had killed a number of communists, was assigned to the Special Forces School as an instructor in demolitions and jungle warfare.

★　　★　　★

Wagner ordered another coffee and Danish when the waitress came over and folded her arms and looked hard at him. After she'd gone off to get these, he thought some more about his present situation. When Geoff had asked him to come spend Christmas with himself and Ursula, he'd very much wanted to go. But that had become impossible. What he now thought of as his Communist Class Consciousness had grabbed hold of him when he heard that Geoff's mother and father were also coming. And then he had learned that Geoff's cousin, Colonel Lowell, was also coming. He might have been able to handle Geoff's parents, but not the Colonel. That had been the deciding factor. Colonels and Lieutenants Don't Mix. Since he knew that Ursula wouldn't agree with him, he'd arranged to miss his plane and then called her to tell her. And then Colonel Lowell had come on the line and said he would fly to Fayetteville to pick him up.

It hadn't been a suggestion, it had been an order.

He didn't know what he was waiting for, just that he was waiting, and he was therefore surprised when he heard a familiar voice behind him.

"Excuse me, Sir," Geoff Craig asked, "but does that silly hat mean you're a Green Ber-ette?"

Karl-Heinz Wagner turned to look at him. And so did a dozen heads, including the six Green Beret noncoms in training. Geoff was wearing a Santa Claus hat, with its tasseled top reaching down to his shoulders, and there was a corsage of tiny Christmas tree balls pinned to the lapel of his suede jacket.

"Ach, Gott!" Lieutenant Wagner said, shaking his head and getting to his feet.

"I bet you eat snakes and everything," Geoff went on cheerfully, enjoying his brother-in-law's discomfort. "Come, let me take you away from all this sordid military brutality."

"You should try to remember that you're an officer," Wagner flared, and was immediately sorry.

Geoff laughed delightedly, snatched up Wagner's luggage, and motioned for Wagner to precede him out of the coffee shop.

The encounter naturally caused some discussion among the Green Beret noncoms in training after they had gone, and then one of them pointed out the window. Lieutenant Wagner and the character in the Santa Claus hat were on the parking ramp, walking toward a glistening civilian twin-engine airplane. A tall, mustachioed civilian was leaning against the fuselage.

When Lieutenant Wagner reached the civilian, he came to attention and saluted. The civilian returned the salute, and then offered his hand, smiled, and motioned Wagner into the airplane.

"I wonder what the hell that was all about?" one sergeant asked.

"With Otto, no telling," a second sergeant replied. "Nice airplane."

"Cessna 310H," a third sergeant said. "Now where the hell is Otto going on Christmas Eve in a civilian Cessna 310H?"

"Ven ve vish you to know," the second sergeant said, "ve vill tell you."

[THREE]
Schloss Greiffenberg
Marburg an der Lahn, West Germany
1900 Hours 24 December 1963

GENERALLEUTNANT GRAF PETER-PAUL VON GREIFFENBERG, retired, was alone in the library of the Schloss listening to the Christmas Eve program on Radio Vienna when the rather burly young man in a well-cut business suit opened the door and stood in the doorway until he was noticed.

"Oh, come in, Willi," the fourteenth Graf von Greiffenberg said. *"Fröliche Weihnachten!"*

The Graf was a tall, thin man in his early sixties. He was wearing an ancient tweed jacket, frayed at the cuffs, and mussed gray flannel trousers.

"Fröliche Weihnachten, Herr Generalleutnant Graf!" Major Wilhelm von Methes-Zach of the Bundeswehr Intelligence Service said, bobbed his head, and advanced on von Greiffenberg, who was sprawled in a Charles Eames chair. He bobbed his head again before handing the Graf a dozen small printed telephone message forms. "The messages since noon, Herr Generalleutnant Graf."

"Thank you," the Graf said. "There's a bottle of Marnier Lapastolle on the bar. Pour some, will you? For both of us. I always feel depraved to drink alone."

"The Herr Generalleutnant Graf is most kind," the Major said.

Von Greiffenberg went through the messages one by one, his lips unconsciously pursed in thought, and then bobbing his head at each one as he read it and agreed with the "disposition taken or recommended" block. Then his lips tightened, his eyes grew very cold, and the vein over his temple throbbed.

"Your cognac, Herr Generalleutnant Graf," Major Wilhelm von Methes-Zach said as he handed von Greiffenberg a crystal brandy snifter.

"Be so good," von Greiffenberg said, thrusting one of the telephone message forms at him, "to explain this one."

Von Methes-Zach took the small sheet of paper and read it.

"I took that call myself, Herr Generalleutnant Graf," Methes-Zach said. "Colonel Felter asked if he could be put through to you, and I told him that it was of course impossible on Christmas Eve. He was calling from Brussels. He said that he would come to Frankfurt and asked if it would be possible for you to fit him into your schedule on the twenty-sixth. I told him that I would pass the word to your secretary and that he should call again on Thursday—that's the twenty-sixth—to see if you would have time for him."

"That's all?"

Major von Methes-Zach was a very bright young officer, and although he had not been assigned to Generalleutnant Graf von Greiffenberg very long, he had been around him long enough to sense that something was amiss.

"Colonel Felter is American, Sir," he said. "He speaks remarkably good—Berliner—German."

"Sonofabitch," the fourteenth Graf von Greiffenberg said in English, and then switched to German. It was a brief, colorfully obscene and profane outburst (the Graf had been a cavalry officer), the gist of which was that he had proof of the deterioration of the aristocracy and the officer corps standing before him, and that the reason behind such incredible ineptness and stupidity was quite obviously that von Methes-Zach's ancestors had been canines who copulated with swine.

Von Methes-Zach had been warned that the old man had an awesome temper, but he was not prepared for anything like what he had just heard. Von Methes-Zach stood at attention, white-faced.

The Graf got his temper under control.

"Sorry," he said. "Obviously Colonel Felter's name means nothing to you, Willi?"

"No, Herr Generalleutnant Graf, I regret that it does not."

"Phrased somewhat euphemistically," the Graf said, "Colonel Felter has interesting contacts at the very highest levels of the American intelligence community."

"I regret that I was not aware of that, Herr Generalleutnant Graf."

"You are now. And there's something else, Willi. If it were not for Colonel Felter, I would still be—presuming I were still alive—a clerk in the supply office of Camp No. 263, near Kyrtymya, Siberia. I had been reported dead. Even General Gehlen believed that to be the case. Colonel Felter finally convinced Gehlen that I was alive, and Gehlen, in his good time, got me out."

Methes-Zach's pink face flushed red. He had learned about General Gehlen early in his intelligence career. Gehlen was a German intelligence officer on the Russian Front during World War II. When defeat was imminent, he had arranged for his files, and what was left of his organization, to be turned over to the U.S. Army. The Americans had provided funds for "the Gehlen Organization," which provided much, if not most of U.S. intelligence data vis-à-vis the Russians until the Gehlen Organization was turned over to German control.

"I regret I was unaware of any of this, Herr Generalleutnant."

"So do I. One test of a good officer, Willi, is how much and how quickly he salvages what he can from a disaster. Do you know how Colonel Felter plans to come to Frankfurt?"

"No, Sir."

"Or where he plans to stay?"

"No, Sir."

"Get on the telephone to the duty officer in Frankfurt," the Graf said. "Tell him to call in as many people as he needs. I want Colonel Felter located. When he is located, the duty officer is to personally go to him, offer both my compliments and my profound apologies for the ineptness of my aide, and ask Colonel Felter if he would do me the great honor of being my guest here for as long as he can stay in Germany."

"*Jawohl, Herr Generalleutnant Graf.*"

"Finish your brandy, Willi," the Graf said. "It's Christmas Eve. And I'm sorry I snapped at you."

IV

[ONE]
227 Melody Lane
Ozark, Alabama
1745 Hours 24 December 1963

FIRST LIEUTENANT KARL-HEINZ WAGNER'S fears that Geoff and Ursula's house would be full of people were more than justified.

Because of the cars that overflowed the driveway and the street in both directions from the long, rambling frame house, Geoff had to park his Oldsmobile station wagon halfway down the block. Most of the car bumpers carried Fort Rucker registration decals, and one, an Oldsmobile station wagon almost identical to Geoff's, was particularly discomfiting: It carried the number *1*, which meant that it was the personal automobile of the Commanding General of Fort Rucker.

And there were several other single- and double-digit registration stickers, indicating the presence of other senior officers. Karl-Heinz Wagner, who had received his officer training in a different society, was uncomfortable in the company of those greatly superior in rank.

They entered the house through a sliding glass door from the carport. A ruddy-faced man in a sports coat and open-collared woolen shirt stood just inside beside a striking, silver-haired woman.

"Ah, the prodigals," the woman said, smiling, when she saw them.

Colonel Lowell wrapped his arms around her and kissed her. She didn't object, but the ruddy-faced man obviously didn't like it.

"You've met Geoff, Bob?" Colonel Lowell asked.

"Yes, certainly," the ruddy-faced man said. "Merry Christmas, Craig."

"Merry Christmas, Sir," Geoff said.

"I love your Christmas outfit," the woman said, "especially all those green balls on your chest."

"Bob, this is Ursula's brother, Karl-Heinz Wagner. Karl, I'd like you to meet my very good and very old friends, General and Mrs. Bellmon."

Karl-Heinz Wagner came to attention and stiffly offered his hand. "It is a great honor, Sir."

"I'm very glad to finally meet you, Wagner," General Bellmon said in German, offering his hand. "I've heard a good deal about you."

His German was fluent and easy. High German, Karl-Heinz thought approvingly.

"The *Herr General* speaks German very well," Karl-Heinz blurted.

"I spent three years in a POW camp."

"My husband, Karl," Mrs. Bellmon said, "is notorious for saying the first thing that pops into his mind."

"Where is the booze?" Lowell asked. "I have just gone through a harrowing experience."

"What was her name?" Mrs. Bellmon asked.

"I let the fledgling birdman here," Lowell explained, "fly my airplane. I am too old for emotional trials like that."

"I thought you were in rotary-wing school, Craig?" General Bellmon asked Geoff.

"Since it is against some absurd regulation against students taking unofficial instruction," Lowell said, "I will rephrase. You did not hear me say that Geoff flew my airplane."

"There's a reason for the regulation," General Bellmon said.

"Nobody heard you say anything about who flew what," Barbara Bellmon said firmly. "Nobody who expects to go home with me, at least."

General Bellmon threw up his hands in surrender.

Ursula came trotting over and kissed her brother. *She looks good,* Karl-Heinz thought. She seemed to glow. And then he noticed that she was expensively dressed in a black woolen dress. There was a string of pearls around her neck, and he quickly judged they were genuine. As was the large, square-cut diamond in her engagement ring.

"Come say Merry Christmas to Geoff's mother and father," she said.

"With the *Herr General*'s permission?"

"Of course," General Bellmon said, and then added, "Karl, a word of advice. I hope you'll take it as coming from a friend of the family. A good friend of the family. We save that 'with the *Herr General*'s permission' sort of business for times when we are on duty and in uniform."

"On the other hand, Karl," Colonel Lowell said, "if you fail to call him General he will have you shot!"

Barbara Bellmon laughed delightedly.

"Come on, Casanova," she said to Lowell, "we'll get you a drink."

There were some other junior officers and their wives in the house, and Karl-Heinz learned they were classmates of Geoff's. And some were in uniform, which made him feel easier about being in uniform himself. There was a buffet, an awesome display of ham and turkey and roast beef and cheeses and shrimp.

Karl-Heinz had a couple of stiff drinks of cognac, which put him at ease, and then a hand clapped his back.

"Dutch, you old sonofabitch!"

It was an officer he had known in Vietnam, a Green Beret, who asked if he had been sent to flight school, too.

"No, I am here because this is my brother-in-law's house and I have been invited for Christmas."

"Geoff Craig is your brother-in-law? I'll be damned. I didn't know that. Come on, I got the wife—I want you to meet her."

Finally he realized that he was glad that he came, and that Colonel Lowell had offered him no choice in the matter. Otherwise he would have spent Christmas in the BOQ, alone, watching television.

Gradually the party petered out. Karl-Heinz noticed that, contrary to what he understood the Customs of the Service to be, people left before the Commanding General did. But at ten o'clock General Bellmon was sitting on a couch with his wife and Colonel Lowell and showed no inclination to leave.

And then Ursula moved among the fifteen or so people remaining, handing each a stemmed glass, which Geoff then filled with champagne. As he did that, he asked each person to hold off drinking it until the speech.

Finally Geoff called for everyone's attention.

"My cousin, the Colonel," he said, and there was the expected laughter, and he waited for it to subside before going on, "has told me of the Army custom of raising a glass on such occasions to 'absent friends.'"

"Hear, hear," General Bellmon said and stood up. The others quickly followed suit.

"Absent friends," Geoff said, and raised his glass.

"Absent friends," everybody parroted, and sipped, the champagne.

"New friends," Geoff said, and raised his glass again. That wasn't expected, but the others raised their glasses again.

"And finally," Geoff said, "to friends-to-be."

"What the hell does that mean?" Colonel Lowell asked, curiously, on the edge of disapproval.

"I was worried no one would ask," Geoff said. "What it means is that in about six months . . . I can't think of anything clever to say. Ursula's pregnant, and we couldn't think of a better way to make the announcement than here and now."

[TWO]
Der Bechewald
Near Marburg an der Lahn, West Germany
25 December 1963

LOTHAR HASBERGER, the six-foot-two, 230-pound, forty-five-year-old Jägermeister—Chief Hunter and Game Warden—of the Bechewald, a nine-hundred-hectare forest in the hills above Marburg, was dressed in the traditional garb of his profession—knickers and stout shoes, a leather coat, and a hat with a long feather. He was armed with a Mauser sporting rifle, based on the Mauser Model 1898 rifle. It had been rebarreled, converted to 7x57mm, restocked, and equipped with an Ernst Leitz, Wetzlar telescopic sight with a magnification power of four, and a pillar and post sight.

Beside him in the back seat of an ex–U.S. Army World War II jeep was Major Wilhelm von Methes-Zach of the Bundeswehr Intelligence Service. He was wearing a tweed jacket, a sweater, a shirt and tie, knickers, and boots reaching over his ankles. He was armed, in addition to the Walther 9mm automatic pistol which he always carried, with a Circassian-walnut-stocked Franz Deiter (Ansbach, Austria) *Drilling*. It had two .30-06 rifle barrels, and there was a 16-bore shotgun barrel beneath the rifle barrels. An Ernst Leitz, Wetzlar 2.5-power telescopic sight with crosshair optics was mounted low over the barrels. The

Drilling (from the German *Drei,* and meaning three-barreled) had cost Major von Methes-Zach the equivalent of nearly four thousand American dollars.

The driver of the jeep, the fourteenth Graf von Greiffenberg, and the man beside him, Colonel Sanford T. Felter, were dressed nearly identically in plaid woolen shirts, U.S. Army field jackets and trousers, and L.L. Bean & Company lace-up hunting boots. They were armed identically, with Sturm, Ruger and Company Super Blackhawk .44 Magnum caliber single-action revolvers.

Several years before, Generalleutnant Graf von Greiffenberg had asked Colonel Felter if the legendary recoil of the .44 Magnum cartridge was really all that bad; if it "really should be on wheels." Felter had told him that it took a little getting used to, since the revolver had a tendency to rise on firing, but that he personally liked his Ruger Super Blackhawk .44 Magnum revolver.

"That's the one that looks like the old Colt six-shooter?" the Graf had asked.

"Uh huh," Felter said. "I've got one with a 7.5-inch barrel. It has adjustable sights, and the springs are coil springs. It's not a copy, you understand, but an improvement on the Colt."

"So I've heard," the Graf had said.

When he went home, Felter went to the Alexandria, Virginia, Ace Hardware Store to buy the Graf a Ruger Super Blackhawk .44 and a couple of hundred rounds of ammunition for it. Felter had few friends, and the Graf was one of them, and he owed him a thousand favors and courtesies and had never before seen an opportunity to repay them. He didn't buy the Ruger at the Ace Hardware store. He shut off the salesman's enthusiastic recital of the Ruger's virtues by telling him he knew, he had one. This one he intended to send to a friend in Germany.

The salesman had then told him he couldn't do that. You couldn't export either firearms or ammunition without a license from the Department of Commerce, approvingly endorsed by the Arms Control Administration of the Department of State.

Felter checked and then gave up. The salesman was right.

Several days later he had a conversation concerning the Graf von Greiffenberg with the Director of the Central Intelligence Agency, and almost as an idle afterthought had mentioned his inability to send the Graf a pistol.

The Director chuckled and then said, "Write down what kind, Sandy.

We can take care of that. The next time you get to Frankfurt, go by the office and it'll be there. Or you want it delivered?"

"This is sort of personal," Felter had replied. "I'd like to give it to him myself."

"It's done, Sandy."

The next time he had gone to Frankfurt, he had gone by the Frankfurt Station, where he found three crates waiting for him. He opened the smallest one first. It contained a mahogany case, lined with green felt. When he opened that he found a pair of glistening Ruger Super Blackhawk Caliber .44 Magnum revolvers and a small typewritten note: "Colonel Felter, these are clean."

It did not mean that they had recently been cleaned and oiled, but rather that they could not be traced as to their source.

The largest crate contained a case (500 rounds) of Remington .44 Magnum cartridges, with 240-grain semijacketed hollow-point bullets. The third crate contained a Bianchi shoulder holster; a Bianchi hip holster and matching belt, both embossed in a basket-weave pattern; and a Douglas Brothers, El Paso, Texas, two-gun belt-and-holster set, engraved in a floral pattern, as worn by the heroes of motion picture Westerns.

There was very little the Director of the Central Intelligence Agency would not do to keep his German counterpart happy.

There was nothing to do but turn it all over to the Graf and tell him what had happened. The Graf had been amused and pleased. He liked the Rugers. He was carrying his now in the shoulder holster, and Felter was carrying the other one in the Bianchi belt holster.

The cowboy holsters had been given to the Graf's grandson, Peter-Paul von Greiffenberg Lowell, then thirteen, and Felter had been able to ship to him, without involving the Departments of Commerce, State, or the CIA, a pair of Crossman Model 1861 "Shiloh" CO-2 powered BB-pistols to go with them.

The Graf von Greiffenberg stopped the old jeep with a squeal of brakes on a dirt road near the top of a hill, and he and Felter got out.

"If you would be so kind, Herr Jägermeister Hasberger," the Graf said, "to wait for us at the bottom, at the narrow point by the stream. Colonel Felter and I will work our way down to you."

"*Jawohl, Herr Graf,*" the master hunter said, and then looked at Felter: "May I be so bold as to remind the *Herr Oberst* that only mature boar are permitted to be taken?"

"I understand, Herr Jägermeister," Felter said. "Thank you very much."

Major von Methes-Zach and the Jägermeister got in the Jeep. The Major turned it around and started down the hill.

"Do you sometimes feel that the Jägermeister doesn't quite approve of me?" the Graf asked.

"I wonder whether it's the pistols," Felter said, "or me?"

"I don't think it's you, Sandy. Our clothes, maybe, and probably the pistols. The lower classes are frightfully snobbish and hate to see standards fall. I guess you noticed the way von Methes-Zach was dressed? And his drilling?"

"Gorgeous," Felter said. "The rifle, I mean. It must have cost a fortune."

"I thought he looked rather gorgeous himself," the Graf said. "When he saw us, he felt a little foolish. I guess he wasn't briefed on my barbaric hunting practices. But I lost my temper with him yesterday, and I thought it might make it up to him a little if I asked him to join us."

"'Excuse me,'" Felter quoted, chuckling, "'but does the *Herr Generalleutnant Graf* intend to *hunt* with that *pistol?*'"

Von Greiffenberg snorted his amusement.

"Now if Craig were here," Felter said, "the Major would approve of him. He has his hunting clothes made in London."

Von Greiffenberg laughed. "He called yesterday. In great good spirits . . . any way you chose to interpret the word. From Fort Rucker. There was a party, and the Bellmons were there. I had a chance to speak with Bob and Barbara."

"He's the Army Aviation officer at Strike Command," Felter said. "I guess you know?"

"I knew he was there," von Greiffenberg said. "I didn't know what he was doing."

"Grumbling. He wanted to go to Vietnam."

"I know he hated going to college," von Greiffenberg said. "I found it a little strange, frankly, myself."

"'Ours not to reason why,'" Felter quoted jokingly. "Ours but to give in to the idiocies of the paper pushers."

Von Greiffenberg smiled.

"Speaking of strange," Felter said, "there are those who might find *this* whole business a little strange. A Jew, armed with a pistol, setting out to hunt, on Christmas morning, a dangerous animal whose flesh his religion forbids him to eat."

"Hunting, with a good friend, who is also a good hunter," the Graf said, "is a pleasure few people ever get to enjoy."

"I'm flattered," Felter said, the flush on his face showing he meant it.

"It'll take them ten, fifteen minutes to get in place," the Graf said. It was not a casual comment, although he would have shown no indication had Felter taken it as one, rather than a suggestion that here, where no one could hear them, was a good place to speak his mind.

"I just came from Africa," Felter said. "Specifically the Congo—and Rwanda-Burundi."

"I was there," von Greiffenberg said. "Years ago, when it was German East Africa."

"I was about to bring that up," Felter said. "I drove from Bukavu in the Congo, through Rwanda to Bujumbura in Burundi. I was going to tell you I came across an immaculately tended German military cemetery. From World War One. A small one—I stopped and looked—with perhaps twenty or thirty tombstones. Concrete with brass markers. The concrete had been whitewashed and the brass had been cared for. Not polished, but not corroded either. Very curious. I would have guessed something like that would have been long overgrown and reverted to the jungle."

"A missionary, perhaps," the Graf said. "Or some African with a sense of duty who passed it on to his sons, who are still waiting for the *Herr Hauptmann* to come back and give over their back pay."

"Maybe you should send someone over from Monkoto and settle up," Felter said casually.

The Graf's face momentarily registered surprise, and for a briefer moment his eyes grew cold. West Germany was conducting rocket-launching tests, forbidden by the Peace Treaty, in a three-thousand-square-mile area in the absolutely uninhabited center of the Congo. Until this moment, von Greiffenberg had been convinced they were doing so in absolute secrecy.

"I, of course," the Graf said finally, smiling broadly, "have no idea what you're talking about."

"Well, it's not much of a secret. Even the CIA knows about it."

The Graf laughed heartily. "Is that what you were doing in the Belgian Congo, Sandy? Running down outrageous rumors?"

"The Democratic Republic of the Congo," Felter corrected him.

"What do you want to know about Monkoto that you don't already know?"

"I'm not interested in rockets," Felter said, "but I do need a favor. More or less out of school."

"In school or out—what do you need?"

"I think there is a very good chance that Major Michael Hoare may have to be called from his well-earned retirement," Felter said dryly. "I want to put somebody in to watch him."

Von Greiffenberg's face grew thoughtful. Michael Hoare was a controversial and legendary character in the Congo and South Africa.

Until 1960 there had been two Congos, French and Belgian. On June 30, 1960, in Leopoldville, King Baudouin had granted independence to the former Belgian colony, which immediately proclaimed itself the Democratic Republic of the Congo. There were at the time thirty citizens of the new republic who possessed a college degree.

Joseph Kasavubu was elected as President and Chief of State. Patrice Lumumba became Prime Minister. Joseph-Désiré Mobutu, whose previous military service had been as a corporal in the Belgian-officered Force Publique was promoted colonel and named to head the Armée Nationale Congolaise (ANC).

Twelve days later, on July 11, 1960, President (we would call the office Governor) Moise Tshombe of the Katanga Province declared the province independent. Katanga was by far the wealthiest and the most industrially advanced of all the Congolese provinces. Enormous and enormously profitable tin and copper mines were in Katanga, operated by the Belgian firm Union Minière. Tshombe could see no reason to share Katanga's wealth with the rest of the new republic.

When the Leopoldville government had taken steps to suppress the rebellion with the Armée Nationale Congolaise, Tshombe had countered by commissioning Michael Hoare into the Gendarmerie de Katanga as a major.

Hoare, born in Northern Ireland, had served with the Chindits in Burma during World War II. After the war he had moved to Durban, South Africa, where he opened an automobile dealership. Hoare had promptly recruited a force of mercenaries in South Africa, elsewhere in Africa, and in Europe, and taken them to Katanga, where they had quickly proven themselves more than capable of dealing with the ANC.

In November 1961 the United Nations demanded the reunification of Katanga Province with the rest of the country. Tshombe responded by making preparations for all-out war, and it was not an idle bluff, for he had powerful Belgian and other European backers who were willing and able to provide whatever Michael Hoare's mercenaries and the other Katangese military forces required.

All-out war seemed quite possible. It would have been not only bloody, but it would have caused havoc by interrupting the flow of Katangese copper, tin, and other raw materials, into the just-recovering European economy.

In December 1962, with the approval of the United States, UN forces began military operations against Tshombe in Katanga. Surprising everybody, he gave up the next month.

Hoare's mercenaries were disarmed and ordered out of the Congo. But he, and they, had remained a wild card in what had happened since.

"You think it would come to that?" von Greiffenberg asked.

"I think it's entirely possible," Felter said simply.

"And so you want to watch him?"

Felter nodded.

"I'm surprised the Company hasn't already done that," the Graf said, and then, after a moment's thought, added: "As a matter of fact, we're rather counting on it."

"I was in Durban, too," Felter said. "I talked to him. If Hoare doesn't know who the Company's man is, Hoare is far more stupid than I think he is. Leaving the Company's man in place, I want to put my own man in."

"How can I help?"

"I heard that Hessische Schwere Konstruktion is building a new bank building in Durban. Is that all there is to it?"

"At the moment, yes," the Graf replied without hesitation. "We plan to be so pleased with the prospect of future business, however, that we will open a permanent Durban office."

"Would another construction engineer raise questions?"

"Presuming he were German, or really fluent in German, no."

"The man I have in mind used to be in the East German Army Pioneer Corps."

"Then he would be right at home," the Graf said. "How do you plan to send him in?"

"I think if he were here, and sent to Durban by Hessische Schwere Konstruktion, it would be less suspicious than if he were to show up in Durban and be hired there."

The Graf nodded his agreement. "Let me know when you're ready," he said. "Can I count on getting from you what he gets . . . now that you've sown the seeds of less than full faith in the Company?"

"Of course," Felter said.

"Anything else I can do for you?"

"That's it."

"Then let us hunt. If they're not in place yet, they will be in a minute or two."

The wind was blowing toward them, which was a lucky circumstance. Boar have acute senses of smell. But they also have acute senses of hearing, and when Felter and the Graf von Greiffenberg had been walking fifteen minutes through the forest, they heard the unmistakable sound of a herd of boar crashing through the underbrush ahead of them.

"Damn!" the Graf swore in English.

Five minutes later there was the sharp crack of a .30-06, followed a moment later by another. The boar had reached Major von Methes-Zach and the Jägermeister, where they were backing them up.

Felter and the Graf moved more slowly now through the forest, pausing every few steps to listen for the sound of the herd of boar, having been re-turned, coming back.

Finally it came, and they froze in their tracks and took the pistols from their holsters.

The boar would now be excited. A big boar would go three hundred, three hundred and fifty pounds, the sows seventy-five pounds lighter. They had no fear of attacking men anyway, they were now excited, and their tusks used against a man who lost his footing were deadly.

They waited a long time, absolutely silent, breathing with a conscious effort, slowly and through the nose.

And then they heard the herd coming to them.

Felter saw nothing, but then he heard the peculiar click of the Ruger Super Blackhawk revolver as it is cocked. He snapped his head around and smiled. The Graf, in the classic pistol marksman's position, the pistol extended at arm's length, the other hand in his trousers pocket, was aiming at something Felter couldn't see in the trees.

And then there was a sound immediately before Felter and he saw a boar coming toward him quickly and with surprising delicacy.

He threw his pistol up, holding it with both hands, drew a quick bead, and fired. The boar didn't even hesitate. Felter fired again, more carefully, and hit where he had aimed, in the eye. The boar fell over dead.

There was a rush of sound and fleeting glimpses of other boars and sows rushing past him through the trees, and then the sound of the Graf's pistol firing, once, twice, and then a third time.

And then all was silent except for the diminishing sound of the herd moving away from them in the forest.

"You all right?" the Graf called.

"You?"

"I got a double," the Graf called back, pleased.

Felter walked to his boar and could see from the condition of the skull that it had to be dead. And then he saw the chest. He hadn't missed. There was a nearly half-inch hole on the boar's chest. What it was was that the most powerful handgun cartridge ever developed could not penetrate the layer of gristle over the chest cavity of a 325-pound wild boar.

The Graf walked over.

"Mine aren't nearly that big," he said. "That'll go a hundred and sixty kilos."

Felter was aware that his heart was beating fast, that he was excited, even exulted.

"Well, now that we've done this," he said, "can we go find something to eat—and drink?"

The Graf von Greiffenberg laughed aloud and then put his arm around Felter's shoulders and hugged him.

There came the sound of electronic beeping. The Graf took a small radio from his pocket.

"*Ja?*" he asked, and then told Major von Methes-Zach that everything was fine; that they'd had some luck; and to bring the jeep. He put the radio back in his pocket and took out a monogrammed silver flask.

Generalleutnant Graf von Greiffenberg and Colonel Sanford T. Felter sat on the ground and emptied the flask of Marnier Lapastolle cognac between them before the jeep found them.

[THREE]
Headquarters, United States Strike Command
McDill Air Force Base, Florida
5 January 1964

GℰNERAL MATTHEW J. EVANS, a tall, well-built, silver-haired man in his middle fifties, walked into the Secure Reading Room of the Classified Documents Section, trailed by his junior aide-de-camp. Both were wearing khaki trousers and open-collared short-sleeve khaki shirts.

Evans was Commander-in-Chief, (CINC), pronounced "sink," U.S. Strike Command (STRICOM) charged with the exercise of United States Military force—Army, Navy, and Air Force—in the Middle East, South Asia, and Africa . . . one-third of the world. STRICOM was a multiservice headquarters, but it was only a staff. When the Joint Chiefs of Staff issued marching orders, Army, Navy, and Air Force units normally assigned elsewhere were put under CINC-STRICOM's command, otherwise STRICOM was the headquarters of a phantom force.

General Evans had been heard to quip, "Never have so many stars [four stars were on each of his collar points] commanded so few."

There were four people at tables in the Secure Reading Room, a lieutenant colonel and two master sergeants in khaki, and a full colonel in greens. The Colonel had removed his blouse, revealing that he held up his trousers with red suspenders. The Lieutenant Colonel and the two Master Sergeants started to get to their feet when the Commanding General, Strike Command, entered the room. General Evans smiled and waved them back into their chairs. The Colonel seemed oblivious to General Evans' presence.

Evans walked to his table. The Colonel, slumped back in a chair with a thick folder propped on his stomach, did not raise his eyes from it.

General Evans smiled and chuckled.

"I like your suspenders, Felter," he said. "What did you do, steal them from a fireman?"

Colonel Sanford T. Felter got quickly to his feet.

"I'm sorry, Sir," he said. "I didn't know you were there."

"What are you reading?" Evans asked.

"OPLAN 515, Sir," Felter said. "Ready Move."

"There's a sequel," General Evans said. "Five Fifteen Slash One, Ready Move Two."

"Yes, Sir," Felter said. "I have that too."

"Why don't you bring them over to my office, Felter?" General Evans said. "It's more comfortable and I'll throw in a cup of coffee."

"I don't want to interfere with your schedule, General."

"Question of priorities," Evans said. "Right now a Counselor to the President is the closest thing I have to a VIP around here."

"Yes, Sir," Felter said. "Thank you, Sir."

General Evans looked at his aide.

"Sign those documents out, Eddie," he ordered. "I think I'll want to have a look at them when Colonel Felter is finished."

"Yes, Sir," the aide-de-camp said.

"You'll have to put your blouse on, Felter, I'm afraid," General Evans said with a smile. "Those suspenders would raise eyebrows around here."

Years before, when he had first met Felter, General Evans had decided that he liked him. He thought of him privately as a mean little sonofabitch, but that was more in approval of him as a man and an officer than a reaction to Felter's reputation as an officer who could not be safely crossed.

Felter didn't look much like a warrior, but it was the General's experience that few warriors looked the part. And from what he knew of Felter (which included what he had heard and what he had taken the trouble to find out for himself), Felter was a warrior, with the Purple Hearts and the medals for valor, including the Distinguished Service Cross, to prove it.

"General Dyess, my J-3, was a little disappointed you didn't have the time to say hello," General Evans said.

Dyess was plans and training staff officer. The numerical designation was preceded by an S- at battalion and regimental level; by a G- (for General) at Division, Corps and Army level; and by a J- (for Joint) on a multiservice staff, such as Strike Command, which included Navy and Air Force components.

(What General Dyess had in fact said was, "General, I just found out that that goddamned little Jew, Felter, is snooping around in the War Plans. And I thought you'd want to know.")

"It was my intention, Sir," Felter said, as he buttoned his blouse, "to pay my respects to General Dyess and you if you had the time to see me, before I left."

"That's what I told him, Felter," General Evans said. "I told him I was sure you would make every effort to fit us into your busy schedule."

"General, if I've offended you, I'm sorry," Felter said. "I wanted to look at those plans before I saw you. I certainly intended no disrespect."

"Hell, Felter, I'm just pulling your leg," Evans said. "I know if you wanted to sneak in here, you wouldn't have flown in in a White House Special Missions jet . . . and wearing fireman's suspenders."

They were nearly at the head of the stairs from the basement by then, and General Evans' aide-de-camp, carrying the OPLANs, rushed past them to open the door.

And then he walked quickly down the corridor and opened the private door to General Evans' office.

General Evans gestured for Felter to sit down on a couch facing a coffee table, and then walked behind his desk and sat down.

A woman master sergeant appeared at a door.

"Get us some coffee, will you please, and then call General Dyess and ask him to keep himself available?" General Evans ordered courteously. He turned to his aide. "Find something to do, Eddie. Colonel Felter and I are about to start singing bawdy songs and I wouldn't want you to be embarrassed."

General Evans waited until the coffee was delivered, and until the aide had closed the door after him. Then he said, "OK, Colonel, what the hell is going on?"

"The President's asked me to keep an eye on the Congo," Felter said, "and authorized me to take certain precautionary, contingency, actions."

"Any special reason? Or is something going on over there I'm not important enough to be told about?"

"I would like to think this is in response to a report I gave him on what I think is liable to happen over there," Felter said, "but more likely, he's reacting to Senator Goldwater."

General Evans grunted.

"You mean that 'change sides' speech?"

"Yes, Sir."

"Are you telling me that nothing is going on over there?"

"Nothing, Sir, that your man in the Congo hasn't already told you."

"I gather you've met Colonel Dills?"

"I just came from the Congo, Sir. I spent a day with him when I was there, Sir. Good man."

"Yes, he is. He's retiring, I guess you know, in August?"

"Yes, Sir, he told me."

"And I don't have any funds to replace him," General Evans said. "Did you know that?"

"No, Sir," Felter said, "I didn't." He paused, just perceptibly. "I think funding can be found, Sir."

"Can I count on that?"

"Yes, Sir."

"Then there *is* something going on over there. Or you think there will be."

"I have a gut feeling, nothing more. The communists tend to try to fill a vacuum."

"But enough of a feeling to come down here and look at the OPLANs?"

"Yes, Sir," Felter said. "Sir, before we go any further. If you have no objections, I'd like to get Lieutenant Colonel Lowell in here."

"Why?" General Evans asked simply.

"Do you know Lowell, Sir?"

"I met him when he reported in," Evans said. "And I know that the opinion of the Army is about equally divided about him. There are those who believe that he's a no-good sonofabitch who should have been thrown out of the Army years ago. And there are others for whom he is sort of a reincarnation of Georgie Patton with traces of Ernie Harmon and I. D. White thrown in for good measure. I haven't had a chance to make up my mind about him."

"Sir," Felter said, "how do you feel about the old saw that says the truth is usually equidistant from the extremes?"

General Evans did not respond to that.

"I've also heard that you two are great buddies, Felter," he said. He waited a moment and then went on. "But I *do* know enough about *you* to know you would not let that color your judgment."

He picked up a telephone.

"Sergeant, go find Lieutenant Colonel Lowell. Get him over here right now."

"Thank you, Sir," Felter said.

"Or does he already work for you, Colonel? Is that why he was sent here?"

His tone of voice was cold, as if he had just thought of the possibility, considered it likely, and didn't like it at all.

"No, Sir. I understand his assignment here may have been influenced by General E. Z. Black—who is an admirer—but I had nothing to do with it. He knows nothing about why I'm here."

"OK," General Evans said.

"Sir, I'm going to need a contact here. And Lowell possesses unique qualifications. He's an aviator, with contacts with them. He has close contacts within the Green Berets. And he's a fine staff officer."

"I have a dozen other officers meeting those qualifications," Evans said. "You left out he's a pal of yours."

"I also omitted mentioning his father-in-law is Generalleutnant Graf von Greiffenberg."

"I thought he was a bachelor."

"Mrs. Lowell was killed some years ago, Sir," Felter said. "But he and his father-in-law have remained close."

"The Germans are involved in this?"

"Yes, Sir, but I'm not in a position to discuss that further at this time."

Evans looked at him a moment and then nodded his head as if he'd just made up his mind.

"OK."

One of his telephones rang. He picked it up and said his last name, grunted, and hung up.

"Lowell's on his way. Take him a couple of minutes. While we're waiting, why don't you tell me what you think of the OPLAN 515/1, Evacuation of American Nationals from Leopoldville, Democratic Republic of the Congo?"

"I wasn't quite through it, Sir, when you came down," Felter said. "I was curious that it calls for a platoon of airborne infantry."

"It originally called for two companies," General Evans said. "Plus a third in reserve. A light battalion, in other words. That got shot down in Washington. The State Department apparently feels that many men would be provocative. JCS as usual, caved in to their superior wisdom."

"Two PFCs in uniform would be provocative," Felter said. "And just about as effective as a platoon."

"You're preaching to the already converted, Felter," General Evans said. "But that was the decision. Unless *you* can get some minds changed. . . ."

"I don't think that's possible, Sir."

"I'm disappointed in you, Felter. Rumor has it that you have the Commander-in-Chief's ear."

"Purely for planning purposes, General. Not to go as far as submitting it anywhere else for comment, it might be interesting to get into the logistics of beefing up Five Fifteen Slash One to a battalion-sized force."

"Huh!" General Evans snorted.

"All the Americans in the Congo are not in Leopoldville, Sir. There's some all over the Kivu Province. We have a consulate in Stanleyville, too. I think we have to be concerned about their welfare, too."

"I take your point, Colonel."

"May I suggest that Colonel Lowell might be helpful in drawing up the plan?"

"I thought you might have something like that in mind," Evans said dryly.

"When I spoke with Colonel Dills, he told me that one of his problems is getting around the Congo. It's as big as the United States east of the Mississippi, you know. No roads, and not much scheduled air transport."

"He's supposed to have access to the planes assigned to the embassy," General Evans said. "But you know how that works. The tea-and-crumpet crew gets priority."

"The Ambassador mentioned that he was short of aircraft, but that his request for another L-23 was turned down."

"Drop the other shoe, Colonel."

"I told him I thought I could arrange for another L-23 and crew," Felter said, "with the understanding that it go to Colonel Dills. I made the point, I think, that I don't want Colonel Dills to have to justify his use of the airplane."

"And he went along?"

"After some discussion he seemed to understand that if Colonel Dills had his own airplane, he wouldn't be competing with the embassy staff for one of theirs. And that I was not in a position to get him an aircraft for general embassy use."

"What do you want from Colonel Dills, Felter? Which means, what do you want from me?"

"I want copies of everything Dills sends you."

"You can get that anyway."

"If you could make Dills's reports available to Lowell, I could probably get them quicker."

"OK."

"And there may be, from time to time, certain things I'd like to have Colonel Dills do for me," Felter said. "Things I would prefer did not get into either diplomatic or military channels."

"Requests which would pass through Lowell?"

"Yes, Sir."

"Such as?"

"Take people here and there to have a look at things."

"Spooks? Goddamn it, Felter. I don't want Dills involved in something like that."

"I understand Special Forces is going to conduct some training exercises overseas," Felter said. "I thought maybe you would want some of them to take place in the Congo."

"And without letting the JCS know about the foreign training-areas having been changed, of course?" Evans said sarcastically.

"I don't think you routinely advise the JCS about training missions involving so few people," Felter said. "I'd really be surprised if they ever became cognizant of these missions."

"And who would get burned if they found out? They'd come after me," Evans said. "And I'd have to tell them."

"Tell JCS I was responsible."

"Tell your Green Berets to be very discreet, Colonel Felter," General Evans said, "and pray we don't get caught."

The telephone rang again and Evans picked it up.

"Send him in," he said, and hung up.

The door opened. Lieutenant Colonel Craig W. Lowell, in a superbly tailored tropical worsted uniform, entered the room. He marched within twenty-four inches of General Evans's desk, saluted crisply, and formally announced: "Lieutenant Colonel Lowell reports to the Commander-in-Chief as ordered, Sir."

Evans returned the salute. He noticed with approval that Lowell wore his double-starred Combat Infantry Badge above his Senior Aviator's wings. Whatever faults he might have, Lowell had his priorities in order.

"I believe you know Colonel Felter, Colonel?" General Evans said.

"Yes, Sir. I have that privilege. Good afternoon, Sir."

"I also heard you're old buddies."

"Yes, Sir," Lieutenant Colonel Lowell said. "The Colonel and I go back to when he had hair."

He walked quickly to Colonel Felter, wrapped his arms around him, and picked him off the floor.

"*Damn*, I'm glad to see you, Mouse!" he cried happily.

"For God's sake, Craig!" Felter said furiously, struggling to free himself.

General Evans, with a valiant effort, suppressed a smile. It wasn't exactly the decorous behavior to be expected of two senior field-grade officers, but if the story were true—and Evans believed it to be—that Lowell had plucked Felter off the beach at the Bay of Pigs ten minutes before that operation went down the tubes, it could be overlooked.

V

[ONE]
U.S. Army Reception Center
Fort Leonard Wood, Missouri
5 January 1964

RECRUIT JACQUES EMILE PORTET, US 53 279 656, had been in
the United States Army not quite seventy-two hours. He had nevertheless already formed two conclusions about the experience: that he didn't
like it and that it was the intention of the United States Army to as
quickly as possible send him to Indochina where he would be killed.

He had gotten in a fight with the system within hours of having taken
one step forward (signifying his willingness, however reluctantly, to
accept the opinion of his friends and neighbors, those faceless
sonofabitches, that he should be inducted into the Army) and raised his
hand to swear that he would not only defend the Constitution of the
United States against all enemies, foreign and domestic, but that he
would obey orders of the officers and noncommissioned officers appointed over him.

He and the other inductees with him had been taken by Greyhound
bus from Saint Louis to Fort Leonard Wood, where they had been given
a welcoming speech, which included a long litany of what the Army
could and would do to anyone who decided to go home, or talk back to a
sergeant, or consume controlled substances, or have in their possession
lethal weapons or pornographic material.

They had then been assigned to a processing company, where they had been assigned to a barracks and issued a mattress cover, two sheets, a pillowcase, and two blankets. A specialist fourth class, drunk with his own authority, had then demonstrated the correct manner of making a GI bed and provided his own list of dire consequences for anyone failing to come up to his high standards.

They were then marched to a building where there were white-jacketed GIs, armed with chrome-plated devices, powered by air. These were intended to administer the required regimen of inoculations against disease.

Jack Portet was a believer in inoculations against disease. He had seen with his own eyes what happened to people in the Congo who let slip their appointment with the doctor to bring their international certificate of inoculations up to date. His own ICI was up to date, and that was what posed the problem, for he had also seen what happened to people who took shots that reacted with inoculations they already had.

He had no intention of letting himself be injected with something that moments later might cause him to pass out, or writhe on the floor. Or to be, conceivably, dead.

"I'd like to see a doctor before I take any of these," Jack had said as politely as possible.

"Fuck you, lemme have that arm."

"Not until I see a doctor."

"Hey, Sarge! I got a wise guy!"

The first physician to whom Recruit Portet explained his problem and showed his international certificate of immunization was a young first lieutenant who had obviously never seen an ICI before. Nor was he familiar with several of the immunization inoculations Recruit Portet's ICI said he had received against the vast array of diseases common to Africa.

Telephone calls were made. The duty officer at the base hospital said that probably the best thing to do was send the kid over there, where they could have a look at his ICI; he would send a staff car. As Recruit Portet's peers, who had taken *their* shots without causing any trouble, were lining up preparatory to being marched back to their barracks, they say him, accompanied by a medical corpsman, being loaded into a Ford staff car and driven off.

The Chief of the Hematology and Immunology Service of the Fort Leonard Wood Base Hospital was a pleasant youngish lieutenant colonel who told Recruit Portet that he was lucky he had refused the usual regimen of inoculations.

"Or we'd have probably had you over here wrapped in rubber sheets, getting iced down."

He himself administered a tetanus booster, all that Jack needed to satisfy the Army's requirements, and then did what he could to make sure there were no problems in the future. He had the shots on Jack's ICI transferred to his Army inoculations record and added a comment to the effect that no immunization inoculations should be administered to Recruit Portet without a careful review of his immunization record.

"This is serious, Portet," the Colonel said. "Don't let them give you anything until *you're* sure they know what they're doing."

And then he sent Recruit Portet back to the reception center in a staff car.

The damage, as Jack suspected, was done. He had had experience with being an oddball before, at Culver and at the lycée in Brussels. He was an oddball, and therefore a troublemaker, because he was different.

He was not at all surprised that night when he was chosen to be a fire watch, which required that he walk up and down through the barracks for two hours, twice, to make sure that if there was a conflagration there would be someone to shout "Fire" and pull the fire alarm.

On his first morning in the Army he received a partial pay of fifty dollars, with which he was expected to purchase necessary toiletries. Then they were marched to a warehouse, measured, and issued uniforms. In the afternoon they were subjected to a battery of tests designed to measure their intellectual, comprehensive, and visual skills.

On his second night in the Army he was selected to be a runner in the orderly room, which required that he stay awake to answer the telephone while the charge of quarters slept.

He was therefore sleepy and a bit out of sorts when he sat down at shortly after nine that morning in a small cubicle facing the desk of Specialist Fifth Class Roland P. Kohlman.

The enlisted ranks of the Army, above PFC (pay grades E-4 through E-7) were then divided into noncommissioned officers and specialists. Specialists ranked immediately below noncommissioned officers of the same pay grade. E.g., a specialist-5 (spec-5) ranked immediately below a sergeant; a spec-7 immediately below a master sergeant.

"Have a seat," Spec-5 Kohlman said to Jack Portet with a smile. "What happens now is that we put your civilian education and your civilian job skills on your form 20. And then we add to those your scores on the intelligence and aptitude tests, and then we decide where you would best fit into the Army's needs."

Jack Portet gave him an uncertain smile, but did not reply.

"Did you finish high school?" Kohlman asked.

"Yes."

"Any college?"

"Yes."

"How much?"

"Four years."

"What's your degree?"

"History."

"I meant AB, BS?"

There followed a discussion of the differences between the degree-awarding procedures of the Free University of Brussels and those of American institutions of higher learning. Kohlman was told that the Free University of Brussels awarded a diploma in a given subject, such as history, but not a degree. The only degrees they awarded were doctoral degrees, and he had not completed that program.

Spec-5 Kohlman was suspicious of Recruit Portet from that point onward.

His suspicions that he was dealing with either a wise guy trying to award himself a background to which he was not entitled or a pathological liar deepened as the interview proceeded.

If Portet were to be believed, he was fluent in German, French, and had some knowledge of Flemish.

So far as Kohlman was concerned, the straw that broke the camel's back came when he asked Portet if he had any civilian work experience, and Portet told him that he had been a pilot.

"A commercial pilot?" Kohlman asked doubtfully.

Jack Portet was no fool. He knew that he was being disbelieved.

"A commercial pilot with an ATR."

"A what?"

"An Airline Transport Rating."

"You were an airline pilot?"

"That's right."

"Who did you work for?"

"Air Simba," Jack told him. "In the Congo."

"You don't happen to have your pilot's license with you, do you?"

Shit! Jack Portet thought. *Now he will be absolutely convinced I'm bullshitting him.*

"It's with my passport and other papers I didn't think I'd need in the Army. In a safety deposit box in the First National Bank of St. Louis."

Spec-5 Kohlman thought over the best way to handle this character for a moment before he went on.

"I think you ought to know that it's a court-martial offense to tell me something to be entered on your official records that isn't true."

Fuck you, Jack Portet thought. *Check it out.*

He said nothing.

"Is there anything you've told me here that you would like to change before we go any further?"

"Yeah," Jack said, "about the languages?"

"What about them?" Kohlman asked, convinced that he had now opened the floodgates of truth.

"Add Swahili to the list," Jack Portet said. "I speak pretty good Swahili."

Recruit Jacques Emile Portet posed something of an administrative problem for the reception center. Interviews with both the sergeant major and the assistant personnel officer for classification and assignment did not get from him an admission that he was telling a tale. The assistant personnel officer was prone to believe him.

He spoke a little French himself, and Portet had replied with obvious fluency when the Lieutenant asked, "Parlez-vous Française?" that he did indeed speak the language.

In the end it was decided to turn the whole matter over to the CIC (Counterintelligence Corps) for an official investigation. The CIC wanted to hear about anybody being inducted who had a "foreign association," and if Recruit Portet had indeed gone to the Free University of Brussels, that was certainly a foreign association.

Several days later Recruit Portet was placed on orders transferring him to the 3rd Armored Division (Training) at Fort Knox, Kentucky, for basic training as an Armored Infantryman.

His records were flagged with a coded notice saying that he was currently the subject of a CIC investigation.

[TWO]
Fort Belvoir, Virginia
13 January 1964

First Lieutenant Karl-Heinz Wagner was in the copilot's seat of the DeHavilland L-20 Beaver when it landed at Fort Belvoir's Army Airfield, under verbal orders of the Assistant Adjutant of the U.S. Army Special Warfare School to report to Room 23-B-19 in the Pentagon.

"I don't know what the hell they want," the Assistant Adjutant said. "You ever hear what they say, 'Yours not to reason why . . .'?"

"Yes, Sir," Karl-Heinz had said. Then he went to the BOQ and put on a class-A uniform and threw two changes of linen into a plastic overnight bag he had been given for having his Volkswagen repainted. Then he drove the Volkswagen to Army Ops at Pope Air Force Base and caught the regularly scheduled, if unofficial and technically illegal, morning courier flight to Washington.

The Army was forbidden by the Key West Agreement of 1948 to operate regularly scheduled air transport service. Doing so would step on the Air Force's prerogative of providing aerial transport to the Army. When the Army utilized the daily Air Force flight from Pope (which touches the Fort Bragg Reservation) to Washington, they billed the Army for each passenger seat at a rate only microscopically less than charged by civilian airlines.

The Army had Beavers: six-place, single-engine aircraft designed for the Canadian-Alaskan bush country and first used by the Army in Korea. It cost much less to fly a Beaver from Fort Bragg to Washington than the Air Force charged for flying five people there. The Air Force could not tell the Army when or where to schedule their training flights, so every day the Army scheduled a Beaver cross-country training flight from Bragg to Belvoir (which is outside Washington) and gave the pilots permission to take along any military personnel who needed a ride to Washington.

Karl-Heinz Wagner got to ride in the copilot's seat because he was senior passenger and it took only one man to fly a Beaver. The other passengers were all enlisted men, one on leave, the others running errands to the Pentagon.

Fort Belvoir is the Army Engineer Center, but its Army airfield served primarily as the primary (and again, technically illegal) air terminus for the Pentagon. When the Beaver touched down, there were perhaps thirty Army aircraft—Beechcraft twin-engine L-23s, more Beavers, and a flock of Cessna L-19s, single-engine, two-seater observation aircraft, sitting on the transient ramp. Their vertical stabilizers bore representations of all the armies and of all the divisions based in the United States.

The Pentagon operated regularly scheduled bus service between Belvoir and Washington and assigned a half dozen olive-drab staff cars to ferry colonels and generals arriving at the Belvoir airstrip to the five-sided building on the other side of the Potomac from the District of Columbia.

Lieutenant Wagner, who had never been to either the Pentagon or Washington before, was told about the bus, told to take it to the Pentagon, and once inside to look for a map of the building hung on a wall. That would show him how to get where he was supposed to go.

But when he climbed down from the Beaver, a black civilian wearing a blue suit was waiting for him.

"Lieutenant Wagner?"

"That's right."

"I been sent to fetch you."

"To take me to the Pentagon?"

"To fetch you," the black man repeated. "You got any bags or anything I can help you with?"

"Just this," Karl-Heinz replied, holding up his "I Had My Car Painted by Earl Schieb" plastic overnight bag.

He got in the front seat of the new-model, but already well-worn (like the taxi it was), olive-drab Ford staff car. Within minutes they were on a heavily traveled expressway, and not long afterward, the Pentagon building appeared on the left.

It grew larger as they approached, and Karl-Heinz had time to reflect on just how huge it was.

It was surrounded by a complicated system of access roads, and Karl-Heinz was not particularly surprised when the Pentagon fell behind. He had learned that on American expressways it was often necessary to head in the opposite direction to ultimately reach your intended destination.

But then they crossed a bridge, and there was a sign, WELCOME TO OUR NATION'S CAPITAL.

"Hey," he said. "We passed the Pentagon."

"You ain't going to the Pentagon," the driver said.

"I'm supposed to go to the Pentagon," Karl-Heinz said flatly.

"Your name Lieutenant Karl Dash Heinz Wagner?"

"That's right."

"Then you ain't supposed to go to the Pentagon," the driver said with absolute certainty. "You going to State-War-and-Navy."

When he looked at the driver, he gave him a broad, if tolerant, smile—the city boy dealing with the country boy unfamiliar with the big city.

The Ford turned left, and almost immediately Karl-Heinz realized that they were driving past the White House. He looked at the building with fascination, wondering if the President of the United States was in there at this moment. Then he noticed a sparse line of men and women, some neatly dressed and others looking like beggars, all of them carrying signs, marching slowly and unevenly on the sidewalk outside the fence.

Gottverdammte Kommunisten! he muttered.

"Communists or cowards," the driver said. "One or the other."

Karl-Heinz looked at him curiously.

"I done my hitch in 'Nam," the driver said.

Karl-Heinz was surprised but said nothing.

They turned left again, right then, and stopped before a substantial, steel-barred fence. A policeman came to the car, carrying a clipboard.

The driver rolled down his window.

"Wagner," he said to the policeman. "Lieutenant Karl Dash Heinz."

The policeman ran his finger down a list on his clipboard and then lowered his head to look through the window.

"May I see your AGO card, please, Lieutenant?"

As Karl-Heinz fished it out, he glanced at the driver, who had pushed himself out of the way so that Karl-Heinz could hand the identity card to the policeman. In doing so, his jacket opened. The driver had a .45 Colt Model 1911A1 pistol in a cross-draw holster on his left hip.

The policeman compared the photograph on the AGO card with Karl-Heinz's face and then gave it back. He gave a signal and the sturdy gate rolled open to the left.

They went inside the compound and stopped before the broad sandstone stairs of a large, and Karl-Heinz thought, quite ugly Victorian building.

"There's a reception desk right inside," the driver said. "Just give her your name."

Five minutes later, wearing a visitor's badge and accompanied by a

White House policeman, Karl-Heinz Wagner was shown into the small and simple office of Sanford T. Felter.

The last time he had seen Felter had been what now seemed to be a very long time ago, at Fort Bragg, when Karl-Heinz had been just about to graduate from the Basic Course at Camp Mackall, and Felter had recruited him to go to Berlin. Felter was now in civilian clothes, but Wagner saluted him anyway.

There was a flicker of surprise on Felter's face, but he returned the salute.

"How are you, Wagner?" he asked. "Good to see you again."

"Fine, thank you, Sir."

"I just heard the good news in the Craig family," Felter said, motioning for Wagner to sit down.

"My sister, you mean, Sir?"

"Yes, of course. I saw Colonel Lowell at McDill, at STRICOM, and he is now acting very much like a prospective grandfather."

Wagner could think of nothing to say in reply.

"How's Camp Mackall?"

"I would rather be in Vietnam, Sir," Wagner said.

"So would I," Felter said, "but that wasn't my question."

"It is difficult to make the men serious," Wagner said. "To make them understand what they will be facing."

"I suspect that someone like you in Roman Legions said very much the same thing about Centurion boot camp," Felter said. "The human mind tends to alter that which it does not want to believe."

"May I ask why you sent for me, Sir?" Wagner asked.

"I have a job for you, if you'd be interested."

"Sir, with respect, I am a soldier."

"So'm I," Felter said. "Soldiers do what they're ordered to do."

"I am not, then, being given a choice? With regard to the job you mentioned?"

It was a moment before Felter replied.

"Yes," he said finally. "I wouldn't want you there unless you understood the importance of what you were doing and were willing to take the assignment. I did not say 'wanted the assignment.' I said 'were willing to take' it. There's a distinction."

"Have I the Colonel's permission to speak frankly?"

"Certainly."

"Colonel, I am a soldier. I don't want to be a spy."

"The first obligation of a soldier is to do what is best for the Army," Felter said. "Even if that includes being a spy. Or, for that matter, being a Counselor to the President."

"It was not my intention to offend the Colonel, Sir."

"When you offend me, you'll know," Felter said matter of factly. "Actually, I appreciate your candor."

"Yes, Sir."

"Over the objections of a G-2 colonel, Wagner, who acted as if the KGB had been invited to bring their cameras while we showed them around the Situation Room . . ."

"Sir?"

"What?"

"The Situation Room?"

"It's next door, five floors underground. The Commander-in-Chief's CP."

"Yes, Sir."

"I was saying that you now have a Top Secret clearance, with an 'Eagle' endorsement," Felter said. "What follows is classified Top Secret Eagle. Do you understand?"

"I do not understand the 'Eagle,' Sir."

"Eagle is a contingency plan for the Democratic Republic of the Congo, the ex–Congo Belge. I am the action officer, and so far, except for the President and my secretary, you are the only other person cleared for it."

"I don't know what response is expected of me, Sir."

"Just sit there and listen," Felter said, not unkindly. "I'll tell you when I want a response."

Felter delivered a ten-minute lecture on the history of the Democratic Republic of the Congo from its birth, including a precise description of the mercenary operations, under Major Michael Hoare, in the Katanga Province.

"If there is a resurgence of the Katanga rebellion, which I think possible, even likely," Felter said, "or some other internal warfare, which is less likely but still possible, I think Hoare will be involved again. I hate to use the word, because it makes me sound like a State Department bureaucrat, but if that happens, there will be important 'geopolitical' consequences."

"Sir, I am shamed to tell you I know little of the problems there."

"You're not alone, Karl-Heinz," Felter said and chuckled. "But let me try to put it in military terms. It is of great importance, 'geopolitically,' for the President to know the capabilities of any new mercenary force that Hoare might organize—or even that we might ask him to organize—for employment in the ex-Congo Belge. I just came back from Africa and I wasn't at all impressed with the man the CIA has charged with keeping an eye on Hoare. For one thing he used to be a naval officer, and for another, I thought he was a *Scheisskopf*."

"You want me to go to the Belgian Congo?" Wagner asked, but it was more of an accusation than a question.

Felter nodded. "South Africa. Hoare's got a Rover agency in Durban. He has a loose collection of ex-mercenaries and would-be mercenaries— not formally organized, but capable, I think, of being quickly pulled together whenever he wishes. If that happens, I need an evaluation—a soldier's evaluation—of that organization. From Hoare down to the private in the ranks, weapons, training, transportation, morale. . . ."

"Yes, Sir," Karl-Heinz said.

"Pardon me?"

"I said, 'Yes, Sir.' Have I the Colonel's permission to ask questions?"

"Shoot?"

"What will my Army status be?"

"I haven't even outlined what role I would like you to play in this."

"I am to go to South Africa as a defected officer of the DDR Volks-armee Pioneers," Karl-Heinz said. "And become a member of the loose organization Major Hoare has established."

Felter nodded his head approvingly. "You will be assigned to the ROTC detachment at Texas A and M and placed on further TDY to the Army Language School at the Presidio of Monterey. And on further TDY here. I've arranged for you to be hired as an engineer for a West German company now building a bank in Durban. You will go from here to Germany and then travel to South Africa with a West German passport. That should cover your tracks. You will draw full pay and allowances, plus per diem, plus hazardous-duty pay. The checks will go to an account we'll open for you in the Riggs Bank here. And when you come back, I will write your efficiency report."

"Yes, Sir," Wagner said.

"I'm a little curious, Wagner. . . . A few minutes ago I had formed the opinion you would not be interested in this at all."

Wagner understood the question but took a moment to frame his reply.

"Sir, I have taken the oath. For a moment I forgot that I did, that I have been given a second chance as an officer."

"If you're talking about swearing to 'obey the orders of officers appointed over me,'" Felter said, quoting the officer's oath of office, "I thought I had made it clear that if you take this job it will be as a volunteer. There's no order involved."

"I have sworn," Karl-Heinz Wagner said, quoting, "'to defend the United States against all enemies, foreign and domestic.'"

"The phrase," Felter corrected him, "is to defend *The Constitution*, etcetera."

"The meaning is the same," Wagner said seriously. "Without the Constitution, there would be no United States and nothing worth defending."

Felter looked at him thoughtfully.

His first thought bordered on the flippant: *You can take a German out of the country, but you can't take the German out of the German.* He immediately regretted it, and realized why it had come to his mind. Then he understood. Like most American officers he was uneasy when someone talked about the officer's oath, or their obligations under it. It didn't mean that they held the oath, or their obligations, in scorn, but rather that it wasn't the sort of thing one talked about, for fear of sounding like a fool, a dunce wrapped in the flag and dancing to the sound of a trumpet.

Karl-Heinz Wagner had been conditioned to quite the reverse. He had been raised in a totalitarian state. He had even prospered under the German Democratic Republic. He had been educated by it, commissioned into its army, and served it with distinction. And he had betrayed it. Not casually, Felter thought, but only after what must have been a good deal of painful thought, and not, Felter believed, for material reasons. But for freedom, another word that most American officers were reluctant to discuss seriously.

The price of freedom for Karl-Heinz Wagner had been the loss of his honor and his property. And if they had caught him, it would have meant his life. And that of his sister. It had taken courage to put his sister behind the cement bags in the truck he'd stolen to crash through the Berlin Wall. . . .

When Felter reflected philosophically about his country, his thoughts usually turned to the revolution and to the revolutionaries. They had not been a bunch of malcontents hoping to get something material out of it when the revolution succeeded. They had been the aristocracy.

And they had been, many of them, soldiers. Colonel George Washington had taken the King's shilling, swearing loyalty to the British State in the person of His Most Britannic Majesty, George III. He had been a rich Virginia planter, and so had Thomas Jefferson. When they had pledged their lives, their fortunes, and their sacred honor, they had something to lose, and they had not considered themselves too masculine, or too sophisticated, to use words like liberty and freedom and honor.

Colonel George Washington, Felter decided, would both understand and approve of Lieutenant Karl-Heinz Wagner, and so did Colonel Sanford T. Felter.

"OK," he said finally. "Thank you. I'll get the paperwork going. Any reason you can't leave Bragg in the next couple of days?"

"No, Sir."

"I've got an Afrikaans instructor laid on at the Language School," Felter said. "He says he can teach a German-speaker enough to get by in three weeks. You'll go there first."

"Yes, Sir."

"But now it's lunchtime," Felter said. "I think under the circumstances that I should buy you a lunch."

"The Colonel is very kind, but that is unnecessary."

"I think we'll go to the Army-Navy Club. The food's not all that good, but I like to go there every once in a while and look at all the memorabilia. A career officer such as yourself, Lieutenant Wagner, should be able to say he's eaten lunch there at least once."

[THREE]
Cairns Army Airfield
Fort Rucker, Alabama
19 January 1964

THE ARMY had purchased a half-dozen Aero Commanders—sleek, lush, high-winged, relatively fast, twin-engine, six-place executive aircraft—"off-the-shelf" and designated the aircraft L-26. The justification for the purchase was that Beech Aircraft (which manufactured the military version of the Twin Bonanza, the L-23, which was the standard Army personnel transport) could not deliver sufficient quantities of them to meet the Army's needs. This was true, but few soldiers were surprised when the L-26 Commanders wound up assigned to transport very senior officers. In some ways the Aero Commander became a sort of U.S. Army marshal's baton, a symbol of high rank and great responsibility.

There was one exception. By direction of the Chief of Staff, one L-26 Aero Commander was assigned to the U.S. Army representative to the Federal Aviation Agency, a colonel, for his use in the execution of his official duties. This surprised few soldiers, too. It was generally accepted that the Army representative to the FAA was the recruiting officer for the CIA's airline, Air America, and that he had other CIA connections.

U.S. Army L-26 Tail Number 209 was at ten thousand feet over Eufaula when the pilot reached for his microphone.

"Cairns, Army Two Oh Nine."

"Two Oh Nine, Cairns," the tower came back immediately.

"Cairns, Two Oh Nine is VFR at one zero thousand over Eufaula. Estimate Cairns ten minutes. Request approach and landing."

"Two Oh Nine, Cairns, we have you on radar. Maintain your present heading. Descend to two thousand feet. Report five minutes out. The altimeter is three zero zero zero. The winds are negligible."

"Cairns, Two Oh Nine, understand two thousand, three zero zero zero. There is a code six aboard. We will require ground transport at the board parking ramp. No honors."

There was aboard L-26 Tail Number 209 a device known as a transponder. It was state of the art. When triggered by the Cairns Army Airfield radar it responded electronically in such a manner that the air-traffic controllers were informed what type aircraft it was and its call sign.

Two Oh Nine had told the tower it had a full colonel (code six) aboard and that he wanted a staff car to meet him. Full colonels are not expected to stand around waiting for a bus or for someone to send a car for them. The "no honors" meant that the car was all the Colonel wanted; it would not be necessary for the AOD (Aerodrome Officer of the Day) to meet the airplane when it landed to officially welcome him to the Army Aviation Center.

"Roger, Two Oh Nine," Cairns replied. "Sir, may I have the name of the code six?"

The pilot of L-26 Tail Number 209 wore the silver eagles of a full colonel on the epaulets of the blouse on a hanger in the cabin behind him. The blouse also carried the crossed flags of the Signal Corps and an impressive array of colored ribbons, the ordinary "I Was There" ribbons, and five, including the Distinguished Service Cross and the Distinguished Flying Cross, for valor. There were also parachutist's wings, the Combat Infantry Badge, and two silver badges testifying to the Colonel's skill with small arms.

Colonel Richard C. Fulbright believed that if you've got 'em, flaunt 'em.

He was a tall, lithe, ruddy-faced officer with intelligent eyes and a mischievous smile.

He flashed the smile as he looked, his eyebrows raised in question, at the man in the copilot's seat. This was another full colonel. His blouse, on its hanger in the cabin, wore the crossed rifles of infantry, parachutist's wings, and the Combat Infantry Badge, but no ribbons.

Colonel Sanford T. Felter indicated with his finger that Colonel Richard C. Fulbright should identify himself as the code six aboard.

"Christ," Colonel Fulbright said, "if I didn't know better, I might think you're a spy or something."

Then he pushed the mike button.

"Cairns, Two Oh Nine. Fulbright. I spell. Eff You Ell Bee Are Eye Gee Aicht Tee."

"I think, Colonel," Felter said, smiling, "the way you're supposed to do that is Foxtrot Uncle Love etcetera."

"Fuck 'em," Colonel Fulbright said cheerfully. "You realize you just ruined Bob Bellmon's day?"

"Bob loves you, Dick," Felter said, chuckling. "Everybody knows that."

"Two Oh Nine, Cairns. Colonel Fulbright, ground transportation will be waiting for you at the board ramp."

"Cairns, Two Oh Nine, Roger. Passing through eight thousand."

It was the SOP (Standard Operating Procedure) for the Cairns tower to report by telephone the arrival of any full colonel or more senior officer to the office of the Fort Rucker Commanding General, specifically to his aide-de-camp.

They did so now.

Captain John C. Oliver, a good-looking, young, recently returned from Vietnam Armor officer who was aide-de-camp to Major General Robert F. Bellmon, walked into the General's office and waited until General Bellmon raised his eyes from a staff study, an inch-thick stack of typewritten pages held together with a sheet-metal clip.

"Sir, a Colonel Fulbright is about to land at Cairns," Oliver said.

"Johnny," General Bellmon said almost kindly, "there is only one Colonel Fulbright liable to come here."

"Yes, Sir."

"I think it highly unlikely that Colonel Fulbright will do me the honor of paying his respects, either to the Commanding General or to me personally, but if he does show up here, we will keep the sonofabitch waiting at least fifteen minutes."

"Yes, Sir," Captain Oliver said, smiling.

"Anything on Colonel Felter?" Bellmon asked.

"No, Sir. With your permission, Sir, I thought I'd take the H-13 and meet the Southern 1430 flight in Dothan." The H-13 was a two-place, bubble-canopied Bell helicopter.

"Go ahead, Johnny," Bellmon said. "I won't be needing you."

Bellmon knew that one of two things was true about Oliver wanting to take the Bell to meet the Southern Airlines flight from Atlanta on which Sandy Felter might, just might, be arriving. One was that he was just doing his job, that he understood that Colonel Felter was entitled to VIP treatment not only because he was in a very high place, indeed, but also because he was an old, close friend of Bellmon. The other was that if he took the Bell, rather than laying on someone else, it would give him a chance to fly. Not much, but fly. As his aide-de-camp he didn't get much chance to fly.

Bellmon liked Captain Johnny Oliver. Not only was he a very bright young officer who had done well in 'Nam and almost certainly had a rewarding career ahead of him, but he was a pleasant, happy, and so far as Bellmon knew, highly moral young man. It had entered his mind more than once that Johnny Oliver would make a welcome addition to the family as the husband of his only daughter, Marjorie.

Oliver was Regular Army, and a graduate of Norwich University, which to Bellmon's mind was the equivalent qualification for a potential son-in-law as being a West Pointer. The Military College of Vermont had been turning out regular Army Cavalry and Armor officers of distinction for a long time. Bellmon had served in the 2nd Armored "Hell on Wheels" Division until he had been captured in North Africa. His division commander had been Major General Ernest Harmon. Harmon was now President of Norwich. And he had turned over the 2nd Armored to another Norwich graduate, I. D. White, who had wound up with four stars on his epaulets. Marjorie could do a lot worse than Johnny Oliver.

Marjorie had, at twenty, just graduated from college, Southern Methodist, getting through in three and a half years with a 3.8 grade average. She was going to need a strong, intelligent man, somebody like Johnny Oliver. Bellmon agreed with his wife that the worst thing he could do would be to let either one of them know how he felt, but he thought about it. God forbid that she fall for one of the locals and be doomed to spend her life in Ozark, Alabama. It was a possibility. Marjorie had taken a job with the First National Bank of Ozark, and the locals seemed to be fascinated with her.

Fifteen minutes later Johnny Oliver walked back into Bellmon's office.

"General," he said, "Colonel Felter is here."

Felter walked into the office and saluted.

Bellmon made a vague gesture in the general direction of his forehead as he got up and came around the desk.

"How are you, Sandy?" he asked, punching Felter's shoulder. "It's good to see you."

"Good to see you, General," Felter said.

"Johnny, you haven't met Colonel Felter, have you?"

"I spoke with the Colonel briefly on the telephone, Sir."

"Sandy, Johnny Oliver. I probably shouldn't say this where he can hear it, but he's the best aide I've ever had."

They shook hands.

"I've heard a good deal about you, Sir," Oliver said. "I'm pleased to meet you."

"Coffee, Sandy?" Bellmon asked. "Sit down."

"I'm coffeed out, General," Felter said. "Thank you, anyway. There were two thermoses—thermi?—in the plane, and we emptied both of them."

"Fulbright's airplane?" Bellmon asked.

"Yes, Sir."

"Johnny, let this be a lesson to you," Bellmon said. "You cannot always judge a man by his friends. Despite the friends he keeps, Colonel Felter is really a very nice fellow and a good officer."

"Yes, Sir," Oliver said, smiling.

"Colonel Fulbright asked me to pay his respects," Felter said.

"While he's down here stealing my best pilots, right?" Bellmon said.

"Is that what he's doing?" Felter inquired innocently.

"There is a rumor around that he's the recruiting officer for Air America," Bellmon said dryly. "Otherwise known as the CIA Air Force."

"Is there really?" Felter said. "I wonder how that got started?"

"To change to a less obscene subject, Sandy," Bellmon said, "what can I do for you?"

"After that, General, I'm almost afraid to bring it up."

Bellmon looked at him curiously but didn't reply. He looked at his watch, then leaned forward and dialed one of the three telephones on his desk.

"Oh," he said, when someone answered. "You're home. Good. Uncle Sandy just walked in the door. I was going to ask your mother to meet us at the club for lunch. Have you got time, too?"

He covered the mouthpiece with his hand and said, "Marjorie."

Felter nodded and smiled.

"Well, bring her, too," Bellmon ordered the telephone. "Obviously. Twenty minutes."

He hung up.

"Marjorie's got the afternoon off," he explained. "She has to work Saturday mornings, so they give her one afternoon off."

"Where's she working?"

"At the bank in Ozark," Bellmon said. "She's got Ursula Craig with her. They've become pals."

"Oh, good," Felter said. "I was going to call them of course."

"How long can you stay?"

"My ride's leaving tomorrow afternoon," Felter said, smiling.

"You were telling me what we can do for you?"

"I'm recruiting, too," Felter said.

"Not for Fulbright?" Bellmon challenged.

"No," Felter said. "For something else." He stopped. "I was about to ask you to excuse us, Captain, but I suppose both that you have been cleared for Top Secret—"

"Yes, Sir," Johnny Oliver said.

"—and that you might as well hear this, anyway," Felter finished.

"I'd be happy to leave, Sir," Oliver said.

Felter shook his head no and then went on: "The staff of the Military Attaché at the U.S. Embassy in Leopoldville, Democratic Republic of the Congo, is about to be augmented by one L-23 and two pilots to fly it. It's in connection with Operation Eagle, but the Military Attaché doesn't know that. The L-23 and the two other pilots were on his wish list, and so far as he knows he's getting what he asked for."

"'Operation Eagle'?" General Bellmon asked.

"It's a classified operation," Felter said, "and that's all you have to know about it right now."

Bellmon's face showed that he didn't like being denied the secret, but he simply nodded his head in understanding.

"The airplane has been acquired 'off-the-shelf,'" Felter said. "It's at Beech in Wichita. They're installing auxiliary fuel tanks so that it can be flown over there. It will have to be brought here and painted in Army colors. He whose name cannot be safely mentioned will arrange with SCATSA to equip it with radios and navigation equipment necessary for operation over there."

The Signal Corps Aviation Test and Support Activity, an agency of the Chief Signal Officer of the Army, was stationed at Fort Rucker to provide avionic support to the Army Aviation Board. It was whispered about that its highly skilled technicians did work on aircraft not assigned to the Board, or even the Army, which arrived and left by night.

Bellmon smiled and chuckled at the "he whose name can not be mentioned," but then the smile vanished.

"In other words it is one of Dick Fulbright's operations? I think I have the right then, to know more about it."

"It's my operation, General," Felter said. "The only thing Fulbright has to do with it was acquiring the aircraft with his funds and having it run through SCATSA."

"OK," General Bellmon said, "so what does it have to do with us? Why are you telling me all this?"

"DCSPers," Felter said, referring to the Deputy Chief of Staff for Personnel, pronounced Dee Cee Ess Purse, "has come up with the names of three aviators, here, who are about to be reassigned and meet the qualifications for the assignment. They are L-23–qualified, have done a Vietnam tour, and speak French."

"In other words," Bellmon said coldly, "I *am* about to lose another two highly qualified pilots to Fulbright and the CIA?"

"No," Felter said. "They will not be under the CIA. This is a routine assignment. They will be designated assistant Army attachés and have diplomatic status."

"Fulbright provides the aircraft, SCATSA provides special electronics, and you're involved. And I'm to believe the CIA isn't involved?"

Felter shrugged but did not reply to the question.

"I want to talk to all three of them, pick the best two, and make sure they are the ones that go, that they are not suddenly declared essential and replaced by two bodies two jumps ahead of an elimination board."

"What if they were legitimately essential?" Bellmon asked.

Felter ignored this question, too.

"In the Congo, they will work for Colonel Tony Dills, who is the STRICOM officer in that area," Felter said.

"General Evans is on this?" Bellmon asked.

"He knows about it," Felter said. "Craig Lowell's handling it for him at McDill."

"And Lowell doesn't know what's going on over there either, right?" Bellmon asked sarcastically.

"He knows precisely what I'm telling you and no more," Felter said. He gave Bellmon the opportunity to look at him and then went on: "So far as I know, really, nothing is going on over there, but I have a gut feeling something is going to happen, and I want good men who know the area on the site."

"'Know the area' can be interpreted in a number of ways," Bellmon said.

"They will be expected to do nothing more than assistant military attachés do anywhere," Felter said. "Keep their eyes and their ears open, of course, and make the usual reports. I don't want them for agents."

"I don't suppose it would matter if you did, would it?"

"No, but I'm telling you the truth."

Bellmon looked at Felter thoughtfully.

"You didn't have to say that," he said. "And if you hadn't shown up with 'he whose name cannot be safely mentioned,' I don't think I would have given you such a hard time."

"They also serve who skulk and spy," Felter said with a smile.

Bellmon chuckled.

"All you want to do is talk to these three officers and pick your best two, is that it?"

"They'll have to be trained in long-distance flight without the usual navigation aids. Will that be any trouble to arrange?"

Bellmon shook his head no.

"I thought you could have me introduced to them as the Army liaison officer to the State Department," Felter said. "Sent here to interview them."

"Sure," Bellmon said. "Have you got their names?"

Felter reached in his pocket and handed Bellmon a sheet of paper.

"You want to use my office, Sandy?" Bellmon asked.

"Let's keep it informal. What about over a beer, at the club, after lunch?"

Bellmon nodded and handed the list to Captain Oliver.

"Johnny, get in touch with these people. Go through their department heads and inform them it is the General's desire that they attend him in the bar of the club at 1330. If you're asked for details, as I suspect you will be, tell them there is some Washington big shot here who wants to talk to them. OK, Sandy?"

"Make that State Department big shot," Felter said, smiling.

VI

W HEN FIRST LIEUTENANT KARL-HEINZ WAGNER came to Washington from the Army Language School in California, he traveled in civilian clothing. He took a taxi from Washington National Airport into the District of Columbia, and to a somewhat seedy motel almost on the Maryland border. There he called the number he had been given.

Colonel Sanford T. Felter, in a baggy suit, arrived at the wheel of a battered Volkswagen thirty minutes later.

"You just leave your uniforms here and I'll take care of them," Felter said. "What did you tell Ursula?"

"That I was going to Panama on TDY to the Jungle Training School and that I would probably be gone six months."

"And she believed you?"

"My sister does not expect me to lie to her," Wagner said evenly.

Felter nodded.

"We're going to go from here to the airport," Felter said. "You'll take the shuttle to New York, to LaGuardia and then take the bus to Kennedy. You're on the seven-eighteen Lufthansa flight to Frankfurt. When you have cleared customs, put your American passport in this and drop it in the Poste Restante."

"Yes, Sir."

Felter then handed Karl-Heinz a manila envelope that looked German—slicker, less substantial than an American envelope. It had a Frankfurt address written on it and there were German stamps on it.

"Yes, Sir," Wagner repeated and put the envelope in his jacket pocket.

Felter handed Karl-Heinz a second, smaller envelope. It contained a West German passport, issued in West Berlin.

"Is this counterfeit?" Karl-Heinz asked.

"No. Not the passport. The Exit Berlin stamp is homemade, but that's all."

"That suggests, Sir, that the German government is involved?" Karl-Heinz said, making it a question.

"Just one very highly placed German, in whom I have absolute confidence."

"And some members of his staff."

"Just one man," Felter conceded. "This is a private operation."

Karl-Heinz nodded.

"After you've gotten rid of the American passport, take the bus into Frankfurt. Buy some clothes. Something that ex-Oberleutnant Wagner would buy. Not that I don't admire the suede jacket. . . ."

Wagner smiled. *"Danke schön, Herr Oberst."*

"Then go to the offices of Hessische Schwere Konstruktion," Felter went on. "It's on the sixteenth floor, Erschenheimerlandstrasse 190. That's not far from the Farben Building, so there will be a slight risk you might run into somebody you know. Be prepared for that." Felter looked up to see if Wagner understood. He nodded once that he did. What he understood was that during the war, the enormous corporate headquarters of the I.G. Farben corporation was purposefully spared destruction when Frankfurt was bombed so that it could be used as the American headquarters for occupied Germany. The U.S. Army has occupied it since 1945.

"When you get to HSK," Felter went on, "ask for Herr Neider. He will expect you, and he will be under the impression that you've just come from Berlin."

Wagner nodded.

"They will put you up for a day or two while they take care of the paperwork and then give you a ticket to Durban via Johannesburg," Felter went on. He handed Wagner two envelopes. "There's five thousand dollars in American money in one and the equivalent in South Africa rand in the other."

"What is it for?"

"Necessary expenses," Felter said, and then added dryly, "The clothing, for one thing."

"Very nice."

"There is an elaborate accounting procedure set up for these funds, Karl-Heinz, but no one has ever asked me how they were actually spent, beyond 'necessary expenses.' Far be it from me to suggest that you consider them a bonus, and I have every confidence that you won't spend a dime of it that is not in the interests of the United States government."

"It would be suspicious if a recent East German defector had a lot of cash."

"On the other hand it might explain why he defected," Felter said. "People are generally far more willing to accept that a man is a thief or an embezzler than that he risked his skin for something as unimportant as freedom."

"You think that is what I should say?" Karl-Heinz asked.

"I think you should think about it. You know what you're supposed to do. How you do it is up to you. If you really get into trouble, or learn something you feel I should know right away, contact the Embassy in Johannesburg. Ask to speak to Mr. Edward T. Watson."

"Who is he?"

"He doesn't exist," Felter said. "But that will get you put through to either the Ambassador, the Chargé d'affaires, or the CIA Station Chief. When you get through to one of them, tell them to open the Eagle envelope. That will be in the Ambassador's safe. It will inform them who you are and that you are working for me, and instruct them to immediately do what they can for you, and to get in touch with me. It also directs them to transmit whatever message you want to send. But until that envelope is opened, no one at the embassy will know you're in South Africa."

"Edward T. Watson," Wagner said, and then repeated it several times to fix it in his memory.

"Durban is a resort town," Felter said. "Vacationers send a lot of postcards. You will send one every week to Mr. Watson. If there is no postcard from Mr. Watson in any seven-day period, the Ambassador has been instructed to open the Eagle envelope."

"OK."

"I wish I had some clever suggestion, beyond buying a car from him, about how to get you up close to Michael Hoare," Felter said. "But I don't."

"If there are soldiers, or ex-soldiers, in Durban," Karl-Heinz said, "there will be a soldiers' bar. I will find it."

Felter grunted his approval.

Forty-five minutes later Karl-Heinz Wagner boarded the Eastern Airlines New York shuttle at Washington National Airport.

[TWO]
The U.S. Army Armor Center
Fort Knox, Kentucky
18 February 1964

RECRUIT JACQUES EMILE PORTET was in the sixth week of the eight-week basic training cycle which would see him designated as a light weapons infantryman when he was called out of a lecture on the care and cleaning of the U.S. Rifle M16A1 and ordered to report to the orderly room.

He found the First Sergeant, the Company Commander, and a young man in civilian clothing about his own age waiting for him.

"This is Mr. Gregory," the Company Commander said. "You are to go with him."

Mr. Gregory did not smile or offer his hand. Instead, he gave Jack a brief glimpse of a gold badge and an identification card in a leather folder.

"Will you come with me, please?" he asked.

Gregory had a car. It was a Ford four-door sedan, and it was immediately clear to Jack that before it had been repainted an unpleasant shade of blue, it had been painted olive drab. Gregory, who seemed very impressed with his own status, was obviously some kind of an Army cop, an Army detective. Jack was curious rather than upset.

I have the strength of ten, he thought, amused, *because in my heart I'm pure.*

Since his run-in with the medic who had tried to give him the full array of inoculations at Fort Leonard Wood, he had stayed out of trouble with the Army. Indeed, he was privileged to be the platoon guidon bearer as an indication of his Platoon Sergeant's opinion that he was less a complete fuck-up than his peers.

The 3rd Armored Division (Training) was housed, several miles from the main post, in frame buildings, their paint showing the ravages of the hundreds of thousands of soldiers who had passed through them since the early days of World War II.

Mr. Gregory, without saying a word to Jack, drove him to the main post, which Jack had seen before only out the windows of a bus or from the back of a truck.

It was a pleasant, tree-shaded area looking very much like an upper-class neighborhood of Saint Louis, its streets lined with substantial red-brick office buildings and homes and even a theater. There were women pushing baby carriages on sidewalks. It was civilization, Jack thought.

Gregory parked the robin's-egg-blue staff car behind one of the Williamsburg-style office buildings and spoke Jack's name for the first time.

"Come with me, please, Portet."

"Por-*tay*," Jack said. "It's pronounced Por-*tay*."

Mr. Gregory looked at him without expression and did not reply.

Then he led Jack into the building and down a glistening linoleum corridor to a door over which hung a neat sign reading G-2.

Even before the lecture on the organization of the Army, Jack had known that G-2 meant Intelligence. That explained Gregory's badge. That goddamned clerk at Fort Leonard Wood had started some sort of bureaucratic mess that was going to mean trouble.

There was a sergeant behind one desk and a rather good looking secretary behind another in an outer office.

"Is the Colonel free?" Mr. Gregory asked. "This is Recruit Portet."

He pronounced it, Jack noticed, "Por-tet."

The Sergeant pushed a button on his intercom.

"Colonel, Gregory is out here with the fellow you wanted to see."

"Send them in," a deep voice replied.

"Report to the Colonel," Mr. Gregory said. Jack had recently been instructed in the proper way to report to a commissioned officer, but had never actually done it before, except in practice with another basic trainee.

He knocked on the door, waited until he was told to enter, and then marched in, located the commissioned officer, marched to his desk, stopped two feet before it, came to attention, raised his hand in salute, and barked: "Sir, Recruit Portet reporting as ordered, Sir!"

Then he waited for the salute to be returned before lowering his hand, meanwhile staring six inches over the commissioned officer's head.

The Colonel waved informally toward his forehead and said, "At ease, son. Take a seat."

The Colonel was a full colonel, a man Jack judged to be in his early forties, getting a little bald and a little plump. His blouse wore a large display of ribbons, topped by a Combat Infantry Badge and parachutist's wings. There was an oblong plastic name tag on the blouse with MARX etched into it.

"Sit down, Portet," Colonel Marx said when he saw that Jack had made no move toward one of the two chairs facing his desk. "And relax—we're not going to shoot you right now. Would you like a cup of coffee?"

Jack thought Colonel Marx was the friendliest officer he had encountered since the doctor at Fort Leonard Wood.

"Yes, Sir, I would. Thank you."

"Gregory?" Colonel Marx asked.

"No, thank you, Sir," Gregory said, which removed the last question in Jack's mind that Gregory was a soldier, or an officer, in civilian clothing. An enlisted man, Jack realized. Otherwise the Sergeant outside would not have dared call him by his last name.

Colonel Marx raised his voice: "Two coffees, please, Sergeant Towe!"

The Sergeant delivered two china mugs of coffee and handed one to Jack.

"Portet, you are currently the subject of a CIC investigation," the Colonel said. "You know that CIC stands for Counterintelligence?"

"Yes, Sir."

"There are some people who (a) find your background fascinating," the Colonel said, "and (b) tend to disbelieve your qualifications as you gave them to the personnel assignment clerk."

"I had the feeling, Sir, that he thought I was making it up."

"Were you?" Colonel Marx asked not unkindly.

"No, Sir."

"The problem is compounded by the CIC's inability to find out much about you," Colonel Marx said. "You actually have a commercial pilot's license, with an ATR rating?"

"Yes, Sir."

"If you had to prove that, how would you go about it?"

"I'd check with the FAA, Sir. Or the Department of Commerce."

"The American FAA? I thought you told the clerk you had a Congolese license."

"I've got a Belgian license, Sir. But the Americans recognize them. And the Congolese, of course."

"*The* Americans?"

"*We* Americans, Sir."

"And the FAA has a record of your licenses?"

"Yes, Sir. I was on several ferry crews with my father, importing and exporting aircraft. We had to put our license numbers on the paperwork."

"I think that if Mr. Gregory had thought of that," Colonel Marx said, "checking with the FAA, I mean, the investigation would be a bit further along. He checked with the Congolese Embassy and they said they had never heard of you."

"They like a little gift before they look for anything," Jack said. "No gift, no information."

"You mean a bribe?" Mr. Gregory asked in disbelief.

"Ten dollars would probably have done it."

"This is an official U.S. government investigation—"

Colonel Marx interrupted him: "Your father, I understand, is a Belgian national who lives in the Congo?"

"Yes, Sir."

"What does he do there?"

"He's Chief Pilot of Air Congo, and he owns Air Simba."

"But you were born here?"

"My father was here during the Second War, Sir. When I was born, he was in the—*our*—Army Air Corps."

"Private Portet is looking less and less like a threat to the security of the United States, Mr. Gregory," Colonel Marx said. "Did it occur to you to run his father's name through the computer?"

"It was scheduled, Sir," Mr. Gregory said. "I can't say for sure that it's actually been done."

"In other words, no?"

"Not yet, Sir. I'll get right on it."

"Good idea," Colonel Marx said, and then turned to Jack. "You don't have any living relatives in the United States? Is there anyone here who knows you?"

"I have an aunt and uncle in St. Louis, Sir."

"Before you leave, make sure Mr. Gregory has their names."

"Yes, Sir."

"And it would also be handy if you could give Mr. Gregory the names of some people—preferably Americans, and preferably American officials—in both Brussels and Leopoldville who would be willing to state that as far as they know, you are not, for example, a KGB agent cleverly trying to infiltrate the enlisted ranks of the U.S. Army; maybe even that they know you to be a patriotic American who, when his draft board sent for him came home and allowed himself to be drafted. Can you think of anybody?"

"Yes, Sir," Jack said. "The Ambassador in Leopoldville plays golf with my father. Mr. Kent Rowley."

"Mr. Rowley would be fine," Colonel Marx said. "Anybody in Brussels?"

Jack had to think for a moment, and then came up with the name of a consular official who had once been stationed in Leopoldville.

"Gregory, wait outside for a moment," Colonel Marx said. "I want to talk to Portet alone."

Gregory obviously didn't like to be dismissed, but he left.

"A nice young man," Colonel Marx said. "Unfortunately he hasn't been doing what he's doing very long, and before he came in the Army, I don't think he was ever out of Ohio."

"Did he really think I was a spy?" Jack asked.

"I think he hoped you would be. Tell me, why aren't you an officer? Don't they give commissions to people with your background and experience?"

"I asked about it . . . the Military Attaché in Brussels looked into it for me. No direct commission, but I could have gone to Officer Candidate School. But that meant three years after I got the commission."

"And you didn't want to put three years in?"

"I didn't want to put *two* years in, Colonel," Jack said. "But two is better than three."

"And being an enlisted man hasn't made you rethink it?"

"Yes, Sir, but the bottom line is that I'm already down to one year, nine months and some days. If I applied for OCS, that would take six months, plus the three years when I'd been commissioned."

"I'm not saying the Attaché was wrong, but I think it's worth looking into," Colonel Marx said. "It doesn't make a hell of a lot of sense to me to make a rifleman out of a highly qualified pilot and at the same time to spend all that money training some rifleman to be a pilot."

"I would much rather be a pilot, Sir."

"If my sergeant comes up with something," Colonel Marx said, "and if there is anything to be found in the regulations, he'll find it and I'll get in touch. And in the meantime I don't think you should be worried about this investigation."

"Thank you, Sir."

"Now I can send you back to your company with Gregory. Or you can walk. If you walked, I don't think anybody would notice if you took the rest of the afternoon to get there, and found it necessary to refresh yourself in the snack bar en route."

"Thank you, Colonel."

Colonel Marx offered his hand.

In early March, in his last week of basic training, Recruit Jacques Emile Portet was summoned back to see Colonel Marx.

Jack thought it was reasonable to presume that Marx had come up with a regulation which would permit him to become an officer and serve as a pilot. Having had enough of basic training, and faced with the strong possibility that the Army was going to load him on a charter flight to Vietnam for service in the infantry, he now saw much to recommend that, even if it would mean putting more time in the Army.

It was certainly possible that the Army would take advantage of his experience and assign him to fly what he thought of as the only full-sized airplane in the Army inventory, the DeHavilland Caribou. The Caribou was a piston-engined transport aircraft about as big as the old DC-3, but with a short takeoff and landing capability.

He still didn't want to give the Army another goddamned year of his life, but if he was flying, at least it wouldn't be entirely wasted time. And he would much rather be flying *over* the bush in Vietnam than running around *in* the bush over there, with an M16A1.

Colonel Marx quickly shattered that bubble of pleasant anticipation.

"There's bad news on two fronts, Portet, I'm sorry to say," he said. "The first is that there's a flag on your records by order of the Assistant Chief of Staff for Intelligence. And I can't find out why. All they'll tell me is that you've been cleared for a 'Secret' clearance. Maybe—probably—they want to assign you to teach Swahili or something like that. The result of that is that you will be assigned to the replacement company when you finish basic training. The other shoe is that Army Aviation is not, for reasons that I don't understand, at all interested in your service as a pilot . . . except if you want to apply for Warrant Officer Candidate School and become a helicopter pilot. That takes about ten months, and you'd have to serve three additional years when you finished."

"Ouch."

"I'm not through with Army Aviation yet," Colonel Marx said, and Jack sensed that the Colonel had taken a personal affront. "I have a couple of old pals who were honest cavalrymen before they sprouted wings, and one of them, who happens to be a general officer, promised to look into this and see what he could do. That should take a couple of weeks. Don't get your hopes up, but maybe something can be done."

"Thank you, Sir," Jack said. "I appreciate your interest."

"I just hate to see the Army waste money. If I had my druthers, you would apply for OCS—and go, because I'm president of the examination board—and that would be the end of it."

"Sir—I hope I can say this without sounding like a wise guy—I would love to fly for the Army. But I don't see why that should cost me nearly three or four years more of my life. I don't really understand why they just don't give me a checkride and send me to Vietnam to fly Caribous."

"Neither do I," Colonel Marx said. "And that is the point I made to my friend the formerly honest cavalryman. But that brings us to the next thirty days."

"Sir?"

"You'll be reassigned to the replacement company until they take the hold off your records . . . until they decide what they want to do with you. The hold is for thirty days. They might assign you on day two or they might extend the period of the hold. That means you will be policing the area, or on KP, or whatever, until you do get your orders."

"That sounds like a lot of fun."

"There is one alternative. Have you ever considered becoming a parachutist?"

"No, Sir."

"It's a three-week course at Fort Benning," Colonel Marx said. "I can get it for you, which means that you would be running around Benning, and you'd be getting taught how to parachute—some people think it's fun—rather than whitewashing rocks and picking up cigarette butts in the replacement company."

"It never entered my mind," Jack said.

"Prospect scare you?"

"The prospect of the replacement company scares me more. Yes, Sir. Thank you, Sir."

"Now that you've volunteered, I'll tell you: I can now tell my old friend that you are a real hard charger who volunteered for jump school. That may help you into a cockpit."

"Thank you, Sir."

[THREE]
The State-War-and-Navy Building
Washington, D.C.
25 February 1964

COLONEL SANFORD T. FELTER, Counselor to the President of the United States, had a staff of two—a bishop and a nun. Although he deeply regretted telling Lieutenant Colonel Craig W. Lowell about this, he had to admit it sounded a little funny. Lowell, predictably, thought it was hilarious and had taken to calling Felter His Holiness, Moses I, the First Jewish Pope.

The Bishop was truly a bishop, though of the Church of Jesus Christ of Latter-Day Saints and not of the Roman Catholic Church: James L. Finton was a career soldier who had risen to chief warrant officer, W-4, in twenty-three years. There are four grades of warrant officers, who are paid approximately what second lieutenants through majors are paid. W-4 is the senior grade. Finton was a cryptographer by training. Felter had found him in the Army Security Agency and arranged for his transfer to the White House Signal Detachment. He was a devout Mormon; the church had saved his sanity after his wife had died of cancer, he told Felter. And he spent his free time in one Mormon church function or another in the District. Finton had come to Felter with a Top Secret clearance, and a number of endorsements to that—a cryptographic endorsement, a nuclear endorsement, and several others.

The nun was really a nun, and of the Roman Catholic Church. Mary Margaret Dunne had been temporarily relieved of her vows to provide for her aged and senile father. When he died, she would return to the cloistered life as Sister Matthew. Mary Margaret Dunne spent her time in one of three places: with her father in a small apartment, on her knees in Saint Mary's church, or in Felter's small but ornate and high-ceilinged office in the State-War-and-Navy Building. (This somewhat grotesque edifice is now known as the Executive Office Building.)

Mary Margaret Dunne had been taken on by the Kennedy White House following a quiet word from the Bishop. She needed a job and she could type like a whiz. She had gone to work for Felter the same morning President Kennedy had introduced Felter at a briefing as the only man in the White House who didn't answer his phone.

The Bishop and the nun were fiercely devoted to Felter. And, about as important, they were both quietly convinced that the communists were representatives of the Antichrist, and that what Felter was doing—what they were helping him do—was as much the Lord's work as it was the government's.

When Felter walked into the office, both of them stood up. He had told them this was unnecessary, but had been unable to convince them to stop.

"Anything interesting?" Felter asked as he glanced at the stack of reports Finton had handed him.

"No. Routine."

"Sister?"

"Master Sergeant Gomez of DCSPERS called," Miss Dunne replied. "He said he didn't know if you would be interested, but he has the name of some soldier who used to live in the former Belgian Congo."

"Just now, Colonel," Finton said, "I was about to call him when you walked in."

"Get back to him, will you, Jim? See what that's about? Oh, hell, get him on the phone. I'll talk to him."

Master Sergeant Gomez told Colonel Felter that he'd been the one assigned to search for officers for the Congo Assignment. He said that he had remembered Colonel Felter's interest when something else had come up. There was a draftee undergoing basic training at Knox. They were about to send him to Vietnam but couldn't because his records were flagged pending the conclusion of a CIC investigation. He had called the CIC and asked when he could expect the investigation to be concluded, and the CIC said they didn't know, the trainee was from the Belgian Congo, and they were having a hell of a time getting any information about him.

"I didn't know if you would be interested or not, Colonel," Master Sergeant Gomez said.

"You're a jewel, Sergeant Gomez," Felter said. "You get both ears and the tail. CWO Finton's on the extension. Give him this guy's name, would you please?"

"Yes, Sir."

[FOUR]
The Twin Bridges Marriott Motel
Alexandria, Virginia
7 March 1964

CWO-4 JAMES L. FINTON paid far less for his small suite in the Twin Bridges Marriott Motel than the going rate. He thought of this deal somewhat wryly as The Mormon Connection. And in truth, fellow adherents to the teachings of the Church of Jesus Christ of Latter-Day Saints seemed to find ways to take care of each other.

He had met the manager of the Twin Bridges several times on church business around the District. At one of these there had been a chance to ask him if he knew of some inexpensive, clean, and quiet place he could rent in the area. He explained that he spent a lot of time in the Pentagon (across the highway from the Twin Bridges) and the rest of it in the State-War-and-Navy Building, and that he needed just a room to sleep and keep his clothing, and a place to park his car where he could expect to find the hubcaps and antenna in place in the morning. He added that he thought people who worked in the Twin Bridges might know of something like that.

The manager was sure he could help, and asked Finton to come by the office the next time he had a free minute.

Two days later Finton stopped by en route from the Pentagon to Felter's office.

The manager showed him a suite in the rear of the motel complex, one designed for salesmen who needed a place to display their wares as well as a place to sleep. It had a small bedroom as well as a larger sitting room, equipped with a small but complete kitchen.

"Very nice, but I couldn't afford something like this," Finton said.

"You don't know that," the manager said. "What do they give you for a housing allowance?"

Finton told him.

"I can let you have this for that much."

"How can you do that?"

"Because the boss said to," the manager smiled. "He said to tell you he appreciates what you're doing, both for the church and the government."

There was no question whom the manager meant by the boss. The chain that owned the Twin Bridges (and a number of other hotels, restaurants, and other food and lodging enterprises) bore his name.

When Finton's eyebrows rose, the manager nodded. "The Old Man himself," he confirmed.

Finton moved in the few good pieces of his own furniture (and then gave the rest to a Church of Latter-Day Saints Thrift Shop in the District), and he liked it there, even though he had to do most of his own cooking. There were nice restaurants in the Twin Bridges, but Finton used them only when he had to. The Old Man Himself had issued orders not to take his money, and Finton was reluctant to take advantage of his generosity.

Finton slid open the folding door to one of the closets in the living room of his suite and searched through a row of plastic drycleaning bags until he found one holding a green uniform. He almost never wore a uniform since he'd gone to work for Colonel Felter, but Felter had suggested that "it might be a good idea to go in uniform" today.

The brass was tarnished, and he polished it. Then Finton gave into what he realized was probably vanity. He would not only go in uniform, he would go as a parachutist. He took parachutist's wings from his insignia box and pinned them to the blouse. Then he put on jump boots and bloused them. And instead of his leather-brimmed cap, he put on an overseas cap with the parachutist's insignia sewn to it.

There were two stars on his parachutist's wings, "combat jump stars." He hadn't actually jumped in combat, as part of an armada of aircraft filling the skies with parachute canopies. But twice, in the dead of night, alone, he had jumped into hostile territory.

He did not pin on any of his ribbons. He thought the stars on the jump wings would be enough vanity. And he always remembered what an old sergeant had told him, years before, about people who wore the Purple Heart ribbon along with their "I Was There" ribbons: "What that means is not only was I there, but I forgot to duck."

When he was dressed, he called the Pentagon dispatcher and said if the Belvoir bus wasn't coming by the Twin Bridges on its next run, he was going to need a ride.

"I'll send a staff car by," the dispatcher told him.

By the time he had had two soft-boiled eggs, toast, and orange juice in The Twin Bridges coffee shop, an olive drab Chevrolet was out in front under the marquee.

When he got to the Belvoir Army Airfield, the pilot of a Benning-bound L-23 was waiting for him in Operations.

"Where the hell have you been? And where's the big shot from the White House?"

"He couldn't make it," Finton said. "I'm going instead."

"If I'd known that," the pilot said, "I'd have been long gone, and you'd be sitting on your ass waiting for another plane."

"I'm sorry, Captain," Finton said.

There was no need for an apology. He was the big shot from the White House for whom a seat on the first aircraft departing Belvoir for Benning and points south after 0800 had been reserved. And he had arrived at 0755.

There was a staff car and a lieutenant colonel waiting for him at the Army Airfield at Fort Benning.

"I know where you came from, Mr. Finton," the Lieutenant Colonel said significantly, "but no one told me why."

"Sir, I want to talk to a young man, Private Portet, Jacques E., who's in parachute school."

"If they'd passed that word down here, I would have had him here waiting for you."

"Sir, do you suppose it would be possible for me to get a car and then just go where he is?"

"Whatever you want, Mr. Finton," the Lieutenant Colonel said. "Would you like me to go along and smooth your way?"

"I don't think that will be necessary, Sir," Finton said. "Thank you just the same."

The Lieutenant Colonel, who was the Deputy G-2 of the U.S. Army Infantry School at Fort Benning, was naturally very curious why a chief warrant officer from the White House had come to Benning to talk to a lowly private soldier in jump school. But he knew enough not to ask. If they wanted him to know, they would tell him.

Twenty minutes later the sedan pulled up near the parachute towers. These are training devices essentially identical to the parachute-jump amusement ride at Coney Island. Five-dollar-a-ride jumpers at Coney

Island are strapped onto benches, which are then hauled to the top of the towers and released, after which they return to the ground, below already deployed parachute canopies. At Fort Benning riders are strapped into standard parachute harnesses.

Frankly curious, Finton got out of the car and watched several minutes as parachutist trainees got their ride. Then a deeply tanned, crew-cutted young sergeant saw him out of the corner of his eye as he led a hundred young men in yet another sequence of fifty push-ups.

The Sergeant continued the push-ups until the fifty had been completed. Then he sprang to his feet.

"Ree-cover!" he barked. The one hundred would be parachutists, many of them breathing hard and all of them with flushed, sweaty faces, got to their feet and stood to attention.

The Sergeant raised his balled fists to the level of his chest and then double-timed to where the CWO stood. There he came to attention and saluted crisply. "Good afternoon, *Sir!*" he barked. "Sergeant Tannley, *Sir!*"

Finton returned the salute as crisply as he could. He saw the Sergeant's eyes drop to his jump wings and, he thought, widen when he saw the combat jump stars.

"Good afternoon, Sergeant," Finton said. "I hate to interrupt your schedule, but I'd like to borrow one of your students for an hour or so."

"Yes, *Sir!*"

"But not if it means he'll have to drop back for missing something important."

"Which one, *Sir?*"

"Portet."

"He's one of the better ones," Sergeant Tannley said softly, as if to make sure Portet would not hear him. "I'm going to sweat their asses a little for the next couple of hours. It won't hurt Portet none to miss that. He's in pretty good shape."

"Good," Finton said.

Sergeant Tannley did a perfect about-face and bellowed "Port-ay! On the double, front *and* center, Harch!"

Private Jacques E. Portet, who was at the left rear of the formation, balled his fists, raised them to chest level, and then double-timed over to where Finton and Sergeant Tannley stood. He came to attention and saluted.

"You will go with this officer," Sergeant Tannley proclaimed.

"Yes, *Sir!*"

Finton remembered that to instill a proper degree of respect for their instructors, aspirant parachutists were required to use "Sir," which was normally reserved for officers.

"With your permission, *Sir?*" Sergeant Tannley barked.

"Carry on, Sergeant," Finton said.

"Yes, *Sir!*" Tannley barked. "Airborne, *Sir!*"

Finton knew that there was an expected response to that, but he had no idea what it was. He searched his mind desperately for a moment and came up with nothing.

"Right!" he barked.

Sergeant Tannley gave him a look of surprise and wonderment and finally, Finton thought, of suspicion. For a moment he was afraid the Sergeant was going to challenge him, or at least his authority to take one of the trainees committed to his charge off somewhere. But then he looked behind Finton and saw the staff car with its sergeant driver and the HQ FT BENNING tag. He did another about-face and double-timed back to his trainees.

"What was I supposed to reply when he said 'Airborne'?" Finton asked Portet very softly.

"'All the way!'" Portet said. He was still at attention, but he was smiling.

"When I went through here," Finton said, "Sergeant Tannley took his nourishment from a bottle, through a rubber nipple. That's new to me."

"I'm afraid you disappointed him, Sir," Jack said. "That 'Airborne—All the Way' business is very important to him."

"Oh, stand at ease," Finton said. "And then we'll go take a little ride."

"May I ask what this is about, Sir?"

"I think you better get in the front, with the driver," Finton replied.

When they were in the car, the driver looked over his shoulder for directions.

"Where could we go where I can talk privately to Portet?" Finton asked, "and maybe get some lunch, too?"

"Rod and Gun Club has a snack bar, Sir," the driver said. "Hamburgers, fries, that sort of thing."

"And a place to talk privately?"

"Yes, Sir."

"Then the Rod and Gun Club."

When the car was moving, Finton took a small leather wallet from his blouse pocket, opened it, and tapped Portet on the shoulder with it.

It was the credentials of a Special Agent of the Counterintelligence Corps, a gold badge and a plastic-coated identification card with Finton's photo on it. Colonel Felter had obtained the credentials for Finton, who was not and never had been in the CIC. They came in handy in situations like this or when it was necessary for him to go armed. If necessary he would have shown them to Sergeant Tannley if Tannley had challenged his bonafides. There were a lot of CIC agents around the Army. There were very few warrant officers equipped with Finton's other credentials—a reduced photocopy of a letter on White House stationery signed by both the President's Chief of Staff and Colonel Sanford T. Felter, stating that CWO Finton was engaged in carrying out special missions for the Office of the President of the United States and that any inquiries regarding his activities should be directed to one of the two signatories and no one else.

"You're in uniform," Jack Portet said. It was a question.

"What's wrong with that?"

"The last one of those I saw," Jack Portet said, "was shown me by a guy I suspect was a Spec-4 who desperately wanted me to think he was either a civilian or an officer in civilian clothes."

Finton chuckled.

"What you see is what you get," he said. "Just a tired old warrant officer."

"He thought I was a spy," Jack said. "Is that what this is all about?"

"No," Finton said. "We know you're not a spy, Portet. I had a look at the roughs of your investigation yesterday. Except for a certain tendency to ignore the thou-shalt-not commandments about adultery and coveting your neighbor's wife, you seem to be a pretty decent fellow."

When they got to the Rod and Gun Club snack bar, the driver said, "If you don't mind, Mr. Finton, I'll eat with a buddy of mine."

"Fine," Finton said.

When they were seated at a small table in a corner of the room, Finton took a bite of his hamburger, nodded his approval, and then took a swallow from a half-pint waxed cardboard container of milk.

"There was a story in the *Reader's Digest*," he said, "that said that there's nothing wrong with hamburgers. They give you a balanced diet."

"I suppose," Jack said.

"I know all there is to know about you, son," Finton said. "So we can save a lot of time."

"Fine. What's this all about?"

"You have something the Army wants."

"A strong back and a weak mind?"

"There's an old saw that you get out of the Army what you put into it," Finton said. "Oddly enough, it's true."

"I don't think you're here to tell me I really should apply for OCS or flight school."

"You know a lot about the Congo. Right now I'd say there are few people in the Army with your knowledge of the Congo."

Jack looked at him curiously but didn't reply.

"What we're thinking of doing is sending you back there," Finton said. "Assigning you to the Military Attaché's office in the embassy in Leopoldville."

"Oh, Jesus Christ," Jack said, making it clear the idea had no appeal at all for him.

"Just off the top of my head, I would have thought, with the alternative being running around in the boondocks of Vietnam, with people shooting at you, that getting sent home to Leopoldville would seem like a pretty good deal."

"Do I have any choice in this? Can I appeal or something?"

"I don't know," Finton said. "There's another old Army saw that you get assigned where you can do the Army the most good. Oddly enough, that's often true too. You want to tell me why you don't want to go back to the Congo?"

"*Because* I live there," Jack said. "There's three kinds of white people who live in the Congo. The *colons,* the colonials, the Belgians who used to run the place for their own advantage. And are still running things because there's just no Congolese who can. . . . The Congolese hate them, and as soon as they're able, they're going to get rid of them. The second kind are the people like my father. Not only do we live there . . . I mean, we're not from Brussels, or someplace, working abroad. We *live* there. It's home. And we're in business with the blacks. And the third kind, the ones the Congolese really hate, are white men with guns and uniforms. The Belgian officers of the Force Publique; the mercenaries, when they were there; and the others . . . the military officers assigned to the embassies. The Congolese think—and maybe with reason—that they're just waiting for an excuse to take over again."

"And you're afraid that if you were assigned to the embassy, it would cause trouble for you when you get out?"

"It would," Jack said simply.

"Well, like I said, you get out of the Army what you put into it. For openers, you wouldn't be a private. I can get you a warrant officer's bar right away. When you're over there we can probably arrange to get you on flight status."

"No, thanks."

"We don't have to ask you, you know," Finton said. "All we have to do is cut a set of orders and put you on an airplane. As a private. You're in the Army. Privates do what they're ordered to do."

"You can put me on a plane to Vietnam tomorrow morning," Jack said. "As either a private, as a 'light weapons infantryman,' or to fly whatever the Army wants me to fly, and I'll go and do what I'm told to do. But the only way you'll get me back to the Congo in a uniform is in handcuffs. And the minute you take the handcuffs off, I'll desert."

Finton looked at him for a moment, his face coloring.

"Bullshit," he said.

"No bullshit," Jack said.

"Let me put it this way. You're in the Army, Portet. And the Army doesn't really give a damn whether the Congolese get pissed off at you or not. The Army is taking other nice young men like you and handing them M16s and sending them to Vietnam, where it knows a certain percentage of them are going to get blown away. Compared to getting blown away, having the Congolese pissed at you doesn't seem all that important."

"I don't think there's much of a chance that some Vietnamese patriot is going to sneak up to somebody's house in America and throw a gasoline bomb through the dining room window," Jack said levelly. "Or catch somebody's stepmother or little sister at the supermarket and rape them, and/or hack them into pieces with a rusty machete."

"Your imagination's running away with you."

"Think what you want," Jack said. "I'm telling you how it is. And that I am not going to the Congo."

He's telling the truth, Finton thought. *And this is a very tough young man who means it when he says he'll desert if that's what he thinks he has to do.*

And he realized that he was of two minds about Private Jacques Emile Portet. CWO-4 James L. Finton, U.S. Army, was torn between contempt and anger toward a young man who had sworn the oath and was now threatening desertion rather than obey an order he didn't like. As a Christian, as a bishop of the Church of Jesus Christ of Latter-Day Saints, Finton approved of a young man who would rather face disgrace and imprisonment than put his family in jeopardy.

"Finish your hamburger," Finton said. "Then I got to find a phone."

"I think I saw one as we came in."

"I need a scrambler phone."

Twenty minutes later, in the office of Assistant Chief of Staff, G-2, Headquarters, the U.S. Army Infantry Center at Fort Benning, Georgia, Private Portet was handed a telephone.

"Yes, Sir?"

"My name is Felter," a voice said to him. "Mr. Finton works for me."

"Yes, Sir?"

"Do I correctly understand your position to be that you would have no objection to providing, without reservation, any information you have, and that what you're reluctant to do is go to the Congo?"

"I refuse to go to the Congo, Sir."

"OK, refuse. What about providing information?"

"I'll tell you or Mr. Finton anything you want to know."

"OK. I don't know right now how we'll arrange to pick your brain, or where, but you'll be told. I'm giving you the benefit of the doubt that you'll be as helpful as you can. The minute I suspect you're playing games with us, you'll be on the next plane to Vietnam. You read me?"

"Yes, Sir, loud and clear."

"You are to tell no one of the substance of the conversation between Mr. Finton and you or that you have talked to me. If somebody asks what Mr. Finton wanted with you, you say that it was in connection with your CIC background investigation."

"Yes, Sir."

"If it gets back to me that you've been running off at the mouth—and if you do, it will—you'll be running around two days later in the jungle in Vietnam."

"Why don't you just do that now?"

Laughter came over the line.

"Finton was right, I see," Felter said. "You are a real hard-nose, aren't you? Sometimes that is an admirable quality. Put Mr. Finton back on the line, please, Portet. And watch yourself in jump school. I don't want you either dead or with a broken leg."

VII

[ONE]
Durban, South Africa
8 March 1964

D. INGENIEUR KARL-HEINZ WAGNER of Hessische Schwere Konstruktion (Sud Afrika) was put up for a week in a small but pleasant and comfortable hotel room overlooking the beach and the Indian Ocean.

And then he found a small apartment not far from the hotel. He could no longer see the beach, but he could smell the salt air.

The day he moved into the apartment, he was given the day off. And since there was nothing to do in the apartment but hang his clothing in the closets and stock the refrigerator, he had most of the day free. He went looking for an automobile.

He found the car, but he didn't find what he was really looking for at Durban Motor Cars, Ltd., on West Street. The car he decided to buy was a lemon yellow, right-hand drive, Volkswagen convertible. What he was looking for was Michael Hoare, late Major of the Katangese Army. But there was no one around the used-car showroom who looked even remotely like the photograph of Hoare Felter had shown him.

The car was priced at the Rand equivalent of $2200, but Wagner decided not to use the money Colonel Felter had given him to pay cash for it. The salesman patiently explained the hire-purchase scheme available to him. One-third down would be required, with the balance to be paid over eighteen months at a 10 percent interest rate.

Karl-Heinz managed to feed the salesman the information that he was newly arrived in Durban, from Germany, as a new employee of Hessische Schwere Konstruktion (Sud Afrika). Wagner was sure that before they gave him the car on time, they would run a credit check on him. The result of that would be that HSK would not only vouch for his credit, but would relate the story of his defection from the East German Army and his crashing through the Berlin Wall. It was reasonable to presume that story would get to Hoare.

And Michael Hoare was there when Karl-Heinz went to take delivery of the Volkswagen. He introduced himself as the proprietor, but gave no indication that he knew anything more about Wagner than that he had just bought a Volkswagen on Hire-Purchase.

Wagner's impression of Hoare was that he was highly intelligent and that he smelled like a soldier. He liked him.

It took him two weeks of saloon crawling to find where Hoare did his drinking, and another four days before Hoare spoke to him.

"You're Mr. Wagner, aren't you?" Hoare said, coming to where Karl-Heinz stood at the bar. "I'm Michael Hoare. You bought your convertible from me."

They shook hands.

"Give this gentleman another of what he's having," Hoare ordered.

"Right you are, Major," the bartender said.

"'Major'?" Karl-Heinz quoted questioningly.

"Late of the Chindits," Hoare said with a smile. "And more recently of the Katangese Army."

"I was a soldier," Karl-Heinz said. "In Germany."

"Were you really?" Hoare asked. He didn't seem to be especially interested, and Karl-Heinz volunteered nothing more.

Four days later he ran into Hoare at the Greyville Race Course, where according to Felter Hoare was a regular. Hoare was in a good mood, his horse had come in. He greeted Karl-Heinz warmly and offered to buy him a drink. And there was another man with him, another man who smelled like a soldier.

"Edward Fitz-Mallory," Hoare made the introductions, "late lieutenant of Her Majesty's Special Air Service. Karl Wagner, late Oberleutnant of Herr Walter Ulbricht's East German Pioneer Corps."

They had a couple of drinks at the racetrack bar. And Karl-Heinz went home and sent a postcard to Edward T. Watson at the U.S. Embassy in Johannesburg.

"Finally getting the fish to bite. Wish you were here. W."

He had said nothing to Hoare, or his salesman, about being from East Germany or about having been an officer in the Pioneer Corps. Hoare had apparently checked him out.

[TWO]
Dothan, Alabama
3 April 1964

WHETHER HIS EXPERIENCE is limited to a Piper Cub or whether he is deadheading to Frisco to be pilot-in-command of a Pan American Airways 707 on the Over-the-Pole Route to Tokyo, only one pilot in five hundred ever completely trusts any other pilot to make a safe landing.

Newly designated Light Weapons Infantryman (Airborne) Private Jacques Emile Portet was no exception. As Southern Airlines Flight 321, thirty minutes out of Columbus, Georgia, turned on its final approach to Dothan, he sat tensely in the last single seat on the left side of the Super DC-3's cabin and peered with rapt fascination out the window, seriously questioning the ability of the pilot, who was obviously either sick or drunk, to get the ancient Gooney-Bird back on the ground in one piece.

Private Portet was fully accoutered with the regalia to which he was now entitled. His feet were shod in spit-shined Corcoran jump boots. There was a strip reading "Airborne" sewn to the shoulder seam of his blouse sleeve, and a circular embroidered representation of a parachute was sewn to his overseas cap. Plus, of course, the silver wings of a parachutist were pinned to his breast.

He had never heard of Dothan, Alabama, until yesterday, when he had been summoned to the orderly room and presented with a set of orders relieving him from 3rd Replacement Company, 3rd Armored Division (Training) Fort Knox, Kentucky, and TDY to the U.S. Army Infantry School and transferring him in grade to the U.S. Army Aviation Board, Fort Rucker, Alabama.

The First Sergeant said it was a hundred miles or so down the road, and that he would be flown from Columbus, which was outside Fort Benning, to Dothan, Alabama, the nearest commercial airport to Fort Rucker. There would be an Army bus to carry him from the Dothan Airport to Fort Rucker.

Aside from Colonel Marx, there had been only one thing to recommend Fort Knox. It was reasonably close to Louisville, which, if it wasn't Brussels, at least offered decent hotels and good places to eat. So far as Jack had been able to determine, Columbus, Georgia, offered neither. And from what he had seen of the metropolis while the pilot flew over it hoping to come across the airport, neither would Dothan, Alabama.

As the Super DC-3 pilot finally got the wings more or less parallel to the ground and remembered at the last possible moment to lower the wheels, he told himself that he should stop bitching. He could be landing in San Francisco, where after a splendid meal in a superb restaurant, the Army would load him on a plane for Saigon.

He didn't know what the Army was going to do with or to him at Fort Rucker, and he now knew enough not to get his hopes high, but it was unlikely that anyone would be shooting at him.

The Super DC-3 pilot finally got it on the runway, the tail too high. It was so far down the runway they would probably have to lay over while the brakes were replaced.

Then he taxied it to the terminal, which had apparently been acquired as Army surplus. There were two Army helicopters, a Huey, the standard light-transport chopper, and a plastic-bubbled Bell two-seater sitting on the parking ramp beside a motley collection of light civilian aircraft. As Jack had walked out to board the aircraft at Columbus, he had seen two lieutenant colonels looking out the windows; the choppers were apparently waiting for them.

The moment the airplane stopped moving, almost all the passengers got to their feet and started to retrieve coats and packages. Jack stayed where he was. He often thought that if there was one thing he had learned from his lifelong experience with commercial aviation, it was that standing in the aisle didn't get you off the airplane much quicker than keeping your seat and waiting for the herd to get off.

He looked out the window at the Huey and wondered if he was going to get a chance to fly one.

Jack presumed that his assignment to the Aviation Center meant that Colonel Marx had done something for him. Otherwise he would be boarding a charter flight in Frisco for Saigon, or Mr. Finton or Mr. Felter, whoever the hell he was, would have had the Army send him someplace else.

There had been a somewhat smug character in basic training who had let it be known that on graduation he would be assigned to the CIC Center, so the Army apparently had a post set aside for their Intelligence people. It was entirely likely that as soon as he unpacked his duffle bag at Fort Rucker, there would be another set of orders sending him to the CIC Center to have his brains picked.

As he forced the faint hope that the Army would relent and let him fly as his two-year contribution to National Defense, he turned his eyes from the window and found himself looking at a young woman.

She had been looking at him, but had quickly, rather suavely, Jack thought approvingly, looked away. She was beautiful. Black haired. Absolutely fascinating face. Smooth-skinned, just the right amount of tan. Gray, soft, intelligent eyes. Wholesome. Gentle. And absolutely marvelous knockers.

And then the stewardess remembered how to get the door open, and the girl went down the aisle and got off. Jack watched with rapt fascination as she walked from the airplane to the terminal. Her gait was graceful, and her derriere was every bit as much an example of God's genius as her breasts.

Jesus H. Christ!

Then he got up and got off the airplane himself and walked into the terminal. He looked for her at the baggage counter, but she wasn't there.

"Going out to Rucker, son?"

Jack turned to see that one of the lieutenant colonels was talking to him.

"Yes, Sir."

"We've got room on a Huey if you'd like to come along."

"Yes, Sir. Thank you very much."

There was a Spec-4 in a space helmet on the Huey. A crew chief. Jack hadn't known that Hueys came with crew chiefs. He let his hopes rise. At least the Army ought to give him a shot at that, without demanding another two or three years of his life. And if he was a crew chief, the odds were that he would run into a friendly pilot who, as a fraternal gesture between pilots, would give him a little bootleg time.

There was a whine of a starter engine as he sat down on an aluminum-pipe-and-nylon-cloth seat, and almost immediately the rotor blades began to turn. His ears told him that the Huey had a turbine engine rather than pistons, and he hadn't known that either.

And then they lifted off, just a couple of feet off the ground, and the pilot turned it into the wind and dropped the nose and moved across the field, gathering speed. And then it just soared into the air.

"Where are you headed?" It was the Lieutenant Colonel again.

Jack took his orders from his inside pocket and handed them to him.

"Right on my way," the Lieutenant Colonel said. "My wife's meeting me. We'll give you a ride."

"Thank you, Sir."

It was a very short flight, and then the Huey sat down on the grass between a runway and a parking ramp at what was obviously a very busy airport. There were too many airplanes and helicopters to count.

There was a base operations building with a control tower on top. There was a sign reading CAIRNS ARMY AIRFIELD and another reading WELCOME TO THE U.S. ARMY AVIATION CENTER.

The Lieutenant Colonel's wife was driving a Ford station wagon, and she was equipped with an interesting set of mammary glands, too.

It's not so much that I am coveting my neighbor's wife, Jack thought, *but rather that I am suffering from a near-fatal case of Lackanookie. And then there was that absolutely ravishing creature on the Gooney-Bird, which started the juices flowing. I am going to have to get the ashes hauled as a matter of the first priority.*

"That's the Board," the Lieutenant Colonel said, pointing to a two-story, obviously brand-new concrete-block building. "Where you'll be working. But the troops are housed on the main post, and I expect you're expected to report in there."

"Yes, Sir," Jack said, although he had absolutely no idea what the Lieutenant Colonel was talking about.

They left the airfield and passed through a small town which seemed to be devoted to trailer parks, gas stations, and hockshops, and then under a sign reading FORT RUCKER, ALABAMA, HOME OF ARMY AVIATION ABOVE THE BEST.

A mile or so inside the post, the Lieutenant Colonel dropped him off in an area of freshly painted World War II–era barracks. There was an orderly room building identified as HEADQUARTERS COMPANY, U.S. ARMY AVIATION BOARD.

The First Sergeant looked like Jack expected a first sergeant to look, but he was apparently not as prone to breathe fire as the other first sergeants with whom Jack had had contact.

He sent an Sp-5 clerk with Jack to help him draw bedding and get set up in the barracks. Compared to the double-decker bunks two feet from the next double-decker Jack had known at Knox and Benning, the squad bay looked deserted. There were only eight single bunks in the whole place. The clerk waited while Jack made up the bunk and hung his uniforms in the wall locker, and then took him back to the orderly room.

"Colonel McNair's sent his car for you," the First Sergeant said. "I told him you had reported in, and he wants to talk to you." Then he handed Jack a small piece of cardboard. "Pass," he explained. "It's good anytime you're not on duty. You have to sign out and sign in, but you can do it by phone. I wrote the number on the back."

"Thank you," Jack said.

"You can wait outside if you want. Just keep your eye open for a Chevy staff car with a lot of aerials on it."

Jack walked from the orderly room to the main thoroughfare. Across it was an apparently not-in-use landing strip. Toward the end of it he saw construction equipment in use, doing something that would take the strip permanently out of service.

And then he saw a bright-red MGB coming down the road, just like the one he had delivered to K. N. Swayer in Albertville. He remembered what Swayer had said: "Isn't that the cutest little fucker you ever saw?" and smiled.

And then the red MGB passed him, and he saw who was driving. The goddess from the Gooney-Bird. She of the trimmest ass this side of heaven.

And she looked at him with something like recognition on her face.
Come back! I love you! We will ride off in your little red MGB together!
A horn blew behind Jack as the MGB disappeared down the road.

"You the guy Colonel McNair sent me to fetch?"

Jack nodded.

He remembered what the First Sergeant had said about looking for a Chevy staff car with a lot of aerials. This one had a Collins aircraft antenna mounted on its roof and several whip antennae Jack didn't recognize.

He got in the front seat with the driver, an Sp-4, who drove him back out to the airfield and deposited him before the concrete block building. There was a sign on this one, too: UNITED STATES ARMY AVIATION BOARD.

Wondering what that was, and who Colonel McNair was, Jack pushed open the glass door and walked inside.

Colonel John W. "Mac" McNair promptly and snappily returned the salute rendered by Private Jacques Emile Portet when Jack marched in and reported to him, but kept him standing at attention for a long moment before he finally told him to stand at ease.

McNair reminded Jack of a bantam rooster. He was about five feet five inches tall, trim, redheaded and freckle-faced.

"Curiosity damned near overwhelms me, Portet," he said. "But I have been told to keep it under control. Colonel Sandy Felter is an old pal of mine, as you may or may not know, but he tells nobody, including old pals, anything he doesn't have to."

It was the first Jack had heard that Felter was a colonel.

"Well, to hell with it, I'm going to ask anyway," Colonel McNair went on. "You won't fly, but you just went through jump school. You want to explain that to me?"

"Sir?"

"Simple question," Colonel McNair said, on the edge of sarcasm. "It's my understanding that you don't want to fly. And yet, according to your orders, you just went through parachute school at Benning. And according to your records, you're a multiengine pilot with an ATR rating. And according to a TWX that came in here yesterday, you have a Top Secret clearance, with an Operation Eagle endorsement. I don't even know what Operation Eagle is, but as a general rule of thumb, people with a Top Secret clearance are not considered threats to the security of the United States. So how come you're not an officer and a pilot?"

"Sir, I'd love to fly," Jack said. "I just don't want to spend four years and some months more in the Army."

"That, I don't understand."

Jack explained the Army's personnel regulations as he understood how they were applied to him.

"I'll be damned," Colonel McNair said. "I didn't know that." Then he seemed to get angry. He raised his voice: "Annie!"

A good-looking, statuesque blonde with her hair in a bun at the base of her neck put her head in the door.

"Yes, Sir?"

"Get this young man's records, and then get together with the Adjutant and see what you can find out about his eligibility for a direct commission, or a direct warrant. I just can't believe what he just told me . . . I believe *him*, that he's telling me what he has been told. I just don't believe what he was told."

"Yes, Sir."

"Between Mrs. Caskey and the Adjutant, if it's in the regulations, they'll find it," Colonel McNair said. "I'm confident of that."

Jack was confident that Mrs. Caskey and the Adjutant were going to find exactly what Colonel Marx had found, that there was no way the Army was going to let him fly unless he gave them another four years of his life, but he didn't think he should say so.

"Yes, Sir," Jack said again.

"Well, I presume Colonel Felter has told you what is expected of you here . . ."

"No, Sir."

"'*No*, Sir'?" McNair quoted incredulously.

"No, Sir," Jack repeated.

"Well, then, I'll tell you. One of my pilots has been given the additional duty of training two pilots for their expected duties in the Congo. Now, why this should be classified Secret, I have no idea. But since you are cleared for Top Secret, I feel safe in confiding in you. What you are to do is help my man—Major Pappy Hodges—train these two officers."

"Yes, Sir."

"Could I make a wild stab in the dark and guess that you have some experience with the Douglas DC-3? The R-4D?"

"Yes, Sir," Jack said. "A couple of hundred hours in them."

"As pilot-in-command, probably?" McNair asked dryly.

"About one hundred ten as pilot-in-command."

"We've got a couple of them here," Colonel McNair said. "By a strange coincidence, and by another strange coincidence, although the officers in training are going to ferry an L-23 over there, Colonel Felter is very interested that they get checked out in the Gooney-Bird. Quietly, he said."

Jack didn't reply.

"Well, then, without asking you to violate the oath of secrecy to which I presume Colonel Felter has sworn you, could I hazard the guess that what you will help Major Hodges to do is teach these guys how to fly a Gooney-Bird in the Congo?"

"Sir, I don't know."

"I shall relay to Colonel Felter, Private Portet—I am to call him on your arrival—that your lips were commendably sealed. You are a credit to whatever it is that Felter does."

"Colonel, I really don't know why Colonel Felter had me sent here."

"Well, maybe Pappy Hodges will tell you," Colonel McNair said sarcastically. "Maybe Felter has confided in *him*. On paper you have been assigned to Major Hodges as an R-4D crew chief."

"Yes, Sir." Jack was a little confused to hear the Gooney-Bird referred to as an R4-D. That was the Navy designation for the DC-3.

"Well, Portet, why don't you take a walk over to Hangar 104 and ask for Major Hodges?"

"Yes, Sir," Jack said. Thinking he was dismissed, he came to attention and saluted, then did an about-face and headed for the door.

"Portet!"

Jack turned to face him.

"Don't get the wrong idea," McNair said. "Whatever Felter has you doing is important—and I know that. If anything gets in the way of you doing what you're supposed to be doing, you call me. Day or night. You get the picture?"

"Yes, Sir."

"Welcome to the Army Aviation Board, Private Portet," Colonel McNair said. He smiled, then waved Jack out of his office.

Jack found Major Ellwood "Pappy" Hodges standing outside Hangar 104 watching a tug drag a Gooney-Bird from the hangar. He recognized him by a name tag sewn to his ancient flight suit. He was leather-skinned, balding, bucket-bellied, and well into his forties. Jack saluted and told him who he was.

"I understand you been around these airplanes?" Hodges said, waving in the general direction of the Douglas.

"Yes, Sir."

"They just changed the port engine in this one. The engine is older than you are. I'm going to test-fly it. If you know something about it, preflight it."

"Yes, Sir."

Jack recognized in Hodges the old pilot, and he both admired and understood old pilots. Jack went through what he thought was a pretty good preflight examination of the airplane. It was old but well maintained.

"They have a preflight check list," Major Hodges said, "but I didn't see you skip anything on the list. Can you taxi one of them?"

"Yes, Sir."

Hodges gestured for him to get aboard the aircraft.

Jack fired it up and started to taxi to the threshold of the active runway. To taxi the DC-3, Jack's father had told him, was harder than flying one. His father said that he always judged a Gooney-Bird pilot by the way he taxied. And he had taught his son well. Hodges apparently used the same criterion.

"When was the last time you flew one of these?" Hodges asked.

"About four months ago."

Hodges grunted.

"Cairns, Army Seven Nine Zero at the threshold of two eight for takeoff," Hodges called the tower. "Visual, local area."

"Seven Nine Zero, the time is ten past the hour. The altimeter is two niner niner eight. The winds are negligible. You are cleared as number one to take off. Maintain two eight zero degrees. Report passing through three thousand."

"Seven Nine Zero rolling," Hodges said, then gestured to Jack to take it off.

They were three hundred feet in the air when the port engine died.

"Shit!" Jack said. "Call a Mayday! We just lost the fucking engine!"

He dumped the flaps and cranked the wheel hard to port to counteract the drag of the dead engine, trying to pick up what altitude he could before trying to turn back to the field. There was finally time to look at the panel.

"No fire light," he said. "I can't see it. We got any smoke?"

"No smoke," Hodges said. "Stand by to restart."

At that point he realized what had happened. Hodges had cut the engine.

"You sonofabitch!"

"You been flying some time," Hodges said matter of factly. "Felter said you had a lot of time. I wanted to find out what kind of time."

"Jesus Christ!"

"I may have to send you out with these two guys going to the Congo," Pappy said. "I had to be sure it would be safe."

"And cutting my engine on takeoff was the test? Jesus Christ, you could have wiped us both out."

"Nah," Hodges said. "I been flying these things since 1943. I know what to do when you lose an engine that way. I wanted to see if you did. Whoever taught you knew what he was doing."

"My father taught me," Jack said, thinking that Hodges had tested him exactly as his father would have tested someone who was supposedly a good pilot. "I got my license when I was fourteen."

"Well, he knew what he was doing," Hodges said. "The priority is (one) that we—you and me—augment and update the hell out of the Jeppesen charts for the Congo, and (two) that we teach these two as much about the Congo as we can. If you were doing that, teaching these people, I mean, what would be most important?"

"Dead-reckoning navigation," Jack said after a moment. "Navaids over there are unreliable."

"And would you say they could do that better in a Twin-Bonanza or a Gooney-Bird?"

"The Beech," Jack said after a moment's thought. "That's what they'll be flying."

"You must be smart, Portet," Pappy Hodges said. "You think like me. That's the way we'll do it. Now see if you can find our way home."

As Jack taxied the Gooney-Bird to a parking ramp, Hodges said, "I'm curious why they don't just pin a bar and wings on you and send you to the Congo, but I been around the Army—and Sandy Felter—long enough to know not to ask too many questions."

"Colonel Felter had that in mind, I think," Jack said. "But I told him why I couldn't go over there wearing a uniform."

"Why not? Or is that one of those questions I'm not supposed to ask?"

"You've sort of got me on a spot, Major."

"Felter told me your father's got a small air-freight operation in the ex–Belgian Congo," Hodges said. "C-46s and C-47s. And that you told the Bishop you were afraid they'd chop your family up with a machete if you showed up over there in a uniform."

"The Bishop?"

"Finton," Hodges explained. "He's a bishop, no fooling—in the Mormons."

"That's about it," Jack said.

By then he had parked the airplane on the ramp and shut down the engines.

"Let me tell you something about Felter, son," Pappy Hodges said. "I been doing odd jobs for him on and off for years. You do what you're told to do, and keep your mouth shut about it, and he takes care of you. In my case, I was riffed three times . . ."

"I don't know what that means."

"RIF. Reduction in Force. Thank you for your faithful service, and don't let the doorknob hit you in the ass on your way out. I been riffed three times. Every time I told Colonel Felter—and every time they unriffed me."

"You're not close to retirement?"

"The first job I had in the Army was shoveling manure in the horse artillery," Pappy said. "Sure I got my time in. What the hell would I do if I retired? I'm too old for the airlines. Hell, I'm too old for Air America. Only way I could fly if I retired would be on charity."

"I understand."

"So what I'm telling you is that you're now working for Felter. Keep your mouth shut, lay off the booze, do what you're told, and he'll take care of you. Fuck up, and by that I mostly mean diarrhea of the mouth, and you'll wind up in Greenland or someplace counting ice cubes."

"I appreciate the advice," Jack said. "Thank you."

"Or, in your case," Pappy Hodges said, "in the Congo. Felter is one of those people you just don't fuck around with."

VIII

Private Jacques Emile Portet of the Flight Operations Section, United States Army Aviation Board, wearing his only civilian clothes, a somewhat battered tweed jacket, a pair of trousers, and a shirt and tie, went into Ozark to buy a car.

He was reasonably sure that he would be at Fort Rucker for some time, probably as long as he had to stay in the Army. He thought that Colonel Felter had probably come to the conclusion that forcing him to go to the Congo would cause more trouble than it was worth. There really wasn't much he could do in the Congo that he couldn't do here. The rules had been explained to him by Major Pappy Hodges. If he made himself as useful as possible and kept his mouth shut, Felter would take care of him. . . .

He intended to do both. And already the taking care of had started. The First Sergeant had called him in that morning and told him that from that moment on he was on twenty-four call. That had at first sounded a little alarming, but the First Sergeant had gone on to explain that what that meant was that he was to be available to Major Hodges twenty-four hours a day, seven days a week. And since that was true, he was excused from the normal "company duties" expected of a private. There would be no formations to stand, no extra duties like charge of quarters, or anything else. And the First Sergeant had told him that, as of the day before, he was on "flight orders," which meant that he would draw flight pay.

When he'd left the orderly room, he'd called Major Hodges at his quarters.

"The First Sergeant told me I was on call to you twenty-four hours a day. I thought I'd better ask you what that meant."

"Have a good weekend, Jack. If you can't keep your pecker in your pocket, try to stay out of jail," Hodges had said. "I'll see you in the hangar at eight o'clock Monday morning."

Since there was virtually no public transportation on the post, just a couple of buses a day to Dothan, Ozark, and Enterprise, Jack had two options: He could either spend his free time in wholesome GI recreation, bowling, working out in the field house, and treating himself to a banquet in the PX snack bar, or he could go buy a car and see what he could do about getting his ashes hauled.

And even putting his near-terminal case of Lackanookie aside, he would need a car to drive from the Board barracks to the airfield, to get his laundry done, just to get around.

Fortunately, money wasn't going to be a problem. He had sold his Volkswagen to Enrico de la Santiago before leaving Leopoldville, nothing down and whatever Rico figured he could spare from his Air Simba pay.

Hanni had written him faithfully once a week, telling him that Rico had been making regular payments. She had also told him that his grandfather's estate had finally been settled and that there had been a check, deposit slip enclosed, and that she did not agree with his father that he would probably blow the whole thing in the next three weeks on strong liquor and wild women.

The copy of the deposit slip had been a shock. The check had been for $96,545, about ten times what Jack had expected. As soon as he'd recovered, He had called his father from a pay station at Knox (the way the operator had behaved, he suspected it was her very first call collect to Leopoldville 6757 in the Republic of the Congo) and offered the money to his father. Air Simba was about 90 percent in hock to Barclays Bank, Ltd.

His father hadn't wanted to take the money ("We can go broke, you know,"), but in the end he'd agreed to borrow, for the company, $75,000. That still left Jack with more cash than he had ever had in his life, and it was nice to think that if he wanted to, he could walk into the

Ford showroom and buy, for example—and for cash—a red convertible off the showroom floor.

Not that he would, of course. Jack prided himself on his automobile wisdom, which was that only fools drive more car than they have to. The function of an automobile was to carry the human body from point A to point B in reasonable comfort and with reasonable reliability. So far as Jack was concerned, the Volkswagen people, more than anybody else, had best solved that human need.

The proof was the Volkswagen that he had sold to Rico. Cheap, solid, reliable. And he had sold it for as much as he had paid for it. What he would do now, he decided somewhat smugly, was buy another used Volkswagen.

This high resolve, this proof that he was mature and above the foolish vanities of his peers, lasted about ninety seconds from the moment he walked onto the Ford dealer's used car lot in Ozark.

He was drawn like a moth to a candle to something which represented the absolute antithesis of his wise and conservative automobile philosophy. It was also the most maddeningly beautiful thing he had seen since he watched the derriere of the gray-eyed girl on the plane undulate as she walked into the terminal and out of his life.

It was a Jaguar XKE drophead coupé, flaming red, with red leather upholstery and wire wheels. It was desecrated by only one thing, a violation of its beauty as obscene as carving initials in Mona Lisa's forehead. Someone had taken a shoe whitener and written "Sharp! $3,000 down!" on the exquisitely slanted chrome-framed windshield.

Jack did the only thing someone of his maturity and common sense could do under the circumstances. He fled the used-car lot.

A few minutes later he found himself before the First National Bank of Ozark's plate-glass windows.

If he was going to buy *a nice little used Volkswagen*, he suddenly realized, he was going to have to pay for it. And he didn't think he would be able to successfully offer a check drawn on the 1010 Avenue Baudouin, Leopoldville, Democratic Republic of the Congo, branch of Barclays Bank, Ltd.

It was a minor problem and he had gone through it before. There was a Barclays branch in New York—and he probably still had their phone number in his wallet, he thought, pleased—who, when telephoned by one of their customers in America, would vouch for his check. When he'd opened his first checking account with Barclays his father had warned him that Barclays had one simple rule: write a bad check and you were out on your ass. But until that first bad check, they were very obliging about handing you money or vouching for your checks.

He would open an account here, put in enough money to buy a *good used Volkswagen*, and go buy one.

He went inside and searched through his wallet. Not only did he have Barclays' number in New York, but the name of a guy who had vouched for his checks before. Ten thousand years ago, when he and his father had been in San Antonio, Texas, and come across three surplus Wright R-1830-92 Twin Wasp engines in a forgotten corner of an Aero Services warehouse, Aero Services had been unwilling to take a check on Barclays until the Barclays man in New York had said the magic words to a Texas banker.

And if I'm going to do this, I might as well do it just once. I will need more money than for just the good used Volkswagen.

He made out a check for $15,000, leaving the payee blank, and took it to the nearest teller's window.

"Yes, Sir?"

There was no reply from Private Jacques Emile Portet. He was struck dumb.

Looking at him from behind the counter was the girl from the airplane. She of the intelligent eyes, wholesome face, and absolutely flawless body. She was wearing a white blouse through which he could see the lace of her slip. He could smell her perfume.

"Can I do something for you?" she asked.

"I'd like to see an officer about opening an account," Jack said. There was something wrong with his voice. It came out in a croaking whisper.

"What kind of an account did you have in mind?"

"Checking," Jack croaked, and then cleared his voice. "I would like to open a checking account."

This came out very loudly, as if he wished to make everyone in the bank aware of his intentions.

"I can do that for you," she said.

She opened a drawer and handed him several forms and then a ball-point pen.

Jack filled them out, not looking at the girl, but not failing to see that she had long and graceful fingers covered with pure white skin, and that her perfectly manicured fingernails were covered with a transparent lacquer.

He made sure he had his voice under control before he spoke.

"I'm going to give you a check on my Leopoldville bank," he said.

"And the number of a man in Barclays Bank in New York City who will guarantee the check."

She looked at the check, then raised her voice: "Mr. Medgeley. Can I see you a minute, please?"

Medgeley was a thirtyish banker type, Jack decided somewhat unkindly, who bought his suits at Sears Roebuck's Annual Distressed Merchandise Sale. He did not like at all the way the pasty-faced bastard beamed as he looked at the obviously very nice young woman's knockers.

"Yes, Miss Bellmon? How can I be of help?"

"This gentleman wishes to open an account," the girl said. She handed him the forms and the check.

Her name is Bellmon. I know that much now. What's her first name?

Medgeley said, in moral outrage, "The payee is not filled in," then took a better look at the check.

"Captain Portet," he said, "you understand it will take some time for this check to clear?"

"There's the name and phone number of an officer of Barclays Bank in New York. You call him—I'll pay for the call—and he'll vouch for the check," Jack said, and added: "It's Private Portet."

"Is this your check? The name on the check is Captain J. E. Portet," Medgeley said.

"I'm . . . before I got drafted, I worked for an airline," Jack said. "That's where that captain comes from."

Medgeley looked at him suspiciously. "I'm not sure how to go about this. It's more than a little unusual."

The translation of that, you pasty-faced bastard, is that you think I'm doing something crooked.

"Then get somebody who does," Jack snapped, wondering why he was so angry. "Who's in charge here?"

"I'm the head teller," Medgeley said with offended dignity.

"Then get me an officer. A vice president or somebody."

Oh, goddamn you and your runaway mouth! She's now going to think you're some kind of a nut!

But when he stole a look at the girl, he thought he saw a smile in her eyes.

"One moment, please," Medgeley said, and marched off with the check and the forms.

He marched back in a minute, looking annoyed and without either check or application forms.

"Mr. Brewer will see you—you, too, Miss Bellmon—in his office."

The girl smiled at Jack and pointed toward a glass-walled office. A tall, well-dressed man was standing in its door. When he saw that Jack was looking at him, he smiled and gestured for him to come over.

Jack looked for the girl. She was already making her way behind the counter toward the office.

"I'm Arnold Brewer," the banker said, offering Jack his hand. "And if you don't mind, Mr. Portet, we'll let Miss Bellmon watch to see how this is done. She just came with us."

The girl came to the office.

"You watch how this is done, Marjorie," Brewer said. "Then you won't have to bother Mr. Medgeley in the future, the next time it happens."

Marjorie. Her name is Marjorie Bellmon. What a pretty name!

"Yes, Sir," she said. She sat down in one of the leather-upholstered armchairs. She did so, Jack thought, with exquisite grace.

"First, Marjorie, you get some proof of identity. Something with a photograph on it. An Army ID card is fine."

"Yes, Sir."

Jack handed over his ID card. Marjorie Bellmon looked at him. For a brief moment their eyes met and Jack felt his heart jump.

"Then you compare the signatures on the instrument—the check— with that on the identity cards," Brewer went on. "When you're satisfied with that, you go to the next step. If you're not satisfied, check with an officer."

"Yes, Sir," Marjorie said.

"The next step here is to see an officer anyway," Brewer continued. "It takes an officer to approve a telephone approval, if you follow me."

"Yes, Sir."

Brewer made the telephone call. It didn't take long.

"He says Mr. Portet's check is as good as gold, that he's a good customer of Barclays Bank, and"—he turned to Jack—"that I give you his best regards."

Brewer scribbled his initials on the forms.

"That's all there is to it, Mr. Portet," he said. "You are now a customer of the First National Bank. Welcome."

"And I can draw on that money? Now?"

"Absolutely," Brewer said. "Marjorie will get you some temporary checks and then they'll mail you some from the printing company."

There was a small machine that printed account numbers and Jack's name on a thin sheath of checks. It did so far too quickly, long before Jack could think of a way to ask Marjorie Bellmon for a date or even work up his courage to make a desperate try at it.

He was shortly back out on the sidewalk alone, with nothing but the exquisite memory of the softness of her hand when she offered it like a man to him.

Marjorie Bellmon is obviously not the kind of girl who will be impressed with material things like fancy automobiles. But on the other hand, she just might be—and I am desperate. . . .

An hour after he walked away from the bank, Jack returned at the wheel of the Jaguar. He gathered his courage and marched back into the bank.

She smiled at him when she saw him. "Forget something?"

"Will you have dinner with me?"

Marjorie Bellmon surprised herself. "Yes," she said.

"Wonderful!"

He was almost back on the street before he realized he had failed to fix a time and place. He went back into the bank and to Marjorie's window.

She smiled at him, and he felt his heart jump again.

"The parking lot behind the bank at six fifteen," Marjorie Bellmon said.

[TWO]
Quarters #1
The U.S. Army Aviation Center
Fort Rucker, Alabama
1755 Hours 4 April 1964

I F HE MADE A LIST of things he didn't like about being Commanding General of Fort Rucker and the Army Aviation Center, Major General Robert F. Bellmon often thought, it would be headed by Quarters #1.

It was the largest of the family housing quarters built since Fort Rucker had been designated a permanent installation (from "Camp

Rucker," which identified a temporary installation); and it supposedly had the elegance befitting a general officer. But compared to the Commanding General's quarters at forts Bragg, Knox, and Benning (respectively, the Airborne, Armor, and Infantry centers), it was a dump. In civilian life it was the sort of house that a Quaker Oats assistant district sales manager in Kansas City would own.

And he *had* to live there. It was the quarters erected at the direction of the United States Congress for the use of the Commanding General of Fort Rucker—and he was the Commanding General.

He had been stationed at Rucker before, just at the time he had been promoted to colonel. The Bellmons had then lived in a decent house in Ozark, a white-columned, turn-of-the-century semimansion on Broad Street. It had been expensive, but they could afford it.

The Bellmons were "comfortable." There had been Bellmons in the Army for four generations—it was about to be five after Bob Junior graduated from the Point—and to a man they had been frugal and shrewd with money. And Mrs. Bellmon had been Barbara Waterford, the daughter of Major General Porky Waterford, whose family had once owned 5000 acres around Carmel, California, before they sold off all but 120 acres on the beach by the inch at very satisfying prices. The Bellmon income from investments was greater than his pay.

And he had to live like a goddamned salesman in this house.

A house without enough goddamned hot water for two people to take a shower one after the other.

General Bellmon had been flying and had come home sweat-soaked and in urgent need of a hot shower. His daughter had preceded him home and beat him to the shower, and exhausted the supply of hot water. There was something powerfully wrong with a house that denied a man in his position the simple pleasure, the simple necessity, of a hot shower.

Major General Robert F. Bellmon was seated in his bathrobe on the couch in the too-small living room of Quarters #1 when his wife and daughter entered the room from opposite ends.

"Well, don't you look nice," he said, meaning it.

"Thank you," Marjorie said, and curtsied.

"Big date?" Barbara Bellmon asked.

"I don't know," Marjorie said thoughtfully. "It could be."

"Johnny Oliver?" Bellmon asked.

"No," she said. "Of course not."

"Who?" Barbara Bellmon asked quickly, to shut off her husband.

"A fellow named Portet," Marjorie said. "He's kind of cute."

"Where did you meet him?"

"I was swinging my purse under the lamppole," Marjorie said. "And he just walked up and introduced himself."

"At the bank?" her mother asked, smiling.

Marjorie nodded.

"A local?" General Bellmon asked.

"No," Marjorie said. "He's in the Army."

Her father brightened. "Portet, you said?"

"I don't think you've met him, Daddy. He's a private, at the Aviation Board."

"I see."

" 'I see,' " Marjorie quoted mockingly, " 'he said, trying to conceal his disapproval.' "

Barbara Bellmon laughed, earning herself a dirty look from her husband.

"Well, I admire his courage," Barbara Bellmon said. "Most privates would avoid the General's daughter like . . . a leper, I suppose."

"Do you think going out with a private is such a good idea, honey?"

"Don't be such a snob, Daddy. Besides, he's actually pretty dashing. He was an airline pilot in the Congo. And he drives a red convertible Jaguar. He reminds me a lot of Uncle Craig."

Barbara Bellmon laughed out loud. "And the Little Lady wins the all-expense-paid trip to downtown Tijuana for saying exactly the wrong thing to calm her daddy down."

"What's wrong with Uncle Craig?" Marjorie demanded loyally, and then remembered. She blushed. "Well, you're always saying that about Uncle Craig, but I never believed it. And anyway, I didn't mean it that way. I meant he's sort of dashing."

"I never believed it, either," Barbara Bellmon said. "He never made a pass at me."

"Well, you are in a small, select group then," Bellmon said.

"I won't be late," Marjorie said. "I have to go."

"He's not coming here?" General Bellmon asked.

"I'm going to meet him at the bank."

"Why can't he come here?" Bellmon demanded.

"Because he doesn't know who you are and I don't want to scare him off."

And then she was gone.

Barbara Bellmon waited until she heard the sound (she thought it sounded like a lawnmower) of Marjorie's car fade and then turned to her husband.

"You are not," she said.

"I am not what?"

"Not going to call Mac McNair at the Board and check this boy out," Barbara said flatly. "I could read your mind."

"'Airline pilot in the Congo,'" he quoted. "Doesn't that sound a little fishy to you?"

"First of all you underestimate your daughter," Barbara Bellmon said. "And secondly, that's not what's bothering you. What's got you upset is that she said he reminds her of Craig and drives a Jaguar."

"Women, especially girls, are not safe around Craig Lowell."

"That's just not so, Bob. I've told you this before, and you simply refuse to believe it. Women are as safe around Craig as they are in their father's lap. Unless *they* have itchy britches. Craig hasn't said no very often, or sometimes when he should have, I admit; but I'll bet my last nickel that no woman ever had to tell him no more than once."

"We are not betting nickels, we are talking about our daughter," Bellmon said.

"I am going to have to get your mind off this before it gets out of hand."

"And how do you propose to do that?"

Barbara Bellmon threw her husband a credible bump-and-grind and then leered lewdly at him.

"Go take your shower," she said. "Maybe something will occur to me."

[THREE]
The Ozark Cafe
Courthouse Square
Ozark, Alabama
1805 Hours 4 April 1964

J ACK PORTET, wearing an obviously new sports coat and trousers, and Marjorie Bellmon sat on plastic-upholstered benches on opposite sides of a well-worn Micarta table, drinking coffee from china mugs.

A single rose lay on the table. When she'd gotten out of her MGB, Jack had thrust a dozen long-stemmed roses at her.

He was now very much afraid that the roses had been a blunder. He was aware that he had an awesome talent to blunder magnificently when something was really important to him.

"You shouldn't have done that," she said. "I hardly know you."

"That's what I'm trying to rectify."

She had met his eyes, for just a moment, and then looked away.

"Where would you like to go?" Jack asked.

"Over there," she said, indicating the brick wall of the Ozark Cafe.

"That's a dump!" Jack blurted. "I was just in there. Even the coffee is bad."

"Nevertheless," Marjorie said somewhat snappishly, "that's where I want to go."

She pulled one rose from the green paper and put the rest on the front seat of her car.

When the waitress offered menus, she said, "No, thanks, I'm not hungry. Just coffee, please."

"I thought we were going to have dinner," Jack said.

"Just coffee, please," Marjorie repeated firmly.

"One coffee," Jack said.

"You don't want coffee?"

"I've been sitting in here for two hours drinking coffee," he said.

She met his eyes and was disturbed by her reaction to them. She had hurt him or made him angry, and she realized that she hadn't wanted to do either.

"I wanted to talk before we went somewhere else," she said.

"We are going somewhere else? We are not going to have our night on the town right here in the Ozark Cafe?"

She smiled, then chuckled. "The folklore is that what a lonely soldier, far from home, really wants most is a home-cooked meal."

"What this lonely soldier had in mind was a dimly lit room with candlelit tables and a violinist wandering through the place playing Hungarian love songs."

"What you're going to get is a home-cooked meal."

"And I'll bet you've got a dog and a little brother, and everything."

"I do," she said, "but I'm not taking you home. I have a girlfriend, and she has—she and her husband have—a house here in town—and we're going there."

"I'll bet she's ugly or fat or both," Jack said. "It is sacred writ that every incredibly beautiful girl is attached to a fat and/or ugly one."

"I thank you for the compliment," Marjorie chuckled. "And for the roses. And you're wrong. She's really quite pretty."

"And we can play Scrabble or something, right?"

"I wanted to tell you about Geoff, the husband," Marjorie said, "before we go there."

"Oh?"

"He's a really nice guy. I really like him."

"But?"

"He's an officer for one thing . . ."

"And he's actually willing to socialize with an enlisted man?"

"He *was* an enlisted man. Don't be a reverse snob."

"OK."

"And he's very rich."

"That's nice, but so what?"

"So nothing," she replied. "I just wanted to warn you before we went there."

"I have nothing against rich people," Jack said. "I always hope some of it will rub off on me." When she smiled, he asked, "Are you rich, too?"

"My father is in the Army."

"An officer, no doubt? And how does he feel about you socializing with the enlisted men?"

"He is not thrilled, frankly," Marjorie said after a moment.

"He'll get used to it after we're married."

Startled, she met his eyes. There was more in them than a wise-crack.

"My God!" she said softly and stood up. "Pay for the coffee," she ordered and walked out of the restaurant ahead of him.

They got in the red Jaguar and she directed him to a subdivision and finally to a rather large frame house set on a wide lawn a hundred feet from the street.

"Pull in the driveway," Marjorie ordered.

There were two cars in the carport, an Oldsmobile station wagon and a Volkswagen, both new and wearing Fort Rucker blue officer's registration decals.

Before they could get out of the car, Geoff Craig came from inside the house.

"I knew it, I knew it!" he cried. "Ursula! Come out here and see what you did to me!"

Ursula Craig, a dishcloth in her hand, came out. A look of concern was on her face.

"Look!" Geoff said, pointing to the Jaguar. "I told you that if I thought it over, some sonofabitch was going to buy it out from under me."

Ursula shook her head and kissed Marjorie.

"How do you do?" she said to Jack, putting out her hand. "I am pleased that you could come to my home. You will have to excuse my husband—he sometimes acts as if he is five years old."

"*Sind Sie deutsch, gnädige Frau?*" Jack asked, picking up on the accent.

"*Ja,*" Ursula said, smiling, pleased. "*Und Sie?*"

"*Nein, ich bin Amerikaner, aber meine Stiefmutter ist eine Hamburgerin.*"

"Christ," Geoff said. "On top of everything else, now they can talk behind our backs."

He smiled at Jack and put out his hand. "I'm Geoff Craig," he said. "And I'm really glad to see you, even if you did steal this beauty out from under my nose. You're a vast improvement over what Marjorie usually runs by here."

"How do you know?" Jack asked. He had quickly decided he liked Geoff Craig, even if he was an officer.

"Anybody with the taste to buy something like that," Geoff said, pointing to the Jaguar, "for one thing. And for another, I don't think you're going to spend all night talking about the goddamned Army or the Good Old Days at Hudson High."

"Hudson High?" Jack asked.

"Wonderful!" Geoff said. "He doesn't even know what it is. Hudson High is what those of us with the wrong attitude call West Point."

He put his arm around Jack's shoulder and led him into the house.

"I am going to ply you with strong drink," he said. "And then try to talk you out of the car."

"I like the car," Jack said.

"I was afraid you'd say that."

The house was expensively furnished but looked comfortable; there was a sense of pleasant disarray. Books and magazines on the floor beside what was obviously Geoff Craig's chair, instead of neatly arranged on tables or a shelf.

And there was a well-stocked bar.

"What would you like?" Geoff asked. "I'm about to have a straight malt Scotch. To set the tone of the evening. After which, tongue anaesthetized, I will switch to the cheap stuff."

"We have some Rhine wine," Ursula said.

"Scotch sounds fine," Jack said.

Over the fireplace was an ornately framed oil painting of Geoff Craig in uniform. But the uniform was fatigues, on which was sewn the single stripe of a PFC. And it looked as if he had been wearing the fatigues and gone without a shave for a week.

"I love the portrait," Jack said.

"So do I," Geoff said, handing him a drink. "But it thrills neither of the ladies."

"I think it's awful," Ursula said. She went to the bar, pulled the cork from a bottle of wine, and poured glasses for herself and Marjorie.

"It's our very first military heirloom," Geoff said. "Something I shall treasure for the rest of my life. It was painted—from a photo Ursula took of me at Fort Bragg—by one of the very finest artists plying his trade on the sidewalk before the cathedral in Jackson Square in New Orleans."

"I thought I recognized the technique," Jack said. "The subtle brushstrokes, the *je ne sais quois* of the gentle pastels . . ."

Geoff laughed, and Jack saw Marjorie smile.

"It's awful," Ursula repeated, but she was smiling.

"Ursula is always saying—she and her brother, who is in the Army because he wants to be—that I should try to act more like an officer, to adhere to the customs of the service."

"You don't want to be in the Army?"

"I didn't," Geoff said. "I seriously considered protesting American foreign policy from Stockholm when I got my draft notice. But now it seems to be growing on me. At the moment I'm here because I was foolish enough to take a commission and now I can't resign. Watch yourself, Jack Portet, or you'll start hearing their goddamned trumpets."

Their eyes met for a moment and Jack realized that despite the joking tone of voice, Geoff Craig had just confided in him.

"I was talking about the customs of the service," Geoff went on. "Over the Bellmon mantel there hangs a similar portrait. The Gen'rul as a second lieutenant. So I figured, what the hell, if it's good enough for the Gen'rul, it's good enough for me. And I had it painted."

"Oh, Geoff!" Marjorie said.

Geoff looked between them.

"I can see by the pissed-off look on her face, and the confusion on yours," he said, "that until just now you didn't know her daddy was a general—*the* General—did you?"

Jack looked at Marjorie and shook his head no.

"Scare you off?" Geoff said. "That really wasn't my intention."

"No," Jack said. "That doesn't scare me off. I don't think anything's going to be able to scare me off."

"Wow!" Geoff said. "I feel that I am in the Garden of Eden, and Jack has just pulled the apple off the tree. And the way Marjorie's looking at him, a little piece of fruit seems to be just what the doctor ordered."

"God*damn* you, Geoff!" Marjorie said.

"She's blushing," Geoff said undaunted. "There's not many girls can do that these days."

"No," Jack Portet said thoughtfully. "That's true."

"Marjorie told me that you were an airline pilot," Ursula said quickly.

"'She said,'" Geoff said, "'quickly changing the subject.'"

"Before Marjorie throws something at you or slaps your face," Ursula said.

"I was, but it was a six-airplane airline. The pride of our fleet are Curtiss C-46s older than I am."

"But you have an ATR?" Geoff asked. When Jack nodded, he went on: "Then I suppose you're qualified to help somebody prepare for an instrument ticket exam in a light twin? Specifically, in a Beech Twin-Bonanza?"

"I suppose so," Jack said. "But the Army just made me a crew chief on a Gooney-Bird. They've made it pretty plain they don't want me flying their airplanes."

"I'm in advanced chopper school," Geoff said. "I'm also learning to fly twin-engine fixed wings—on my own, I mean."

"They let you do that?"

"Well, I'm going to present them with an FAA certificate and see what happens," Geoff said.

"I've got FAA certificates," Jack said. "They don't seem to be worth much to the Army."

"That's because you're an ignorant, uncouth enlisted man."

"Geoff!" Ursula flared.

"On the other hand, I am a high-class commissioned officer and gentleman, and a rated rotary-wing aviator," Geoff went on. "The guardhouse lawyer in me tells me that I can get away with it. All I need is to get past the exam."

"You're talking—presuming you can fly—eight, ten, maybe twenty hours in the air. Plus ground school. The examination's a bitch."

"I know," Geoff said. "I had a guy teaching me, a captain, but they're running him through some kind of a special course and he's not available. And it's forbidden for officers to teach people how to fly, or crop-dust, etcetera, etcetera."

"Where would you get an airplane? Can you charter something around here?"

"No," Geoff said. "But Beech was more obliging. I've got a Twin-Bonanza on a six month's dry charter sitting at the Ozark airport."

Jack's eyebrows rose in surprise but he said nothing.

"I'll pay you the going rate," Geoff said. "And throw in some unusual employee benefits—such as my wife's cooking and introductions to other hopeful maidens around town."

"If you're serious, sure. I'd be happy to."

"What got to you, the cooking or the introductions to the available maidens?"

"The going rate," Jack said.

"Starting tomorrow morning?"

"Why not? That'll be the end of our Scotch drinking, though."

"OK," Geoff said. He put out his hand. "We have a deal?"

"Deal."

"Now I will cook our supper," Geoff said. "I am one of the world's great beefsteak broilers. And afterward, if she's a good girl, I will get Marjorie an apple."

Barbara Bellmon was watching Johnny Carson when she heard Marjorie's MGB putter up the driveway.

She didn't want to give the impression that she had been waiting up for her daughter, and she started to get up to go upstairs. But then she figured the hell with it, she *wasn't* waiting up for her, and let herself fall backward onto the couch.

"Hi," Marjorie said when she came in the house.

"How did it go?"

"He and Geoff got along like thieves," Marjorie said. "They have the same sense of humor. It was mutual-appreciation night. And he speaks German, so Ursula thought he was just fine."

"But I gather you're not quite so enthusiastic?"

"Geoff made—somewhere among his many other wiseass remarks—the crack that the way Jack was looking at me made him think we were in the Garden of Eden and I was hungrily eyeing the apple."

Barbara Bellmon had to laugh.

"That's awful," she said.

"What's worse," Marjorie said, "so did I."

"Oh, my!" Barbara Bellmon said.

IX

[ONE]
Fort Rucker, Alabama
18 April 1964

"GENERAL," CAPTAIN JOHN C. OLIVER said as he stood in Bellmon's office doorway, "they say they have no Colonel Felter."

"Are they still on the line?"

"No, Sir," Oliver said.

"Get the number again," Bellmon said and picked up his telephone. He listened as his secretary gave the Fort Rucker operator the number he wanted in Washington, D.C. The called party answered on the third ring.

"The White House. Good afternoon."

"I have a person-to-person call for Colonel Sanford T. Felter," the Fort Rucker operator said.

"One moment, please," the White House operator said, and then came back on the line a moment later. "I'm sorry, Operator. We have no one here by that name."

"This is Major General Robert F. Bellmon, United States Army," Bellmon said. "Please put me through to Colonel Felter."

"I'm sorry, Sir," the operator said. "There is no one here by that name."

"Put the duty officer on the line," Bellmon ordered.

"I beg your pardon, Sir?"

"I happen to know that the White House switchboard is operated by the Signal Corps and that a duty officer is always on duty. I wish to speak to him."

"One moment, please, Sir."

It was a good thirty seconds, which seemed to Bellmon considerably longer than that, before a male voice came on the line.

"Major Lemes."

"Major, this is General Bellmon. I command the Army Aviation Center at Fort Rucker."

"How can I be of assistance, Sir?"

"You can either tell the operator to put me through to Colonel Sanford T. Felter or you can call Colonel Felter and tell him I am trying to reach him on a matter of some importance."

Major Lemes hesitated before replying.

"Will you hold, please, General?"

Very faintly, as if Major Lemes had covered the mouthpiece of his telephone with his hand, Bellmon heard: "I need a location on the Mouse."

And then there was nothing for a very long moment but a faint electronic hiss. And then the familiar voice.

"This is Colonel Felter, Sir."

"You're a hard man to get on the phone, Sandy," Bellmon said.

"I'm sorry about that, Sir. You were on the old authorized list. Apparently you were dropped from a new one. I'll look into it. It won't happen again. What can I do for you, General?"

"There's some bad news, Sandy," Bellmon said. "I have just been informed of an airplane crash in Norman, Oklahoma. Both pilots of an L-23 engaged in a cross-country training flight have been killed."

"And the aircraft?"

"Totaled."

"What happened?" Felter asked.

"I don't know," Bellmon said. "All I have is the report from the airport manager at Norman. He called the duty officer here. My Chief of Staff's on the line to Fort Sill right now, asking them to send their accident investigation crew to the site, to at least hold it down until I can get my accident people out there."

"What did the airport manager have to say?" Felter asked.

"Just that it crashed and burned. They had filed a flight plan to here. So he called us. Maybe they lost an engine on takeoff. . . . I just don't know, Sandy."

"Damn!" Felter said.

"Both were married and had small children," Bellmon said.

"I know."

"I assumed you would wish to hear about it as soon as possible."

"I don't know what can be done about an airplane," Felter said, as if thinking aloud. "Something, I'm sure. In the meantime, General, I would be grateful if you would make me up a list of potential replacements. I'll get there as soon as I can. I don't know when that will be. I'm . . . not in Washington. But replacements for plane and crew will have to be found right now."

"That'll be difficult, I'm afraid."

"Yes, I suppose it will. I'll be in touch as soon as I know something," Felter said. "General, have you called McDill? I mean, have you informed Lowell?"

"No, but if you want me to, I will," Bellmon said.

"Would you please? And thank you for calling me, General. And please extend my condolences to the families."

Bellmon put the telephone back into its cradle and then slumped back in his chair. He turned in order to face the window.

He could see the flagpole from his office window, and the headquarters parade ground. There was the reveille and retreat cannon. A Huey sat on the grass, waiting for General Bellmon, as a jeep had once waited for another General Bellmon at Fort Knox, and a stallion had once waited for still another General Bellmon at Fort Riley.

He wondered if his father and his grandfather felt as he did now, that the toughest job in the Army had nothing to do with the battlefield.

He sat there for a moment deep in thought, his shoulders slumped. And then he pushed himself out of his chair.

"Johnny!" he called. "Are we ready to go?"

"Yes, Sir," his aide-de-camp said. "The chaplain and the surgeon are here, and Mrs. Bellmon will be waiting for us on Red Cloud Road."

The toughest job in the Army is knocking on the door of dependent quarters to tell the occupants that their sponsor will not be returning. Ever.

You don't have to tell them, Bellmon thought. *They know the moment they open the door and see the General, and the General's wife, and the aide and the chaplain and the surgeon standing there.*

[TWO]
The Texas White House
18 April 1964

W HEN THE WHITE HOUSE Communications Agency put
through the call from General Bellmon, Colonel Felter was in the company of the President of the United States. The President was in a good mood. He had not only just knocked a little of the smugness out of three members of the Secret Service, but had won twenty-six dollars in the process.

The President had challenged three off-duty members of his protective staff to shoot a little trap.

"Me and Felter," the President had said. "And you three. Dollar a bird. Winner takes all. And me and Felter will shoot from the twenty-yard line. How 'bout it?"

The Secret Service agents had all been thoroughly trained in the use of firearms, including shotguns, of course. And, in addition, one of them thought of himself as a pretty good trapshooter. His concern as they began to shoot was how the President of the United States was going to react if he was beaten and, if the President was serious about the dollar a bird, what he should do if the President started handing him money.

The Secret Service agent's fears that his superior marksmanship might somehow humiliate the President were soon proved to be invalid. Sharing the President's well-worn Winchester Model 12 pump gun, and firing from the twenty-yard line, the President and Colonel Felter both went straight during the first round. That is to say that fifty clay pigeons were thrown into the air and neither President nor Colonel Felter missed one of them.

Of the seventy-five birds thrown from the sixteen-yard line for the three Secret Service agents to shoot at with Remington Model 1100s, ten birds sailed unscathed through the rain of number-seven-and-a-half shot.

The second round was just about as humiliating for the agents. Colonel Felter dropped two birds from twenty yards and the President missed once. The Secret Service dropped fourteen from the sixteen-yard line.

The trapshooting Secret Service agent's question as to whether the President was serious about a dollar a bird was answered when he saw him extending his hand, palm upward, toward Colonel Felter, and then saw Felter put two dollar-bills into it, one for each of his misses.

At that point the telephone rang. More accurately, it buzzed and began flashing a small red light on its side. The telephone was on a long cable that connected to a box in the ground, and the box connected to the switchboard.

Both the President and Felter looked peevishly toward the phone. The President had left word that he didn't want to be bothered when he was on the trap range.

One of the on-duty Secret Service agents answered it, then handed it to the man with the bag, today an Army lieutenant colonel charged with carrying the bag containing today's firing codes for nuclear weapons. His orders were never to be more than three seconds from the Commander-in-Chief.

"Colonel Felter," the Lieutenant Colonel called out, "it's a General Bellmon for you. Will you take it, Sir?"

Felter went to the telephone.

When he was finished, he walked back to the President, who was folding into a neat oblong the money he had just accepted from the Secret Service.

He looked at Felter with his bushy eyebrows raised.

"You look a little unhappy, Sandy," the President said. "Anything wrong?"

The President liked Felter. Deep in his gut he liked the hard-ass little guy. And he was aware that it was strange that he should, and he wondered why he did. The best answer he had come up with was that he could trust Felter.

"An Army aircraft has crashed, Sir, killing the two pilots aboard."

"You on the notification list for airplane crashes, Colonel?"

"No, Sir," Felter said. "This was a special situation."

"I was about to suggest we take these three sharpshooters up to the house and buy them a drink with their own money," the President said, "but I wanted to talk to you about Army airplanes anyhow, and this is as good a time as any." He turned to the Secret Service agents. "Thanks, fellas. I enjoyed it. We'll have to do it again sometime after you've had some practice and can come up with some more money."

They laughed dutifully. The President handed the nearest agent the Winchester Model 12. "Put that in the rack when it's clean, will you?"

"Yes, Mr. President," the agent said.

The President, his arm around Felter's shoulder, started for the house. The man with the bag followed him. The Secret Service agent with the telephone put it in the box in the ground and then ran after him, his walkie-talkie to his mouth, relaying to the other agents the information that John Wayne and the Mouse were en route to the house.

The Presidential trapshooting bothered the Secret Service, for by definition it meant that someone with a loaded weapon and with a finger on the trigger would be in range of the President. It didn't matter that three of the other four shooters were Secret Service agents. There could be an accident. And Colonel Felter was not in the Secret Service.

It had been proposed—and at the last moment decided against—posting an agent with a telescopically equipped high-powered rifle. His mission would have been to keep Colonel Felter in the crosshairs so long as he held a weapon in his hand. In the end, because John Wayne was liable to hear about it and blow his cork, the decision was not to use the sharpshooter, but rather to instruct the Secret Service trapshooters to go to the range with their revolvers and to keep an eye on the Mouse.

Inside the house, the President ordered the Navy Filipino mess steward to prepare drinks, after which he left the room to wash his hands. When he returned to the living room he announced, "Everybody out—I want to talk to Felter."

When they were alone he said, "That was good for them. A little humility is good for the soul. And it cost them. Not much. But enough so they'll remember it. Win or lose, if it's for free, it don't mean a goddamned thing."

Felter smiled.

"Where'd you learn to shoot like that, Felter?"

"A friend taught me," Felter said. "An officer named Craig Lowell. He has a trap range very much like this one."

"That's the one who owns most of downtown New York City?"

"So it is alleged, Sir," Felter said with a smile.

"Where's he now?"

"He's at McDill Air Force Base, Sir. He's the Army Aviation Officer on the staff of General Evans at STRICOM."

"Then he wasn't one of the pilots killed in the plane crash?"

"No, Sir."

"I thought it might have been him," the President said. "Since General Bellmon called you . . . here . . . about it."

"No, Sir."

"I'm a little curious, Felter, about what you're up to."

"Sir?"

"Both the Army Chief of Staff and the head of the CIA are curious, too," the President said. "Both of them have made a point of telling me they could be more helpful if they knew what you were up to. I just smiled my shit-eating grin at them and said thank you. But what the hell are you up to?"

Felter hesitated.

"I'd rather not make that an order, Colonel," the President said, a tinge of impatience in his voice.

"Nothing that should concern the Director or the Chief of Staff, Sir. I'm sorry their intelligence about me is so good."

"I'd hate to think you were pissing around the bush with me, Felter," the President said. "I would be very disappointed with you."

"When I was over there, I wasn't particularly impressed with the CIA people in South Africa or in Leopoldville, ex-Belgian Congo. So I put my own man in Durban and had Special Forces, through General Evans at STRICOM, put a couple more A-Teams into the Congo. I was about to send another airplane and a couple of pilots to the Congo so they would have a means to get around if necessary. That was the plane that crashed. They were on a training flight . . . long-distance flight by the seat of their pants."

"You think something's going to happen over there, don't you?"

"Yes, Sir," Felter said. "There's no doubt that we're going to have trouble over there."

"Gimme a for example?"

"Both the Russians and the Chinese communists stand to gain from any trouble they can cause in Africa, and they can cause trouble both cheaply and in ways that will not arouse public opinion against them. Not that they are, generally speaking, much concerned with public opinion," Felter said.

"Keep talking," the President said.

"The Chinese, for example—and I believe, Mr. President, that we're going to have more trouble from them than from the Soviets—are already extending the hand of socialist brotherhood all over Africa. There's a racial element, of course, which they have been clever enough to exploit: the yellow and black brothers against the white man. The Chicom embassy in Bujumbura, Burundi, which abuts the ex–Belgian Congo—the whole country is about as big as New Jersey—is three hundred men strong. They've sent doctors and teachers and are building dams and roads. The CIA has evidence that some of the crates they've shipped into Burundi, allegedly containing construction equipment, actually contain small arms and ammunition—"

"I've seen the reports," the President interrupted.

"Getting the arms into the ex–Belgian Congo poses no problem at all," Felter went on. "Nor does finding someone to give them to, someone who believes that he can take over the country."

"Both the CIA and the State Department tell me there is virtually no chance whatever of the government in Leopoldville being toppled, now that the Katanga business has been settled."

"I don't think it's been settled," Felter said. "Katanga may revolt again, just as soon as the last of the UN troops leave. And they will leave in June. Katanga is where all the money—in terms of resources and capability—is, and I understand their position. They don't want to share what they have with the rest of the Congo. But whether Katanga is in or out of the Congo doesn't really bother either the Russians or the Chinese, except that another revolt would contribute to what they're really after."

"Which is?"

"Social and economic chaos," Felter said. "Whatever hurts the West's economy—and by the West, I mean Europe, the United States, Japan, plus South Africa—is to their advantage. I don't want to deliver a lecture—"

"Keep talking," the President said. "When I get bored, I'll tell you."

"All right, Sir. The interruption of Congolese raw materials—copper, lead, tin, for that matter, coffee and latex—flowing to the West first of all causes the price of those materials to rise, almost certainly causing an economic disruption, and with a little bit of luck, an inflation. But in addition to that, it absolutely knocks out the Congolese economy. Starvation comes in. And it's *never* very far away. The West, and especially the United States, then finds itself sending money—or foodstuffs, which is the same thing—to replace the Congo's lost income, plus, of course military assistance to keep a government friendly to us in power. For peanuts, the cost of some small arms and explosives, they force us to spend billions."

"That's a pretty gloomy picture, Felter," the President said. "Far gloomier than I've been getting from the State Department."

Felter shrugged.

"What does the shrug mean, Felter?" the President asked sharply.

"That I am not always in absolute agreement with the State Department's evaluation of a given situation, Sir."

The President smiled, then chuckled. He looked at Felter thoughtfully for a moment, then took a swallow of his drink and swirled it around inside his mouth before swallowing.

"If you were the Secretary of State, what would your advice to the President be?" Johnson asked.

Felter's face showed that he recognized the question to be very dangerous.

"I'm a soldier, Mr. President," he said. "I don't—"

"Bullshit," the President said. "Answer the question."

"I would maintain a closer relationship with Joseph Mobutu than is presently the case—"

"*Colonel* Mobutu?"

"Yes, Sir. He runs the Armée Nationale Congolaise," Felter said. "*Colonel* Joseph-Désiré Mobutu."

"I hope I'm not beginning to get the picture," the President said. "Sir?"

"I send one of our *colonels* over there to look around, and he runs into another *colonel,* and comes back and reports that he and the *Colonel* are right, and the State Department is all wrong."

Felter did not reply.

"What about this Colonel Mobutu, *Colonel?*" the President said unpleasantly.

"Sir, I believe that sooner or later, and possibly quite soon, the State Department will have to deal with Colonel Mobutu as head of state."

"Are you suggesting an imminent coup, Felter? That the Army will take over?"

"When Colonel Mobutu decides to take over, he will."

"That's not what I hear from the CIA or the State Department," Johnson said. He waited for a reply, and when none came, went on: "You don't seem concerned over the prospect of another military dictatorship, Felter," he said.

"Aside from the King of Morocco, I'd say Colonel Mobutu's our best friend on the African continent. He's really impressed with George Washington, for one thing. And it's not a superficial or sentimental thing. He'd like to do for his own country what Washington did here—"

"How do you know that? You know him?"

"I paid a courtesy call on Colonel Mobutu when I was in Leopoldville," Felter said. "He was kind enough to have me to dinner. Just the Colonel, Dr. Dannelly—"

"Who?"

"Dr. Dannelly is a physician, a Mormon, from Salt Lake City. I'd say Mobutu is impressed with him as a friend, a Mormon, and a physician, in that order."

"CIA put him in there?"

"You mean is he working for the CIA? Or the State Department? No, Sir. He went over there as a missionary. He got together with Mobutu and he now considers it his duty to stay there."

"His duty to who?"

"To God," Felter said evenly.

"Not his duty as an American, for Christ's sake?"

"No, Sir. His religious duty. He's over there to help the Congolese people. And he has obviously decided that the way to do that is through Colonel Mobutu. I understand that's been difficult for State and the CIA to understand. Or accept."

"Meaning what?"

"Since he has made it plain that he intends to take no 'suggestions' from State or the CIA, they tend to pretend he isn't there."

"I've never even heard of the sonofabitch!" the President said angrily.

"Mr. President," Felter said cautiously, "if you brought Dr. Dannelly up to Mr. McCone or Mr. Rusk"—the Director of the CIA and the Secretary of State—"I think they would both feel obliged to do something about Dr. Dannelly. If they did it would destroy my relationship with both Dannelly and Mobutu."

"Not to mention that they would be even more pissed at you than they already are," the President said. "They would know where I got it."

"Yes, Sir," Felter said, smiling. "That, too."

"So far as you're concerned, Dannelly is all right?"

"As I understand it, our interests in the Congo are to keep the Katanga Province in the union, and to keep the communists—Russian and Chinese—from causing us more trouble than we can easily handle."

The President nodded.

"Dr. Dannelly told me he believes the Congo would be an economic nightmare without Katanga," Felter said.

"What did he have to say about the communists?" the President asked dryly. "Chinese or Russian?"

"He didn't have to say anything, Sir. He's a devout member of the Church of Jesus Christ of Latter-Day Saints. They regard the communists as the Antichrist."

The President grunted.

"Pity Benson wasn't Secretary of State," the President said. "Maybe he could have sown some of those seeds in Foggy Bottom."

Felter smiled. He also respected Ezra Taft Benson. Benson had been the very conservative Secretary of Agriculture in the Eisenhower administration. A devout Mormon, he later headed the Mormon Church.

"If Mobutu can take over the government, why doesn't he?" the President asked.

"There are several reasons, I think," Felter replied. "He doesn't want to do it without the proper preparation. And it's not time yet. And the Colonel is aware what our State Department thinks about colonels."

The President grunted and then smiled. "What shape is his army in?"

"He's got a regiment of parachutists that aren't nearly as good as he thinks they are."

"You saw them, I suppose?"

"Yes, Sir. I was given the honor of jumping with them."

"Colonel Mobutu arranged that?"

"Yes, Sir. He jumped, too."

The President snorted again.

"And the rest?"

"If anything happens soon, Mr. President, they're not going to be of much use."

"You're not suggesting that mercenaries will have to be used again?"

"Yes, Sir, I'm afraid that would be necessary if anything happens in the next six months or a year."

"Do you know what that means politically? White soldiers in use against black Africans?"

"I also know what the fall of the Congo, or a renewed civil war, would mean politically, Sir."

"Jesus Christ! Damn it, ten minutes ago I was feeling pretty good. Now you come in here and tell me the CIA and State have it all wrong, that Mobutu is the real power in the Congo, not Kasavubu, and that the Congolese Army is not prepared to put down another rebellion. And that I'm going to have to use mercenaries, which will piss off every country in Africa except Israel and South Africa. And," he added, "it will do me no damn good with the black voters here, either."

"That, Sir, is the situation as I see it."

"If I had McCone and Rusk in here, and they heard you say what you have just said, you know what they would say? Politely, of course, because they're gentlemen, but what they would say would mean you're full of shit, Colonel."

"Yes, Sir, I think that's probably true."

The President drained his drink.

"OK," he said, obviously having come to a decision. "I hope you're wrong, Felter, but I can't take that chance. Do what you think you have to do. Keep me advised. I'll keep the heat off you."

"Thank you, Sir."

[THREE]
Cairns Army Airfield
22 April 1964

1015 hours:

"CAIRNS, Air Force Three Eleven."

"Three Eleven, Cairns, go ahead."

"Cairns, Air Force Three Eleven, a Learjet at flight level two five thousand sixty miles north of your station. Estimate ten minutes. Approach and landing, please."

"Roger, Three Eleven, we have you on radar. Maintain your present course, begin descent to flight level five thousand now. Report five minutes out. Ceiling and visibility unlimited. The winds are negligible. The altimeter is two niner niner three."

"Understand five thousand five minutes. We have a code six aboard. No honors. But please advise General Bellmon, I spell Baker Easy Love Love Mike Oscar Nan, that Colonel Felter, I spell Fox Easy Love Tare Easy Roger, is aboard."

"Roger on your Colonel Felter, and we know how to spell Bellmon, thank you, Three Eleven."

1018 hours:

"Air Force Three Eleven, Cairns."

"Three Eleven."

"Three Eleven, we have you at one six thousand feet due north indicating four two zero knots. Please advise Colonel Felter that General Bellmon will meet him."

"Cairns, Three Eleven. Passing through one five thousand. Roger on the message."

1020 hours:

"Cairns, Air Force Three Eleven. Passing through ten thousand. Estimate Cairns five minutes."

"Three Eleven Cairns, understand ten thousand and five minutes. Maintain present course and rate of descent. You are cleared to two thousand five hundred. Use runway two eight. Look out for local fixed- and rotary-wing traffic."

1024 hours:

"Cairns, Three Eleven at twenty-five hundred. We have the field in sight."

"Three Eleven, Cairns, you are cleared as number one to land on runway two eight. The winds are negligible, the altimeter is two niner niner three. Report on final. Army Four Four Two, you are number two after the Air Force Lear on approach. Beware of jet turbulence."

"Four Four Two understands number two after the Learjet. I have him in sight."

"Three Eleven turning on final to two eight."

1025 hours:

"Cairns Approach Control, Air Force Three Eleven on the ground at two five past the hour. You want to close us out with Atlanta, please?"

"Air Force Three Eleven, affirmative. We will close out your flight plan. Three Eleven, take the next convenient taxiway and proceed to Base Operations. Ground control personnel will direct you to parking. Will you require fuel or other service?"

"Need some go juice, thank you."

At 1028 hours Major General Robert F. Bellmon, trailed by Captain John Oliver, walked out of the Base Operations building across the concrete parking ramp to the glistening Learjet. The fuselage door opened and a young black woman wearing the chevrons of an Air Force staff sergeant climbed down.

She saw Bellmon and saluted. Crisply, but not in awe. Learjets of the Air Force's Special Missions Squadron got to see a lot of brass. The day before, Air Force Three Eleven had carried two four-stars, an admiral, and the Commander-in-Chief of the Strategic Air Command.

"I don't believe Colonel Felter is quite ready to deplane, Sir," she said to Bellmon.

"May I go aboard, Sergeant?" Bellmon asked.

"Yes, Sir."

Colonel Sanford T. Felter was not quite ready to deplane because he was in the process of changing into a uniform.

"I am suitably awed, Sandy," Bellmon said.

"I asked my boss if I could come down here for a couple of days," Felter said as he tied his necktie in a mirror, "and he asked why, and I told him, and he said, 'Take a jet and be back tomorrow.'"

He shrugged into his jacket.

"I will admit I have learned to like traveling like this," he said.

"The memorial service is at eleven," Bellmon said.

"I know," Felter said. "That's one of the reasons I'm here."

"And the other?"

"I need replacement pilots," Felter said. "One of Dick Fulbright's people will deliver another airplane later today."

[FOUR]
Quarters #1
Fort Rucker, Alabama
1345 Hours 22 April 1964

GENERAL ROBERT F. BELLMON was surprised when Colonel Sanford T. Felter accepted Barbara's offer of a drink.

"Please, Barbara," he said. "Scotch, no ice. As much water as ice."

Felter sensed Bellmon's surprised eyes on him.

"I learned that from Craig," he said. "He said it makes no sense to kill the taste of expensive whiskey by making it cold."

"Well, certainly I won't question the argument that Craig Lowell knows more about whiskey than most people, but why are you so sure that's going to be expensive whiskey?" Bellmon replied.

"Because he knows I love him," Barbara said, handing Felter a glass. "Isn't that right, Sandy?"

"Thank you," Felter said.

Bellmon raised his glass. "Absent companions," he said.

"Absent companions," Felter said. "Including those two we just buried."

"Now don't *you* start it," Barbara said sharply.

"Start what?" Felter asked.

"What Bob started this morning when he was putting on his dress uniform," Barbara said, and quoted her husband: "'If I hadn't given Felter their names—'"

"I picked them," Felter said. "If it wasn't for me, they wouldn't have been in that airplane."

"No, they probably would have been run over by a truck," Barbara said. "Now the both of you stop it—and I mean it."

Bellmon put up his hands in a gesture of surrender.

"Bob," Felter said, "we have to talk about replacements."

"We do?" Bellmon replied suspiciously.

"The names you gave me are not satisfactory," Felter said. "So I had to look elsewhere."

"I may be able to help," Bellmon said. "How would you like to have, as a replacement pilot, a young man with several thousand hours of multiengine time—"

"That's not funny, Bob!" Barbara interrupted furiously.

"—who not only speaks French and German but—"

"Now damn it, Bob, you stop!"

"—is also very familiar with the Congo," Bellmon concluded.

"There is no Army aviator with those qualifications," Felter said. "Or at least none known to DCSPERS."

"There is that little problem," Bellmon said. "He is not a rated aviator, or for that matter an officer, but I've been around you a long time, Sandy, and know that you can cause administrative miracles to happen. . . ."

"Oh, you mean *Portet*," Felter said, and chuckled. "He's not available for this, Bob."

"You know about him?" Bellmon asked, visibly surprised.

"I'm surprised that you do," Felter said. "I'll have to ask you how he came to your attention."

"That sounded official, Sandy," Bellmon said thoughtfully.

"He's Marjorie's new boyfriend," Barbara said.

"Is that it, Bob?" Felter pursued. "That's how he came to your attention?"

"Marjorie has a bad case of puppy love for him," Bellmon said. "I should have guessed that there was more of a reason for the sonofabitch being here than his unwillingness to take a commission."

"Bob!" Barbara said in mingled anger and concern, and then she turned to Felter. "I think you had better explain 'not available,' Sandy. If you can, that is. Otherwise Bob will turn that into the worst possible scenario."

"'Nothing derogatory,'" Felter quoted after a just perceptible hesitation. "As a matter of fact, Bob, if it puts your mind to rest, everything I have suggests he's a really nice young man. Bright, levelheaded. His family in Leopoldville are nice people, highly regarded."

"I really hope that ruins your day, Bob," Barbara said. "Sometimes you can really be a louse!"

"What is he doing here that I don't know about?" Bellmon asked, smiling. The smile was clearly forced.

"So he and Marjorie have hit it off, have they?" Felter said, as if the question had not been asked.

"Oh, it's old home week," Barbara said. "He met Marjorie at the bank and she took him over to the Craigs', and he and Geoff hit it off."

"He's been giving Geoff Craig illegal instruction to get him through the FAA twin-engine instrument check," Bellmon said.

"I know," Felter said. "Why illegal?"

"How do you know?"

"Because Portet asked Pappy Hodges if it would be all right, and Pappy Hodges asked me," Felter explained.

"Well, it's illegal, with your permission or not," Bellmon said. "I don't know about that officially, of course. If I did, being the louse Barbara thinks I am, I'd have to rack the both of them."

"For what?" Felter asked. "I don't understand."

"We at the Aviation School somewhat immodestly believe that we give student aviators all the instruction they can handle at one time," Bellmon said sarcastically. "They're forbidden to take any off-post instruction."

"Well, then, I'm glad this came up," Felter said. "Because we are going to have to figure out some way to get twin-engined fixed-wing qualification on Geoff's records."

"I just told you it's illegal," Bellmon said. "I can't do that."

"The replacements for the pilots who went down," Felter said, "are Major Hodges and Lieutenant Craig. That's what I started to tell you before we went off at a tangent. And that means he has to be rated in the aircraft. Haven't you got some sort of board you can run him past?"

"Sure," Bellmon said. "And the next thing you know, every other rotary-wing pilot on the post will be taking out a second mortgage to get the money to take off-post fixed-wing flying lessons. Christ, they're told and told it's expressly forbidden! And then some lieutenant, whose wife just happens to be my daughter's best friend, not only does it, but winds up with a plush embassy flying assignment because he did. You realize what that looks like, what it makes me look like?"

"Is there one of these boards at Bragg?" Felter asked. "Could I work this through Hanrahan?"

Brigadier General Paul Hanrahan was Commandant of the Special Warfare School at Fort Bragg, North Carolina. In effect, the head Green Beret.

"There used to be," Bellmon said. "At the expense of a lot of effort, I had it put out of business. The only board authorized to rate people on civilian experience is here."

"Then it will have to be here," Felter said.

"That sounded suspiciously like an order," Bellmon flared.

"Come on, Bob," Felter said. "Put things in perspective. It's not that important."

"As opposed to what you're doing?"

Felter nodded but didn't respond directly.

"It is also common knowledge among the troops that Geoff is rich," Felter said, "and that he is related to the legendary Colonel Craig W. Lowell—"

"What about Lowell?" Bellmon interrupted. "He meets all your requirements and then some. Why don't you send him?"

"I'll tell you what I told him," Felter said. "He was on the phone to me to volunteer his services five minutes after you called him to tell him the plane went in. If you're trying to be inconspicuous, you don't send a lieutenant colonel, especially a flamboyant one like Lowell, to drive an airplane."

Bellmon smiled. "Just a suggestion," he said.

"I'm sorry if giving young Craig an embassy flying assignment makes things awkward for you . . . for the Army, if you like. Actually, from my standpoint there are several things against him. He is a Green Beret, and that will come out inevitably, and so far as the Congolese are concerned, they read 'mercenary' whenever they hear 'Green Beret.' Additionally, I sent Lieutenant Karl-Heinz Wagner to Durban as a recently escaped from East Germany refugee working for Hessische Schwere

Konstruktion. His orders were to infiltrate himself into the good graces of Major Michael Hoare—"

"Major who? Hoare, you said? Who's he?" Bellmon asked.

"An Irishman, a former Chindit, who commanded the mercenaries in Katanga," Felter said. "And who will probably get himself involved again. . . ."

"I remember the name now," Barbara said.

"And I don't like the idea of having Wagner's sister right next door, so to speak," Felter said, "for the obvious reasons. And I can't tell Geoff I'm sorry, but there are no funds for dependent travel to the Congo. Ursula would arrive in the first-class compartment of the UTA flight from Brussels the day after Geoff gets there. There she would be greeted by the upper echelons of the Congo business community paying their respects to the daughter-in-law of Craig, Powell, Kenyon and Dawes, investment bankers."

"Sandy," Barbara said, getting to her feet, "wouldn't you rather that I went and polished pots or something while you talk to Bob?"

"No. I want you to hear this, so maybe you can convince him I wouldn't be about to ask Geoff Craig to go over there if there was anyone I could send instead."

"Oh, hell, Sandy," Bellmon said, sounding contrite, "I know that."

"Well, since I have not been asked to leave," Barbara Bellmon said, "let me throw this into the equation. You know, Sandy, that Ursula's seven months pregnant? Can she go? Isn't there some kind of a regulation?"

"Not in the last six weeks of a pregnancy," Bellmon said.

"Barbara," Sandy said, "you don't really think that a little thing like a regulation would stop her? Didn't you ever hear that the rich are different from you and me?"

"I don't think it would stop her if she didn't have a dime," Barbara Bellmon said. "But I thought I should mention it."

"Did I just hear you say you 'were about to ask' young Craig if he wants to go?" Bellmon asked.

"Yeah, that's what I said. I called Pappy Hodges and told him to buy a new toothbrush, but I couldn't talk to Geoff." He paused. "Ursula told me that he and Portet went right from the chapel to the airport."

"You seem pretty sure he'll go," Bellmon said.

"Of course he will," Barbara said. "*They* will."

"I'm about to call Ursula again and ask her to have a few people in,"

Felter said. "Me. Major and Mrs. Hodges. And Major General and Mrs. Bellmon."

Bellmon looked at him curiously.

"My thinking, Bob," Felter said, "is that if, as you say, people are going to talk about Geoff getting special treatment, for my purposes that's not all bad. I would much rather have the Congolese—and everybody else—think that Geoff is getting special privilege than to suspect what he and Pappy will really be doing over there. If you were there for a party, that would come out. They call that disinformation. But if you'd really be that uncomfortable . . ."

"I know what they call it," Bellmon said sharply.

"Of course we'll be there," Barbara said. "But, Sandy, have you thought that Marjorie's friend will probably be there? Where she is, he normally can be found."

"Goddammit," Bellmon said.

"I've thought of it," Felter said. "I've been looking forward to meeting him. Now, since Marjorie approves, more than ever."

"You little bastard, you!" Bellmon said.

Felter smiled. If Bellmon swore at him, he was no longer angry. And if he was no longer angry, that meant he had accepted the necessity of what he had been told had to be done.

X

[ONE]
227 Melody Lane
Ozark, Alabama
1725 Hours 22 April 1964

U RSULA CRAIG kissed her husband when he and Jack Portet walked through the sliding plate-glass door into the kitchen, cans of beer in their hands.

Ursula had her hair in braids, was without makeup, and looked, Jack thought, wholesome and radiant, like a cover for *Mother to Be* magazine.

"I wonder how we could make that contagious," Jack Portet said to Marjorie Bellmon, who was at the kitchen counter spreading cheese on crackers.

Oh, shit! I didn't mean that the way she's going to think. I meant the kiss!

Marjorie looked at him in surprise, then noticed the horrified look on his face and took pity on him.

"If the cops had seen you riding around with that beer in your hand," Marjorie said, "I'd be passing these to you through the bars of the Dale County jail."

She went to him and started to push a cracker into his mouth. He caught her hand and they looked at each other.

"The kiss we can arrange," Marjorie said quietly, and kissed him, quickly and almost chastely, but still intimately. "I'll have to give a lot of thought to the other suggestion."

Jack brightened immediately. "Every journey," he intoned solemnly, "begins with a first, small step."

"If I didn't know better," Geoff Craig said, "I would think he really meant that he would like to spread a little pollen on her."

"Geoff!" Ursula said furiously, her face coloring.

"Hello, Geoff," Colonel Sanford T. Felter said, walking into the kitchen from the living room. "I hope you don't mind me coming here uninvited."

Geoff, smiling, walked to Felter with his hand extended.

"Don't be silly, Colonel," he said. "It's good to see you, Sir."

"I saw you at the funeral," Felter said, "but you got away before I had a chance to speak to you."

"You were surrounded by the brass," Geoff said. "Ursula been feeding you?"

"Yes, indeed."

"Jack, this is Colonel Sandy Felter," Geoff said. "I'd say he's a friend of the family, but that's a little inadequate. He and my cousin Craig have been buddies since they were second lieutenants."

"We've met," Felter said, giving his hand to Jack Portet. "Or at least we've talked on the telephone."

Jack, taken aback, was about to say something but Felter cut him off. "Since *Craig Lowell* was a second lieutenant," Felter corrected Geoff Craig with a smile. "When we met, my talents had already been recognized and I was wearing a *silver* bar."

"I didn't know you knew Jack," Geoff said.

"I know a good deal about Jack," Felter said. "For example that he's been teaching you how to fly fixed-wing airplanes."

"I gather that's come to the attention of our Supreme Leader?" Geoff said. "You didn't come here to drop a word to the wise in my ear, did you by any chance?"

"Actually, I came here to ask you how you'd feel about an assignment as an assistant military attaché—a flying attaché—in the Congo," Felter said.

"I thought we had a deal, Colonel," Jack said coldly.

"What the hell?" Geoff asked, confused.

"The deal was *you* didn't go to the Congo," Felter said to Jack. "Geoff's not part of that deal."

"Is somebody going to explain what the hell's going on?" Geoff demanded.

"I'm just a little curious, too, Uncle Sandy," Marjorie said suspiciously, "about how come you know Jack."

"'Uncle Sandy'?" Jack asked, softly and incredulously.

"How much time do we have?" Felter asked Ursula, speaking German.

"I made a leg of lamb," Ursula replied, also in German. "It'll be another forty minutes. The Bellmons and the Hodges are due any minute now."

"What did they say, Jack?" Marjorie demanded suspiciously.

"I'm apparently about to meet your father and mother."

"I thought that's what she said. And now I *really* want to know what's going on."

"That will give us a few minutes to talk, Geoff," Felter said. "I really am here on business, I'm afraid."

Geoff looked at him and then at Ursula. Ursula's face showed surprise and concern.

"What kind of business?" she asked softly in English.

"Nothing to worry about," Felter said.

"As Lord Cardigan said to the Light Brigade," Geoff said. "'Just canter down the valley toward Balaklava, fellows. Nothing to worry about.'"

Felter laughed. It was obvious to Marjorie that neither Ursula nor Jack Portet understood the reference to the suicidal charge of the Light Brigade at Balaklava. But Marjorie did. And she had known all of her life that Colonel Sanford T. Felter was in the upper echelons of Intelligence. She wondered first what Felter wanted from Geoff, and then she felt sorry for Ursula. And then she was surprised at the enormous relief she felt when she realized that whatever was going on, it had nothing to do with Jack.

Then Felter added, "You too, Jack, if you don't mind."

"We can use the office," Geoff said.

"That'll be fine," Felter smiled at Ursula. "The Army has to find replacements for the people who died in that plane crash, Ursula. They were about to be assigned as assistant military attachés to the embassy in Leopoldville. I think Geoff qualifies. That's what I want to talk to him about."

"Oh," Ursula said, clearly not sure what that meant.

Marjorie glanced at Jack. He was looking at Felter from eyes that were cold and suspicious.

And then the three of them disappeared down a corridor.

Jack expected to find a bedroom converted to an office by the installation of a small desk pushed against a wall. What he found looked as businesslike, but was far more elegant than the office of the President of the First National Bank of Ozark.

A large, gleaming mahogany desk held a leather blotter pad, a multibutton telephone, and a dictating machine. The chair behind it was high backed and upholstered in light-brown leather. Against the wall was a matching credenza, and at one end of the desk a small table held a typewriter. An IBM Selectric, to judge by the plastic cover. There was a conference table, one end butted against the desk, holding another telephone. There was space for five people, each to be seated in smaller versions of the chair behind the desk.

There were filing cabinets, each with a combination lock, a small refrigerator, and a bar.

Behind the desk was a picture of a very handsome mustachioed young officer having a medal pinned to his blouse by General of the Army Douglas MacArthur. Beneath that photograph a frayed, battered, grease-spotted battalion guidon had been framed. On the guidon were sewn on lettering, 73RD HV TANK, and someone had added, apparently with a grease pencil, the legend TASK FORCE LOWELL.

"What the hell is this place, anyway?" Jack asked.

"When my cousin Craig used this house as a bachelor pad," Geoff replied, chuckling, "he didn't like the office the Army gave him at Rucker. He worked out of here."

"It looks as if he walked out of here five minutes ago," Felter said.

"I don't use it," Geoff said. "I'd feel I was intruding; I sometimes think this is the only home he has."

"That's MacArthur giving him the Distinguished Service Cross," Felter said, walking to and pointing at the photograph. "And the guidon is the one he flew from his tank when he made the breakout from the Pusan Perimeter. They teach that operation at both the Armor School and Command and General Staff."

"I'm awed," Jack said.

"Here is the Colonel as a young man," Geoff said matter-of-factly, pointing at one of the photographs on the wall.

Jack went and looked. Despite a bushy, wax-tipped mustache, the photograph showed an obviously very young Lieutenant Craig W. Lowell. He had an M1 Garand rifle cradled in his arms like a hunter. At first Jack thought the photograph was a joke, posed for laughs, but then he realized that it was no joke. Lowell's foot, like a hunter's foot on a prized lion, was resting on the shoulder of a man lying on the ground. The man's eyes and mouth were open and there was a bullet hole almost in the exact center of his forehead.

"Greece," Colonel Felter said softly. "He was nineteen. When he was wounded and evacuated to the hospital in Germany, I found that roll of film in his things and sent it home to my wife to have it developed. I've always wondered what they thought at the Rexall Drug Store when they saw that snapshot."

There were other photographs. Felter was in some of them. One showed Lowell with a good-looking blonde beside him and a baby in his arms, standing beside Lieutenant Colonel and Mrs. Robert F. Bellmon. And, Jack saw, a pert-nosed little girl who had grown into Marjorie.

"His wife was killed by a drunk driver," Geoff said, "the day he got a battlefield promotion to major and the DSC. How's that for a blow in the ass?"

"My God," Jack said.

Felter pointed to a photograph of Lieutenant Colonel Lowell standing with Sergeant Geoffrey Craig wearing a green beret, holding Ursula's hand.

"I took that," Felter said. "The day Geoff and Ursula were married."

Jack looked at Geoff, who said, "Only for *en famille* discussion, the real story of how I met Ursula is that shortly after I was drafted, I found myself in the Fort Jackson, South Carolina, stockade, about to be locked up forever for breaking my basic training Platoon Sergeant's jaw."

"Really?" Jack asked politely, not sure that his leg wasn't being pulled.

"Really," Geoff said, nodding his head. "My father was somewhat hysterical and got in touch with Cousin Craig. Cousin Craig arrived wearing all of his medals to awe the local brass. A deal was struck and I was offered the choice between Leavenworth and becoming a Green Beret. So I went to Bragg, and met Ursula. And then, knowing that Ursula—not to mention me being in Special Forces—would send my father back into hysteria, Cousin Craig went with me to New York for the great 'Hi, Pop, meet the little woman' scene. We got married the next day. Colonel Felter gave the bride away. He was standing in for

Ursula's brother, who was off doing something mysterious for the mysterious Colonel Felter."

"You do get around, Colonel, don't you?" Jack remarked.

Geoff chuckled.

"I just remembered, Uncle Sandy," Geoff said, "that Cousin Craig once told me that if you ever came to me and said that you had a little job for me, that I was to jump out the nearest window."

"Which brings us to the business at hand," Felter said.

"I think I'm going to have a drink," Geoff said. "Jack?"

"Please," Portet said.

"Sandy?" Geoff asked.

"I'll have a glass of wine with the lamb," Felter said.

Geoff made the drinks and handed one to Jack.

"From this point," Felter said, "this conversation is classified Top Secret—Eagle."

"I don't have an Eagle endorsement," Geoff said. "I don't even know what Eagle is."

"You do now," Felter said. "Eagle is the covering operation for the Congo."

"You do?" Geoff asked Jack. "Know all about this?"

"He knows what he has the need to know," Felter said.

"Which isn't much," Jack said, and then turned to Felter. "Colonel, I don't mean to be rude, but just who the hell are you?"

"He won't tell you," Geoff said. "*That's* classified."

"No," Felter said. "It's not."

He took his wallet, technically a large Moroccan leather passport case, from his blouse and handed Jack a plastic-coated, photographically reduced-in-size copy of his appointment as Counselor to the President.

"Show it to Geoff when you're finished," Felter said.

"I'm impressed," Jack said. "I suppose that's the whole idea."

"What I don't understand is how a friend of Cousin Craig's can be that close to a Democrat," Geoff said as he handed it back to Felter.

Felter ignored the remark.

"Captain Kegg and Captain Askew were working for me," Felter said.

Geoff looked at Jack and said, "None of this seems to surprise you, Jack."

"I've been filling in the blanks in the Jeppesen information," Jack said. The Jeppesen Company provides, with weekly updates, information concerning airfields and their facilities around the world. "Private strips, that sort of thing, about the Congo, and trying to get them—*was* trying—to get them prepared for flying over there.

"He and Pappy Hodges," Felter said. "And now that Kegg and Askew . . . are no longer available, we're going to send Pappy. And you, if you want the assignment."

Geoff didn't reply.

"I've already located another airplane," Felter said. "It should be here by now. SCATSA will install the necessary avionics and auxiliary fuel tanks so it can be ferried over there. As soon SCATSA finishes, you'll take it over there. Seventy-two hours, something like that. I realize that's short notice, but it should be an interesting assignment, Geoff, and I'm in a position to offer it to you."

Geoff did not respond.

"Dependents to follow as soon as possible," Felter added.

"I'll bet it will be an *interesting* assignment. But why me?"

"You speak French, for one thing. You're well traveled. You'd fit in with the embassy crowd. And, as I say, I'm in a position to do you a favor."

"Oh, bullshit!" Geoff said. "I asked why me? I'm not a spy."

"All I want from you is to keep your eyes and ears open. I want you to be my eyes and ears on the spot. No espionage. I want to make that clear. I'm not sending you in there as an agent. That's the truth."

"If you want to tell me what's going on, what I'd be getting myself— and more important, Ursula—into, I'll listen. Otherwise you can stick this job up your ass."

Jack's eyes widened. Lieutenants just do not talk to colonels that way, even if the colonel is called Uncle Sandy.

Felter's face showed no reaction.

"I have given you no reason to distrust me, Geoff," he said. "Or to talk to me like that."

"That's not the case, I'm sorry to say," Geoff said levelly.

"What do you mean by that?" Felter asked coldly. Jack saw that Felter was getting angry.

"You told us that Karl-Heinz was going to the jungle warfare school in Panama," Geoff said. It was an accusation.

Jack saw that whatever that meant, Colonel Felter had been surprised.

"What makes you think he's not in Panama?" Felter asked after a moment's hesitation.

"A friend of mine got on a UTA flight out of Brussels to

Leopoldville," Geoff said. "And there was Karl-Heinz. On his way to Johannesburg, South Africa."

Felter didn't reply.

Jack plunged ahead, warming to his challenge: "And what are we doing with at least three A-Teams in the Belgian Congo?" A Special Forces A-Team consisted of two commissioned officers and eight to ten enlisted men, all of them at least sergeants.

"Your friend talks too much," Felter said, coldly angry. "And so, apparently, does Karl-Heinz."

"Don't worry about it," Geoff said. "The security of what I gather is Operation Eagle is intact. Karl-Heinz gave him the 'you-don't-know-me' eye in the airport in Brussels, and then when he found out they were on the same plane, on the plane, I mean, there was time for him to tell my friend he hadn't seen him."

"Obviously it's not intact," Felter said, "if you know about it."

"I didn't hear the word Eagle until just now," Geoff said. "And Karl-Heinz hasn't opened his mouth."

"Your friend ran off at his, obviously," Felter said.

"Well, we were in 'Nam together and I guess he figured I wouldn't get on the horn to the Russian Embassy and 'guess what, fellas?'"

"Have you told Ursula?" Felter asked quietly.

"No," Geoff said. "I didn't want her to worry."

"I was going to tell you, and ask you to tell Ursula, about Karl-Heinz tonight," Felter said. "And to impress upon her the necessity to keep quiet about it."

"Were you really?" Geoff asked sarcastically.

"So far as Karl-Heinz is concerned," Felter said, "it's possible that Michael Hoare's services as a mercenary will be required," Felter said. "If that happens I want somebody with him who can tell me what's going on."

"In other words he's a spy? Or an agent? Or whatever you call people like that?"

"Yes, he is."

"And the A-Teams? What are they doing?"

"For the moment, gathering intelligence," Felter said. "What you and Pappy Hodges will be doing is moving them around."

"For what purpose?" Geoff asked. "I mean, what are they looking for?"

"Evidence that the Chinese communists are moving into the Congo, or the Russians, or Chinese or Russian surrogates from any of a half dozen places," Felter said. "And to provide the STRICOM officer in the Congo with more information than he can gather by himself in case we have to intervene. The cognizant officer at McDill, incidentally, is a lieutenant colonel named Lowell."

Geoff's eyebrows rose at that, but he didn't respond directly.

"In other words you think something is going to happen?" he asked.

"I have a gut feeling," Felter said. "No hard intelligence."

"Then why all the goddamned secrecy?"

"There are those, in Leopoldville, all over Africa, and unfortunately in high places in Washington, who would regard what I think it is necessary to do over there as outrageous interference in the internal affairs of a sovereign nation," Felter said.

"But not LBJ, I gather?" Geoff said thoughtfully.

Felter did not respond to that.

"Does that satisfy your curiosity, Geoff?"

"One more question. How does Jack fit in all this? Is he going to be there too?"

"No," Jack said flatly.

"It seems to me that you could do this a lot better than either Pappy or me," Geoff said.

"Yes, he could," Felter said. "But he won't go."

"What do you know that I don't?" Geoff asked Jack.

"I live in the Congo. My family lives in the Congo. When my two years are up, I'm going back there to live. I couldn't do that if I showed up there in a uniform or at the embassy. Then I would be a *colon*, an American *colon* maybe, but a *colon*. And so would my family."

"What's the big deal?" Geoff asked.

"Having our planes burned up. Or having a grenade thrown through the dining room window," Jack said. "Or maybe having my little sister chopped in little pieces by some patriot."

"Jesus Christ!" Geoff said. "I have the uncomfortable feeling that you're telling me the truth. And you're asking me to put Ursula in a situation like that?"

"And if you're dumb enough to get involved in this, Geoff, you stay the hell away from my family in Leopoldville," Jack said.

"OK, we'll make that part of the deal," Felter said. "But as far as Ursula—and Mrs. Hodges—are concerned, I don't see any real danger. You will have diplomatic protection of course. And in the worst possible scenario—"

"Which is?" Geoff interrupted.

"The fall of the Leopoldville government, and/or the fall of Leopoldville to insurgents, there would be plenty of notice, plenty of time to put a STRICOM OPLAN into play."

"There is such a plan?"

"Yes. It involves a battalion of parachutists to hold the Leopoldville airport during an aerial evacuation of American nationals. Diplomatic and otherwise."

"Would that work, Jack?" Geoff asked.

"For anybody in Leopoldville it would," Jack said. "What would happen to people in Bukavu, or Kolwezi, or Stanleyville is something else."

"You think it would be safe for Ursula to go to Leopoldville, is that what you're saying?" Geoff asked.

Jack thought it over for a long moment before replying.

"Yeah, I think so," he said. "My father would have shipped the family the hell out if he thought something was going to happen. And you'd be living in the embassy compound. Ursula would be all right. But the first time you hear that something's going on, get her the hell out—don't wait."

Geoff nodded.

"OK," he said to Felter, "I'll go."

Felter nodded. "Now, I would suggest, before Pappy and his wife get here, is the time to tell Ursula about Karl-Heinz," he said. "Do you agree?"

Geoff nodded.

"Jack, would you ask her to come back in here?" Felter said.

Jack left the office and started down the corridor as Ursula came the other way.

"The Hodges are here," Ursula said. "I thought I should tell them."

"Go ahead."

He continued down the corridor and reached the living room as Major General and Mrs. Robert F. Bellmon came in from the glass door to the patio.

"Mother, Daddy," Marjorie said, grabbing his hand and marching him over to them, "this is Jack."

"Hello, Jack," Barbara Bellmon said cordially.

"How do you do, Sir?" Jack said, putting out his hand.

"I've been hearing a good deal about you lately," General Bellmon said.

Private Portet and Major General Bellmon smiled stiffly at each other.

[TWO]
The Dependent Housing Area
U.S. Army Aviation Center
Fort Rucker, Alabama
0715 Hours 27 April 1964

Quarters 3404-A and 3404-B were halves of a frame single-story building. They shared an interior wall and were mirror images of each other, each with three bedrooms, two baths, a living-dining area, and a kitchen. There was a carport on each end of the building.

Major and Mrs. Pappy Hodges, whose children were grown, occupied 3404-B. 3404-A housed a young captain and his wife and three small children. The young Captain did not approve of Major and Mrs. Hodges for a number of reasons. Major Hodges, for instance, refused to cut the grass on their shared lawn until the Housing Officer sent him a formal notice of failure to meet expected standards of quarters maintenance.

He also suspected, but could not prove, that on at least two occasions Major Hodges had soaked his supply of barbecue charcoal with a hose so that it would be difficult to ignite, and as Major Hodges put it, "stink up the area."

The young Captain was delighted to hear the old bastard was getting transferred.

The table in the dining area of Quarters 3404-B was covered with maps when First Lieutenant Geoffrey Craig, wearing a flight suit, walked in. Not only aerial navigation charts from the Jeppesen Company, but also ground maps from the U.S. Army Corps of Engineers and an enormous map, the largest of all, published by the Michelin Tire Company.

Major Hodges was leaning over the Michelin map (Africa, Central & South, Madagascar, 1:4,000,000, 63 miles to 1 inch) watching with close attention as Private Jack Portet made marks on it.

"This ought to be fun," Pappy Hodges said. "It's been a long time since I flew someplace looking for a burned-out area near a ninety-degree bend in a river."

Geoff Craig glanced at the map, saw the notations Jack Portet had made on it, and then looked at Jack.

"I thought he was kidding," he said.

"Welcome to flying in the Congo," Jack said.

Hodges started to fold the map.

"Louise!" he called, raising his voice. "We're going!"

Louise Hodges appeared in a moment, in a bathrobe, holding a cup of coffee.

"You sure you don't want any breakfast?" she asked.

"I'll get a doughnut in the snack bar at Cairns," Pappy said.

"Are they sending a staff car, or what?"

"I'm going to ride out with Geoff," Pappy said.

He stuffed the maps, one by one into his Jepp case (which was a large leather case, like a salesman's sample case, in which the loose-leaf notebooks and other Jeppesen materials were carried), closed it, kissed his wife perfunctorily on the cheek, and then picked up the Jepp case and his other luggage.

"Have a nice flight," Louise Hodges said.

"Yeah," Pappy said and walked out of the living-dining area.

Louise Hodges saw the looks on the faces of Geoff and Jack.

"This isn't the first time he's left me on three days' notice," she said. "You get used to it. You don't like it any better, but you get used to it."

They smiled, somewhat awkwardly, and started to follow Pappy Hodges out of Quarters 3404-B.

"Geoff," Louise Hodges called. "Don't worry about Ursula. Marjorie and I will see that she gets packed and on the plane."

"Thank you," Geoff said.

Geoff's Oldsmobile station wagon was parked in the driveway behind Jack's Jaguar. Ursula and Marjorie were in the back seat. Geoff opened the rear door of the Oldsmobile so Pappy could put his luggage in, and they got in the front seat.

"Mrs. Hodges isn't coming with us?" Marjorie asked when Jack had the car running and was backing into the street.

"She's smart," Geoff said. "She's staying home."

"Thanks a lot," Ursula said softly as Geoff backed out of the drive.

"Oh, honey, I didn't mean anything but that there will be nothing to see at the airfield. You could have just stayed home."

There was something to see at Cairns that Geoff didn't expect. There were two staff cars flying large checkered flags parked beside the Beechcraft L-23D on the parking ramp. One was the aviation-radio-equipped car of the President of the Army Aviation Board and the other was the gleaming Chevrolet, with its two-starred plate uncovered, of the Commanding General, the United States Aviation Center and Fort Rucker.

"Where's the band?" Geoff asked.

"I wonder what the hell that's all about?" Pappy Hodges asked. "I thought this was supposed to be sort of a secret."

It took fifteen minutes to go through the weather briefing, preflight the airplane, and load the luggage. The Commanding General and the President of the Board waited patiently, which was also surprising.

Then they shook hands and Geoff kissed Ursula and got aboard.

A minute later the L-23D taxied toward the active runway.

General Bellmon looked around. He saw Private Portet walking toward Hangar 104, and that Marjorie was with Ursula Craig.

"Johnny," General Bellmon said to his aide, "that young man is Private Portet. Will you run after him and tell him I would like a word with him? There. I'll come to you."

"Yes, Sir," Captain Oliver said.

General Bellmon turned to Colonel McNair.

"I don't think you have to hang around, Mac," he said. "They're as good as gone."

There was the sound of engines being brought to takeoff power, and a moment later the L-23D appeared on its takeoff roll. It rose into the air, retracted its gear, and began a slow climbing turn to the north. Then it was out of sight.

"Can I interest you in a hot doughnut and coffee, General?" Colonel McNair asked.

"No, but you could call Felter and tell him they're off, if you would please, Mac. If they say they never heard of him, tell them you're me. And tell him I was here to see them off."

Colonel McNair smiled.

"Yes, Sir," he said. "I'll tell him we were both here."

General Bellmon walked to where his aide was standing with Jack Portet.

"Well, they seem to have gotten off all right," he said. "But I don't mind saying that I am still not used to the notion of flying a little airplane like that between continents."

"It reminds you of the sailor's prayer when you're halfway between

Newfoundland and Scotland," Jack Portet said. "'God, your ocean is so big—and my airplane is so little.'"

There was no question in Captain Oliver's mind that Private Portet was at least implying that he had flown the Atlantic.

"Johnny, would you ask Marjorie to come over here a minute? And will you keep Mrs. Craig company for a moment?" Bellmon ordered.

Marjorie walked quickly over to where her father stood with Jack. There was concern on her face.

"What's wrong?" she demanded.

"I have something to tell Jack," General Bellmon said. "And I wanted to tell him to his face. And I thought you should be here too."

Marjorie put her hand on Jack's arm.

"Go ahead," she said. "Tell us."

"Orders are being cut transferring Jack to the J-3 Section at STRICOM at McDill Air Force Base. I wanted you both to know that I had nothing to do with the transfer. As a matter of fact, I asked Colonel Felter if it was necessary. He said that it was, that the sooner everybody involved in this is gone, the sooner it will no longer be the subject of idle conversation."

"Damn him!" Marjorie said.

"That sonofabitch!" Jack said.

"He provokes that reaction in me sometimes," General Bellmon said. "I find that I have to frequently remind myself that what he is doing is almost always of enough importance to justify the ruthlessness with which he does it."

"When?" Marjorie asked.

"It'll take two, three days for the orders to come down," General Bellmon said. "And it will take Jack another seventy-two hours, or ninety-six, to clear the post. In the meantime Colonel McNair said that Jack can consider himself to be on pass."

"Well, thank you, Daddy, for trying."

"Yes," Jack said thoughtfully. "Thank you, General."

Bellmon took a quick look at his watch.

"I've got to go to work."

Jack saluted. Bellmon returned it, then marched off.

"Jesus, I'm going to have to watch myself," Jack said.

"What?"

"I saluted him just now without even thinking about it."

XI

[ONE]
Pietermaritzburg, South Africa
2 May 1964

MAJOR MICHAEL HOARE called Karl-Heinz Wagner at the job on Friday and asked if he would like to spend Saturday in the country, shooting tin cans. Karl-Heinz quickly accepted.

"And now that I have you in my net," Hoare said, laughing, "I'll tell you that we'll ride out there in style, in a Porsche, which I just happen to be in a position to offer you dirt cheap."

Karl-Heinz suspected that neither the tin-can shooting nor selling him a Porsche was really what Hoare had in mind. A gut feeling, nothing more, but he would have bet on it.

Hoare showed up at the apartment on time and at the wheel of a nice little all-black Porsche convertible, freshly waxed, and with new Michelin tires all around. Hoare told him that not only didn't the Porsche have many miles on it, but had been well cared for during its four years of life.

Then Hoare motioned him behind the wheel.

"I'd love to drive it, Mike," Karl-Heinz said, "but you better understand that I can't afford it."

"Drive it anyway," Hoare said. "See how the rich people live."

When Hoare was sure that Karl-Heinz had been behind the wheel long enough to appreciate the good shape the car was in, he told him,

"Seriously, Karl, I bought this right, which means I could let it go right, for far less than it's really worth."

"Seriously, Mike," Karl-Heinz replied, gently mocking him, "unless you want to swap it even for my Volkswagen, there's no way I could afford this right now. See me in six months when I have my head above water."

"I would have thought you'd be doing all right with Hessische Schwere Konstruktion."

"I'm still a trainee. The pay scheme was set up for kids right out of university. And when I came over, I was wearing all that I owned. I've got the payment on the Volkswagen to make, and the payment on my furniture, and the payment on my clothes . . ."

"How long will you be a trainee?"

"For six months."

"Then it gets better?"

"Some," Karl-Heinz said, then chuckled. "My training as an engineer taught me to blow things up, not build things."

Hoare laughed understandingly.

"You ever miss the service?" he asked.

Karl-Heinz's mind's eye was suddenly filled with a very sharp memory. He had been on a hilltop in 'Nam and they had sent in a Caribou—a DeHavilland of Canada twin-engine, short takeoff and landing cargo aircraft to pick him up. Charlie had waited until the Caribou was on the ground and then started throwing in mortar rounds. The Caribou pilot had turned it around and immediately started to take off. The rear door was open, and Karl-Heinz had decided to run for it, otherwise he would have had to wait another day to get off the hilltop.

He had made it, but just barely, taking a running dive through the open door and landing on his stomach.

"Father" Lunsford (First Lieutenant George Washington Lunsford, named after the Father of His Country) had been in the back, a blood-soaked bandage on his neck announcing he had been dinged and was being med-evaced. Father had leaned down and waved the neck of a bottle of a Dewar's Scotch under Karl-Heinz's nose.

"Get off your belly, you Kraut honky," Father had greeted him cheerfully, "and Father will give you a little nip."

Father Lunsford had been in the airport in Brussels, dressed up to fit the Nigerian passport he was carrying in a sort of black felt overseas cap, a wildly printed flowing cotton coat, and a turtleneck sweater. There were eight other men on the plane, in an assortment of costumes (including that of a priest), all of them well-built, in good shape, with varying shades of black skin. Karl-Heinz had known before Father Lunsford had told him that they were fellow graduates of the John Wayne School for Boys at Camp Mackall, North Carolina. Father Lunsford had also told him that he'd made captain and was now commanding one of the three A-Teams that had just been ordered into the Congo.

Yes, I miss the service, Karl-Heinz thought.

"Sometimes," he said, "I miss the soldiering. But not the Volks-armee."

"Aren't armies about the same?" Hoare asked.

"I don't want you to think I'm a nut," Karl-Heinz said.

"Why should I think that?"

"Because the Volksarmee is a communist army, and all communist armies are shit."

"Oddly enough," Michael Hoare said, "my sentiments exactly. I've often thought how much it had to cost you when you came over the Berlin Wall. That took balls."

"Not really," Karl-Heinz said. "I just couldn't take it anymore. If I hadn't left, it was just a question of time until I had too much to drink and started running off at the mouth."

"Huh," Hoare grunted.

Near Pietermaritzburg, which is about forty-five miles from Durban, Hoare touched Karl-Heinz's arm and told him to take the next dirt road to the left. Half a mile down the road they came to a steep, natural clay cliff. Two cars and a van were already there, and a sheet of plywood had been set up as a table on sawhorses. The table held handguns, two Colt .45 M1911A1 automatics and an assortment of others, including several small snub-nosed .38s and an enormous Smith & Wesson revolver. There was a large supply of ammunition, some of it in what appeared to be Army cans, and other shooting paraphernalia, earmuffs, cleaning rods, and so on.

Two half sheets of plywood had been set up against the clay bank. Each had a life-size silhouette target stapled to it.

Karl-Heinz recognized none of the men who came up to the car. They were all English or South African. Or maybe Irish, like Hoare. Two of them looked intelligent, somehow cultured. The third, although he was cleanly shaven, struck Karl-Heinz as a thug. He sensed that he was being evaluated by all three, and that there was a degree of resentment on the part of the thug.

They fired the pistols. Karl-Heinz was not a good pistol shot, which became quickly evident, and he was afraid he was losing stature.

"If anybody ever asks you," Michael Hoare said, "you did not see what you are about to see, Karl. Understand?"

Karl-Heinz nodded. Hoare motioned with his head toward the van, and the thug, whom by now Karl-Heinz could identify as a Dutchman named Erik, went to it, opened a compartment in the floor, and came up with three weapons wrapped in canvas. He laid them on the table and unwrapped the canvas. One was an FN 7mm automatic rifle, the second a Russian Kalashnikov AK-47, and the third a U.S. Army M16A1.

"The authorities take a dim view of automatic weapons," Hoare said. "You're supposed to have a permit."

Karl-Heinz picked up the AK-47 and saw that it had been made in China.

"You ever see one of these?" Hoare asked, holding out the M16A.

Karl-Heinz nodded and took it from him.

"And the Fabrique Nationale?" Hoare asked.

"I've heard about them," Karl-Heinz said, and laid the M16A down and took the Belgian rifle. He had in fact put a hundred rounds through one at Fort Bragg, but he could not remember if the FN had been in foreign-weapons orientation class in East Germany.

It was a good weapon, well made and simple.

"Put a clip through it," Hoare said, indicating the cans of ammunition on the table.

Karl-Heinz removed the magazine from the FN, found 7mm ammunition, saw that the ammo had been made in China, and started thumbing cartridges into the magazine.

The thug did the same thing with an M16A magazine and then put it in the weapon and worked the action.

"Watch that muzzle," Karl-Heinz said softly but firmly.

"What?"

"Don't point that thing at me!"

"I know what I'm doing," the thug said.

"Not if you're pointing it at me, you don't."

"Shit!" the thug said.

Karl-Heinz grabbed the M16A1 barrel, jerked the weapon out of the thug's hands, removed the magazine, worked the action to eject the cartridge in the magazine, and then tossed the M16A1 to Hoare.

"Sorry," he said. "I don't like the way your friend handles weapons."

"You sonofabitch!" the thug said. "Who the fuck do you think you are?"

"Someone who doesn't want to get shot in the belly by an asshole," Karl-Heinz said.

"I'll cut you a new asshole, you sonofabitch!" the thug said, squatted, and came out of the squat with a knife in his hand. He had apparently had it strapped to his ankle.

Karl-Heinz turned his back on him and faced Hoare.

"Mike, you better tell your friend to put that thing away before I stick it up his ass."

He heard footsteps behind, spun around, and saw the thug, his face contorted by fury and excitement, coming toward him in a crouch.

Karl-Heinz squatted quickly, scooped up a handful of sand, and threw it in the thug's face as he got to his feet. Then he kicked him in the crotch, bent over the writhing man, snatched the knife from him, and threw it toward the targets.

"If he wasn't a friend of yours, I would have cut his balls off," he said to Hoare.

The other two applauded.

"Erik," Michael Hoare said to the man on the ground, his voice flat and cold, "when you can move, get in the van and stay there." He turned to face Karl-Heinz. "You're very good," he said.

"I think maybe you better take me home," Karl-Heinz said. "I don't know what's going on here, but I don't like it."

"Nothing else like that will happen," Hoare said. "I give you my word." He smiled. "Don't you want to fire the FN?"

"Why not?" Karl-Heinz said after a moment. He put the magazine in the FN, put the rifle to his shoulder, and fired two bursts at the knife lying on the sand in front of the targets. He didn't know if he had hit it or not, but when the dust subsided, the knife was no longer in sight.

"Erik," Hoare said to the thug, who by then was sitting up, white-faced, "I think you should also remember that Lieutenant Wagner doesn't forget quickly." Then he turned to Karl-Heinz again. Smiling broadly, as if making it a joke, he said solemnly, "Let me say, Lieutenant Wagner, on behalf of myself and my staff, that we are delighted that you have changed sides."

"Hear, hear," the other two said.

"And with that, gentlemen," Hoare said, "we *will* take our leave."

The other two came to attention, stamped their feet in the military manner, and barked, "Sir!"

In the Porsche, Karl-Heinz said, "Are you going to tell me what the hell that was all about?"

Hoare looked at him and smiled. "I'm glad you didn't cut Erik's balls off. Good ordnance sergeants are hard to come by."

"Ordnance sergeants?"

"You have been in South Africa long enough to hear that when I'm not selling cars, I am the infamous Major Hoare of the Katanga mercenaries," Hoare said. "Why is it that you've never mentioned it?"

"I figured if you wanted to talk about it, you would."

"Now's the time, then," Hoare said. "Charley—the tall one—was my GSO-2—intelligence officer. And Reggie was my personnel officer."

"*Was?*" Karl-Heinz said.

"There is no question in my mind that very shortly a situation will develop in the ex–Congo Belge which the armed forces of the Democratic Republic will not be able to handle."

"I don't think I want to hear any more of this."

"Let me finish," Hoare said. "The same thought has run through the minds of certain members of the Congo government. Funds have been made available to me to begin setting up another force—"

"I don't want anything to do with it."

"—which would permit me to pay my GSO-3—plans and training officer—two thousand dollars a month. For what really would be part-time work."

"Dollars? American dollars?"

"The funds are available in Switzerland, in dollars," Hoare said.

"I don't want to go to a South African jail," Karl-Heinz said. "And if Hessische Schwere Konstruktion heard of it, I would lose my job."

"We will violate no South African law," Hoare said. "But believe me, Karl-Heinz, unless they heard we were plotting the overthrow of the Pretoria government, there's no way the South Africans are going to bother us. They don't want a communist government on their northern border."

"What kind of communists?"

"Chinese, Russian, Czech, and possibly East German. I would bet on the Russians or East Germans. Would that pose any problems for you— the East Germans?"

"Is that why you want me? Because I'm an East German?"

"What I need is someone to come up with a training schedule," Hoare said, "together with a table of organization and equipment, and then to oversee the receipt of the equipment when it arrives."

Karl-Heinz said nothing.

"I took you to meet Charley and Reggie so they could have a look at you," Hoare said. "After the way you handled Erik—well, that's all they had to see."

"Most of your troops are like Erik?" Karl-Heinz asked. "Knife-wielding thugs?"

"Yes, I'm afraid so," Hoare replied honestly. "They need really special officers to keep them in line. You're obviously the kind of officer we need."

"Ach, Gott!"

"I have two more arguments," Hoare said. "I am in a position to pay a recruitment bonus—"

"What kind of a bonus? How much?"

"You're driving it," Hoare said. "And if it becomes necessary to field the commando, the two thousand five hundred dollars will seem like peanuts."

"What does that mean?"

"To the victor goes the spoils," Hoare said evenly.

"And if HSK finds out and I get fired, then what?"

"I think it would be best if you stayed on with HSK," Hoare said. "But if something should happen, no problem. You'd have a job the next day."

He put out his hand. After a moment Karl-Heinz took his hand from the leather-covered steering wheel of the Porsche and shook it.

[TWO]
Rhine Main Air Base
Frankfurt am Main, Germany
16 May 1964

BARBARA AND MARJORIE BELLMON had driven Mrs. Louise Hodges and Mrs. Ursula Craig to the airport in Dothan and put them aboard a Southern Airways flight to Atlanta. There they changed to Eastern and flew to Newark. From Newark they traveled by bus to McGuire Air Force Base, which is adjacent to Fort Dix, New Jersey. At

McGuire, when Mrs. Craig's condition was noticed—as coached by Mesdames Bellmon and Hodges—she firmly stated she was five months, no more, into her pregnancy. A visibly disbelieving medical officer finally cleared her to board a DC-8 of World Airlines, under government charter, for the flight to Frankfurt am Main.

Ursula was uncomfortable in her narrow seat and could not sleep, but there were no real problems. She didn't even get sick to her stomach, and she would have bet that she would.

In the Military Terminal at Rhine Main, an Army Transportation Corps sergeant examined their orders and issued them a voucher. Lufthansa would honor that, he said, and issue their tickets from Frankfurt to Brussels and from Brussels to the Congo. He pointed out the door through which they should go to find a bus to the civilian side of the field and added that he was sorry but they were going to have to worry about getting their luggage over to Lufthansa themselves.

They got on the bus, rode across the field, and unloaded their luggage at the Lufthansa Terminal.

"You sit on the bags, honey," Louise Hodges ordered. "I'll go see what's going on. You all right?"

"Fine," Ursula said, forcing a smile.

Louise Hodges didn't see anything resembling a skycap inside the Lufthansa Terminal, so she went to the nearest counter and spoke to a rather startlingly beautiful black-haired counter girl.

"I'm going to need some help with some luggage."

"Are you booked on Lufthansa?"

"I will be as soon as I hand over an Army travel voucher," Louise said a little snappishly.

"May I seě the voucher, please?" the beautiful girl said.

Louise handed it over.

"Hurry it up, will you?" Louise said. "The lady with me is in the family way."

There was a near miraculous change in attitude, but it was not caused, as Louise thought, by sisterly concern for a pregnant woman.

"Just one moment, please, Mrs. Hodges," the beautiful girl said with a warm smile. She disappeared through a door. When she returned, she was accompanied by a well-dressed man holding a rose in each hand, and a nurse in whites.

"My dear Mrs. Hodges," he said. "Welcome to Germany!"

He handed her a rose.

"And where is Mrs. Craig?"

"Outside, sitting on our bags," Louise said, eyeing the rose almost suspiciously.

"Oh, my," he said. "I trust everything is all right?"

He headed for the door, trailed by the nurse, the beautiful young woman, and two baggage handlers.

He went to Ursula, bowed, and handed her a rose. The nurse grabbed the hand holding the rose and took Ursula's purse. There followed a three-way conversation in German, far too fast for Louise to comprehend.

"What's going on?" Louise Hodges asked.

Ursula looked a little uncomfortable.

"I just told them I'm fine and that I don't want to go to a hotel here," Ursula said.

"They're giving you trouble about getting on the plane?" Louise asked.

"Oh, no," Ursula answered. "He wants to know if I would be more comfortable on a helicopter between here and Brussels."

"I'm sure you would," Louise said. "How much would that cost?"

"It's been taken care of," Ursula said softly.

"Geoff?" Louise asked.

"Geoff's father."

"Oh."

"And a car will meet us in Brussels and take us to the Westbury Hotel for the night, then back to the airport in the morning," Ursula said. "There will be another nurse, and a doctor if I need one. What should I do, Louise?"

"Say a little prayer," Louise said. "'Thank you, God, for a rich father-in-law.'"

[THREE]
Leopoldville, Democratic Republic of the Congo
18 May 1964

THREE SEPARATE GROUPS of people, each recognized by the authorities to be of sufficient importance to permit them to be on the tarmac instead of inside the terminal behind the customs barrier, were on hand when the UTA DC-8 touched down at Leopoldville's airfield from Brussels.

Lieutenant Colonel and Mrs. Gregory Sutton of the Office of the Military Attaché to the United States Embassy had a nodding acquaintance with the others, who were Mr. and Mrs. Kenneth Doane-Foster of Barclays Bank Ltd. and Captain and Mrs. Jean-Philippe Portet of Air Congo.

But they didn't speak other than to say good morning, and it wasn't until the plane had stopped and the stairs had been rolled up to the aircraft door that they learned they were all at the airport on the same mission. As the door opened, Mr. Kenneth Doane-Foster's chauffeur unrolled a sheet of paper on which had been neatly lettered MRS. GEOFFREY CRAIG and held it over his head.

"Kenneth," Captain Portet said in the hearing of Lieutenant Colonel and Mrs. Sutton, "what are you doing here?"

"Meeting an American lady," Doane-Foster said.

"I think we're meeting the same one," Jean-Philippe Portet said.

"You don't say," Doane-Foster said.

"I think we all are," Lieutenant Colonel Sutton said.

"There's Louise," Mrs. Sutton said, and then raised her voice. "Hello, Lou!"

Louise Hodges spotted her and smiled, then waved.

Mrs. Sutton went to the foot of the stairs, and when Louise came down them, trailed by Ursula Craig, kissed her.

"Long time no see," she said. "Welcome to the Congo. Pappy and Geoff got weathered in at Kolwezi."

"That figures," Louise said. "This is Geoff's wife. She's very tired and very pregnant. Is there some way you can get us through this customs crap quickly?"

"You'll be staying with us until we can find someplace for you to live," Mrs. Sutton said. "Quarters are nonexistent. As soon as we get to our place, I'll have the surgeon have a look at her." She put her hand out to Ursula. "I'm Dottie Sutton."

"How do you do?" Ursula said, looking at the sign with her name on it with confusion.

"Mrs. Craig," Kenneth Doane-Foster said, "I am Kenneth Doane-Foster of Barclays Bank, and this is my wife, Daphne."

"How do you do?" Mrs. Doane-Foster said, extending her hand to Ursula.

"Ursula," Hanni Portet said, *"ich bin Jacks Stiefmutter. Und hier ist sein Vater."*

"I say, we do have a situation here, don't we?" Doane-Foster said. "I couldn't help but overhear something about a problem about quarters and a doctor. Let me quickly offer the ladies the Barclays guest house for as long as they need it. And I can have our doctor there by the time we get there."

"I don't need a doctor," Ursula said, "I feel fine."

She looked at Hanni with what Hanni thought was a plea for help in her eyes.

"I claim stepmother's rights," Hanni said firmly, switching to English. "These two have been feeding Jack, and I intend to make it up to them." She turned to Ursula and switched back to German.

"You hungry? Or would you rather go right out to our house?"

"I'm hungry," Ursula said. "When's Geoff going to be here?"

"Maybe tomorrow, the day after for sure. By then we'll have you rested up and pretty."

"Danke schön," Ursula said.

"I say, I'm sorry, I don't speak German," Doane-Foster said. "I missed most of that."

"My wife, Ken, just stole the prize," Jean-Philippe Portet said.

The issue of who stayed where was finally settled over lunch at the Cercle Sportif, Leopoldville's country club. Louise Hodges would stay with her old friends the Suttons. Ursula Craig would stay with the Portets. Kenneth Doane-Foster signed the tab; Mrs. Doane-Foster said that the moment they had their feet on the ground she would have a lunch to introduce them to the other ladies of the community; her husband said that was a splendid idea, and the moment he got to the office, he would get on the phone—he knew some people—and see if he couldn't come up with an apartment. And he would of course have his physician drop by the Portets' that afternoon.

When Doane-Foster got back to his office, he went to the file and got out the confidential file on Air Simba, to which the bank had lent a rather substantial amount of money in a transaction it regarded as rather risky. He made a note that Jean-Philippe Portet had a previously unknown very close personal relationship through his son with Geoffrey Craig, the only child of Porter Craig, Chairman of the Board of Craig, Powell, Kenyon & Dawes, the investment bankers. He dictated a confidential memorandum to that effect for telex transmission to London and then called in his real estate man and told him he needed an apartment suitable for a young junior officer just assigned to the U.S. Embassy.

"His name is Geoffrey Craig," Doane-Foster said. "His father is Porter Craig, of Craig, Powell, Kenyon and Dawes. Sir Edward called me, Tom. He said he thought it might be a good idea if I did what I could for him in behalf of the bank. And I rather got the idea he had more in mind than my picking up the odd luncheon chit. Do you take my point?"

[FOUR]
The Hôtel du Lac
Bukavu, Democratic Republic of the Congo
18 May 1964

MAJOR PAPPY HODGES and First Lieutenant Geoffrey Craig had been in their room not more than fifteen minutes, just long enough to strip out of their flight suits and take a shower, when there was a knock at the door.

Pappy went to the door wrapped in a towel. An African stood there, a large man wearing a white cotton jacket, a round red felt cap, baggy black trousers, and sandals.

"What can I do for you?" Pappy asked suspiciously.

"M'sieu would like to buy jade?"

"No."

"Well, then, how about a thirteen-year-old virgin? We're running a special on slightly damaged thirteen-year-old virgins."

"Father!" Geoff cried. Rushing naked and dripping to the door, he wrapped his arms around the African and pulled him into the room. "Jesus Christ, how the hell are you?"

"Parched," the African said, closing the door and turning to offer his hand to Pappy. "Captain Lunsford, Sir."

"I'll be damned," Pappy said.

"Won't we all?" Father Lunsford said. "Have you guys got anything to drink?"

"There's a bottle of Scotch in my bag."

"They have room service," Lunsford said. "Get us some beer."

"I didn't expect to see you here," Geoff said as he picked up the telephone and ordered a half-dozen bottles of beer.

"Tell them Simba," Father Lunsford said. "They have two kinds of beer here, Simba and elephant piss."

"Simba," Geoff said to the telephone.

"And I would dearly like a cigar. I don't suppose either of you—"

Pappy went to his Jepp case and came out with a box of cigars.

"Genuine Havanas," he said. "I bought them in Greenland. They're terrible. The communists seem to have fucked that up, too."

"Expatriate life does tend to make one a terrible chauvinist, doesn't it?" Lunsford said in a mock English accent as he bit the end from his cigar.

"What the hell are you doing here?" Geoff asked.

"Reconnoitering," Lunsford said. "I had a guy at the airport and he said that an L-23 had landed. I figured it was probably you, and since I was in the neighborhood . . ."

"We had a hell of a time getting across the border," Pappy said.

"Well, Major, you're clearly a pair of mercenaries," Lunsford said, "bent on bringing back colonialism." He exhaled and looked at the cigar. "Kicking the gift horse in the teeth, that is pretty disappointing, isn't it?"

"And they were six bits apiece," Pappy said.

There was a knock at the door. Lunsford went quickly into the bathroom and stayed there until the waiter with the beer had gone.

"Reconnoitering?" Geoff asked as he handed him a bottle of beer.

"Roads and drop zones," Lunsford said. "And then I was over in Bujumbura having a look at the Chinese. Jesus, I hope we don't get involved in anything here. This is the tail end of a very long supply line."

"You think we will, Father?" Geoff asked.

"I don't know for sure, but if I were Mao Tse-tung and wanted to fuck things up over here, I'd sure know how to go about it."

"How?" Geoff asked.

"I would ship in a couple of crates of AK-47s as embassy furniture and then pass them out to the most convenient savage who sees himself as the leader of his country," Lunsford said. "He would take it from there."

"'Savage'?" Geoff quoted softly.

"Savage," Lunsford said. "There are some exceptions—they've got a first-rate colonel named Leonard Mulamba, who knows what he's doing . . ."

"I never heard that name," Pappy said thoughtfully.

"He stays the hell out of Leopoldville," Lunsford said. "Dills arranged for me to meet him. I guess you've met Colonel Dills? The Strike Command guy?"

"We're getting our orders from him," Pappy said, and added, "Some of them."

"Good man," Lunsford said. "Anyway, I got to meet Mulamba, and we hit it off, and I asked him how he would recommend I get around. So he put me in an ANC uniform"—the Armée Nationale Congolaise—"as a major, Major ———. And we went around together. He could teach some of my instructors at Leavenworth how to conduct an IG inspection. No bullshit. Right to the heart of what they call combat readiness. Or the lack of it—which is about all we found."

"You went to Leavenworth?" Geoff asked. The U.S. Army Command and General Staff College is at Fort Leavenworth, Kansas.

"'Went?'" Lunsford asked. "My good fellow, I was the honor graduate of my class. And I have a suitably engraved sword to prove it."

"I'm awed," Geoff said.

"You damned well should be," Father Lunsford said. "You're looking at a certified future senior leader of our armed forces."

He held out his hand for another bottle of beer.

"If I'd known what I was getting into over here," Lunsford went on, "I'd have taken my sword off the mantelpiece and brought it with me. The savages are impressed with swords. They have some trouble grasping things like automatic weapons."

"So did I when I was drafted," Geoff said.

"You are not listening to me," Lunsford said. "I'm talking *savages*."

"For example?"

"Well, for example, I got this from Colonel Mulamba during the Katangese rebellion. The rebel forces entered battle against the mercenaries with great confidence. They had *dawa*."

"What's that?" Pappy asked.

"Well, the officers take a recruit and they make little cuts on his forehead and chest. Then they rub magic dust in the wounds."

"Magic dust?" Geoff asked, chuckling.

"Shut up and let me finish. Then they drape an animal skin, lion—simba—is best, of course, but goat will do in a pinch. Then they tell the recruit to walk away. They pop a couple of rounds in the air and tell the recruit the ceremony worked, he now has *dawa*. He is now immune to bullets. And he believes it, because he has heard the shots himself and is still alive."

"That's hard to believe," Geoff said.

"You better believe it, Geoff," Lunsford told him seriously, "or you'll wind up in little pieces, *à l'italienne*."

"What does that mean?" Geoff asked. "'Like the Italians'?"

"You're an aviator," Lunsford said incredulously, "and you never heard about the Eye-talian aviators?"

Geoff and Pappy shook their heads no.

"The Italian Air Force sent people down here . . . to Kamina, an ex-Belgian air base—"

"We've been there," Pappy said.

"—to teach the Congolese how to fly," Lunsford picked up. "And half a dozen of them did not pay some hookers the agreed upon price. They disappeared. The Eye-talians, I mean. They turned up in the market. Neatly sliced into roasts and chops."

"Really?" Geoff asked incredulously.

"Really. A lot of these people came out of the trees last week, my innocent young friend. To coin a phrase, this is a whole new ball game. I won't say the rules are different, because there are no rules. If we get into something over here, it's going to be a mess."

"You think the Chinese are going to start something, Lunsford?" Pappy asked.

"I don't know. Felter obviously does, and from what I hear of that guy, he's usually right."

"Felter told us you were training Congolese paratroopers," Pappy said.

"And so we are," Lunsford said. "It goes a little slow. You have to start with the basics. 'This is a boot. You put the boot on your foot.'"

"Three A-Teams?" Geoff asked. "That's all?"

"You don't think that's enough?" Father Lunsford asked. "Oh, ye of little faith! We are here to save the world for democracy, and the Green Berets shall not fail or my name is not Maxwell Goldberg. Fuck it—let's eat! The steaks here are not at all bad, and you guys are buying."

"I thought you didn't want to be seen with us," Geoff said.

"I will now leave," Captain Lunsford said, "and go downstairs. And then, when you come in the dining room, I will come to your table and offer to sell you jade, and this time, Major, you will try to cheat this poor and ignorant savage out of it."

XII

Leopoldville, Democratic Republic of the Congo
22 May 1964

HANNELORE PORTET could think of a number of reasons why Ursula and Geoff should not move into the apartment Kenneth Doane-Foster found for them in a seven-story building downtown near the Mobil Oil Building.

For one thing it wasn't that nice an apartment. The nicest thing that could be said about it was that it was available. The rooms were small and dark, and the balcony faced the sun, which meant that it would be unusable except very early in the morning and at night. And it was downtown, which meant that no matter how hard the concierge tried to keep them out, there would be a steady stream of salesmen knocking at Ursula's door. And she didn't like the idea of Ursula being there alone when Geoff was out of town. And then there was the problem of servants.

On the other hand, the Portet house could swallow Geoff and Ursula—and the baby when it came—without a hiccup. The house was just too big for the three people who lived there. Jean-Philippe even admitted that. But he refused to sell it because of the tennis court and the swimming pool. A pool and a tennis court would just not fit in in a neighborhood of houses small enough for the three of them, he argued. And besides, he used the house to entertain for business purposes, and the Congolese would wonder what trouble he, or Air Simba, was having if they sold the place and moved into smaller quarters.

He was right, of course, but she considered that the pool and the tennis courts and an excess of houseboys were just another reason why it made sense for Geoff and Ursula to just stay.

And there were personal reasons, too. Jeanine was eleven, about to cross over into womanhood, and Hanni thought Jeanine could learn more from Ursula about love and babies than she ever could from maternal lectures. Jeanine and Ursula had hit it off from the beginning, and Hanni was always pleased when she came across them speaking German.

And Geoff and Jean-Philippe had hit it off from the very beginning. It was not hard to understand why Geoff and Jack had become friends, and with Jack gone, Geoff seemed to be standing in for him.

Hanni had sensed from the very beginning, from the day Jean-Philippe had met Geoff at the airport and brought him to the Cercle Sportif for dinner, that Geoff was somehow uncomfortable with them. She had no idea why—for he *obviously* liked them—but she was sure of her feeling.

The opportunity to bring up the subject came when Hanni walked out of the living room and found Geoff and Jean-Philippe sitting beneath an umbrella on the upper patio. They were drinking beer in what Hanni thought of as American style. They had their feet up on chairs, and their beer bottles rested in ice-filled champagne coolers, one per drinker, and they were drinking it from the necks of the bottles. They took a swallow and then buried the bottles in the ice.

Jeanine, Ursula, and two of the dogs were in the swimming pool. Ursula was in up to her neck, for two reasons. The water seemed to take away some of the strain . . . and for modesty. She was much too large for a bathing suit, so she wore a slip over her underwear.

Hanni walked over to the men and took her husband's bottle from him, carefully wiped the neck on her dress, and took a pull.

"She does that, you understand," Jean-Philippe said, obviously pleased to have the opportunity to explain, "to give the impression there is no intimate contact between us."

Hanni poured a little beer in her husband's lap, and when he stood up, smiled and handed him the beer bottle.

"There should be a special medal for men married to German women," he said.

"I have a proposition to make," she said.

"I'm all ears. Any lewd proposals will be carefully considered."

"I was talking to Geoff," Hanni said. "The proposition is that since the dogs won't have nearly so much fun if he moves Ursula out of here, that they should stay, permanently."

"I second the motion," Jean-Philippe said immediately. "If Ursula wasn't in there with Jeanine, the damned dogs would be standing here shaking themselves dry."

They both looked at Geoff and were both surprised at the look of discomfort on his face.

"What did I say wrong?" Hanni asked.

"Jack told me to stay away from you," Geoff said. "He said there would be resentment."

"That's ridiculous," Hanni said. "Who would be resentful? Was he talking about the embassy?"

"The Congolese. He . . . . uh . . . said it might involve some pretty unpleasant stuff."

"Nonsense," Hanni said immediately.

"Does Jack know something I don't?" Jean-Philippe asked. "Are you in the CIA?"

"No," Geoff said.

"Then there's nothing to worry about."

"But I'm not just flying airplanes for the embassy, either," Geoff said.

"No one thinks that any assistant military attaché in anybody's embassy is around just to watch parades," Jean-Philippe said. "Jack's concern is touching but misplaced."

"He was worried, and I mean worried, about physical violence," Geoff said. "He talked about you getting your airplanes blown up . . . and worse."

"As long as the present government is in power, we're in no danger of any kind," Jean-Philippe said. "And so far as you're concerned, you and Ursula, you're probably safer here than you would be in New York City."

"How do you figure that?"

"Kenneth Doane-Foster, which is to say Barclays Bank, met Ursula at the airport. Mobutu's Service de Sécurité didn't miss that, and by now they've found out what that was all about. Mobutu knows that his government is going to have to borrow enormous amounts of money, and I don't think he wants to ruin his welcome on Wall Street, or on Threadneedle Street, which he would if anything at all, from a traffic ticket up, happened to you or Ursula."

"I think you overestimate my father's influence," Geoff said.

"I never heard of your father," Jean-Philippe said. "But Doane-Foster has, and when I asked him what he was doing at the airport, he was honest enough to tell me. Is it really true that your father owns Manhattan Island south of Washington Square?"

Geoff took a moment to reply. Then he met Jean-Philippe's eyes.

"No," he said. "That's a gross exaggeration."

"Well, let's not disillusion either Doane-Foster or Colonel Mobutu," Jean-Philippe said. "For your sake and mine."

"Excuse me?"

"Doane-Foster has been much nicer to me since you came to stay with us," Jean-Philippe said. "You're the social catch of the 1964 Leopold-ville Social Season."

"Jesus!" Geoff said.

"And I have been led to believe by Mobutu's brother-in-law, who's got a piece of Air Simba, that the Colonel would be pleased to be invited to dinner . . . to meet the man whose father owns Manhattan Island south of Washington Square."

"You didn't tell me that," Hanni said.

"I didn't think Ursula would be up to a dinner," Jean-Philippe said.

"No, of course not," Hanni said quickly.

"Why don't we ask her?" Geoff said. "If we're going to be living here, we should meet the neighbors." He met Jean-Philippe's eyes again. "I didn't like the idea of her being alone in the apartment with me gone all the time. But I didn't know what the hell to do about it. I'm very grateful."

[TWO]
Albertville, Democratic Republic of the Congo
14 June 1964

MARTIN LUTHER NSAGAMDO was short, slight, and twenty-eight years old, but looked older. He had had rickets as a result of malnutrition as a child, and by the time he had been taken in by the Lutheran Mission of St. John (Missouri Synod), the damage was beyond repair.

The Lutherans had taught him English, and how to read and write, and that God had sent his own son, Jesus Christ, to save sinners, black and white.

Martin Luther Nsagamdo had been an unusually bright child, and there had been talk of sending him to the United States on a scholarship, but in the end there had been no money. He finished the missionary school, which went through the equivalent of eighth grade, and then he was sent to Kolwezi, to the Belgian Catholics, who ran a high school, Saint Agnes's, for bright youngsters.

That hadn't worked out either. He lasted two years, just long enough to more or less master French and to operate a typewriter. But he had great difficulty with mathematics; and Father Henri had gently explained to him that perhaps God had other plans for him than becoming a clerk. And that it was now time for him to leave school, as place had to be made for others.

Martin was then, so far as he knew, about fourteen. He returned to Albertville and tried to find work in the mines, but they would not have him because he didn't look strong enough. So he found work in the kitchen of a Belgian mining engineer. He did the kitchen laundry, shined the pots and pans and stoves, and saw that the Belgian's dog got what the Belgian wanted him to have and that the food just didn't disappear from the kitchen.

And he learned how to cook. Not fancy—that involved secrets the Belgian's cook was not foolish enough to share with him—but simple. He could fry eggs, broil ham and chicken, and make roasts of pork and beef. He stayed with the Belgian and his family eight years, then worked for another Belgian for two.

Then he went to work for K. N. Swayer, the *chef Américain* who had come to Albertville to put trucks together. Because he was loud and took the Lord Jesus' name in vain very frequently and sometimes drank himself into oblivion, K. N. Swayer at first frightened Martin Luther Nsagamdo. But he came to understand that he was really a good man, that the Americans who put the huge trucks together were different from the Americans of the Lutheran Mission of St. John (Missouri Synod) and from the Belgians. Not worse, just different.

Martin Luther's cooking pleased K. N. Swayer. He liked steak and potatoes and a tomato, or roast pork and potatoes and a tomato, and for a sweet ate ice cream flown in from Leopoldville, over which he sometimes poured chocolate syrup and sometimes Benedictine.

And he taught Martin Luther Nsagamdo to drive his car, and he put him in charge of keeping it spotless. K. N. Swayer repaired the car himself, and Martin Luther watched him, and thus came to understand something of how it worked.

On one memorable occasion, K. N. Swayer told him to get behind the wheel of the car and then ordered him to drive to his village so that he could see what it looked like.

It was a grand and glorious feeling to drive into the village at the wheel of a red MGB. On the way home, K. N. Swayer asked him why he had never married, and Martin Luther Nsagamdo explained that a wife cost so many head of cattle, and he had not yet been able to save up quite that much money.

The next day K. N. Swayer told him that he had been thinking it over, and that he really thought Martin Luther would be a much better boy if he had a wife to help him around the house. And exactly how much more money did he need than he had?

Martin Luther Nsagamdo concluded that K. N. Swayer was really a Christian gentleman after K. N. Swayer told him he could consider the money he had lent him to be a wedding present, and came to the wedding and sang in a loud voice "Jesus Loves Me" and "Onward, Christian Soldiers" from memory.

Martin Luther Nsagamdo was happier as K. N. Swayer's number-one boy than he had ever been in his life, and he was very sad to realize that this part of his life was coming to an end.

He found K. N. Swayer sitting on the back porch of the house, watching darkness fall on Lake Tanganyika. He was drinking beer from a bottle and munching on cheese and crackers.

"May I speak with you, Sir?"

"Now what did you break, for Christ's sake?"

"Evil is coming," Martin Luther Nsagamdo said.

"What the fuck are you talking about?"

"The Simbas are here," Martin Luther Nsagamdo said.

"The lions?" Swayer asked, confused.

"They call themselves the lions," Martin Luther Nsagamdo said.

"Who the hell are they?"

"Evil men," he said, "who have gathered around Nicholas Olenga. He used to be a clerk for the railroad."

"Why is he evil?" Swayer asked. His curiosity was now aroused.

"He says he will kill all white men," Nsagamdo said. "Especially Americans."

"Why?"

"Because you are here in the Congo to make slaves of everybody."

"And you say this character is here? You mean in Albertville?"

"He and two hundred Simbas," Martin Luther Nsagamdo said. "Mister Swayer, Sir, I think you should gather the Americans and leave."

"You think this guy is serious about killing people?"

"Yes, Sir, he is serious."

"Just Americans or all white people?"

"Americans for sure, other Europeans, maybe. He is a little man, but he could do much harm before the Force Publique could come and help."

I'll be damned, K. N. Swayer realized. *He believes everything he's saying.*

Five minutes later Swayer had Captain Jean-Philippe Portet on the telephone.

"Tell me about a character named Olenga, Philippe," Swayer said.

"Joseph Olenga?"

"Yeah."

"Bad news. What about him?"

"Why bad news?"

"He's a Kitawala," Portet said.

"A what?"

"They mixed *The Watchtower* with jungle gods, if you follow me. Let me try this: They're anarchists, in the name of Jesus Christ, who is coming back tomorrow, *and* in the name of whatever pagan diety happens to fit the situation at the moment. And, of course, the white man is the biggest devil of them all."

"Jesus!"

"Why do you ask about him?"

"He's here in Albertville," Swayer said. "My number-one boy just told me he thinks I should get everybody out of here."

Swayer had really expected Captain Portet to chuckle and say something about not believing everything you heard from your houseboy.

Instead there was a long silence before Portet replied.

"Have you got all your people where you can get your hands on them?" Portet asked, evenly, but deadly serious.

"You think there's something to this? Something dangerous?"

"I'll have an airplane there at first light," Jean-Philippe Portet said. "You have your people at the airport. They are *not* to pack any bags. Just what they're wearing."

"Holy Christ!"

"You heard what I said . . . no suggestion that there is mass evacuation?"

"Yeah. I heard you," K. N. Swayer said. "Where are we going?"

"Unless you want to come here, I'll call the Hôtel du Lac in Bukavu and tell them to expect you," Portet said. "How many of you are there?"

"Thirty-two," Swayer said.

"First light, Ken," Portet said.

"What about the Belgians at Union Minière?" Swayer asked. "Should I tell them?"

"Absolutely not!" Portet said immediately and firmly. "Thirty-two people will just about fill my Commando. And I don't want a mob scene at the airport."

"But aren't they also going to be in danger?"

"Probably not," Portet said. "Even *les sauvages* seem to understand that the mines produce money. Usually they leave the mines—and the breweries—alone."

"But we're working for the mines," Swayer said.

"You're Americans."

"Then you really think this is serious?"

"You want to take the chance it's not?"

"No," Swayer said.

When you get right down to it, he thought, *this is what I'm being paid for, to take care of my people. Putting trucks together isn't that important. And if they don't like it when they get Portet's Air Simba bill in Tulsa, fuck 'em.*

[THREE]
Jan Smuts International Airfield
Johannesburg, South Africa
1730 Hours 14 June 1964

ARTHUR B. COHEN, Resident Director of Craig, Powell, Kenyon & Dawes, South Africa, Ltd., was on hand when South African Airways Flight 808, which had originated in Leopoldville and would terminate at Durban, landed. Just to be sure, he had arranged for an ambulance to be on hand, but it did not prove necessary.

Mrs. Geoffrey Craig, on the arm of her husband, made it down the stairs from the DC-8 on her own power.

"It's nice to see you again, Mr. Craig," Mr. Cohen said to Geoff, who was in civilian clothing.

"You, too," Geoff said, although he could not recall ever having seen the man before. "This is my wife, and Mrs. and Miss Portet."

"An honor, ladies," Mr. Cohen said. "Now is there anything that has to be done right now? Or can we get on to the hotel?"

"Honey?"

"I feel great," Ursula said.

"We've got you in the Intercontinental," Mr. Cohen said. "Your father led me to believe you preferred a hotel. Mrs. Cohen and I would have been of course delighted to have you with us."

"We didn't want to intrude," Geoff said.

"It would be no intrusion at all, I assure you."

"The hotel's fine," Geoff said. "Thank you just the same. Where's the car?"

Cohen looked around and then gestured impatiently. An old but glistening Rolls-Royce moved majestically across the parking ramp.

"Unless Mrs. Craig would prefer to lie down?" Cohen asked.

"I feel fine," Ursula said. "I wish everybody would stop treating me like I'm made of glass."

It was a fifteen-mile ride from the airport into Johannesburg. Jeanine sat on one of the jump seats, her eyes solemn and wondering as she looked at Ursula.

"I can't hear the clock," Geoff announced.

"Excuse me?" Mr. Cohen said.

"I said, I can't hear the clock. Rolls-Royce advertises that the loudest thing at sixty miles an hour is the clock. I can't hear the clock."

"Quite," Mr. Cohen said.

"Did you know, Mr. Cohen," Geoff said, "that Rolls pays a royalty to Cadillac for the suspension on these things?"

"No, I can't actually say I'd heard that."

"Shut up, Geoff," Hanni said fondly. "You're more trouble than Ursula."

"It's going to be all right, honey," Ursula said. "I'm fine."

"Dr. Kloepp will come to the hotel just as soon as you're settled," Mr. Cohen said. "Spare you a trip to his office, you see."

"He doesn't have to do that," Ursula said. "I'm perfectly able to get around on my own two feet."

"You're as graceful as a cow on ice," Geoff said. "Let him come to the hotel."

"Geoff!" Hanni snapped.

Ursula and Jeanine giggled.

There were fresh flowers in each of the rooms of the suite on a high floor of the Intercontinental Hotel, and a large bowl of fresh fruit on the coffee table in the sitting room.

Geoff inspected each of the rooms before sitting on the couch in front of the bowl of fruit.

"No liquor?" Hanni asked.

"I'm sure there is somewhere," Mr. Cohen said, a little taken aback. He pulled on the door of a credenza and it came open, revealing a complete bar.

"What may I offer you, madam?" Mr. Cohen asked.

"Nothing for me, thank you," Hanni said. "But pour something strong into Daddy-to-Be before he drives us all crazy."

"Mr. Craig?"

"Geoff, for Christ's sake," Geoff said. "And yeah, a little nip would be just the thing. Bourbon if they have any."

"I'm going to lie down," Ursula said.

Geoff was instantly on his feet.

"You all right, honey?"

"I just want to lie down."

"You hungry or anything?" he persisted.

"I wish I could unplug him," Ursula said, then laughed and disappeared into the bedroom and closed the door.

Cohen handed Geoff a drink.

"Wild Turkey," he said. "I don't think I've ever had any before."

"Good stuff," Geoff said. He took a sip and then reached for the telephone on the coffee table. "Operator, I want to speak to a Mr. Karl-Heinz Wagner, at Hessische Schwere Konstruktion in Durban."

The operator said she would call him back. He hung up and found Hanni's questioning eyes on him.

"Ursula's brother," he said. "But that was a confidential call. Understand?"

She nodded.

"You, too, Mr. Cohen," Geoff said. "You are hearing none of this. And if he can come, you didn't see him. Do you understand?"

"Certainly."

It took ten minutes to get Karl-Heinz on the line.

"We're ready with your party, Mr. Craig," the operator said.

"Karl? Geoff."

"You are not supposed to call me," Karl-Heinz said.

"Ursula is about to have her baby," Geoff said. "Anytime, they say, within the next week or so. We're at the Intercontinental in Johannesburg, on the off chance that you could get up here."

There was a long pause before Karl-Heinz called back.

"When it happens, call me. At the company. My home line may be tapped. I will find a way to get up there."

The line went dead.

"Ursula didn't tell me her brother was in South Africa," Jeanine Portet said. "She didn't even tell me she had a brother."

"She must have forgot, honey," Geoff said. "But don't ever mention it to anybody, OK?"

"I'd love to know what the hell that's all about," Hanni said.

Geoff met her eyes but didn't say anything.

Then he got up and walked to Ursula's bedroom door.

She was standing by the bed, her back to him.

"I just talked to Karl-Heinz," he said. "He says he'll come when you've had the baby."

Ursula turned to face him.

"Then you better call him back," Ursula said. "I just broke my water."

"Hanni!" Geoff shouted.

"Take it easy, I heard her," Hanni said, pushing past him. "Have the car brought around."

[FOUR]
Penthouse Suite Two
The Intercontinental Hotel
Johannesburg, South Africa
0430 Hours 15 June 1964

GEOFFREY CRAIG had Miss Jeanine Portet slung over his shoulders like a bag of cement when he entered the suite.

"Just dump her on the bed," Hanni ordered. "I'll undress her."

"Poor kid," Geoff said.

"She wanted to wait, she waited," Hanni said. "And I'm sure when she wakes up she'll be glad she did. Did you see her face when she saw the baby?"

"Did you see *his* face?" Karl-Heinz Wagner said.

"Yes, indeed," Hanni said.

"There must be champagne around here someplace," Geoff said.

"It's half past four in the morning!" Hanni protested.

"I intend to toast my son and his nephew," Geoff said. "I don't care what time it is."

A search of the premises revealed no champagne. Two bottles were ordered from room service.

"Anyone else hungry?" Geoff asked, holding his hand over the mouthpiece.

Hanni looked surprised. "For some reason I'm famished," she said.

"Steak and eggs, sunny side up," Geoff ordered. "Three times. Whatever goes with it."

"I've got to be thinking of getting back," Karl-Heinz said.

"You can't go until you see Ursula, for Christ's sake," Geoff said. "I mean, awake. I want to get a picture. Geoffrey Craig, Jr., with his mommy, daddy, and uncle Karl."

"*I* am not on administrative leave," Karl-Heinz said.

Hanni picked up on that and looked at him curiously.

"Oh, for Christ's sake!" Geoff said. "Don't be such an ass. How often do you get to be an uncle? And they wouldn't dare start the war without you."

"I must get back," Karl-Heinz said relentlessly. "Perhaps it will not become known that I was gone."

"Tell them you were in Johannesburg with two good-looking German blondes. That sounds credible."

"I must get back," Karl-Heinz said. "There is an UTA flight at 1105."

"OK, that'll give us time," Geoff said. And then he thought of something. "Christ, my father!"

He picked up the telephone and gave the operator the number in New York.

"Do you know what time it is in New York?" Hanni asked.

"Who knows, who cares? God is in his heaven and all is right with the world," Geoffrey Craig, Sr., said.

[FIVE]
Albertville Airfield
0500 15 June 1964

K. N. SWAYER had gotten very little sleep during the night. He had called in his assistant, Denny Fitzwaller, a tiny, fifty-year-old Scot with whom he had installed rigs all over the world and told him what was going on. It was something they had been through before, constipated natives making a flaming pain in the ass of themselves and that it would probably turn out to be a waste of everybody's time and a hell of a lot of the company's money, but nothing more.

But it was better to be safe than sorry, and that what had to be done was to spread the word that at quarter to five in the morning, everybody from Unit Rig was to get in their car and drive to the airfield. No suitcases or anything else that would give away their intention to get on the Air Simba airplane and get out.

"There's no need to panic," Swayer had concluded. "Just tell them to play it cool and do what they're told to do."

Most of the Unit Rig people, who had worked for Swayer or Fitzwaller before, took the evacuation news calmly, but two brassy wives and a Detroit Diesel tech rep were difficult. The wives arrived at Swayer's cottage together to demand a fuller explanation than what Fitz had given them. When Swayer patiently provided it, they told him they could see no reason—if there was no real problem, as he said—for them to go off anywhere with nothing but the clothing on their backs and to leave all their things for the niggers to steal.

The tech rep, who came to Swayer's house while the women were raising hell with Swayer, announced that he didn't give a damn what either Fitzwaller or Swayer said, if there was a plane coming in in the morning, he intended to be on it, and with all his things, because he had had enough of Albertville, the Congo, and Unit Rig and was going home. He didn't, he said, need Detroit Diesel's job that much.

Swayer told the women to go home and pack two suitcases and to put them in the trunk of their car so that no one would see them.

Fitzwaller came in and announced that everybody had been notified.

"Give it an hour, Fitz," Swayer said when the women had left, "and then let the air out of their tires."

"You sonofabitch!" the Detroit Diesel tech rep said.

Swayer walked up to him and grabbed his shirt front and slapped him, twice, with his open hand, so hard that when Swayer let loose of the shirt, the Detroit Diesel tech rep fell down.

"You can't do that to me!" the Detroit Diesel tech rep said furiously, glowering up at Swayer from the floor.

"I just did," Swayer said without raising his voice. "And if you open your mouth one more time I'll do it again. Sit yourself in a chair and stay there unless I tell you you can move."

He waited until the Detroit Diesel tech rep had, after some hesitation, done what he had been told to do, and then turned to Fitzwaller.

"In the morning, Fitz, pick up this guy and those women and their husbands in the GM carryall and take them—without luggage—to the airport."

"Got you," Fitzwaller said.

"You realize what's going to happen when I make a report of this?" the Detroit Diesel tech rep said.

Swayer ignored him.

At four o'clock in the morning Martin Luther Nsagamdo made breakfast for Swayer and the Detroit Diesel tech rep. Orange juice, a small steak, eggs, toast, and coffee.

Swayer went to his safe and took out his emergency-cash envelope and put all of it but five hundred dollars in his pocket. He gave the five hundred dollars to Martin Luther Nsagamdo and told him to see after the houseboys of the other Unit Rig people in case they had "forgotten" to do it themselves.

He told Martin Luther Nsagamdo that if things looked bad, he should put his wife in the MGB and drive her to his village.

At quarter to five he put the Detroit Diesel tech rep into the MGB, and with Martin Luther Nsagamdo riding precariously behind them, his rear end on the trunk, drove out to the airport.

There were, he thought, an unusual number of what he thought of as bush Africans on the streets of Albertville. So far as Swayer was concerned, bush Africans, as opposed to the Albertville natives, most of whom seemed to make an effort to dress and behave like Europeans, *looked* as if they lived in the bush. They wore animal skins and strange hats, went barefoot, and carried sticks. More important, they seemed sullen and hostile, whereas the Albertville natives were polite, smiling, and happy.

The Air Simba Curtiss Commando appeared right on schedule, making Swayer wonder whether the pilot had arrived early and circled out of sight and hearing until the time set for his arrival. Swayer was not surprised when the Commando landed and the door opened and Captain Jean-Philippe Portet fitted the stairs in place. He would have been surprised if Portet had sent someone else.

The Unit Rig people were quickly loaded aboard.

Swayer shook Martin Luther Nsagamdo's hand, told him not to run the MGB into a tree, and climbed aboard.

Captain Jean-Philippe Portet, who had shut down only one of the Commando's engines, restarted it as he taxied to the end of the runway, and when he reached the end and turned, immediately began his takeoff run.

Martin Luther Nsagamdo watched the Commando grow small in the sky and then got behind the wheel of the MGB.

He drove with great care back to the house, where his wife would be all packed and waiting for him. It would be her first visit home since they had been married and she had come to work for Mister Swayer.

A mile from town the road was blocked by perhaps fifty people. Several of them were wearing parts of Belgian Army uniforms, a brimmed cap, or a blouse, or a shirt worn with the tails flapping. And several of them were armed, Martin Luther Nsagamdo saw with concern as he drove close and slowed down.

He stopped and smiled politely and greeted the apparent leader as *"Chef."*

"What are you doing?" the Chef said. He was wearing a Belgian officer's blouse, complete to Sam Browne belt, from which hung a sword and a brimmed cap. But he wore no shirt and tie, the trousers were civilian, and he was barefoot.

"I have taken my boss to the airport," Martin Luther Nsagamdo said. "And now I go to put the car away."

Martin Luther Nsagamdo did not see the machete which came swinging from behind at his head until he sensed something moving near him in the last split second. There was not even time to raise his hand to protect himself or to duck.

The blow severed the right side of his neck and his spinal cord and most of the left side of the neck, but not all of it. His head remained connected to his body by a thin sheath of muscle and tissue. Arterial blood, for three or four heartbeats, spurted six inches up from his shoulders.

His body was dragged from the MGB.

The *chef*, the man in the Belgian officer's blouse and Sam Browne belt, reached in the car and dipped his finger in the blood. He touched it to his forehead and then painted a cross with it on the passenger-side windshield.

Then he got behind the wheel and, cheerfully blowing the horn, drove slowly into town with his men trotting along beside and behind him.

An hour later another patrol of Lieutenant Colonel Nicholas Olenga's People's Army of Liberation found Mrs. Martin Luther Nsagamdo in the kitchen of K. N. Swayer's house. She was waiting for her husband, all dressed up in a flowered print dress she had seen in a Montgomery Ward catalog, and which K. N. Swayer had sent for.

She was raped and shot and dismembered.

[SIX]
United States Strike Command
McDill Air Force Base, Florida
17 June 1964

CINC STRICOM had been at Fort Hood, Texas, visiting the 2nd Armored Division, and it was half-past three in the afternoon when his L-23 landed at McDill. Two days before, impulsively, when it had been time to either get on with the visit or cancel it, he had told his aide to ask Lieutenant Colonel Lowell if he would be free to fly the airplane.

CINC STRICOM's aircraft was normally flown by company-grade officers, because he believed it was a waste of a more senior officer's time and skill to be an airborne taxi-driver. But in this case he went against his own unofficial rule. For one thing he wanted to get to know Lowell better, and having him around at Hood would accomplish that. And for another, Lowell was an Armor officer and would be another set of eyes.

Taking Lowell along had been a good idea. Lowell had turned out to be an even better spare set of eyes than he had hoped he might be, zeroing in like a bird dog on several things the 2nd Armored probably hoped would not be noticed, and which he himself would probably have missed. Combat-readiness items, not chickenshit; and with the attitude of helping, not catching somebody with his hand in the cookie jar or asleep.

And additionally, he had been a pleasant companion. General Evans thought he might make a habit of having Lowell fly when he visited other units. His ability to fly the airplane was icing on the cake.

It was Wednesday, and on Wednesday afternoons he liked to play golf. What General Evans wanted to do was go to his quarters, take a shower (he had worked up quite a sweat before leaving Hood, and the L-23 had been full on the long ride home), and then at least knock a couple of buckets of balls down the driving range.

But he told his driver to take him to the office. There were some things about Hood that he wanted to get down on paper while they were fresh in his mind, and maybe with a little luck he could find time tomorrow to sneak away for a couple of hours to the golf course.

"Colonel," he said, just as Lowell was about to close the door of the staff car, "unless you've got something really pressing, I'd like you to come along. I normally type up notes-to-myself when I'm back from someplace like 'Hell on Wheels,' and I'd like you to have a look at them."

"Yes, Sir," Lowell said, and went around and got in the other side of the car.

The STRICOM Chief of Staff, and General Evans' senior aide-de-camp and secretary were waiting for him when he got to the office. He dealt with his Chief of Staff first, listening to what had been done in his name in his absence and nodding his approval as the actions were reported one by one. The definition of a good chief of staff was an officer who would take the actions the boss would take if he were around to take them, and General Evans thought again that his present Chief of Staff, even if he were in the Air Force, was the best he had ever had.

When he was through with his Chief of Staff, Evans made his aide-de-camp wait until he dictated to his secretary his thoughts on what he had seen and what had to be corrected at Fort Hood. Two memoranda would be typed up. One, the "Memorandum for Record," would be duplicated and circulated to the staff and to Fort Hood. The other, "Notes, Ft Hood, 15-17 June 64," would not leave his office, and no one but his secretary would ever see it. He would refer to it later to refresh his memory.

Then he dealt with his senior aide-de-camp. Most of that conversation dealt with his schedule for the next ninety-six hours. And, as he was supposed to, the senior aide-de-camp gave Evans a summary of the gossip that had come his way while CINC STRICOM had been at Hood.

Rear Admiral (upper half) Ralph H. Summerall, USN, STRICOM J-2, appeared at that time. Evans would have preferred that Admiral Summerall put off whatever was on his mind until the staff conference in the morning. If anything important had happened, he would already have heard about it from his secretary, his senior aide, or his Chief of Staff. *And probably in that order*, he thought somewhat cynically as he smiled at Summerall.

"Come on in, Ralph," he said. "Would you like some coffee?"

"No, thank you, Sir," Admiral Summerall said. "I'd like just a moment of your time, General."

By that, he meant in private. It was easier to send the aide to fetch coffee than to explain, yet again, to Admiral Summerall that his senior aide was privy to everything going on. And CINC STRICOM was tired.

"What have you got, Ralph?" Evans asked when the aide left, closing the door behind him.

"I may be carrying coals to Newcastle, General," Admiral Summerall said, "but I decided you might not know, and I thought I should tell you, even though I hope you won't ask my sources."

"Wouldn't dream of it, Ralph," Evans said.

"General Westmoreland is being sent to Indochina, *vice* General Harkins," Summerall said.

"I heard rumors about that," CINC STRICOM said. "But it's official now, huh?"

"It will be, as of 20 June."

"Interesting," CINC STRICOM said. "Westy's a good man."

"And General Taylor is going to Saigon as ambassador," Admiral Summerall said. "As of 1 July."

"I hadn't heard that. *Very* interesting."

What the hell was that all about? Was Max Taylor being sent over there as the ambassador or to keep an eye on Westy? Maybe both?

"Well, then, I'm glad I decided to drop by," Admiral Summerall said.

"I'm glad you did, too," CINC STRICOM said. "What else have you got for me?"

"Nothing that won't wait until the staff conference, General," Admiral Summerall said. And then, as if he had just remembered, he reached in his pocket and came up with a sheet of folded paper. "Crypto called just as I was leaving my office to come here. And I volunteered to pick it up. I'm not sure how important it is, but it's classified Eagle. . . ."

"Let me have it," STRICOM said.

FROM MILATTACHE US EMBASSY LEOPOLDVILLE
DEM REP OF CONGO
FOR CINC STRICOM MCDILL AF BASE FLA
FOLLOWING FROM COL DILLS CLASSIFIED SECRET DASH EAGLE QUOTE SOURCES RELIABILITY ONE STATE REBEL FORCE ESTIMATED STRENGTH 300 [THREE HUNDRED] OCCUPIED ALBERTVILLE ON LAKE TANGANYIKA DURING NIGHT FOURTEEN DASH FIFTEEN JUNE. BELIEVE ALL AMERICANS IN AREA ESCAPED BY AIR. FORCE BELIEVED TO BE LED BY NICHOLAS OLENGA SELF APPOINTED LEADER PAREN LT COL PAREN OF PEOPLE'S ARMY OF LIBERATION. STRONG POSSIBILITY ARMED BY CHICOM IN BUJUMBURA. CONGOLESE ARMY HAS MOVED TOWARD ALBERTVILLE WITH INTENTION REESTABLISH LEOPOLDVILLE CONTROL. DO NOT REPEAT NOT BELIEVE CONGOLESE ARMY AS PRESENTLY CONSTITUTED WILL PREVAIL. FURTHER DETAILS UPCOMING AS AVAILABLE. DILLS COLONEL ENDQUOTE END MESSAGE

CINC STRICOM picked up one of the telephones on his desk and dialed a single digit.

"Would you ask General Dyess to step in here right away, please? And if Colonel Lowell's out there, send him in, too." He turned to Admiral Summerall. "I presume General Dyess has not seen that?"

"No, Sir, he has not. Am I missing something here, General?"

"Right now, Admiral, you know as much as I do," CINC STRICOM said.

There was almost immediately a knock at the door. A moment later Major General George Dyess, STRICOM J-3, entered without waiting for permission.

"Have a look at this," Evans said, handing the message to him. "It just came in, Ralph brought it over."

General Dyess read it. "The natives are restless, I see. You think this is important, Sir?"

"Give it to Colonel Lowell, George," Evans said, and then answered Dyess's question: "I'm worried by the 'strong possibility' that the natives have been armed by the Chinese communists."

"What would you like me to do?" General Dyess said.

"Get OPLAN 15-6 out of the file," CINC STRICOM ordered. He looked at Lowell. "Any suggestions, Lowell?"

"Private Portet, Sir," Lowell said.

Both General Dyess and Admiral Summerall looked at him in curiosity.

General Evans snorted and then nodded. "Yeah," he said. "Show OPLAN 15-6 and this message to Private Portet. See what he has to say. Have him put it on paper. When we have that—and I want it as soon as you can get it—you come by the house. Bring Portet with you."

"Yes, Sir," Lowell said.

"Who is Private Portet?" Admiral Summerall asked.

"He's a draftee who used to live in the Congo," CINC STRICOM explained. "Right now he's our resident expert on the place."

"Apparently you don't think much of either your, or the Navy's, area intelligence specialist for the Congo?"

"I know this young man lived in the Congo, where he flew for a cargo airline, and that he speaks the language," Evans said. "And I strongly suspect that when I telephone Colonel Sanford T. Felter and read him this TWX from Dills, the first thing he's going to ask me is what Portet has to say about it."

XIII

COLONEL SANFORD T. FELTER came to Camp David on the Presidential Sikorsky H-34 helicopter sent to Washington to fetch Presidential Press Secretary Pierre Salinger. He was not the only hitchhiker. The Director of the USIA and a CIA briefing officer were also aboard.

Felter had to wait until Johnson had seen all of these people before he was able to see the President.

When it was his turn, he saw that the President was wearing a loud, flower-patterned, Hawaiian shirt with its tail hanging out. And he was making himself a drink. From the look on his face Felter could tell he was not in a good mood.

"Good afternoon, Mr. President," Felter said.

The President grunted. He did not offer Felter a drink.

"I will try to be brief, Mr. President."

"Go ahead."

"I don't know, of course, how far the CIA briefing went with regard to Albertville—"

"He never heard of it," the President said. "I asked him and he didn't know one fucking thing about it. I sent him to find out."

"Sir?" Felter said, confused.

"Albertville, in the Congo? That *is* what you're here to tell me about?"

"Yes, Sir."

"The Senator from Oklahoma took time from his busy schedule to call me and ask what I intended to do about his people getting run out of there. I told him I was working on it. I told you to keep me advised, goddamn you. How come you're coming in now?"

"Mr. President, I got my information thirty minutes before I got on the chopper."

"Maybe I better ask the Senator from Oklahoma to keep me advised. He's apparently better informed than you are."

Felter did not reply.

"Well, let's hear it, Colonel. Better late than never, to coin a phrase."

"I have my information from two sources, Mr. President," Felter said. "From Colonel Dills, who is the STRICOM liaison officer in the Congo, and from Captain Lunsford, a Green Beret officer in the area. I would therefore rate my information as wholly reliable."

"Late, but *reliable*," the President said sarcastically. "I suppose that's something."

"Perhaps I could save some of your time, Mr. President, if I knew what the Senator has already told you."

"He said he had a telephone call from one of his more important constituents who had his balls all up in an uproar. The constituent just had a telephone call from his man in the Congo, who said he had to charter an airplane to get his people out of some town because it had been taken over by some rebels."

"That would be Mr. Swayer, of Unit Rig, Mr. President, and it explains why the Senator heard about this so quickly. Mr. Swayer apparently telephoned Tulsa as soon as he got to Leopoldville. My information came by radioteletype."

"Next time tell them to get on the phone," the President snapped.

"With respect, Mr. President, I think we have to give Colonel Dills the benefit of the doubt and that he considered the telephone and decided it would be better to collect all the facts and use radioteletype."

The President, not mollified, glared at Felter. "Well, let's have *all the facts*."

"Yes, Sir. Sir, Albertville is a small town on Lake Tanganyika, just about in the middle of Africa. Lake Tanganyika forms the international border between the ex–Belgian Congo and Tanzania and Burundi."

"What are Americans doing there?"

"Unit Rig is supplying heavy earth-moving equipment, huge trucks, to Union Minière for use in the mines. The trucks were disassembled for shipment and air-freighted in. They are being reassembled on site. Mr. Swayer is Unit Rig's supervising engineer."

"So what happened?"

"My information, Mr. President, is that a Congolese named Nicholas Olenga has taken over the town."

"Who the hell is he? What does he want?"

"We don't know much about him, Mr. President. He is a member of the Maniema tribe, in his early thirties. Before independence he was a clerk, which would indicate that he is literate. Colonel Dills believes that since he did not receive a position of importance under the Leopoldville government, he now intends to topple that government and take over himself."

"He was a goddamned clerk? And thinks he he can take over the government? Is he nuts? How long will it take your Colonel Mobutu to get over there and throw his ass in jail?"

"I don't believe that will happen anytime soon, Mr. President," Felter said. "Colonel Dills reports that the ANC, the Armée Nationale Congolaise, 'is planning action to bring the situation under control.' But he reports that he does think that they will be successful in the near future. I concur with his evaluation of the situation."

"Jesus Christ!"

"The Red Chinese, Mr. President, have been engaged for some time in a propaganda effort, the gist of which is to convince the Congolese that the United States intends to step in to replace the Belgians as their colonial masters. It has been successful among the Maniema and some other tribes in that area of the Congo. They are now violently anti-American. Olenga has apparently used this as his rallying point."

"Let me get this straight," the President said. "An ex-clerk with delusions of grandeur has convinced a bunch of jungle bunnies that we're the bad guys and they have taken over some backwater town in the middle of nowhere. Right so far?"

"Yes, Mr. President."

"You really think those Unit Rig people were in danger?"

"Yes, Sir, I believe they were."

"And the entire Congolese Army can't stop this foolishness?"

"Not in the foreseeable future, Mr. President."

"So what happens now? You're not suggesting that he can actually take over the whole Congo? How many men does he have?"

"My information is that he took over Albertville with a force of approximately three hundred, Sir."

"*Three hundred?*" the President parroted incredulously. "And the Army can't take them on—put them behind bars?"

"Colonel Dills believes, as does Captain Lunsford, and I concur, that as soon as they realize the ANC has not done anything about Olenga, the natives—that is to say the uneducated tribesmen who live in the bush—will rush to join him."

"What makes this Captain Lunsford an expert?"

"He has been in the area, Sir. He is there now. He speaks the language. Captain Lunsford reports that Olenga is now wearing a Belgian officer's uniform and calling himself 'colonel,' and his organization 'the People's Army.'"

"He's there now?"

"Yes, Sir. He requested permission to remain in the area, and I gave it to him."

"How come the Unit Rig people were in danger and he's not?"

"He is in some danger, Sir. But he speaks Swahili and several of the local dialects and believes he can pass himself off as a Congolese."

The President's eyebrows rose at that. "You mean he's black?"

"Yes, Sir."

"I'll be damned," the President said. "OK, Felter, worst possible scenario. Let's have it."

"The tribesmen, Maniema and others, will join Olenga. They will march on the small towns in the area. They may be able to take Bukavu and possibly even Stanleyville. If they are able to take Bukavu, which I consider possible, I believe this will open the very real possibility of substantial assistance from the Chinese communists in Burundi. If they have arms, they can take Stanleyville. If they take Stanleyville, and they haven't been given arms before, I am sure they will get them then."

"They have not yet been supplied with arms?"

"Not so far as I know, Sir. One of the reasons I gave Captain Lunsford permission to stay was in the hope that he could find out about that."

"What about Chinese advisers?" the President asked. "I'd like to get my hands on one of them involved in this."

"I don't think they will send either advisers or substantial shipments—in other words, attributable shipments—or arms until they see how he's doing. What they call face is involved, Sir. They are not, in my judgment, going to make their involvement known until they are sure of success. They do not wish to lose face."

"So we just wait to see what happens, huh?"

"I don't see what other alternatives there are, Mr. President."

"What about your friend Mobutu's paratroopers? Could they put this lunatic down?"

"I don't believe Colonel Mobutu will use them until the situation is worse than it is. By then it may be too late. But he will not risk letting them get too far from Leopoldville, not now."

"Well, we'll see how hard the Ambassador can lean on him about that," the President said. He raised his eyes to Felter. "I'm sorry I jumped on your ass when you walked in, Felter."

"Yes, Sir."

"Keep doing what you're doing. It may not sound like it from time to time, but I appreciate it."

[TWO]
30 June 1964

AP NEW YORK NY

30JUN205P

FOR NATIONAL AND INTERNATIONAL WIRES

UNITED NATIONS NEW YORK—JUNE 30—UN SECRETARY GENERAL U THANT REPORTED TO THE GENERAL ASSEMBLY AT TWO PM THIS AFTERNOON THAT THE LAST ELEMENTS OF THE UNITED NATIONS PEACEKEEPING FORCE IN THE DEMO-CRATIC REPUBLIC OF THE CONGO HAVE BEEN WITHDRAWN.

U THANT PRAISED THE EFFORTS OF THE PEACEKEEPING FORCE IN "MAINTAINING THE PEACE AT GREAT COST," BUT SAID HE "HAD TO TELL THIS BODY THAT THE IMMEDIATE OUTLOOK IS NONE TOO PROMISING."

THE MULTINATIONAL FORCE HAD BEEN IN THE FORMER BELGIAN CONGO ALMOST FOUR YEARS. KNOWLEDGEABLE OBSERVERS HERE BELIEVE IT HIGHLY UNLIKELY THAT THE UN WILL AGAIN DISPATCH A MILITARY FORCE TO THE STRIFE-TORN AFRICAN NATION.

[THREE]
Conference Room 6-14
The Central Intelligence Agency
Langley, Virginia
0815 Hours 7 July 1964

SINCE THE FOURTH OF JULY had fallen on Saturday, and since government employees already had Saturdays off, and since it was the intent of the Congress to provide government employees, including themselves, with a paid day off for the celebration of the birth of the nation, Monday, July 6, 1964, had also been declared a holiday, so that those who had not elected to celebrate the nation's independence on their own time could celebrate it on the taxpayers' time.

Those employees of the Central Intelligence Agency whose duties required that they come to work on Monday, July 6, would be paid at overtime rates in the case of hourly employees; and those on the General Schedule of Professional Employees would be given compensatory time off. The idea, presumably, was that they would celebrate the nation's independence on, say, the third of August—or whenever they could be spared from their duty.

But those CIA GS employees who had worked on Monday had everything ready for the Director's senior staff conference. The maps in the room had been updated, the files from around the world edited, or condensed, or analyzed, or all three. Estimates and scenarios had been prepared. The conference room itself had been swept, once with a Hoover vacuum cleaner, and again by a man looking for electronic bugs. The paper shredders had been checked to make sure that when documents were fed into them they would be sliced into narrow strips and fed into burn bags. Pencils (six per chair at the table) were sharpened, and pads of note paper were laid out.

Coffee was brewed; and cups, non-dairy creamer, sugar, and saccharine were arranged in convenient places. A small pitcher of real cream had been placed near the Director's chair. He had found out what was in non-dairy creamer and would have nothing to do with it.

There were five people in leather upholstered chairs at the large, glossy, eight-place mahogany table when the Director walked in, smiled, and said "Good morning," and sat down. They were the Deputy Directors for Overt Operations, Covert Operations, Counterintelligence, and Administration, and the Executive Administrative Assistant to the Director. The Executive Administrative Assistant to the Director, who was the only female in the room, was seated right next to the Director and had brought a brand new stenographer's notebook.

In chairs against the wall were more than a dozen other people whose presence it was believed would be required during the meeting. They were desk officers for various areas of the world and other specialists of one kind or another.

It was understood by them that they were not supposed to either smoke or expect a cup of coffee. Rank hath its privileges.

The Director had just settled himself in the chair, cleared his throat, and reached for the first of the folders his Executive Administrative Assistant had placed before him on the desk when a red lamp on one of the telephones began to flash.

The Executive Administrative Assistant answered it and then whispered to the Director, "Colonel Felter is outside, Sir."

"Shit," the Director said, then, "OK, OK."

"Ask Colonel Felter to come in, please," the Executive Administrative Assistant said.

Felter, in a baggy gray suit, came into the room.

"Good morning, Sandy," the Director said. "Glad you could make it. Pull up a chair." He gestured to one of the empty leather-upholstered chairs at the table.

"Good morning, Sir," Felter said, sat down, pulled one of the stainless steel thermos jugs to him, and poured himself a cup of coffee.

"You just sitting in, Sandy? Or is there something particular on your mind?" the Director asked. "You want some cream for that coffee?"

"No, thank you," Felter said. "Did you get to the Congo yet?"

"Haven't got to anything yet," the Director said. "So we'll start with the Congo."

His Executive Administrative Assistant leaned forward in her chair and went through the stack of folders so she could pull out the Congo file for him.

One of the men sitting in the chairs along the wall stood up, went to the chair at the end of the conference table, took a thick sheath of papers from his briefcase, laid them on the table, and then put the briefcase on the floor beside him. He was the African Desk Officer.

"You know Tommy, of course, Sandy?" the Director asked.

"Sure do," Felter said.

"You want me to go directly to the Congo, Mr. Director?" Spottswood J. Thomas II, the African Desk Officer asked. His area of responsibility was the entire African continent.

The Director nodded. He was searching through the African folder for the material dealing with the Congo.

"I would guess that Colonel Felter is interested in the activity in Central Africa, around Lake Tanganyika—" Spottswood J. Thomas II began.

"*Particularly* interested, Tommy," the Director interrupted. "We all have learned that Colonel Felter is interested in everything."

Felter smiled. He admired the Director, and by and large had a good relationship with him. But the Director was human, and he did not like Felter's presidential authority to know whatever the CIA knew, nor his responsibility to tell the President when and how he disagreed with a CIA assessment of a situation and its proposal to deal with it.

"To sum up," Spottswood began, "on the night of 14-15 June, a rather motley force of Africans, the majority of them members of the Maniema tribe and numbering between two and three hundred, took over the Force Publique police station in Albertville . . . the seat of municipal government, as it were. The only Americans in the area, aside from missionaries in the countryside, were employees of Unit Rig, who were there for the purpose of assembling mining trucks. They heard about what was happening somehow and managed to get out by air.

"The best information we have is that the leader of this force is a man named Nicolas Olenga, a self-appointed lieutenant colonel of something he calls the People's Liberation Army.

"Efforts by the Congolese Army, called the ANC, for Armée Nationale Congolaise, have so far been unable to suppress the minor rebellion. I say minor because there is no, repeat no, information that they have been armed by the Chinese communists in Bujumbura or anywhere else. The ANC is having a hard time getting its act together, primarily, I believe, because of the distances involved and the very bad, practically nonexistent transportation network. The rebellion, if it can be described by that word, pending the arrival of the ANC to put it down, has spread. They have moved into Kasongo and Kindu.

"A thumbnail assessment would be that there's nothing that can be done for the moment until the ANC gets in gear, but that until that happens the situation is by no means desperate. The worst possible scenario is that the Chinese communists may decide to arm this Olenga.

I consider that unlikely, and every day that doesn't happen is a day closer to the time when, inevitably, the ANC will resume control."

Spottswood J. Thomas II looked at the Director and then at Felter.

"How does that fit in with what you have, Sandy?" the Director asked.

"Two companies of the ANC met Olenga's force on the Kasongo Road," Felter said, "and broke and ran, leaving their weapons—mostly FN 7mm assault rifles—behind. So they have three, four hundred automatic rifles. When they got to Kasongo, they rounded up and executed a little over two hundred Congolese who had either worked in some capacity for the government and/or who had some education and could read and write. By beating them to death with clubs and rifle butts."

"Where did you hear that?" Spottswood J. Thomas II asked incredulously.

Felter ignored him.

"Then, on vehicles he requisitioned in Kasongo," Felter went on, "Lieutenant Colonel Olenga moved on Kindu. His column ran over another ANC unit—this one a more or less reinforced company—and took Kindu with no opposition. There he repeated his rounding up of the educated and/or of the local bureaucrats, another two hundred of them, and beat them to death. In Kindu, having acquired the uniform of a Belgian lieutenant general somewhere—including a Sam Browne belt and a dress saber—he promoted himself to lieutenant general and announced his intention to march on both Bukavu and Stanleyville, where it is his announced intention to kill all the Americans he finds and establish a people's democracy."

"Where, may I ask, are you getting all this, Colonel?" Spottswood J. Thomas II asked.

"I don't think he's going to answer that, Tommy," the Director said. "But maybe he'll tell me how he would rate his source?"

"Sources," Felter said, holding up his index finger, signifying _1_. Intelligence sources are rated one through five, with one indicating the most reliable.

"Ouch," the Director said. "What do you think's going to happen?"

"I think they are going to take Stanleyville unless something stops them," Felter said. "And who knows after Stanleyville?"

"I can't accept that, Colonel," Spottswood J. Thomas II said.

Felter shrugged.

"They are not being supplied by the Chinese communists," Thomas argued. "I therefore rate their chances of moving as far as Stanleyville as not very likely. And if they did, deferring to Colonel Felter's expertise, manage to take Stanleyville, what would they have?"

"A United States consulate for one thing," the Deputy Director for Covert Operations said.

"And the airfield," Felter said. "Capable of night operation. Capable of handling practically any aircraft."

"Why would the Chinese communists wait until then to supply them? Why wait?" Thomas asked.

"If he manages to take Stanleyville," Felter said, "I think the Chinese—or for that matter any number of other people—would then be able to reason that he was worthy of their support. Until now, until he does something significant, supplying him would be too risky."

"How would you stop this fellow, Felter?" the Director asked.

"That's not my area. I collect and furnish information. That's all."

"Just for the hell of it, Sandy, if this were a sandtable problem at Leavenworth, what would be your recommendation?"

"In a hypothetical situation like this, and speaking as an infantry officer, I would ask the Air Force to interdict General Olenga's columns on the march."

"You know damned well we can't send the Air Force into the Congo!" Spottswood J. Thomas II snapped.

"We were talking hypothetically," Felter said. "This was a sandtable exercise at Fort Leavenworth."

"And if that caused the Chinese communists to take the gloves off and start supplying Olenga now?" Thomas countered.

"I don't have any assets to speak of over there, Felter," the Deputy Director for Covert Operations said. "A handful of T-28s."

T-28s were single-engine (Wright Cyclone 1425hp piston) two-seater aircraft built by North American originally as trainers, but which were often utilized as a ground-support aircraft. They had six underwing hardpoints to which gunpods, rockets, and bombs could be attached.

"Hypothetically speaking, B-26s would be better," Felter said.

"I repeat," Spottswood J. Thomas II said, his voice now a little tight, "what if, hypothetically speaking, T-28s or B-26s, which they would know came from us, caused the Chicoms to take the gloves off?"

"What about B-26s?" the Director asked the Deputy Director for Covert Operations.

The B-26 series were twin-engine medium bombers built by Douglas and first flown in 1942. They saw service in World War II and in Korea and Vietnam as well, most often in a low-altitude role.

"I don't know," he replied. "I'd have to ask Fulbright."

"Honey," the Director said to his Executive Administrative Assistant, "see if you can reach Fulbright."

The African Desk Officer started to say something but changed his mind when he saw the look in the Director's eyes.

"Hypothetically, Sandy," the Director said, "how many B-26s would you guess would be needed?"

"Hypothetically," Felter said, "a friend of mine in Florida said half a dozen would probably do it."

"I have Colonel Fulbright," the Executive Administrative Assistant said.

"Tell him to get on a scrambler phone," the Director ordered.

That took a very long thirty seconds, but finally a light on one of the other phones began to blink. The Director picked it up and then pushed a button which caused the conversation to be amplified through a speaker so that everyone in the room could hear it.

"Dick," the Director said, "apropos of nothing whatever: If there was a requirement for half a dozen B-26s to be washed and given away halfway around the world, how long would it take from 'go' to get them there?"

"If I was really pushed, I could have a dozen of the new K models—"

"What's that?"

"That's the counterinsurgency version," Fulbright said. "An outfit named O-Mark took some old ones and replaced everything but the windshield. It has two 2500-horse engines, wing tanks, good avionics—"

"I get the picture," the Director said. "How soon did you say?"

"I'd have to run some kind of a quickie school at Hurlburt," Fulbright said, "but I could have them washed and delivered in a month from 'go.'" Fulbright said.

"I must say, Dick," the Director said, "that I am really impressed that this information was right at your fingertips."

"Well, Mr. Director," Colonel Fulbright said, unabashed, "I was a Boy Scout, and as you know, our motto is Be Prepared."

"Don't get too far from a phone, please, Dick," the Director said. "I think someone may want to talk to you in about an hour."

"We are at your service, Mr. Director," Fulbright said.

"Those aircraft were supposed to go to Vietnam," the Deputy Director for Overt Operations said. "They were rebuilt using military-assistance funds. If Fulbright grabs them, we're going to have to pay for them."

"Perhaps we could get the President to pay for them out of his discretionary funds," the Director said. "How much is involved?"

"A quarter of a million a plane. A million and a half," the Deputy Director for Overt Operations said.

"Do you think the President is going to share your concern about what's happening on Lake Tanganyika to the extent of say, two million, Sandy?" the Director asked.

"All I could do would be to ask him, Mr. Director. I'm supposed to see him in an hour. I could ask him then if you'd like."

"Why don't you do that? And get back to me?"

"I'd be happy to, Mr. Director," Felter said. He stood up. "Thank you for the coffee."

"Anytime, Sandy. The welcome mat is always out."

Felter left the room.

"If anybody in here does not believe," the African Desk Officer fumed quietly, "that that little bastard didn't have the whole thing set up with Strike Command and with Fulbright before he walked in here, I have some oceanfront property in Arizona that I would like to offer for sale to him."

"It isn't really nice of you, Tommy, to refer to the Counselor to the President as that little bastard," the Director said.

"Sorry," the African Desk Officer said.

"What really burns me up," the Director said, looking right at the African Desk Officer, "is that the little bastard walks in with better, more up to date, and more comprehensive intelligence than my people have been able to provide. I find that really humiliating."

The Director let the African Desk Officer squirm for a full fifteen seconds and then got on with the staff conference.

[FOUR]
McDill Air Force Base, Florida
1030 Hours 10 July 1964

COLONEL SANFORD T. FELTER called General Matthew J. Evans, Strike Commander-in-Chief, on a scrambler phone to tell him that he had just heard from Colonel Dick Fulbright that the first of the

B-26Ks for the Congo would be ferried to Hurlburt Field, Florida, almost immediately. A second would arrive no later than Monday, the third and fourth on Wednesday, and the final two no later than Friday.

Almost as soon as Felter's voice came over the line, General Evans had signaled his senior aide-de-camp, Lieutenant Colonel Dennis V. Crumpette, to listen in on the conversation.

"The Air Force will make sure that the Eagle pilots are competent in the aircraft before they go over there," Felter explained. "So far he's come up with eleven people, six Americans and five Cubans, all with B-26 experience, and he promises that he'll have all we need, which means enough of them so there will be a flight engineer for each airplane by Wednesday or Thursday. In the meantime he's arranging to borrow from the Israelis both spare parts and mechanics and ground-handling equipment until we can get our own over there. They'll be at Kamina by the time the first two B-26Ks get there."

"Kamina is the ex-Belgian air base in the Congo?" General Evans asked.

"Yes, Sir," Felter said. "In the Katanga province."

"How long will the washing and training take?" General Evans asked.

"I told him to make it as quick as he could. No more than seven days, I would say, so the last plane should be able to clear Hurlburt for Nicaragua eleven days from Monday."

"Add two days to the Congo?"

"Three to be safe," Felter said. "So the first B-26K should arrive at Kamina ten days from Monday—in other words on 24 July—with the others following on 26 and 28 July. We may be able to shave a couple of days off that. With a little luck we might be able to have all of them there by say the twenty-sixth."

General Evans grunted.

"I was thinking that Portet might be useful if he was at Hurlburt," Felter said. "He's ferried aircraft to the Congo before. And I don't know what kind of pilots Dick can come up with on such short notice. Could you send him up there?"

"Sure," General Evans said.

The conversation turned to other things. When Felter was off the line, General Evans looked at Lieutenant Colonel Crumpette thoughtfully.

"I can't think of a thing we have to do, Dennis," he said, "except letting Lowell in on that conversation and getting the Portet boy up to Hurlburt. Can I still send him VOCG"—Verbal Order of the Command-

ing General—"or has the AGC"—the Adjutant General's Corps—
"usurped that commander's prerogative in the name of efficiency, too?"

"With your permission, Sir, I'll go see Lowell right now. I'm sure we
can arrange to have Portet up there by the time the first B-26 gets there,"
Crumpette said.

Lieutenant Colonel Crumpette was not surprised when Lieutenant
Colonel Lowell was not in his office but on the flight line. Neither was he
surprised when he'd reported the substance of Felter's telephone call to
General Evans and the requirement to get PFC Portet to Hurlburt that
Lowell volunteered to take him himself.

"Consider it done. Send him over. I've been looking for an excuse to
get some cross-country time in a T-37. He got his orders and everything?" The T-37 was a side-by-side, two-seat jet trainer manufactured
by Cessna.

"He's going VOCG," Crumpette said. "I'll call headquarters company and tell them to get him over to the field as soon as they can."

All the First Sergeant of Headquarters Company, who fetched PFC
Portet from a mandatory lecture, "This Is What We Are Defending,"
knew was what he had been told. That had been relayed to him by the
Headquarters Company Commander. The Strike Commander-in-Chief
had personally ordered the immediate transfer of PFC Portet to
Hurlburt Field. He had not been told why, but it was obviously of great
importance. A jet, to be flown by the STRICOM Army Aviation officer
himself, was at that very moment waiting for him at Base Operations.

"How long am I going to be gone? Why am I going?"

"Just shove your gear in your duffel bag," the First Sergeant said. "If
they wanted you to know, they would have told you."

"What about my car?"

"Fuck your car. You can worry about that once you get to Hurlburt."

Lowell was preflighting the T-37 when a pickup dropped Jack off at
the flight line.

Jack saluted.

Lowell returned it casually.

"Am I allowed to ask what's going on?" Jack asked.

Lowell told him about the B-26Ks.

"I guess they want you there to help with the pilot briefing," Lowell
said. "The same sort of thing you did when they sent Geoff and Pappy
over there. I didn't talk to Felter myself."

"Why the big rush?"

"That's the Army," Lowell said. "You never heard 'hurry up and wait'?"

Jack chuckled. "Where is Hurlburt, anyway?"

He saw Lowell's eyes light up.

"Thataway," he said, making a vague gesture toward the north. "You can't hardly get there from here."

"The reason I asked, Colonel, is because I hate to leave my car here."

"They call that the exigencies of the service," Lowell informed him. "In other words, sorry about that."

When there was no response, Lowell went on. "If the Army wanted you to have a red Jaguar, PFC Portet, they would have issued you one."

Jack laughed dutifully, although he didn't think the legendary Colonel Craig W. Lowell was nearly as witty as Colonel Craig W. Lowell obviously did.

"Go over to flight-crew equipment and get a helmet for yourself and 'chutes for us both," Lowell ordered. "I have to make a phone call."

"Yes, Sir," PFC Portet said.

At 1155 hours McDill Departure Control cleared Air Force Two Seven Three VFR (Visual Flight Rules) direct to Hurlburt.

"Are you prone to airsickness, son?" Lowell asked PFC Portet when they were airborne and over the Gulf of Mexico.

"No, Sir," PFC Portet said.

"I'd like to try a few aerobatics. But not if you're liable to throw up."

"If I start to get sick," Jack said, "I'll let you know, Sir."

Lowell flew aerobatics for about thirty minutes and then set a course for the Florida panhandle coast, making landfall at Cape St. George. There he dropped down to wave-top level and completed the trip to Hurlburt Field along the beach. As the crow flies, it is three hundred and twenty miles from McDill to Hurlburt, or about forty-five minutes in a T-37. With thirty minutes added to the flight time by the aerobatics, PFC Portet was delivered to Hurlburt Field one hour and twenty minutes after he climbed into the T-37 at McDill.

Lowell told Jack he was sorry, but he had no idea what Jack was supposed to do now that he was here.

"Check in with Base Ops," Lowell said helpfully. "Maybe they could help you. If not, eventually I'm sure, somebody will come looking for you."

"Thank you very much, Colonel," Jack said, a hair's width away from overt sarcasm.

"My pleasure, son." Lowell beamed at him and then turned his attention to the refueling of the T-37.

Jack carried his duffel bag what seemed like a very long way to Base Operations and went inside.

A sergeant and an officer were on duty behind the counter. The Sergeant glanced at him, and then returned his attention to *Time* magazine.

"I'm PFC Portet," Jack said.

"Is that so?" the Sergeant said.

"I've just been dropped off here," Jack said. "I don't know what I'm supposed to do next."

"You got orders, I guess?"

"No, I don't."

At that moment, for the first time, Jack gave more than a casual glance at the air-distance chart glued to the wall behind the counter. This was a large map, with a means (usually a cord) to permit pilots to roughly measure the distance between where they are and where they wish to go. Until that moment, he had known nothing more about the location of Hurlburt Field than that it was on the Gulf of Mexico.

He now saw that it was practically around the corner from Fort Rucker. Maybe eighty miles. No more.

If I only had my car, I could be with her in an hour and a half!

"No orders?" the Sergeant demanded incredulously.

"I'm traveling VOCG."

"You're ordered to report here?"

"Right."

"Then hang around, why don't you? Somebody'll come looking for you sooner or later. You a Green Beret?" the Sergeant asked.

"No."

"We got some Green Berets here," the Air Commando Sergeant said. "Maybe they're expecting you."

"I don't think so," Jack said.

"Then we're back to you sticking around and waiting until somebody comes looking for you, aren't we? Wait outside, Mac. Go to the PX and have a cup of coffee. If somebody comes looking for you, I'll tell them where to go."

"Can I leave my duffel bag here?"

"You can leave it, but somebody'll steal it, sure as Christ," the Sergeant said.

Fuck it! Jack thought furiously. *Let them steal the sonofabitch. Fuck the Army and the Air Force!*

He walked out of the building, located the PX, and started walking toward it. Two hundred yards en route, he came to a pay phone.

It took just a moment for the call to be put through.

"General Bellmon's quarters, Lieutenant Bellmon speaking, Sir."

"I have a collect call for Miss Marjorie Bellmon from PFC Portet, will you pay?"

"I beg your pardon?"

"PFC Portet is calling collect from Florida for Miss Marjorie Bellmon," the operator said somewhat impatiently. "Will you accept charges?"

"Just one moment, please," Lieutenant Bellmon said. And then— faintly—Jack heard him call, "Mother! Some soldier is calling Marjorie collect."

There was surprise and, Jack decided, disapproval in his voice. This was obviously the little brother, three weeks or so out of West Point.

A female voice came on the line.

"We'll accept," she said. "Hello, Jack. This is Barbara Bellmon. Is something wrong?"

"I'm sorry to call collect, Mrs. Bellmon, but I don't have any change."

"It's all right," she said. "Are *you* all right?"

"I'm alive," Jack said. "But aside from that, things aren't going too great. Could I speak to Marjorie?"

"She's at the bank," Barbara Bellmon said. "She's working."

"*Damn!*" Jack said, furious with himself for not thinking about that before he called. "Sorry, Mrs. Bellmon."

"When she comes home I'll tell her you called. Is there someplace she can call you?"

"No, ma'am," Jack said. "I'll have to try her later."

"Do that, Jack."

He hung the telephone up, swore, and left the booth. He resumed his journey toward the PX snack bar.

There was a squeal of brakes and someone called his name.

He turned, for a moment not able to accept that Marjorie Bellmon in her MG was fifteen feet away from him.

He walked up to the car.

"What the hell are you doing here?" he blurted.

"I'm fine, Jack," Marjorie said. "Thank you for asking."

"Sorry. What are you doing here?"

"Uncle Craig called me at the bank. He said you were going to be at Base Ops here and needed me desperately. I just got here."

"Oh, that sonofabitch!"

"What's the matter, Jack?"

"Now that you're here, nothing. And he was right. I do need you desperately."

She met his eyes. Her face flushed.

"Thank you for coming, thinking I was in trouble," Jack said.

"That's what you do when you love somebody," she said softly.

"Jesus!"

"No, 'Marjorie.' Jesus is the one with the beard. Get in the car."

XIV

[ONE]
Hurlburt Field, Florida
10 July 1964

MARJORIE BELLMON was an Army brat and she knew what
to do.

"We go back to Base Ops," she said. "And if they still don't know
what to do with you, then we call the OD, and if he doesn't know, then
we call Uncle Craig."

PFC Portet was expected at Base Ops. Specifically, a Green Beret
major, smiling broadly, was waiting for Jack when he went back inside.

"You're Portet?"

"Yes, Sir."

"And *somebody*, I guess, did finally show up for you?" He made an
"OK" sign with his fingers, signifying his approval of Miss Marjorie
Bellmon.

"Yes, Sir," Jack said.

"You have any money?"

"Yes, Sir."

"You're sure?"

"Yes, Sir."

"Enough to rent a motel room and feed yourself over the weekend,
plus some walking-around money?"

"Yes, Sir."

"OK, then you can take off. You are to report Monday morning at 0800 to Building T-6101," the Major said. "Have a nice weekend."

"That's all?" Jack asked, remembering at the last moment to append "Sir?"

"That's it," the Major said. "Except, of course, when you see the Duke, you tell him Operation Cupid went off like clockwork."

The Duke was obviously Lieutenant Colonel Craig W. Lowell.

"Yes, Sir, I'll do that."

Jack went outside and got back into the MGB with Marjorie. The hem of her skirt had pulled up over her knees, and his eyes were drawn to it. She either saw him looking, or sensed it, and pulled the hem down.

"I'm off until eight o'clock Monday morning," he said.

"Oh."

"I called your house just before you showed up. I didn't have any money and had to call collect—and your brother answered the phone."

"Oh," she said. "And he was very conscious of being an officer, right?"

"What I was thinking was that your mother doesn't know you're down here, does she?"

"Yes, she does," Marjorie said. "Or she will when I don't come home from work."

"She does?" Jack parroted, surprised.

"When Uncle Craig called," Marjorie said, "I called her and asked her what I should do. She said that I would have to decide that for myself."

Their eyes met. Jack felt giddy.

"I just thought of something," he said.

"What?"

"We haven't kissed," he said. "After."

"After what?"

"After you told me you loved me."

"You mean like in the movies, when they do it slow motion, and the man and woman run—float—toward each other, usually on some beach?"

"I guess," he said.

"I didn't feel like it," she said. "Did you?"

"I don't know," he said. He put his hand out and ran the balls of his fingers against her cheek. She put her hand up and caught his and kissed his knuckles, very tenderly.

"I don't have a whole hell of a lot of experience in what I should do after I tell a guy I love him," she said. "Actually, I have zero experience."

"Baby," he said.

"That isn't the only thing, romance-wise," Marjorie said, "that I have zero experience in."

It took him a minute to take her meaning. And when she saw on his face that he finally understood, she nodded. "Ain't that amazing? I thought it was time to add that to this equation."

He touched her face again, and she caught his hand and held it there, then suddenly pulled away and sat up.

"I think we have an audience," she said, gesturing with her head toward the door to Base Ops. Jack turned and looked. The Green Beret Major and the Air Force Lieutenant were standing in it. The Major had his arms over his head, hands joined, in the gesture a winning prizefighter makes.

Marjorie spun the MGB's wheels as she backed out of the parking spot, and again as she started down the street.

"I don't care," Jack thought aloud, "if the whole damn world knows."

"It's not a spectator sport!"

He wondered where she was driving him. She was obviously familiar with the base. But, on the other hand, she just might be escaping from their audience.

"If Uncle Craig flew you up here," she said, "obviously your car is still at McDill."

"You're a regular Sherlock Holmes."

"Well, I suppose then that the thing to do is go get the car," she said. "I can drive you to the airport and you can fly down there and be back tomorrow sometime."

"Oh, to hell with the car. I'd rather be with you."

"Or," Marjorie said. "We can both fly to Tampa and get your car and drive back tomorrow."

She met his eyes.

"What about your mother?" he asked. "What would she think, do, if you just didn't come home overnight?"

"I think she had a pretty good idea that if I came down here I might not come home," Marjorie said quietly.

She turned to look at him, looked into his eyes longer than was safe for someone driving a car, and then turned her attention back to the road. The tires squealed and she jerked the MGB back in the right lane. There was the blare from a Buick's horn, and Jack heard someone angrily shout, "Goddamned dumb broad! Keep your eyes on the road."

"*Or* we can go to a motel right now," Marjorie said. "And worry about the car tomorrow."

"Oh, Jesus Christ!"

"What's the matter?"

"I'm very afraid that no matter how I respond to that, it will be the wrong way."

"Give it a shot," Marjorie said. "I'm playing hardball. Are you?"

"I'll wait as long as you want me to," Jack said nobly, and then blurted, "Oh, Jesus, Marjorie, I want to so bad it hurts."

She looked at him again.

"There's motels all along the beach," she said. "And just for the record, that was exactly the right answer."

They passed the MP guard shack at the base entrance and left Hurlburt Field. As they turned east on Highway 98, an airplane made its approach to Hurlburt's Runway zero five, the edge of which abuts the shoreline highway. The aircraft flashed over the beach and then the highway at no more than a hundred feet, the roar of its twin engines deafening.

Jack was in love, but he was a pilot. He had taken his eyes from what he was absolutely convinced was the most beautiful and perfect female God had ever made when he heard the roar of the airplane, and he watched it until it was out of sight.

"That's one of them, obviously," he said.

"One of one what?"

"The B-26 that just landed was, I'm sure, one of those we're sending to the Congo. It looked brand damned new and there wasn't a mark on it. Identification numbers, I mean."

"I thought they had to have identification numbers," Marjorie said.

"They do," Jack said.

"Are you going to the Congo?" she asked levelly. "Is that what you're doing here?"

"I'm not going," Jack said. "Right now I am delighted the United States Military Establishment does not let me fly their airplanes."

"Thank God!" Marjorie exhaled, and then, jokingly, added, "We can go back and look if you like. I mean, if you're getting bored or anything . . ."

"Oh, no," he said.

[TWO]
Ocean Breeze Motel
Fort Walton Beach, Florida
2105 Hours 10 July 1964

"HANG ON a minute, will you?" Jack Portet said to the telephone and then covered the mouthpiece with his hand. "How far are we from Eglin Air Force Base?"

"It's right here," Marjorie said.

"This is Captain Portet of Air Congo," he said to the telephone. "Any chance that my wife and I can deadhead?"

He was stark naked, leaning on the wall of the motel room with his hand on his hip. She was in bed, stark naked, but with a sheet pulled modestly over her. He had told her she was the most beautiful thing he had ever seen in his life, and she thought, looking at him now, that he was beautiful, even if the word didn't seem appropriate for a man.

She had been more than a little surprised at how easy it had been for them, and at her reaction afterward. No regrets. No embarrassment. She had always believed that she had an overdeveloped sense of modesty, and all of a sudden being naked with a man in a motel room seemed to be the most natural thing in the world. And the second time had been better than the first. And the third better than the second.

Jack smiled happily at her.

"You're very kind," he said to the telephone. "Thank you very much." He hung up and smiled at Marjorie. "I can't believe I'm saying this," he said, "but get out of bed and put your clothes on. We're on an Eastern flight to Tampa in fifty-five minutes."

"You're not Captain Portet of Air Congo, and I'm not your wife," Marjorie said. "If anybody finds that out, what happens?"

"I've got an Air Congo ID card," Jack informed her just a little smugly. "My father, you will recall, is Chief Pilot. And if anybody questions you—and they won't—I guess I'll just have to make an honest woman of you."

She threw the sheet away from her, aware—and pleased—that he was watching her hungrily, and lifted herself out of the bed.

"I'm tempted to say to hell with the Jaguar," he said.

"Put your pants on, Captain Portet."

*   *   *

The Eastern plane was nearly empty. The pilot came back shortly after they took off from Eglin and eyed Jack suspiciously.

"Captain Portet?"

"That's right."

"Are there two of you?"

"Me and my dad," Jack said. "He's Chief Pilot."

"OK, everything falls in place. I met your Dad in—either Cairo or—in Beirut. It was Beirut. I got a chance to do three months as an IP for Air Lebanon when they got their first DC-6s. He was there doing something for them for Air Congo."

"I remember," Jack said. "The ones they bought from Mexicana?"

"Right," the pilot chuckled. "They still smelled of tacos. You working when we make Tampa?"

"No," Jack said. "On sort of a vacation."

"Dolores," the Captain said to the stewardess. "Give these people some of the good booze. His father's an old friend of mine." He reached over and gave his hand to Marjorie. "Nice to meet you, Mrs. Portet."

"Thank you," Marjorie said.

"I like the sound of that," Jack said when the pilot had gone back to the flight deck. "'Mrs. Portet.' How does it set with you?"

The stewardess showed up with splits of champagne before she had to answer.

When they got to Tampa they took a cab to McDill and picked up the Jaguar. And then, because they agreed it would be nicer to drive in the morning, and they were tired, and they'd had all that champagne on the airplane, they went to another motel.

The next day, Saturday, they drove far up in the Florida panhandle as far as Panama City and took another motel room. Marjorie needed underwear and a bathing suit, and Jack insisted on going to a small shopping mall with her to buy it. The only way she could have kept him from paying for it would have been to cause a scene, so she gave in. Afterward, in the car on the way back to the motel, she realized that she had very much liked his being with her, shaking his head until she had picked a bra and panties that pleased him and then grinning happily when she showed him a nearly translucent set in white that was probably not going to make it home, much less through a trip inside a washing machine.

They swam and made love and ate dinner and made love and walked on the beach and made love and slept in each other's arms. And she wondered if he had made her pregnant. And she wondered what she would do if he had. She decided after a while that though she really hoped she was not, if she was, that was it and she wouldn't be sorry. Monday she would go to a doctor and get a diaphragm. She hadn't gone before for the simple reason that she never had the intention, pre-Jack, of sleeping with anybody. She wondered if what had happened between them qualified as "saving it till marriage."

At eight o'clock, after Jack had wakened and they had made love, and he was happily singing in the shower, she called her mother and told her she was sorry she hadn't called, but she had gone to Tampa with him to get his car and there hadn't been time, and that she would be home late that night.

From her mother's response, she knew that her father was in hearing, and from her mother's tone of voice, she knew her mother knew what had happened between her and Jack. She was embarrassed, which she expected to be, but not ashamed, and that surprised her.

And she was not surprised when Jack talked her into staying over and leaving early in the morning.

"Or, if you want, I'll follow you up there and face the Gen'rul tonight," Jack said. "Aside from tearing me limb from limb, what can he do to me?"

Her father, Marjorie thought, was not going to be angry with Jack. He was going to be disappointed with her. That was probably going to be worse.

They checked out of the motel, drove onto Eglin Air Force Base, reclaimed her car, and took a motel on the beach a thousand yards from the fence around Hurlburt Field.

Early in the morning she told him that she was going to have to talk to her father, maybe after talking to her mother—who she was sure was on their side—and that she didn't want him to come to Rucker until she told him he could. He agreed, but she knew he would come whenever he wanted to anyway.

They went to a McDonald's for breakfast.

Marjorie sensed Jack's eyes on her and looked up from her Complete $1.29 Breakfast.

"Now that we're back in the real world," Jack said, "eating plastic food from plastic trays . . ."

She smiled, as much with her eyes as her mouth.

"Yes?"

"I think we had better get right at the subject of me making an honest woman of you. When you see the Gen'rul, I mean."

"I already was honest," Marjorie said. "And you making a woman of me was everything, thank you very much, that I hoped it would be."

"At this hour, and in this place," Jack said, "if that's what you would like, I am perfectly willing to get on my knees and make a proposal right out of *True Romance*. Even if that means soiling my nice clean uniform by kneeling in the spilled coffee."

She laid her fork down and took his hand.

"Oh, Jack."

"May I take that as a yes?"

"No," she said. "Not exactly."

"What?"

"Comment ça va, Jacques?" a male, Spanish-accented voice said softly.

Jack looked up at the man standing by the table. There was confusion on his face for a moment.

"Jesus H. Christ!" He got to his feet and put out his hand. "Rico, what the hell are you doing—wherever we are—here?"

Enrico de la Santiago smiled warmly and then gave Jacques a quick hug. He didn't respond directly to the question. Instead he said, "I saw you come in, but I just didn't think . . ."

"Sweetheart, this is a friend of mine from the Congo—Enrico de la Santiago," Jack said. "Rico, this is Marjorie Bellmon, my . . . we were just discussing what exactly is our relationship . . ."

"You said it," Marjorie said. "'Sweetheart.' If you're who I think you are, Jack's talked a lot about you. I'm happy to meet you."

"You are very beautiful," de la Santiago said.

"Thank you," Marjorie said.

"What the hell *are* you doing here?" Jack demanded.

"I don't work for your father anymore, Jacques," de la Santiago said.

"Now you fly B-26s, right?" Jack said, suddenly understanding. " *Unmarked* B-26s. And how do you like Hurlburt Field, home of the Air Commandos and God alone knows what else, *Señor* de la Santiago?"

"Jack, for God's sake!" Marjorie protested.

"Jacques, don't ask me more," de la Santiago said. "Please."

"It's all right, Rico. Just as soon as I get Marjorie to agree to marry me, I'm going out to Hurlburt myself."

"And they didn't tell you to watch your mouth?" de la Santiago asked.

"He says a lot of things without thinking," Marjorie said.

"How long have you been here?" Jack asked de la Santiago.

"I came in last night—"

"From the Congo?" Jack interrupted.

"Yes," de la Santiago said after a moment's hesitation. "And took a motel." He nodded to indicate across the street. "And now I am going to call a taxi and go out there."

"I've got a car," Jack said. "I'll take you out there. But you really picked a lousy moment to walk up. Marjorie here was just about to tell me why she won't—exactly—marry me."

Marjorie colored, just visibly, and her eyes flashed at Jack, and she glanced at de la Santiago.

"I'm not going to go run off to some justice of the peace with you," she said evenly. "Which is what I think you had in mind."

"And what if I ask the Gen'rul, and he says, 'You're out of your mind, no way, José'?"

"I want to do it right, honey," Marjorie said. "If there is any way I can."

"You'll notice, Rico," Jack said, "she called me honey. You would be amazed how that scrap of affection, far short of an unqualified 'Oh, yes, whoopee!' gives me hope."

De la Santiago shook his head and smiled.

"I've really got to go out there," he said. "Is it far?"

"And I have to go," Marjorie announced. "I've got to go to work. I don't want to lose my job."

"My offer, of course, includes room and board plus all my worldly goods," Jack said. "And anything else needed to clinch the deal."

She chuckled and laughed, and then suddenly got up, leaned across the table, kissed him quickly.

"You stay," she ordered. "Call tonight at seven thirty."

"I can be up there by seven thirty," he protested, getting to his feet.

"Sit," she ordered. "Stay. And don't come, call."

And she quickly left the restaurant.

"I have the feeling," Enrico de la Santiago said, "that that one was not one of your usual bedwarmers."

"Christ no!" Jack said. "That's the *one*. I knew that the first time I saw her." He looked at de la Santiago. "I suppose that sounds pretty goddamned silly, doesn't it?"

"Not at all," de la Santiago said. "I first saw my wife when she was fifteen, in church. I knew then."

Jack remembered that de la Santiago's wife and children were still in Cuba.

"Any word on them, Rico?"

"They are alive," de la Santiago said. "And Fidel Castro, that miserable sonofabitch, has no intention of letting them go."

"Shit," Jack said.

"She is very beautiful, that one," de la Santiago said. "And in her eyes, I can see that she loves you."

"Change the subject, huh?"

De la Santiago shrugged. "We have said what can be said about my family," he said. "I will tell you what I know of the Congo, and you will tell me what you know of Hurlburt Field and Colonel Richard Fulbright."

"I know nothing about Hurlburt Field," Jack said. "And I never heard of Fulbright. On Friday I was listening to a typical bullshit Army lecture, at McDill Air Force Base in Tampa, and they called me out of it, told me to pack my bags, and flew me up here. In a Cessna T-37, with an Army colonel who played fighter pilot and did aerobatics over the Gulf. I don't know for sure, but what I think they want me to do is brief the B-26 pilots on the Congo, help with the ferry flight planning, that sort of thing. They don't let me fly."

"I am to report to Colonel Fulbright," de la Santiago said. "For a thousand dollars a month and a hundred-thousand-dollar insurance policy, I will fly his B-26s and teach other people to fly them."

"Christ, we paid you fifteen hundred a month," Jack said.

"Two thousand. After you left. But being an Air Simba captain wasn't doing anything to get my family out of Cuba. Or kill communists."

Jack looked at him but said nothing.

"Where are you supposed to report?" de la Santiago asked.

"Building T-6101, at 0800."

"That's where I am to report to Colonel Fulbright," de la Santiago said.

[THREE]
Building T-6101
Hurlburt Field, Florida
0805 Hours 13 July 1964

THE FIRST TIME PFC JACQUES PORTET saw Colonel Richard Fulbright, the Colonel was sitting on a desk in an office in the old frame World War II barracks building, talking on the telephone. When he spotted Jack and de la Santiago, he waved them into the room.

Jack's first, somewhat irreverent thought was that Colonel Fulbright had more medals than Patton; there were row after row of them on his blouse. And a battery of wings, both pilot's and parachutist's, above both blouse pockets. Before Fulbright leaned over and hung up the phone, there was time to examine one interesting set of pilot's wings and decide they were intended for pilots of the Chinese Nationalist Air Force.

Then, when he saw Fulbright looking at him, he remembered to salute. Fulbright returned it casually, examining him carefully as he did.

"Clever fellow that I am," Fulbright said, "I deduce that you are PFC Portet. I think I should begin this little chat by telling you that your father is a little pissed with me."

Jack didn't know what to say, so he said nothing.

"For stealing de la Santiago," Fulbright said, "of course. I should have guessed that you two would find each other."

When there was no reply, Fulbright looked between the two of them and smiled.

"I don't think he is as pissed as he originally was. I think I managed to convince him that what we've got going here is important. Am I going to have a lot of trouble convincing you of that, Portet?"

"Sir, I don't know what you're doing here," Jack said.

"We are going to send six B-26Ks to Kamina Air Base, on loan to the Congolese government, which is going to use them to put down a rebellion against the duly constituted government."

He waited for Jack to reply, and when he didn't, asked: "No comment?"

"I saw an unmarked B-26, Sir," Jack said. "And I came here from McDill. I don't know what to say."

Fulbright turned to de la Santiago.

"How long will it take you to check him out in a B-26?"

"Colonel, I'm not current in a B-26."

"That's not what I asked. Let me explain the situation to you. Until midnight I have the services of one, only, Air Force guy who is a qualified B-26 IP. Right now, of the pilots available to me for this operation, I have two with current ATRs. Guess who?"

"No one else is B-26 qualified?" de la Santiago asked, genuinely surprised.

"Used-to-be-qualified," Fulbright said. "Some of the Americans flew twenty-sixes in Korea, that's ten years plus ago. Some of the Cubans— I'll give you a list, maybe you'll know somebody—flew them before the bearded bastard came out of the mountains. None of them have done any flying to speak of since. You flew B-26s in Cuba, and you've got a current ATR, so by default you're the head IP. Getting the picture?"

"Yes, Sir," de la Santiago said.

"So I repeat the question," Fulbright said. "How long will it take you to get Portet checked out in a B-26?"

De la Santiago thought it over for a moment before replying.

"Jacques is a good pilot," he said finally, thoughtfully. "Not even getting into ground school, I'd like eight, ten, twelve hours in the air with him."

"And how long do you think it will take our one Air Force IP to check you out?"

"These are -D models?"

"-Ks," Fulbright said. "They've got 2500-horse Pratt and Whitneys and some really nice avionics. They're essentially brand-new airplanes, rebuilt from the wheels up."

"God, I'd like a week!" de la Santiago said.

"You're got until midnight," Fulbright said. "When you walked in, I was on the phone begging to keep the IP. The Air Force told me to go fuck myself. They want nothing to do with this. And not only because I stole these airplanes from them."

"I will do what I can," de la Santiago said.

"Take Portet with you," Fulbright said. "Maybe some of it will rub off on him."

"Yes, Sir."

"You have any civilian clothing, Portet?"

"Yes, Sir."

"OK. Get into it. I mean right now. Go into the latrine and change

before anybody who already hasn't seen you as a PFC does. I don't want
to see you in a uniform again. If anybody asks, you're an employee of
Supportaire, Inc. If anybody gets really curious, refer them to me."

"Can I do that?" Jack asked. "Fly and wear civvies?"

"My boy," Colonel Richard Fulbright said, "you are now assigned to
an operation directed by Colonel Richard Fulbright." He raised his
hand as a priest raises his in a blessing. "With Fulbright, All Things Are
Possible," he intoned sonorously. "Now go forth and do good."

Jack chuckled and then laughed.

"By the time you get back," Fulbright went on, "I'll have ID cards and
the rest of the crap ready for you. There's a pickup outside. He'll take you
to the field, and our very self-righteous, holier-than-thou Air Force IP.
Don't tell the sonofabitch anything but your name. Your *first* name."

Jack looked at him and saw that he was dead serious.

"We're operating out of the same strip, as a note of historical interest," Fulbright said, "on which Jimmy Doolittle trained his people to fly
B25s off aircraft carriers in War Two."

"Really?" Jack asked, impressed. General Jimmy Doolittle was one of
his father's few heroes. He had often heard the story of Doolittle's bombing raid on Japan in the early days of World War II: Doolittle hadn't done
much physical damage, but he had dealt a real blow to Japanese pride and
morale, and at the same time given American morale a badly needed boost
after it had been severely damaged by the Pearl Harbor attack.

"An operation not unlike this," Fulbright said. "The essential difference
being that if Doolittle had been caught, all they would have done was behead him. If we get caught, we'll really be up shit creek without a paddle."

Fulbright was smiling brightly, as if proud of his wit. But Jack saw in
his eyes that he was serious about that, too.

[FOUR]
Villa Sans Regrets
Cap d'Antibes, France
16 July 1964

HELENE (MRS. PORTER) CRAIG'S smile was a little strained
when she saw her first grandchild being carried down the stairs of the

Air France DC-8 at Cannes by an enormous coal-black female in an ankle-length, flamboyantly flowered flowing dress.

She quickly kissed her daughter-in-law, making a quick judgment that she looked a little wan and tired, and then made it plain she wished to take the baby. The enormous black woman eyed her suspiciously and didn't hand the blanket-wrapped infant over until she had looked at Ursula and Ursula had nodded.

"He's precious," Helene Craig said. "Just precious."

"He's also dirty and hungry," Ursula said. "Mother Craig, these are our friends, Hanni and Jeanine Portet. And Jiffy's best friend, Mary Magdalene."

Helene Craig decided she liked the Portet woman and her daughter. They looked wholesome and were well dressed, and the little girl made a polite curtsy.

"I'm so grateful you could make the time to come with Ursula," Helene Craig said, "and I'm very happy to finally meet you."

"There was no way," Hanni Portet said, "that Jeanine was going to let her godson out of sight."

Helene Craig smiled. She hadn't been exactly thrilled that the baby had been christened in the Congo without her presence. But, as her husband had pointed out, it was now done, and he understood the whole idea was to get the child dipped rather than make a social event of it.

"Hello, honey," Porter Craig said, wrapping his arm around Ursula's shoulders. "It's good to see you."

Hanni's reaction to the Craigs was that Geoff didn't look at all like his father or mother—except for his eyes. She hoped Jiffy would not grow up to look like his grandparents.

"Give your baggage stubs to my husband—"

"Who I wish everyone would call 'Porter,'" Porter Craig interjected with a smile.

"—and the houseman will take care of the luggage."

"We'll need diapers," Ursula protested. "Jiffy already smells."

"Jiffy?" Porter Craig asked.

"Mary Magdalene has trouble with 'Geoff,'" Hanni explained. "It was 'Jeefe' and then 'Jiffy.'"

Mary Magdalene, Helene Craig decided, must be the African woman.

"There's diapers and everything else I thought you might need at the house," Helene said. "It's been a long time, but I think I got everything."

There was a Bentley and a Peugeot station wagon outside the terminal. Ursula took the baby from her mother-in-law and got in the back of the Bentley, followed by the Craigs and Hanni Portet. Mary Magdalene and Jeanine would wait until the luggage was claimed and ride to the house in the Peugeot.

"That's quite a nurse," Helene said as the Bentley moved off.

"She raised Jeanine," Hanni said. "Good solid woman."

"She's wonderful," Ursula said.

Helene Craig had just decided she would say nothing else about the African woman when her husband said, "I'd hate to have her mad at me."

"So would I," Hanni laughed. "She comes from a warrior tribe. Once someone grabbed her purse at the market. She ran him down, knocked him on his back, and then broke a liter bottle of Perrier over his head."

Helene Craig smiled wanly.

"I'm surprised she didn't kill him," Porter Craig said.

"So was Mary Magdalene," Hanni laughed.

"It's beautiful here," Ursula said quickly.

"I'm sorry Geoff couldn't get away," Porter Craig said.

"Well, he's a soldier," Ursula said. "He just can't take off whenever he wants."

"What exactly is he doing?" Helene Craig asked.

"He's flying a lot."

"I think it's really unfair that they wouldn't let him out of the Army when he came home from Vietnam," Helene Craig said.

"He likes what he's doing."

"How is he going to fend with you gone, honey?" Porter Craig said.

"In great hardship," Hanni laughed.

"He calls the Portets' 'The Resort,'" Ursula said. "It has a swimming pool and a tennis court. And people to fetch beer for him."

"You were very kind to take them in the way you have," Helene Craig said.

"They did the same for my stepson in Alabama," Hanni said. "And it really is a joy to have a baby in the house. When he wakes up crying at night, I know he's not mine, and I can just roll over and go back to sleep."

"Well," Porter Craig said, "we intend to do now what we can to repay you. We've taken the house for the rest of the summer, and if it gets too warm here, the bank has a place in Norway where it never gets above seventy."

"Oh, we can't stay all summer!" Ursula protested.

"We'll see," Helene Craig said and patted her daughter-in-law's hand.

XV

[ONE]
Stanleyville, Democratic Republic of the Congo
17 July 1964

Pappy Hodges made a very slight adjustment to the trim-tab wheel of the L-23 Twin-Beechcraft and turned to his copilot.

"Do you *have* to smoke that fucking thing? It smells like a smoldering rope."

"You are looking at one of the world's most widely traveled cigars," Geoff Craig replied. "Rolled between the thighs of some Cuban belle, it was transported to the Orient, there to be purchased by my cousin Craig and brought to the United States. Then it was flown from Florida here as a suitable gift to mark the birth of his first nephew, at God alone knows what cost to the taxpayers. I respectfully put it to you, Major, Sir, that such a cigar is entitled to stink a little."

"You left out illegal," Pappy chuckled. "It's illegal to import Cuban cigars into the United States."

"Cousin Craig doesn't allow patriotism or the law to interfere with the simple pleasures of his life."

"And he probably gave them to you because he couldn't stand the stink either. But gimme one anyway," Pappy said. "Maybe if I smoke one myself, it will mask the noxious odor."

Geoff unwrapped a cigar, handed it to Pappy, and then extended a cigar lighter.

Pappy puffed appreciatively.

"I gotta admit it tastes better than it smells," he said. "But I guess it would have to, wouldn't it?"

Geoff chuckled.

"What are you reading?" Pappy asked. Geoff handed it to him.

> *Memorandum Re: Punia*   *15 July 1964*
> *For: 1LT Craig*
> *From: Capt Weaver*
>
> *Until the discovery of tin near Punia, and its exploitation by Union Minière, Punia did not exist. It lies in the Equatorial jungle, approximately one hundred miles north-northeast of Kindu and thirty miles east of the Lualaba River, which, in a more or less straight line, cuts across the jungle between Stanleyville and Kindu.*
>
> *To accommodate Union Minière, the government of the Belgian Congo first cut a road from Punia to the Lualaba River so that tin could be shipped on the river. Later, roads from Punia to Kindu and due north to Lobutu, where there is a junction with the main highway between Bukavu and Stanleyville, were built, whereupon the Punia-Lualaba road was allowed to revert to the jungle.*
>
> *All but twenty miles of the Kindu-Punia road is classified "partly improved," which is the euphemism for a widened path cut out of the tropical forest. All of the road from Punia to Lobutu is "partly improved."*
>
> *To accommodate its administrators and mining engineers, Union Minière cut a 2000-foot swath through the forest and bulldozed a 2000-foot runway. This was an enormously expensive project. Not only do the trees in this area often top three hundred feet, but it was later determined that it cost more to get the two Caterpillar-3 bulldozers into Punia than they had cost, delivered to the docks at Matari. It was decided that it was not economically sound to remove the bulldozers once the landing strip had been leveled. They were left there.*
>
> *During the Katangese rebellion, Union Minière temporarily abandoned mining operations in Punia and in nearby Yumbi and removed all Europeans from the area. Operations have not been resumed to date. It must be presumed that jungle and Equatorial rain have begun to reclaim the small town and its improvements, and that the airstrip will not be usable. So far as is known, Punia is uninhabited, although there may be one or more Congolese caretakers present.*

"Weaver is the AIS?" Pappy asked, referring to the Area Intelligence Specialist.

"Yeah," Geoff said.

"You asked him about Punia?"

"I thought casually. I didn't expect him to come up with that."

"He's nosy," Pappy said.

"He didn't get curious," Geoff said.

"Maybe asking him wasn't such a good idea," Pappy said. "He could run to the Attaché and tell him 'Hodges and Craig are involved in something in Punia.' That would get him two brownie points with the Attaché."

"When I got that, I called him back, thanked him profusely, and asked if he could do the same thing for me for Luashi," Geoff said.

"Where the hell is that?"

"On the South African border."

"You learn quick, don't you?"

"Some things I already know," Geoff said.

"Meaning what?"

"Well, I know you taught Lindbergh how to fly, Major, Sir, and I don't want to piss you off, Major, Sir . . ."

"But?"

"I think I should fly the O1E," Geoff said. The O1E was a single 213hp piston engine, two-seater observation and liaison aircraft manufactured by Cessna and originally designated L-19.

"Why?" Pappy asked reasonably.

"I've been picked up in situations like this," Geoff said, "and I know Father Lunsford."

"You got what? Ten hours in an L-19?"

"I've been picked up in situations like this," Geoff repeated, "and I know Father Lunsford."

"I don't want you doing anything dumb," Pappy said after a moment's thought, "like taking a chance on landing before you know the field's OK."

"I'll be careful."

"You dump that airplane, you won't be able to walk out," Pappy said. "I guess you thought of that?"

Geoff nodded.

"He don't clear you to land, you just dump the stuff and come home," Pappy said. "And you don't loiter if he ain't there."

"It's one five zero miles," Geoff said. "Call it an hour ten. Call it two hours thirty minutes round trip. That'll give me an hour to loiter and a half-hour reserve."

"When you get back here, you better have an hour's fuel aboard," Pappy said, "which means you loiter no more than thirty minutes."

"OK."

"If he's not there, he's not going to be there. And I don't want to find myself explaining what happened to the L-19. Not to mention trying to explain to Lou why I let a brand-new daddy dump his airplane so he'd have to wander around the jungle dodging lions and cannibals."

"In the new Army, Major, Sir, the aircraft is known as 'O1E.'"

"Fuck you, Lieutenant," Pappy said.

When they landed at Stanleyville a half hour later, they each had five inches or a little more of the original seven inches of the H. Uppmann Corona Corona clenched between their teeth.

"If you had to bet," Pappy said between his teeth, "which of those guys would you say was the diplomat?"

There were four men standing in the shade of the overhang of the terminal building. One of them wore a snap-brim straw hat, a blue-and-white cord suit, and carried a briefcase.

Geoff chuckled. As soon as Pappy had parked the L-23 and shut the engines down, the man in the cord suit walked over. "I'm Mr. Manley, Sir, from the U.S. Consulate."

"How do you do?" Geoff said, offering his hand. "Geoff Craig."

"My orders are to show you the aircraft, Sir, and then take you over to the Immoquateur. The Consul would prefer, unless it is necessary, that you not visit the consulate."

"The Consul? I thought you were the Consul," Pappy said as he jumped to the ground from the wing. "We were told he'd meet us."

"No, Sir," Manley said. "I'm the crypto officer. *Warrant Officer* Manley, Sir. The Consul asked me to handle this."

"I guess the Consul doesn't want to be seen with a couple of scruffy soldiers," Pappy said.

"Just between us . . . scruffy soldiers," Manley said, "he's really pissed about this, whatever it is you guys are doing. He fired off a TWX every hour on the hour to Leopoldville, 'protesting in the strongest possible terms,' until he got an Immediate from the Ambassador himself telling him to shut his mouth and do what he was told."

"We didn't hear that of course," Pappy said. "But thanks. Where's the airplane?"

Manley pointed. Geoff saw that the O1E, parked with a line of light aircraft, had been stripped of its paint and that it had no markings.

"It came in that way?" he asked. "Without markings?"

"Yeah," Manley said. "I never even saw who brought it. I was duty officer at the consulate and a guy—an American, I'm sure—called up and said the package we were expecting was at the airport. And then hung up. What the hell are you guys doing?"

"Photographing emergency airstrips in the jungle," Pappy said.

"Yes, Sir," Manley said dryly. "I knew it was something like that."

"Well, let's have a look at it," Pappy said. "And then I'm for a cold beer."

They had a very nice dinner in the restaurant of the Hôtel des Chutes and then went to the Immoquateur, a nine-story apartment building overlooking the docks on the Congo River. It was Warrant Officer Manley's apartment, furnished simply but comfortably.

There was a balcony looking down on the river, and once—inevitably, Geoff thought—the two old soldiers turned up mutual ol' buddies, they sat there telling war stories over ice-cold Simba beer, while Geoff made do with the local citron pressé, a sort of carbonated lemonade.

At daylight they were back at the airport. The O1E had hardpoints under each wing, and the two drop bundles were attached to them. They contained rations and batteries for Father Lunsford's radios. And ammunition.

Geoff emptied his pockets of everything but matches and four of Cousin Craig's H. Uppmann Corona Coronas. If he was captured, or killed, there would be nothing on him or his body to identify him as an officer of the United States Army.

And then he got in the O1E, fired it up, and took off. The takeoff took him over Stanleyville. It looked, he thought, like someplace in Southern California. The only thing that was missing was flashing signs for gas stations, motels, and Monsterburgers.

But five minutes later there were absolutely no signs of civilization whatever, just a sea of treetops stretching to the horizon. If he went down here, he thought uneasily, he never would be found. Even if the plane exploded and burned, it would leave only a tiny black mark in the forest.

"'Take not counsel of your fears,'" he quoted aloud. "Thank you, General Patton, for that wise observation. Otherwise I would be wondering what the fuck I am doing here."

Thirty minutes out of Stanleyville, he turned his AN/ARC-40 radio to the frequency he hoped Father Lunsford might be using. He wouldn't be transmitting on it in any way that would allow Geoff to use the signal to home in on him. But it was possible, presuming Father's batteries were still hot, that he would periodically press the mike button a couple of clicks and then listen for Geoff's call.

There was nothing in his earphones but a hiss and an infrequent pop; not the sound of a carrier.

An hour out of Stanleyville, he saw a road—just short stretches of it not covered by the forest, but enough to convince him it was the now deserted road between Punia and the Lualaba River.

And then, less than a minute later, he flew across the southern end of the Punia airstrip. He came across it suddenly, shaming him for being so goddamned dumb that he hadn't thought to fly a couple of thousand feet higher to give him a wider view of the ground.

He flew out of sight of the field and then dropped even lower, now very much aware of his limitations as a pilot. It was his intention to fly across the field at a very low altitude so he could see better. That would require him to find the field by seat-of-his-pants navigation. Pappy could have done it easily, and so, he thought, could Jack Portet. But he wasn't either of them. He was a brand-new pilot and over his fucking head.

And then he saw what looked like a wave in the treetops and banked toward it.

He'd found it.

A hundred feet off the treetops, he made a wide turn to the left and then lined up with the clearing and flew directly over it, as slow as he dared.

He didn't see a goddamned thing. Father Lunsford wasn't there.

And then he saw bulldozer tracks. Someone had worked on the runway. And then, just before he pulled up to get above the trees, he saw Father Lunsford near the end of the runway at the treeline, standing on the hood of a bulldozer and frantically waving his arms.

"Jesus," Geoff said, wiggled his wings, and stood the O1E on its wing to turn and line up with the runway. Sixty seconds later he was on the ground. Father Lunsford trotted out to the runway and to the plane as Geoff shut it down and climbed out.

They stood looking at each other for a moment. Geoff forced a smile: Father Lunsford looked like shit. He was wearing what once had been a white dress shirt. The sleeves had been ripped off just above the elbows, and it was stiff with filth. Over that he wore an unbuttoned vest, once part of a suit. He had a light-brown snap-brim felt hat on his head. His cotton trousers looked as if they once might have been white. Around his waist was a brown leather belt from which hung a saber and a small .32 caliber automatic pistol with its trigger guard fastened to a snap fastener. And finally there was an FN 7mm assault rifle hanging from a frayed web strap around his shoulder.

Sores and scabs, some of them suppurating, covered his face and neck and legs and belly.

"I look like shit, huh?" Father Lunsford said. "Well, fuck you, Lindbergh."

"How are you, Father?" Geoff asked.

"Don't let it go to your head, white boy," Lunsford said, "but I'm glad to see you."

Geoff nodded, unable to find his voice. And then they were hugging each other. An unpleasant smell, acrid, animal, came off Lunsford.

"You stink," Geoff said.

"You been running around in the jungle like Tarzan, you'd stink, too," Lunsford said. "You got any booze?"

Geoff went to one of the hardpoints and released one of the drop packets.

"There's two quarts of booze, one gin and one Scotch, in here," he said. "More or less cleverly disguised as medicinal alcohol."

"What about the real thing?"

"A quart of that, too. And there's penicillin and some other antibiotics, pills and stuff I can shoot you with. And some rations."

"What I need is some slant-eyed lovely in Bangkok cooing sympathetically as she gently dabs at my skin with some ancient and mysterious balm," Lunsford said. "Remember that? The hot water? The tile bath?"

"I remember," Geoff said. "And she stole three hundred bucks."

"Well, that shit she had, whatever it was, worked. It was worth the three hundred. I wish I had some of it now."

He stripped out of his clothing.

"Since I'm stuck with you, soak a bandage in alcohol and wipe the sores," he said.

"What are they?" Geoff asked. "Just insect bites?"

"Who the fuck knows?" Lunsford said, holding up two plastic quart bottles filled with clear liquid. "Which is which?"

"The label on the one with the gin has a corner torn off," Geoff said.

Lunsford handed him the other one, unscrewed the cap of the one with gin, and took a healthy swallow.

"I don't suppose you brought me any mail?" Lunsford asked.

"Yeah, in the other drop bag."

Lunsford's eyes lit up.

"Father, I got to take it back with me," Geoff said. "Or burn it."

"Take it back," Lunsford said. "I'll read it later."

"Why don't you come back with me? You're all fucked up."

"Jesus, I'd like to, Geoff."

"Then come. Just get in the goddamned airplane. In an hour you can be in a hot bathtub. I can probably even arrange for a native damsel to rub balm on you."

"Lieutenant, you are speaking to an honor graduate of the Command and General Staff College. What would my fellow future leaders of the Army think of me if it got out that I quit my post before being properly relieved, just because I was being eaten up by hordes of mysterious and poisonous insects?"

"Fuck 'em."

"With an attitude like that, Lieutenant, you will never rise to a position of great trust and responsibility."

"Fuck 'em, Father, come on out. I'll bring you back in a couple of days."

"When I get out of here, Geoff, I'm never coming back," Lunsford said, his voice now serious.

"Send in somebody else, then. Your exec."

"He'd last about three minutes. He speaks Swahili only, for one thing. And that badly. I don't particularly like the fucker, between you and me, but I don't think that's enough reason to put his liver on the Olenga ration."

"What the hell does that mean?"

"It means that certain elements of General Olenga's forces practice cannibalism, is what it means. They like liver."

"Christ!"

"And you thought the VCs were bad guys? Or that the 'Nungs were primitive?"

"Another reason to get out, then, for Christ's sake!"

"Not yet, Geoff," Lunsford said. "Give me my mail."

"Why not?"

"They keep talking about 'the arms coming,'" Lunsford said. "I'm beginning to believe them. I want to get my hands on some of those arms. Or catch me a Chinaman delivering them. Proof that some striped-pants sonofabitch in Washington won't be able to explain away."

"You can't do that yourself," Geoff said. "Who do you think you are, John Wayne?"

"I can try."

"Come on, Father, you're talking out of your asshole."

"Lieutenant, no further comments on the subject from you are desired or will be tolerated," Father Lunsford said. "Do I make myself clear?"

Geoff just met his eyes.

"The response expected from you, Lieutenant," Lunsford said, "is, 'Yes, Sir.'"

"Yes, Sir," Geoff said after a moment.

"Now give me my fucking mail and go take a piss or something while I read it," Lunsford said, punching Geoff affectionately on the arm.

Thirty minutes later the unmarked O1E took off from Punia.

When First Lieutenant Geoffrey Craig last saw Captain George Washington Lunsford, C&GSC '63, he was standing at the edge of the jungle, leaning on a tree. At the final moment, as Geoff flashed past him, he took his snap-brim fur felt cap from his head and made a sweeping bow.

He was just a little drunk. Whenever Father Lunsford had half a bag on, he got a little silly.

When Geoff turned and flew over the Punia strip again, Father Lunsford had disappeared back into the jungle.

[TWO]
Leopoldville, Democratic Republic of the Congo
19 July 1964

CAPTAIN JEAN-PHILIPPE PORTET and Lieutenant Geoffrey Craig were having dinner at the Cercle Sportif when Geoff was summoned to the telephone. He was pretty sure he knew who it was.

When Geoff and Pappy Hodges had returned from Stanleyville and reported to Colonel Dills, Dills had told them it was time to let the Attaché in on what was happening. In addition to the brief, relatively informal report they had given to Dills himself and which he would send to STRICOM, he had ordered Pappy to prepare a more formal and comprehensive report, this one addressed to the Ambassador through channels—in other words, through the Military Attaché.

Pappy Hodges had naturally told Geoff to do the report for him, cheerfully admitting that writing anything longer than his signature on a check was beyond his literary talents. By now, Geoff reasoned, the report had had time to reach the Attaché, and the Attaché wanted to talk to him about it before he sent it on to the Ambassador.

Typical Army/Government bullshit, Geoff thought. The Ambassador already knew what the report said. Dills had gone right from the airport, where he had met them, to see the Ambassador. But the Attaché didn't know that; and the Ambassador would probably pretend surprise when he got the report. That was easier than telling the Attaché that things had been going on under his nose that they hadn't wanted him to know about.

"Lieutenant Craig," Geoff answered the phone, in the proper military manner.

"When I called the house," a voice with a slight but unmistakable German accent said, "they told me where you were."

"Where are you?" Geoff asked after a moment's hesitation.

"In a bar on the Boulevard Leopold," Karl-Heinz Wagner said. "The Cricou."

"How much time do you have?"

"A hour, maybe two. But not more."

"OK," Geoff said. "You walk out of the bar. People will try to sell you ivory and jade. Act interested. Stand by the sidewalk. I'll be there in ten minutes, either in a Buick or in a taxi. Watch for it."

Karl-Heinz hung up without another word.

Geoff went back into the dining room.

"I hate to ask, but can I have the car for a couple of hours?" he asked Jean-Philippe Portet.

"Of course," Jean-Philippe said. *If he had asked why,* Geoff realized, *I would have said I couldn't tell him.* But he didn't ask, at least not out loud.

"That was Ursula's brother," he said. "He's at a bar on the Boulevard Leopold."

Jean-Philippe met his eyes. "I heard Hoare was in town," he said evenly. "I think it would be better if you—if we—took him out to the house."

"I didn't know Hoare was here," Geoff said.

"I don't think Tshombe wants it known," Jean-Philippe said. Moise

Tshombe had become Premier on July 15. "I'm surprised they let your brother-in-law out of the hotel."

"Tshombe told you?" Geoff asked, genuinely surprised.

"Who do you think went and got him?" Jean-Philippe said with a smile. "Hoare could hardly arrive on the afternoon flight from Jo'burg and go through customs. People know his face."

"Jesus Christ."

"I didn't know your brother-in-law was with him," Jean-Philippe said. "But I'm not surprised. There's six of them, counting Hoare."

"You didn't say anything," Geoff said.

"I thought it was one of those things we just didn't talk about," Jean-Philippe said. "And I will stay here and catch a ride home if you think that's best."

"To hell with it. Come on. And thank you."

In the Buick during the short ride downtown, Geoff told Jean-Philippe exactly what Karl-Heinz was doing with Hoare.

"I can see the reasoning," Jean-Philippe said. "But does everybody, especially your brother-in-law, know how dangerous that is? Some of the people around Hoare are really dangerous."

"My brother-in-law has the balls of an elephant," Geoff said.

"Elephants get shot," Jean-Philippe said, and then a moment later added: "I'm sorry. I shouldn't have said that."

As he drove past the Cricou Bar, Geoff saw Karl-Heinz on the broad sidewalk, surrounded by four Africans trying to sell him ivory, jade, and native crafts. He tapped the Buick's horn and then continued on down the Boulevard Leopold to the railway station, where he made a U-turn and headed back.

When he pulled to the curb, Karl-Heinz jumped in the back seat and a moment later they were back in the stream of traffic.

Jean-Philippe turned to face Karl-Heinz. "We're going out to my house," he said. "No one will see us there. And I will send you back downtown in a taxi."

"You flew the plane," Karl-Heinz said.

"Yes," Jean-Philippe said. "I did."

"What about your wife?"

"She and your sister and my daughter are on the Cap d'Antibes," Jean-Philippe said.

"And will you take us back?" Karl-Heinz asked.

"Probably," Jean-Philippe said. "And I will be discreet. Geoff has explained the situation to me."

Karl-Heinz thought that over a moment.

"I suppose, under the circumstances, that he had to tell you," he said finally. "I want to get in touch with Colonel Dills. I thought the safest way to do that would be through Geoff."

"We'll call when we get to the house," Jean-Philippe said. "He's in the U.S. Embassy compound. It's not far."

"What do you want with Dills?" Geoff asked.

"We met with Tshombe this afternoon," Karl-Heinz said.

"And?"

"I do not think I should get into that with you," Karl-Heinz said.

"Tshombe's not going to use Major Hoare and his people unless he has to," Jean-Philippe said conversationally. "Using them will cause him a good deal of trouble, inside and out of the Congo. The use of white mercenaries is the one thing a black African politician simply cannot do. He hopes that he will be able to put General Olenga's Simba Army down using the Armée Nationale Congolaise. I don't think he will be able to, even using B-26s against them. More importantly, neither do colonels Joseph-Désiré Mobutu and Leonard Mulamba, probably the only Congolese officers who know what they're talking about. They have been pressing him to get Hoare into action as soon as possible. As of last week. Since Tshombe is unwilling to commit political suicide right now, a compromise has been reached. Belgium will be asked to provide a couple hundred officers to 'advise' the ANC. Put some backbone into it, so to speak."

"You sound as if you have been talking to him," Geoff said.

"Him and Mobutu," Jean-Philippe said. "Let me finish: *And* a quantity of arms and ammunition, plus a good deal of money, will be made available to Michael Hoare just inside the South African border. He is to recruit, to prepare, and to arm his mercenaries, and be ready to send them should they be needed. Tshombe does not think the rebels will even try to take Stanleyville. Mobutu thinks they can and will."

"You seem to be privy to a great deal, Captain Portet," Karl-Heinz Wagner said.

"Everything I have just said is known to Colonel Dills," Jean-Philippe Portet said. "But I think he would be very interested in your assessment of Hoare's potential. So I will, as I said, ask him to come by the house."

"So far as Olenga's—the Simbas'—potential is concerned," Geoff said, "I saw Father Lunsford the day before yesterday. He said they have not as yet received any substantial arms shipments from Bujumbura or anywhere else."

"He's with them?" Karl-Heinz asked.

"I don't know if he's with the Simbas or just watching them from the bush," Geoff said. "He's dressed up like one of them. But he did tell me that most of the Simbas are from thirteen to fifteen years old; they get their strategy from witch doctors; and—I thought this very interesting—after they beat to death anybody who can read or who used to work for the government—or behead them—they cut out their livers and broil them."

"You don't mean eat them?" Karl-Heinz asked incredulously.

"That's what Father Lunsford said."

"I heard that. But I thought it was bullshit."

"If you get it from Father Lunsford, you can believe it," Geoff said.

XVI

[ONE]
Quarters # 1
Fort Rucker, Alabama
1935 Hours 25 July 1964

Wᴴᴱɴ ᴛʜᴇ ᴅᴏᴏʀʙᴇʟʟ ʀᴀɴɢ, the Bellmons had just sat down to dinner. A look of displeasure flashed across General Robert F. Bellmon's face.

"See who that is, Bobby, please," Barbara Bellmon said to her son. "Tell them we're eating."

Bobby was Second Lieutenant Robert F. Bellmon IV, USMA '64, a tall, well-built young man who bore a strong resemblance to his father. In deference to his father's belief that no matter what color it was or what was printed on it, a T-shirt was an undershirt, and gentlemen did not sit at table in their underwear, he was wearing a light cotton, gray, zipper jacket with ᴡᴇsᴛ ᴘᴏɪɴᴛ lettered across the back over his USMA Fencing Team T-shirt. He laid down his knife and fork, rose from the table, and went to the door.

A young man stood there in a light-blue knit polo shirt and khaki trousers. General Bellmon had another sartorial opinion regarding khaki pants. He didn't care what civilians did, khaki trousers were part of the uniform and should not be worn as part of civilian attire.

There was no question in Bobby Bellmon's mind who the young man was. There were not that many flaming-red Jaguar convertibles around.

This was the sonofabitch—it had become clear from overheard whispered conversations—who was fucking his sister.

"Yes?" Bobby Bellmon said. "Can I help you?"

"I'd like to see Marjorie, please," Jack Portet said.

"We're having dinner."

"Would you please tell her I'm here?" Jack said. As he looked at Marjorie's brother's face, there was no question in Jack's mind that Bobby had heard about him and that he disapproved of what he had heard. "My name is Portet." Perversely, he added, "PFC Portet, Sir."

"Just a moment, please," Bobby Bellmon said, closed the door in Jack's face, and returned to the dining room.

"It's Marj's friend," he said. "PFC Portet."

"Where is he?" Barbara Bellmon asked.

"Outside the door. I told him to wait."

Barbara Bellmon glanced at her daughter, saw the look on her face, and quickly got to her feet.

"Oh, Bobby!" she said in exasperation.

"I'm sorry, Jack," they heard her say a moment later, "Bobby didn't know who you were. Come on in and sit down and I'll set a place for you."

When they appeared at the door, Jack said, "Good evening, Sir. I'm sorry to burst in this way." He looked at Marjorie and their eyes locked, but neither of them spoke.

"How are you, Jack?" General Bellmon said.

The telephone rang.

"Bobby, get that," General Bellmon ordered.

"I didn't expect to see you tonight," Marjorie said finally.

"General Bellmon's quarters," Bobby said to the telephone. "Lieutenant Bellmon speaking, Sir."

"Make a place for him, Marjorie," Barbara ordered. "I'll get plates and silver."

"I'm not hungry, thank you," Jack said.

"I'm sorry, General Bellmon is busy at the moment," Bobby said to the telephone. "May I take a message?"

"Nonsense," General Bellmon said. "Sit down. There's more than enough."

"Thank you, Sir," Jack said, and went and stood close to Marjorie. She touched his arm.

"Dad, it's the AOD," Bobby said—the Aerodrome Officer of the

Day. "He said to tell you that a Florida aircraft has just landed and has been put inside the SCATSA hangar."

"Tell him thank you," General Bellmon ordered.

"General Bellmon says thank you, Major," Bobby Bellmon said.

"I guess you're involved with that, Jack?" General Bellmon asked.

"Yes, Sir."

"What's a Florida aircraft?" Bobby Bellmon asked.

"I don't think you've formally met Bob, have you, Jack?" General Bellmon said, rather obviously ignoring the question. "This is our son, who is about to start flight school. And, Bob, this is Marjorie's friend. You should get to know him. He's quite a pilot."

Bobby Bellmon forced a smile on his face and offered Jack his hand. "I'm pleased to meet you."

"How do you do?"

Barbara Bellmon came out of the kitchen with a plate of meat loaf and vegetables. "Sit, I said. You couldn't have timed your arrival better. We just sat down. And I will refrain from saying, 'Next time, call.'"

"Something's wrong," Marjorie said thoughtfully. "What is it, Jack?"

"Nothing's wrong."

"Yes, there is."

"I've got to go away for a little while. I wanted to ask you to take care of the car for me."

"Go away where?"

The telephone rang.

"Bobby," Marjorie said, "tell whoever that is to call back in five minutes."

"That will depend on who is calling," Bobby said as he reached for the phone. "General Bellmon's quarters. Lieutenant Bellmon speaking, Sir." There was a response and then Bobby looked at Jack, extending the phone to him. "It's for you."

Jack took the phone from him and spoke his last name.

"OK, Luis," he said. "Call the tower and have them relay to Atlantic Area Control that we made a precautionary landing at Cairns, and tell them we'll be airborne again in about thirty minutes. You better top off the tanks while you're at it. I'll be out there as soon as I can."

"'Precautionary landing'?" General Bellmon quoted. "Something wrong with your airplane, Jack?"

Jack met his eyes. "No, Sir. There's nothing wrong with the airplane."

"I want to know what's going on," Marjorie said.

"So do I," Bobby Bellmon added.

"It may well be none of our business," General Bellmon said.

"I asked the copilot to bring the airplane here and pick me up," Jack said, "so I could drop the car off. There wasn't time to do it any other way."

"Before what?" Marjorie asked almost angrily. "I want you to tell me what's going on!"

"A pilot got sick," Jack said. "Actually, we found out he's an alcoholic when he fell off the wagon. There's just nobody else available. I have to fill in for him."

"And you're going to the Congo!" Marjorie said.

Jack looked at her and shrugged. "It can't be helped, honey."

"Does Colonel Felter know about this?" Barbara Bellmon asked.

"I don't know," Jack said. "I'm taking my orders from Colonel Fulbright."

"That figures," General Bellmon said a little bitterly.

"You're not supposed to go over there," Barbara Bellmon said. "All you were supposed to do is help them get the planes and crews ready to go over there."

"How do you know that?" General Bellmon asked his wife.

"Craig told me," Barbara said. "When Jack first went to Hurlburt."

"You're going right now, aren't you?" Marjorie asked, making it an accusation. "That's what that airplane's doing at Cairns!"

"Yeah," Jack began. "That's about—"

"Just a moment please, Jack," the General interrupted him. "I have something to say. Primarily to Bobby, but really to all of you."

There was something in his tone of voice that silenced all of them and made them look at him expectantly, as if, Jack thought, they were awaiting his orders.

"We're dealing with a highly classified operation here, Bobby," General Bellmon said, "although to judge by this conversation, you'd never know it."

Bobby Bellmon looked at Jack in righteous indignation.

"Don't look at *him*, Bobby," General Bellmon said. "Or *just* at him. Take a look at your mother and your sister. Your mother put her nose in where she knew it had no business, and as hard to understand as this is, both Sandy Felter and Craig Lowell have told her a good deal that she has no need to know. And Marjorie knows more than she should. Some of that she got from Jack, obviously. The point is, there has been a serious breach of security. And I am obliged to do something about it. The trouble is, I don't know what."

"Bob!" Mrs. Bellmon said almost sorrowfully.

He held up his hand to silence her.

"The first thing you do when you face a situation like this is assess the damage," Bellmon went on. "Marjorie, how much have you talked about Jack . . . about where he is and what he's doing, to your friends?"

"What exactly *is* he doing?" Bobby demanded.

"I haven't asked for questions," Bellmon said flatly.

"I've told some people he's been at Hurlburt," Marjorie said. "But not what he's doing. I know better than that."

"I hope so," Bellmon said.

"But, Daddy, I *know*," Marjorie said. "I know Colonel Fulbright's involved, and Uncle Sandy, and Uncle Craig, and I know about the B-26s, and I guess I've known from the first that they were being sent to Africa. But I haven't said anything to anybody about that."

"And I gather you know at least as much as Marjorie?" Bellmon said to his wife.

"The only thing Craig told me was that they were going to pick Jack's brains at Hurlburt," Barbara said. "Obviously that had to do with Africa. But I didn't hear anything about B-26s until just now."

"And how much have you told Marjorie, Jack?" General Bellmon asked.

"I told her I was flying."

"B-26s? Stripped of identification numbers?" Bellmon asked, and Jack nodded. "No one told you to keep your mouth shut about what you were doing? That the classification is Top Secret?"

"Yes, Sir," Jack said, "But—"

"But what?" Bellmon asked, tiredly, resignedly.

"For God's sake," Jack said, "you're a *general*. She's a general's *daughter*. I wasn't running off at the mouth in a saloon."

"Just to make my point," Bellmon said, "do you have any reason to believe that Second Lieutenant Bellmon here is cleared for Top Secret—Eagle?"

"No, Sir," Jack admitted.

"Then do you think you should have said in his hearing anything at all about flying unmarked B-26 aircraft out of Hurlburt Field?"

"I don't mean to sound flip, General," Jack said, "but I don't think it's very likely that he's a Russian spy."

"He's twenty-one years old and a second lieutenant," Bellmon said.

"I think it's reasonable to presume that with a couple of beers in him at the officer's club, and if the conversation lagged, he might just mention that his sister's boyfriend, a PFC, is flying unmarked B-26s out of an Air Force base. Especially since no one told him it's Top Secret."

"That's not fair, Daddy, to either Jack or Bobby!" Marjorie said.

"Lieutenant Bellmon," General Bellmon said formally, "through no fault of your own you have been made privy to certain classified information regarding Operation Eagle. It is my duty to order you not to divulge, or discuss in any way, what you have heard with anyone, and to inform you that if you should so do, it will render you liable to such punishment as a court-martial may impose."

"Yes, Sir," Bobby said.

"Was that necessary?" Marjorie asked.

"Marjorie, please," Barbara Bellmon said.

"When are you going, Jack?" Bellmon asked.

"Now I'm not sure I should answer the question."

"Don't be flip with *me*, Jack!"

"As soon as I get out to Cairns. We're going over by the southern route, via San Juan and the Cape Verde islands."

"Isn't that stretching the B-26 a little?"

"We've got auxiliary fuel tanks," Jack said, "but it's tight."

"Thirty minutes after you take off, I will have to call Colonel Felter and tell him to what degree I believe security has been breached," Bellmon said.

Jack shrugged.

"Now sit down and eat your dinner," Barbara Bellmon said.

"Mrs. Bellmon, I just . . ." Jack said and stood up, gesturing helplessly at the food.

"I'm going out there with you," Marjorie said.

"I don't think you should," General Bellmon said.

"I don't give a damn what you think!"

She fled the room.

Jack nodded at General Bellmon and then at Bobby. "I'm sorry," he said to Barbara, "about all this."

She went to him and kissed his cheek.

"Take care of yourself, Jack," she said.

General Bellmon came out as Jack was starting the Jaguar engine. Jack looked up at him. Bellmon put out his hand.

"Good luck, Jack," he said. "Take care of yourself."

"Thank you, Sir."

When Jack had backed out of the driveway, Bellmon turned and started back into the house. He ran into his wife coming out. "Where are you going?"

"Where do you think?" Barbara said and got into the Oldsmobile.

He watched her; and then, as she started to go down the driveway, he put out his hand like a traffic cop, stopped her, and got in beside her.

They reached the SCATSA hangar at Cairns Field as the unmarked B-26K, gleaming in the taxiway and hangar lights, taxied toward the active runway, its engines throbbing powerfully.

Marjorie was standing by the hangar door, her arms folded tightly across her breast, her shoulders hunched over. She saw the headlights and turned to look for a moment, long enough for Bellmon to see that she was trying very hard not to cry.

Barbara jumped out of the car and went to her and put her arms around her.

The B-26K disappeared behind the Base Operations Tower building. And a moment later they could hear the sound of the engines revving as the mags were tested, and then the roar as full takeoff power was applied to both engines.

A moment later the B-26K came into view again on its takeoff roll. The wheels started to come up the moment it broke ground, and a few seconds after that the wings dipped to the left and then to the right as Jack waved so long.

Then Marjorie started to sob.

"It's all right, darling," Barbara said to her. "He's a good pilot. He'll be back."

"He won't," Marjorie moaned. "I have a goddamned premonition that I'll never see him again."

"Every time your father went away I thought the same thing," Barbara Bellmon said. "And every time he came back."

That's not true, General Bellmon thought. *We've talked about that. She told me there had never been any question in her mind that I would come back, that it never entered her mind that I would not.*

He waited until there was no longer the sound of the engines, and then went to his wife and daughter.

"You want me to drive Jack's car, honey?" he asked.

"No," she said sharply. "And I'll tell you something else. If he does come back, I'm going to marry him. So you better adjust to that."

"I'm already adjusted," he said.

[TWO]
Kamina Air Base
Katanga Province
Democratic Republic of the Congo
27 July 1964

JACK PORTET greased the B-26K onto the long, wide concrete runway, feeling just a little pleased with himself. The -K had its idiosyncrasies (it had a tendency to veer to the right when you broke ground, and it landed hot), but even his father could have found no fault with this approach and landing nor, so far as that went, with the whole trip. They had hit where they wanted to hit on time and with more than the minimum fuel remaining.

The avionics were first-class, brand-new, state-of-the-art Collins and Sperry. On the across-the-Atlantic leg and then down the west coast of Africa, they had a radio link on the single-sideband with the Strategic Air Command. It had never failed, and it had been as clear as a bell.

Somewhat cynically, Jack had thought that the SAC radio link had been primarily to inform colonels Felter and Fulbright as quickly as possible if they had had trouble; there was very little SAC could have done for them had they had to sit down in the middle of the Atlantic. But even knowing this, it had been comforting to have someone to talk to. It had been a long way at 370 knots across a very wide ocean from San Juan to the Cape Verde islands.

Three quarters of the way down the runway, he turned the -K off onto a taxiway and taxied back toward the hangar area. There were a number of planes on the former Belgian Air Force base, most of them wearing Congolese insignia. He saw some of the B-26s that had preceded him. Several of these had already been painted with Congolese insignia and identification numbers. There were eight T-28s parked wingtip to wingtip, and three Douglas C-118s, the military version of the DC-6, with Congolese markings.

He half expected to see Air Simba markings on a C-46 parked behind a hangar, but when he drew close, he saw the Commando wore UN markings and was a derelict, missing one engine and one tire and wheel. He wondered if his father knew about it. He might be able to buy it dirt cheap and cannibalize it for parts. Or for that matter make a little gift to the proper people, who would look the other way while he helped himself to whatever parts he thought he could use.

Then he saw something else behind the line of hangars. Two USAF C130-E Hercules. (The Hercules was the standard USAF long-range, multirole, heavy-duty airlift transport aircraft.) Their rear cargo doors were open, and they were in the process of off-loading a mixed cargo. Each had apparently carried a partially disassembled Sikorsky H-34, as well as a large assortment of wooden crates.

The crates probably contained the .50 caliber Browning machine guns with which the B-26s would be armed and ammunition for them, Jack decided.

And finally, before a Congolese in a much-too-large-for-him set of white coveralls came running onto the taxiway with wands in his hands to direct Jack to a parking spot, Jack saw a U.S. Army L-23 parked next to the Hercules.

He idly wondered as he moved the -K where it was supposed to go and went through the shutdown procedure if it could possibly be Geoff Craig.

It was. When Jack dropped to the ground from the -K's hatch, Geoff was standing there with Pappy Hodges.

"Dr. Portet, I presume?" Geoff said. "Welcome to the Heart of Darkest Africa."

"Hello, you ugly sonofabitch," Jack said. "How are you?"

"I didn't know they let common enlisted men like you fly fancy airplanes like that," Geoff said.

"Hello, Jack," Pappy Hodges said, offering his hand. Luis Martinez, the former Cuban Air Force captain who had been Jack's copilot, threw their luggage to the ground through the hatch and then dropped down after it. Jack made the introductions.

"I got something for you, Jack," Pappy said. "I don't think you're going to like it."

"What?" Jack asked.

Pappy Hodges handed him a quarter-inch stack of mimeograph paper.

HEADQUARTERS
UNITED STATES STRIKECOMMAND
McDill Air Force Base, Florida

SPECIAL ORDERS: NUMBER   107:
EXTRACT ★★★★★★★★★★★★★

21. PFC PORTET, Jacques Emile US53279656, Hq & Hq Co USSTRICOM, McDill AFB Fla is relieved present assignment and transferred in grade and will proceed to Hq & Hq Co, US Army Garrison, Berlin, Germany, effective 25 July 1964. Auth: TWX Hq Dept of Army dated 25 Jul 1964. EM will travel by US Govt or civilian air, rail, or motor transportation as required. EM is NOT authorized transportation at government expense of dependents, household goods, or private automobile. Tvl is authorized in civilian clothing at option of EM. Travel will be accomplished within seven (7) days of departure. The exigencies of the service preclude the granting of any delay en route leave. Hq & Hq Co, USA Gar, Berlin, is directed to notify Hq Dept of Army (ATTN: PERS-II-A.3) by most expeditious means of acquisition of EM. Service and allied records of EM are being forwarded by registered US Mail.
BY COMMAND OF GENERAL EVANS:
OFFICIAL:
Dennis V. Crumpette
Lt. Col, GSC
Scty Gen Staff

"What the hell is this?" Jack asked.

"I have supplemental verbal orders regarding you, PFC Portet," Pappy said dryly. "I am to lead you personally by the hand to one of those Air Force Hercules and hand you over to the aircraft commander. You will then be flown to Evereux, France. At Evereux, France, you will tell the Air Force people that you have just arrived from the States . . . *directly* from the States. They will then arrange your transportation from Evereux to Berlin by the most expeditious means."

"What the hell is going on?" Jack asked.

"Just guessing," Pappy said, "I would say that somebody wants your ass out of the Congo as soon as possible."

"Why? And why Berlin?"

"Berlin is a puzzler," Pappy said. "Why, I can make guesses. If I were a betting man, and I am, I would bet that Fulbright has his ass in a crack for letting you fly that B-26 over here and that they want to get you as far away from it and from the whole operation as they can, and as quickly as they can."

"How come you did fly it?" Geoff asked.

"The guy that was supposed to fly it crawled into a bottle," Jack said. "There was nobody else to fly it."

"OK, then," Pappy said. "That's it. Presuming that they can get you to Berlin right away, it's deniable. What they call 'credibly deniable.'"

"What the hell does that mean?"

"If some sonofabitch in the State Department, or the CIA, or the White House, leaks it to the press," Pappy said, "or for that matter if the Russians are watching Hurlburt and have found out what's going on, and arrange for some reporter to make a scoop—that U.S. military personnel are flying B-26s over here, it can be credibly denied. 'Portet? Don't be silly. Portet is a PFC—and he's in Berlin, not the Congo.'"

[THREE]
Orly Field, Paris, France
29 July 1964

THE TRANSPORTATION OFFICE at Evereux, an American-operated air base on which several squadrons of C130-E Hercules aircraft were based in support of NATO, provided PFC Portet with a ride on a Gooney-Bird to Orly and a voucher for a ticket on Pan American to Berlin. Pan Am didn't seem at all surprised to have a PFC traveling alone show up asking for a ticket. Jack decided that people apparently hitchhiked rides into Evereux. It was a transport-aircraft base, and that made sense when he thought of it.

There had been no way for him to place a call at Evereux to Hanni and Jeanine on the Cap d'Antibes, or at least none that he could discover. The military switchboard was not equipped to accept pay calls onto a French trunk. He would, he decided, call from Orly.

On the Gooney-Bird to Orly, however, having nothing better to do, he reread his orders assigning him to Headquarters & Headquarters Company of the U.S. Army Garrison, Berlin, wondering what the hell they intended for him there. And then he noticed the line saying "travel will be accomplished within seven (7) days." That meant he had seven days to get there, starting on the twenty-fifth.

Thirty days hath September, etcetera told him that meant he had until the first of August. And they didn't really know when he had left. He could tell them he had left the States on the twenty-eighth, which meant that he didn't have to be in Berlin until August fourth.

Air France said they would be willing to deadhead Captain Portet of Air Congo into Cannes, but the planes were full, and he was liable to be left standing at the gate. He wasn't sure if that was true or whether the French were just trying to weasel out of giving him a free trip, but he couldn't take the chance. He bought a ticket, and there was just time to call the number Geoff had given him at Kamina before he made his flight.

Hanni and Jeanine and Ursula, carrying the baby, met him at Cannes in a chauffeur-driven Bentley.

In direct defiance of verbal orders relayed to him by Major Pappy Hodges not to mention to anyone that he had been anywhere near the Congo, he told them all what had happened, and that he had left Geoff twenty-four hours before, looking trim and healthy.

But on the way from the airport to the Villa Sans Regrets, he decided that telling Geoff's parents about his trip via the Congo would not be wise, and said so.

"I was going to say the same thing to you," Ursula said. "I'm going back to Leopoldville with Hanni and Jeanine on the first. Geoff's mother doesn't like it, and she would use trouble down there as another argument. I've found out that Geoff gets his stubbornness from her."

The Porter Craigs were waiting for them at the villa, standing outside when the Bentley rolled majestically up. Mrs. Craig snatched the baby from Ursula and cooed at it.

"This house is yours, Jack," Porter Craig said, warmly pumping his hand. "We've become family. I realize that sounds a little odd, but it's really true. If you don't see what you want, ask for it."

"How's the phone service to the States?" Jack asked.

"In the study there's a green telephone," Porter Craig said. "It's a tie line to the office in New York. When you get a dial tone, dial 9, and then 0 for the long-distance operator."

"General Bellmon's quarters, Lieutenant Bellmon speaking, Sir."

"This is Jack Portet, Bobby," Jack said. "Is Marjorie there?"

Marjorie came on the line a moment later. "Jack, where are you?"

"In the library of a villa on the Cap d'Antibes. A butler just walked in offering me my choice of beer or booze."

"Damn you, can't you ever be serious?"

"Love me?"

"Yes, of course."

"Say it."

"I can't," she said. "Where are you?"

"In the library of a villa. . . ."

[FOUR]
Flughafen Tempelhof
West Berlin, Germany
2 August 1964

T HERE WAS A CONSPICUOUS SIGN by the baggage claim area directing all incoming military personnel to report to a military-liaison office farther inside the enormous curved terminal building.

Jack Portet, who was in civilian clothing, looked at it with mingled annoyance (he was obviously about to become PFC Portet again) and curiosity (what the hell was he doing in Berlin?) as he waited for his luggage. Then he picked up his bags and shrugged, and headed down the corridor in the direction the arrow indicated.

He didn't quite make it to the counter behind which sat two bored GIs, a sergeant and a corporal.

"I was beginning to wonder if you had been some cannibal's dinner," a voice said softly in his ear.

Jack, startled by the voice turned to see who was talking to him. It was the Warrant Officer who had come to Fort Benning to see him when he was in jump school.

As the man offered his hand, Jack remembered his name: Finton. "Hello, Mr. Finton," he said.

"Over this way, Jack. I've got a car out here."

"I'm supposed to check in at the counter."

"You're supposed to do what I tell you, Jack," Finton said, not unkindly.

There was a black Opel Captain with civilian Berlin license tags parked outside the terminal building. Jack wondered what there was about it that made him absolutely sure it was an Army car. Or at least a U.S. government car. "Are you going to tell me what this is all about?"

"That's why I'm here," Finton said. "You ever been here before, Jack?"

"No."

"Nice town," Finton said. "I like Berliners."

"What the hell am I doing here?"

"You are going to be a German-language interpreter in the G-3 Section of OMGUS, which stands for Office of Military Government, U.S. Technically, Berlin is still under military occupation."

"In other words you're not going to tell me."

"You were never at Hurlburt Field, Florida," Finton said. "And therefore you know nothing about it. You don't know anything about B-26 aircraft or about B-26 aircraft being flown to Africa. You have not been to Africa since you left to get drafted. Get the picture?"

"Everybody on the Gulf Coast knows about those airplanes," Jack said. "Why all the secrecy?"

"I didn't come over here to argue with you, Jack. I'm telling you how it is."

There was steel in his voice, and Jack heard it. "Sorry," he said.

"Everybody on the Gulf Coast knows about those airplanes," Finton said, "but not where they went. They were intended for Vietnam, not for the Congo."

"Without sounding like a wise guy—and I really don't mean to— what's the difference?"

"There are people around the President who are violently opposed to any American intervention in the Congo," Finton said. "And could, and would, use you as a means to stop Operation Eagle."

"Me? *PFC* Portet?"

"You're a soldier. You're military."

"So are Geoff Craig and Pappy Hodges."

"They are military attachés to the embassy. You're not. It would make headlines in the *Washington Post* if it got out—and if any one of fifty people in the White House and the State Department heard about it, it *would* get out—that we were using military personnel to fly B-26 bombers to the Congo."

"That's a little hard to believe."

"If you had heard Felter eat Fulbright's ass out for letting you fly that airplane to the Congo, you'd believe it."

"There was no one else to fly it. The guy that Fulbright hired to fly it turned out to be a lush."

"Then it should have stayed at Hurlburt until they got somebody else.

Take my word for it, Jack, if it had gotten out—if it gets out—it could blow the whole operation out of the water."

They had driven through an area of five- and six-story apartment buildings. Now they were in an area of substantial one-family homes, some of them nearly mansions.

"That sign says Onkel Tom Strasse," Jack said. "Our Uncle Tom, as in Harriet Beecher Stowe?"

"Ours. The Berliners took that yarn to heart."

"Where are we going?"

"To Zehlendorf," Finton said. "We have a house—a compound, really—there. I brought your uniforms with me from the States. You will report in in uniform."

"Who is 'we'?" Jack asked. "As in 'we have a house'?"

"An agency of the U.S. government."

"Why Berlin?" Jack said. "Why couldn't I have gone back to McDill?"

"Why go to all this trouble, you mean?"

"Exactly."

"Because it's that important, Jack, that you vanish into the woodwork."

"Can I tell my girl, my family, where I am?"

"Your girl already knows," Finton said, "so that's not a problem. And Pappy Hodges will explain the situation to your father if he hasn't already. I think the flaming ember has been pissed on. All you have to do is keep your mouth shut."

Jack grunted.

"You'll like Berlin, I think," Finton said as he turned off Onkel Tom Allee onto Sven Hedin Strasse. He then drove the Opel through a gate in an eight-foot-high fence. The gate closed after them. Jack saw a beautiful German shepherd sitting with a stocky man. The dog looked curiously at the car, as if he hoped it contained someone to play with him. And then Jack saw that the stocky man had a submachine gun slung over his shoulder.

"Looks like a lot of fun," he said.

XVII

WHEN THE ALARM BELL went off on one of the battery of high-speed radioteletype machines against the wall, the Army Signal Corps Master Sergeant who had the duty rose quickly out of his chair and walked to it, getting there before the message had been completely typed.

When the last letters had been typed out, the Master Sergeant tore the message—it was an Operational Immediate—from the machine and turned to carry it to the duty officer. A man in a baggy gray suit touched his arm, stopping him, with the obvious intention of reading the message.

That was not the prescribed procedure. Incoming messages, especially those of higher priority—and Operational Immediate was second only to Flash—were to be delivered to the duty officer, who would determine the distribution.

The Master Sergeant had been only recently assigned to the Situation Room. All that he had been told about the man in the baggy gray suit was that he was an Army colonel named Felter and that he worked in some unspecified function "upstairs," in other words, in the White House itself.

By the time the Master Sergeant had made up his mind to politely remind the Colonel of the prescribed procedure, Felter had read the message.

OPERATIONAL IMMEDIATE
TOP SECRET
FROM CINCPAC
TO CNO WASH DC
INFO JCS & WHITE HOUSE SITROOM
USS MADDOX DD134 OPERATING IN INTERNATIONAL WATERS
IN GULF OF TONKIN REPORTS ATTACK AT 0845 ZULU BY TWO
NORTHVIETNAMESE PATROL TORPEDO BOATS. MADDOX RE-
TURNED FIRE, SINKING ONE ATTACKING VESSEL AND
DAMAGING THE OTHER. MADDOX UNDAMAGED, NO CASU-
ALTIES, PROCEEDING.
LOUMA, VICE ADMIRAL USN FOR CINCPAC

"Make me a copy of that, please," Felter said.

He walked away from the battery of radioteletype machines to a Navy master chief electronicsman sitting in front of a computer keyboard.

"Punch up the *Maddox,* DD134," he ordered.

The Master Chief's fingers flew over the keyboard. A map of the coast of the part of Indochina now called North and South Vietnam appeared on the computer monitor. A moment later a dot began to flash on the screen.

"Punch in the international-waters line."

A line appeared on the computer monitor. The blinking dot was well outside it. "How recent is that?" Felter asked, "and how good is it?"

"Within a hundred meters, Colonel," the Master Chief said. He tapped the keys again and a date and time message appeared on the screen. "Thirty-five minutes ago, Colonel."

"Throw it up on the big screen, Chief."

The Master Sergeant appeared. Felter, expecting a photocopy of the Operational Immediate, held out his hand.

"Sir, I'm sorry, but without specific authority I'm not permitted to make copies—"

The Master Chief laughed. "Sergeant, you were just authorized. Take my word for it. What's with the *Maddox,* Colonel?"

"They report they were attacked by two North Vietnamese torpedo boats," Felter said.

"And that's international waters," the Master Chief said. "That's an act of war by anybody's definition."

"Yes," Felter said.

"That would be a shitty place to fight a war," the Master Chief said.

"Yes, it would," Felter said.

The Master Sergeant returned with a photocopy of the Operational Immediate.

"Thank you," Felter said.

"Sir, how do I log that out?" the Master Sergeant asked.

"Log it out to me," Felter said. "Chief, I'm going to take this upstairs. I'll be either there or here for a while. If you could arrange it, I'd be grateful if you could stick around."

"Aye, aye, Sir," the Master Chief said.

An Air Force major general walked up.

"Chief, how quickly can you get me the latest satellite-verified position of the USS *Maddox*, DD134, and its position relative to North Vietnamese waters?"

The Master Chief pointed silently to the left of three large monitors mounted on the wall, which showed the coast of Vietnam, and a blinking dot that indicated the position of the *Maddox*. The Chief winked at Felter as Felter turned and headed for the elevator.

[TWO]
Union Transit Africaine Flight 43
Near Fort Lamy, Union of Central African Republics
1330 Hours 3 August 1964

WITHIN THEIR PEER GROUP—the pilots and copilots of jet passenger aircraft on scheduled intercontinental service (known at that stratified avia-social level as "captains" and "first officers")—pilots flying the Africa-Europe routes consider themselves to be, and are generally regarded as, an elite within an elite.

There are a number of reasons for this. Some have to do with the enormously long "legs" they habitually fly. And which they fly without half the navigation aids available to their brothers flying from, say, New York to Paris, or even from Honolulu to Melbourne.

They know they *fly* their airplanes, while their brothers at the controls of identical aircraft on the New York-Paris run simply don't have to do that. What they mean by *fly* in this case has nothing to do with skillful aerial maneuvers, with gentle landings and smooth takeoffs. There are very few people sitting in the left seat of multi-engine, multi-million-dollar, multi-hundred-passenger aircraft cockpits who are not possessed of remarkable airplane-driving skills.

What they're talking about is the necessity for them to make decisions—important, genuinely life-and-death decisions—one after the other, that their brothers flying back and forth across the Atlantic simply are not called upon to make.

While the weather, present, en route, and forecast for ETA at destination, is certainly nice for a pilot about to fly from Kennedy to Heathrow to know, it really isn't all that important to him.

If Heathrow socks in before he gets there, no real problem. Heathrow has one of the best instrument-landing systems in the world—people and equipment. And if he can't get into Heathrow, he can sit it down somewhere else in England, or fly a little further and sit down in Brussels, or Frankfurt, or Paris, or at any one of a hundred or so other alternate airports, many of which have long, wide runways and skilled people to talk him down through the soup.

There is not much difference, as the crow flies, in distance between Brussels and Kennedy and between Brussels and Leopoldville International.

The difference is that once the Mediterranean is left behind, the skies between Brussels and Leopoldville are comparatively deserted. There is not another airplane a hundred miles ahead, or behind, or which will cross the Leopoldville's path five thousand feet above or below him.

There are far fewer navigation aids, and the ones that do exist are not nearly as reliable as those on more widely traveled air corridors. There are fewer weather stations, reporting less frequently, and often less accurately.

And most important, there are far fewer alternative airfields where the captain of a trans-African flight can conveniently and safely sit down if his destination becomes unavailable.

So he has to make decisions . . . right from the first one, based on his assessment of the en route and destination weather: *Do we go or don't we?*

And he has to pay far more attention to his navigation. For on the African continent there are very few multi-million-dollar, long-range radar sets operated by skilled people who will obligingly report to a captain exactly where he is.

And, en route, he has to constantly reassess his status and consider his options.

At 1330, UTA 43 called Fort Lamy on the VHF.

"Lamy, UTA Four Three, can you give us your latest on the Leo weather?"

"UTA Four Three, Lamy. Stand by, please."

"Can you read him?" the First Officer of UTA 43 asked his captain. The Captain threw up his hands in a gesture of resignation.

Lamy came back on and reported what the Captain of UTA 43 was afraid he would. There were moderate to severe thunderstorms in the area which were not expected to clear before nightfall. The thunderstorms were moving in a southerly direction. They extended one hundred miles either side of a line from Latoursville in Gabon to Salazar in Angola.

"Oh, shit!" the Captain of UTA 43 said. "That knocks out Luanda, too, if they're moving south. We'd get there right in the middle."

"That leaves us Lagos, Stanleyville, and Kampala," the First Officer said. "We won't have enough fuel remaining to go further south."

"See if you can raise Lagos," the Captain said.

Lagos, Nigeria, came over the VHF very clearly, first to answer the call and then to report five minutes later that there were not, repeat not, sufficient hotel rooms to accommodate the passengers of UTA 43 overnight.

"We're apparently not the only people this shit is fucking up," the pilot said. "See if you can raise Stanleyville."

Stanleyville did not come in at all clearly. There was apparently some kind of electrical storm in the area. The Captain of UTA 43 was not surprised. At this time of year there were almost always afternoon thundershowers.

But they could hear him well enough to get his weather—the storm would clear by five—and to learn that the Sabena guest house was available. Sabena maintained a guest house right beside the airfield for just such happenstances as this. In effect, it was a rudimentary hotel capable of feeding and housing, in somewhat cramped circumstances, airplane passengers stranded overnight—or until their flight could continue.

"Stanleyville," the Captain of UTA 43 said, taking the microphone himself. "Please contact the UTA station manager and inform him that UTA Four Three is diverting to Stanleyville at this time. We have eleven, one one, first-class passengers, including one first-class infant, and ninety-six, niner six, tourist passengers, including seven, repeat seven, tourist infants. Plus seven, repeat, seven crew."

He had to repeat the message several times to get it through the electrical interference in the Stanleyville area. Then he called Fort Lamy and had him file the change to his flight plan.

Then he pressed the cabin announce switch.

"Ladies and gentlemen," he said. "This is Captain Damier speaking. There's a rather nasty thunderstorm in Leopoldville. So we've decided to sit down in Stanleyville and wait it out. I'm sorry for the delay, and I can't even guess when the weather at Leopoldville will improve. That's the bad news. The good news is that I have done this before, and I can tell you that the Sabena guest house really puts out a fine meal. And, if we have to spend the night, they're going to put us up in their fine guest house. And if there's time, we'll see if we can't arrange for a bus tour of Stanleyville for those who would like to see it. They call it the Paris of the Congo."

He then repeated more or less the identical message in English.

When Hanni Portet, in the first-class compartment of UTA 43, saw the look of disappointment on Ursula Craig's face, she smiled at her and leaned over and whispered so as not to wake Jiffy.

"We keep an apartment in the Immoquateur," she whispered. "We'll stay there. It's nice, and it overlooks the Congo. These things happen."

Then she got a stewardess's attention.

"I am Madame Portet," she said. "My husband is Captain Portet, Chief Pilot of Air Congo."

"Yes, Madame," the stewardess replied. "How may I help you?"

"When the Captain is in touch with Stanleyville," Hanni Portet said, "would you ask him to get in touch with Air Congo and tell them I'm aboard and to have a car for us at the field? So we can go into town and the Immoquateur?"

"Certainly, Madame," the stewardess said.

When UTA 43 touched down at Stanleyville at 4:45, the stewardess, following the Captain's orders, saw to it that Madame Portet and party were the first to debark. She went down the stairs with them and saw that they were safely aboard a Chevrolet carryall. Then she went back aboard the aircraft.

As the first passengers started to walk down the stairway, the UTA Stanleyville Station Chief came running out of the terminal and pushed his way quickly and somewhat rudely up the stairs. He jerked open the door to the flight deck.

"How much fuel do you have aboard?"

"An hour forty-five, maybe two hours," the First Officer replied.

"That'll get you to Kampala," he said, visibly relieved.

"You mean now?"

"The Simbas are two hours away."

"Who the hell are the Simbas?" the First Officer asked.

"You really think they're going to come here?" the Captain asked. "You sound a little hysterical, frankly."

"They are going to come here," the UTA Station Chief said. "The only question is when."

"I'd like to know a little more," the Captain said.

"I order you to prepare this airplane for immediate flight!" the UTA Station Chief said excitedly.

"You don't order me anywhere," the Captain said coldly.

"Captain," the Station Chief said, "you are responsible for the lives of your passengers."

The UTA Captain, whose face showed he did not like being reminded of his obligations by a groundling, thought that over for a moment.

"Set us up for Kampala, Louis," he said to his First Officer. Then he pushed the stewardess call button, and when one came in the cockpit told her to reload all the passengers.

Hanni and Jeanine Portet, Ursula and Jiffy Craig, and Mary Magdalene had been in the Air Simba apartment in the Immoquateur only long enough to change Jiffy's diapers and for Hanni to start a pot of coffee when the air trembled from the roar of a DC-8 passing over.

Hanni knew the difference between the roar of engines taking off and landing. That had to be the UTA airplane. There had been no other jet on the field.

But there was no sense in worrying Jeanine and Ursula. There was an explanation, certainly, and the worst thing that could happen was that they would have to catch something else, probably East African Airways, for the rest of the trip to Leopoldville.

[THREE]
The United States Consulate General
Stanleyville, Democratic Republic of the Congo
0845 Hours 4 August 1964

CHIEF WARRANT OFFICER JOSEPH F. MANLEY, his white shirt and trousers sweat soaked and stained from the effort of moving the steel drums from their storage area to the side of the swimming pool, rolled the last of seven in place and then looked to the Consul General for orders.

"Go ahead, Joe," the Consul General said.

Manley reached into the nearest steel drum and came up with several sheets of bond typewriter paper. On the top and bottom of each sheet was stamped SECRET in red letters. He twisted the sheets of paper together to form a torch and then took a Zippo from his pocket and ignited it.

He held it to the top of one of the drums.

For a moment nothing happened. And then all at once there was a brilliant white glare and a sound like rushing wind. A sheet of white flame erupted from the barrel, rising a dozen feet in the air.

Some kind of phosphorus, Manley decided.

He expected the flame to die down immediately. It did not.

"Shit!" he said aloud, aware that the vulgarity offended the Consul General's sense of verbal decorum for cryptographic officers.

Manley decided another system of ignition would be required. He went to the second steel drum and took a stapled-together report from it.

He ripped one page from it and, without twisting or crumpling it, ignited one end. He dropped it into the second steel drum and then did the same thing to the third. He was just igniting the next sheet of paper when the second drum went off, and then almost immediately the third.

By the time all of them were ablaze, it was so hot that he had to walk around the other side of the swimming pool in order to get back to the Consul General.

"I think you better stay until you're sure everything has burned," the Consul General said.

"Yes, Sir," Mr. Manley said.

"When you've done that, radio Leopoldville that it's been accomplished."

"Yes, Sir."

[FOUR]
The White House
Washington, D.C.
4 August 1964

TWO HIGH-PRIORITY MESSAGES came over the high-speed radioteletype printers in the Situation Room within minutes of each other.

URGENT

FROM US EMBASSY LEOPOLDVILLE DEM REPCONGO

TO SECSTATE WASH DC

CONSULGEN STANLEYVILLE REPORTS BY RADIO STANLEYVILLE OCCUPIED BY REVOLUTIONARY MILITARY FORCES OF LT GEN OLENGA PAREN SIMBAS PAREN AFTER BRIEF RESISTANCE BY ARMEE NATIONALE CONGOLAISE.

CONSULATE AND CONSULAR RESIDENCE VIOLATED BY OLENGA FORCES. US COLORS RIPPED FROM CONSULATE FLAGSTAFF. CONSULGEN AND SIX MEMBERS OF STAFF FIRED UPON BY OLENGA FORCES. CONSULGEN AND STAFF FOUND REFUGE IN COMMUNICATIONS VAULT. ATTEMPT BY OLENGA FORCES TO FORCE VAULT NOT SUCCESSFUL. CONSULATE AND CONSULAR RESIDENCE PRESENTLY NOT REPEAT NOT OCCUPIED BY SIMBAS.

THIRTY PAREN ESTIMATED PAREN US NATIONALS IN STANLEYVILLE AND IMMEDIATE VICINITY. STATUS UNKNOWN.

AMBASSADOR CURRENTLY MEETING WITH PREMIER TSHOMBE WITH VIEW EFFECTING RESCUE US DIPLOMATIC PERSONNEL AND OTHER US NATIONALS BY CONGOLESE MILITARY FORCES. AMBASSADOR BELIEVES IMMEDIATE RESCUE UNLIKELY CON-

SIDERING ANC INABILITY TO HOLD STANLEYVILLE AGAINST
SIMBAS.

AMBASSADOR BELIEVES CLEAR AND PRESENT DANGER TO
LIVES OF ALL US NATIONALS IN STANLEYVILLE EXISTS, AND
HAS THEREFORE ORDERED US ATTACHE TO PREPARE CON-
TINGENCY PLANS FOR RESCUE OPERATION UTILIZING US
MILITARY FORCES PRESENTLY IN CONGO.

AMBASSADOR WILL FURNISH EVALUATION OF ENTIRE SITUA-
TION

FOLLOWING MEETING WITH TSHOMBE AND OTHERS.

DANNELLY DEPUTY CHIEF OF MISSION

The second message was very similar to one received two days previously:

OPERATIONAL IMMEDIATE
TOP SECRET
FROM CINCPAC
TO CNO WASH DC
INFO JCS & WHITE HOUSE SITROOM
USS TURNER JOY DD163 OPERATING IN INTERNATIONAL WA-
TERS IN GULF OF TONKIN REPORTS ATTACK AT 1045 ZULU BY
TWO NORTHVIETNAMESE PATROL TORPEDO BOATS. JOY RE-
TURNED FIRE, POSSIBLY SINKING ONE NORTHVIETNAMESE
VESSEL AND DAMAGING THE OTHER. JOY UNDAMAGED, NO
CASUALTIES, PROCEEDING.
LOUMA, VICE ADMIRAL USN FOR CINCPAC

[FIVE]
Leopoldville International Airfield
Democratic Republic of the Congo
5 August 1964

J EAN-PHILIPPE PORTET arrived at the airfield in a 1964 Cadillac
Fleetwood sedan. He was preceded by a 1961 Chevrolet carryall and

trailed by a former U.S. Army GMC six-by-six truck.

The carryall and the truck were full of heavily armed, neatly uni-
formed parachutists of the Armée Nationale Congolaise; and an ANC
major was at the wheel of the Cadillac, which was the vehicle assigned
for the use of Colonel Joseph-Désiré Mobutu.

Hurricane fence surrounded the airfield. When the little procession
reached the gate, ANC soldiers there rushed to unlock the padlock in the
chain sealing it. While this was going on, the ANC Major kept his hand
on the horn ring, and then the soldiers saluted, somewhat unevenly, as
the convoy passed through the gate.

"Major," Jean-Philippe Portet ordered, leaning forward, "drive over
to that U.S. Army airplane."

The Major turned and looked at him in surprise and confusion.

"Do what I say!" Portet snapped.

The Cadillac turned toward the L-23, dutifully followed by the GMC
six-by-six. The carryall drove another five hundred yards toward the Air
Simba hangar before the driver became aware he was no longer leading
his convoy. There was a squeal of brakes as the carryall suddenly
stopped, and then a clash of gears and the sound of a siren starting to
whine as the carryall started up again and made a wide, sweeping turn
across the wide concrete parking area in pursuit of the Cadillac and the
truck.

Geoff Craig and Pappy Hodges, both in flight suits, turned from their
inspection of the L-23 as the Cadillac approached.

"Jesus Christ, now what?" Geoff said, and then he saw Jean-Philippe
in the back seat.

Jean-Philippe got out of the Cadillac. He was carrying a leather briefcase. The Major driving the Cadillac got out quickly, setting an example
for the twenty-odd paratroopers in the six-by-six. They jumped to the
ground, working the actions of their FN 7mm rifles at the same time,
then formed a protective circle around the Cadillac and the airplane,
training their rifles menacingly outward. They appeared to be having a
very good time.

Jean-Philippe Portet walked close to Geoff, looked into his face for a
moment, and then impulsively hugged him.

"Well," Geoff said, "what's with you and the chocolate soldiers?"

"Easy, Geoff," Pappy Hodges said, softly but firmly.

Jean-Philippe raised the briefcase. "For Hoare," he said.

"What do you mean, for Hoare?"

"Money—three quarters of a million dollars in Swiss and American money," Jean-Philippe said. "I'm taking it to him. That's why the soldiers. I just left Tshombe and Mobutu."

"You really think he'll be able to do any good?"

"He did the last time he was in the Congo."

"Any word from Stanleyville?"

"The consulate radio is still operating. So is the Belgian Consulate's," Jean-Philippe said.

"That's not what I meant," Goeff said.

"My Hanni and Jeanine are with your Ursula, Geoff," Jean-Philippe said. "I know what you mean."

"Well?" Geoff demanded, ignoring the rebuke.

"I spoke, from the Belgian Embassy, to Nothomb—"

"Who's he?"

"A bright young man, about your age, an acquaintance of mine, who is the Belgian Consul General in Stanleyville. He said that he'd spoken with Hanni. She's in the Air Simba apartment in Immoquateur and doing fine."

"Ursula?" Geoff asked. His voice was at the edge of breaking.

"We have to presume, Geoff," Jean-Philippe said, "that if he talked with Hanni, he knows about Ursula and Jiffy. And I'm sure there would have been some hint if anything was wrong. Nothomb didn't seem especially concerned, to tell you the truth."

"Well, fuck him!" Geoff flared. "'Not especially concerned!' I'll be goddamned!"

"I meant to suggest, Geoff," Jean-Philippe said, "that Nothomb was trying to put me at ease, that he sees no immediate danger."

"I talked to Father Lunsford," Geoff said. "I know Father Lunsford. I don't know about this fucking friend of yours, but I know when Father Lunsford tells me something you can take it to the bank. And Lunsford told me what these fucking savages are doing! Christ, they're cannibals! No immediate danger, my ass! What the hell is the matter with you, anyway?"

"Geoff—" Jean-Philippe began gently.

Pappy Hodges interrupted him.

"Excuse me, Captain Portet," Hodges said. "This is my business." He stepped in front of Geoff. "Look at me and pay attention, because I'm only going to say this one time, kid."

"What?" Geoff snapped.

"The Military Attaché asked me what about you," Pappy said. "He thinks you're too emotionally involved to be reliable. He wants to ship your ass out of here, not only keep you out of the way while people who haven't lost their cool do what has to be done. I told him you were the most levelheaded sonofabitch I had ever known. And I told him how you got your battlefield commission in 'Nam. So you're here, and we're starting to do what has to be done. Like soldiers. One more example of you getting hysterical like that, forgetting you're a soldier, and I'll have the Attaché ship your ass out of here so quick your asshole won't catch up for a week."

Geoff glowered at him. His mouth worked. "Yes, Sir," he said finally.

"I'm telling you like it is," Pappy said. "I can't afford you if you can't control yourself."

"I got the message, Pappy."

"I hope so," Pappy said. He sounded tired.

"What are you up to?" Jean-Philippe asked.

Geoff looked at Pappy. After a moment Pappy nodded.

"We're going to go to Kamina," Geoff said. "And then to Punia. There's four H-34s at Kamina plus a couple more supposed to be en route. We can stage them at Punia. Then we jump in the Berets near Stanleyville at night. They take the consulate and hold it long enough— thirty minutes ought to do it—for the H-34s to land and make the evacuation."

"And what do you think the Simbas will be doing while you're doing this?" Jean-Philippe asked.

"If we can we're going to pick up Father Lunsford and ask him," Geoff said. "It's feasible. Twenty guys who know what they're doing can accomplish amazing things."

Wishful thinking, Jean-Philippe thought. *But saying so will accomplish nothing.*

He looked at his watch.

"The sooner I get airborne," he said, "the sooner Michael Hoare will have his money."

[SIX]
Washington, D.C.
5 August 1964

FLASH FLASH

APWASH 8133

WASHINGTON—THE WHITE HOUSE ANNOUNCED AT 2:13 PM
THIS AFTERNOON THAT US NAVY AIRCRAFT OPERATING
FROM A NAVAL TASK FORCE IN THE GULF OF TONKIN HAVE
BOMBED NAVAL INSTALLATIONS IN NORTH VIETNAM.

PRESIDENT LYNDON B. JOHNSON ORDERED THE "SURGICAL
STRIKE" IN RETALIATION FOR THE NORTH VIETNAMESE
TORPEDO BOAT ATTACK ON THE US NAVY DESTROYERS MAD-
DOX AND TURNER JOY IN INTERNATIONAL WATERS IN THE
GULF OF TONKIN.

SEVERE DAMAGE WAS REPORTED TO DOCKS AND FUEL STOR-
AGE FACILITIES IN PORTS FROM WHICH NORTH VIETNAM IS
KNOWN TO OPERATE TORPEDO BOATS. ALL AIRCRAFT IN-
VOLVED IN THE ATTACK RETURNED SAFELY FROM THE MIS-
SION.

[SEVEN]
The Immoquateur Apartments
Stanleyville, Democratic Republic of the Congo
6 August 1964

ONCE THE SIMBAS HAD LEFT the Consulate Building, Warrant
Officer Joe Manley had volunteered to go into town and have a look
around.

The polite fiction was that he was to establish contact with the Armée
Nationale Congolaise and learn from them their plans to either recapture

the city or make an attempt to rescue the consulate and other American personnel.

As he made his way through the backyards of the comfortable houses lining the Avenue Eisenhower, the only members of the ANC he saw were dead, their corpses lying where they had fallen. Many of them were mutilated. They had been slashed, he judged, by machetes.

Since he had been in the vault when the consulate was invaded, and the door was of course closed, he had yet to get a look at any member of General Olenga's Army of Liberation, the Simbas. Now the Simbas— the first ones he had ever seen—were all over, and they were worse than he expected.

Some of them wore uniforms. This suggested at least that they were officers. Some looked like incredibly slovenly troops. And some looked, Manley thought, like extras in a old Johnny Weissmuller Tarzan movie. They were barechested and barefoot, their faces were marked with mud, and they had animal skins draped over their shoulders.

It was difficult to accept that this rabble had defeated armed, organized troops, but that seemed to be the simple truth.

And then some Simbas saw him.

They set out, from Avenue Eisenhower, after him. Not quite sure where he was going, he ran up and down alleys expecting any moment to hear a burst of automatic weapons fire. But none came, and finally when he looked over his shoulder to see if his pursuers were gaining on him, there was no one in sight. He ran a little farther until he could run no more, and then stepped inside what had only the day before been a stationery store. The shelves had been ripped from the walls toward the center of the room, and their contents were scattered everywhere.

Manley climbed to the center of the room over the rubble and found a sort of cave, where the high shelves from one wall had fallen onto a desk. He would stay there out of sight until dark, he decided,

By the time he got his breath back, there had been time to reach an unnerving conclusion. The Simbas who had been after him had given up the chase not because he had gotten away from them, but because further pursuit on their part would have been a waste of effort. He was a white man in a city surrounded by hundreds of miles of jungle. There was no way he could get out of town, and even if he could do that, no way to get through the jungle.

It finally grew dark, and then to his great surprise, the street lights came on. When he finally gathered his courage enough to look very carefully out the door, he saw lights in homes and offices, and then, incredibly, Europeans walking along the streets. Quickly and nervously to be sure, obviously anxious to get where they were going as quickly as possible, but still on the streets.

He thought that over for a couple of minutes.

Lieutenant Craig, the young Army aviator who had flown the unmarked L-19 into Punia, had told him when he returned that he had heard from an absolutely reliable source that the Simbas actually practiced cannibalism. Young Craig obviously believed that, whether or not it were true.

Manley resolved, very calmly, that if it were true, and these fucking people did decide to hack him up with a machete prior to broiling his liver, he would do a John Wayne. He would take as many of them with him as he could.

And the way to do that was to get to his apartment in the Immoquateur. There, in a carefully hollowed out book, *The Indian Campaigns of General Philip Sheridan* ("borrowed" from the library at Vint Hill Farms Station, Virginia, where he had undergone the last stage of cryptographic training), was a Colt 1911A1 automatic pistol and two spare magazines. He had taken the pistol from the body of a Marine lieutenant as X U.S. Corps had retreated from the Yalu in December of '50. It was in the hollowed-out book because, among other chickenshit regulations that went with this assignment, there had been a regulation that absolutely forbade personally owned firearms.

He got as far as the elevator in the Immoquateur without being seen, and there he found himself looking down the open end of an FN 7mm barrel.

"*Que voulez-vous?*" the Simba asked.

Shit, that bastard doesn't speak French any better than I do.

"*Ici, mon maison,*" Manley said.

"*Maison?*"

"*Oui, mon maison,*" Manley said imperiously.

"*Bon,*" the Simba said, smiling and lowering the Fabrique Nationale. "*Bonsoir, M'sieu.*"

"Bonne soir yourself, you cocksucker."

Manley got on the elevator and rode to the fourth floor.

Someone had been in the apartment. His Zenith Transoceanic portable radio was gone, he saw immediately.

But nobody had bothered his books.

He went and took *The Indian Campaigns of General Philip Sheridan* from the bookcase, opened it, and shook the Colt loose. He removed the magazine, saw that it was full, replaced it, and worked the action. Then he took the two spare magazines and put them in his trousers pockets.

Then he sat there in the dark, holding the pistol.

The telephone rang.

He looked at in disbelief. A telephone, with cannibals running the town?

But then he remembered the power plant was obviously still in operation, so why not the telephone?

He picked it up.

"Manley."

It was the Consul General. He had been "concerned" about him and thought he would "give the apartment a try."

"Did you plan to come back here tonight?"

"Not unless you want me to," Manley said.

"No need," the Consul General said. "If you think you could, why don't you check out the building and see if you can find out how many Americans are there."

"Yes, Sir," Manley said.

"I'll see you in the morning then," the Consul General said and hung up.

He did not, Manley thought, even ask if he had found the ANC, and if so, what the ANC had had to say.

[EIGHT]
Johannesburg, South Africa
7 August 1964

E MBASSY OF THE UNITED STATES OF AMERICA, good morning."

"Mr. Edward T. Watson, please," the caller said. He had a slight German accent.

"Just one moment, Sir."

"Hello?"

"Mr. Edward T. Watson, please."

"I'm sorry, he's not here at the moment. May I take a message? Or have him return your call?"

"Would you please tell him that I wish he were here, the wild geese are flying?"

"You must be Ed's Cousin Karl."

"That's right."

"Well, I'll get that message to him within a few minutes."

"You're very kind."

"Karl?"

"Yes?"

"Good luck, Karl. Take care of yourself."

"Thank you."

That afternoon the following advertisement appeared in the Johannesburg, South Africa, *Times of South Africa:* "Any fit young man looking for employment with a difference at a salary well in excess of 100 Pounds monthly should telephone Johannesburg 2323 during business hours. Employment is initially offered for six months. Immediate start."

The next day the same advertisement, differing only in the telephone number to be called in Salisbury, Rhodesia, appeared in the *Salisbury Morning News and Bulletin.*

XVIII

[ONE]
The Immoquateur Apartments
Stanleyville, Democratic Republic of the Congo
5 August 1964

THERE WAS A THREE-QUARTER MOON reflecting off the sheet-steel roofs of the warehouses on the other side of the Congo River. The surface of the river itself was so smooth that there was a remarkably clear reflection of the moon on it. Hannelore Portet, leaning on the concrete railing of the balcony of the Air Simba apartment, could smell hibiscus.

A few minutes earlier she had heard the washing machine start up, which meant Ursula was washing the day's diapers, and she was not surprised when Ursula came out onto the balcony a minute or so later.

"I guess his Royal Highness has given his slaves the rest of the night off?" Hanni said, speaking German.

Ursula made a grunting noise that could have been a chuckle.

"Mary Magdalene is rocking him to sleep," she said. "Jeanine is asleep. She fell asleep reading *Playboy*."

"When I was her age, my parents had a doctor book," Hanni said. "We used to sneak it out and look at the pictures."

Ursula made the grunting noise again.

"What's going to happen to us, Hanni?" Ursula asked.

"I wondered when you were going to get around to asking," Hanni said. "About the only answer I can give you is that we wait."

"That's not much of an answer."

"I both like and love you," Hanni said. "I love you because you're sweet and a good mother, and you're good for Jeanine. And I like you because you're tough. I don't think many people, including Geoff, know how tough you are."

"I'm not tough," Ursula said. "I'm scared to death."

"But you're competent. You get done what needs to be done. And you're not hysterical. You haven't started crying."

"I have," Ursula said. "I woke up in the middle of the night and cried. I want to go home!"

"You haven't let Jeanine see you," Hanni said. "Or Mary Magdalene."

"What good would that do?"

"I'm scared too," Hanni said. "And I know that us being here is my fault."

"Don't be silly."

"Why silly? If I hadn't played the *grande dame,* been *Madame Chef Pilote,* we would have been aboard that airplane when it took off."

"That's ridiculous," Ursula said.

"But I was, and here I am with my daughter, and you, and Jiffy, surrounded by *les sauvages* on a rampage."

"I don't want to hear any more of that," Ursula said. "I want you to tell me what's going to happen. And I'd rather you hadn't said 'the savages,' thank you just the same."

"But that's what they are," Hanni said. "I'm a mother. I understand them."

"You're a mother?" Ursula said, incredulously. "You understand them?"

"I've raised a child," Hanni said. "And as you are about to find out, I've seen signs already. Children are savages. They have to be taught how to behave. No one has ever taught *les sauvages* to behave."

"You're serious, aren't you?"

"Absolutely," Hanni said. "It was sinful what the Belgians did here, granting independence overnight. It was like giving a loaded gun and the keys to a car to a six-year-old. Something like this was bound to happen. And you can no more blame the savages who came out of the bush and who think they're freeing their country from colonialism than you can blame a small child for cutting himself after you gave him a knife. They just don't know any better."

"They know how to use their knives," Ursula said.

Hanni didn't reply for a moment. "I don't know what's going to happen," she said finally. "I don't have any idea. You never know what's going to happen in the Congo."

"They are killing people every day," Ursula said. "Beating them to death. Cutting them up with big knives . . . what do you call them? 'Machetes.'"

"So far no Europeans," Hanni said.

"So far," Ursula said. "But how long will that last?"

"I have been thinking positive," Hanni said. "Did you ever read that book?"

"What?"

"A book. Written by an American. *The Power of Positive Thinking.*"

"No, I haven't," Ursula said, a tone of impatience, even annoyance, in her voice.

"The idea in it is that you think of the best that you can do rather than of the worst things that can happen."

"That's foolish."

"Olenga and the Simbas are mad at the Americans," Hanni said, ignoring her. "They seem to be going out of the way not to offend the Belgians or any other Europeans. Because of my husband, I've got a Belgian passport, and Jeanine is Belgian, and you still have your German passport. That's positive."

"But I came here on an American passport and there's no Congolese visa on my German one. And Jiffy's on my American passport."

"I've hidden your American passport," Hanni said. "Just to be safe. Your German passport will be enough. If you are actually asked for it, the man who asks will probably be illiterate. If it is not an American passport, that will be good enough."

"Hanni!" Ursula said, sadly, disbelievingly.

"We have food, and we can buy more," Hanni said. "There was five thousand dollars in Swiss francs in the safe here. Fuel money, in case we had to send an airplane somewhere where you needed cash for fuel."

Seeing the look on Ursula's face, she decided to try humor.

"When the plane arrives tomorrow to take us home, I don't know what we'll do with all the condensed milk. Mary Magdalene took me at my word when I told her to buy all she could. We have eight cases. There's no shortage of bread or chickens. Beef may not be on the menu for long—"

"And if the plane doesn't come tomorrow?" Ursula interrupted, not amused. "Or the day after that? Or next month? Or never?"

"There will be a plane," Hanni said. "Jean-Philippe will probably be flying it."

"I hope it gets here before the Simbas run out of Congolese to hack to death," Ursula said, "and start coming after the Europeans."

Hanni met her eyes. "So do I, *Liebchen*," she said finally. "And I really think it will."

"Geoff must be going out of his mind."

"See, you're learning," Hanni chuckled.

"Huh?"

"You're thinking positively," Hanni said. "You're feeling sorry for somebody else, not yourself."

"Ach, Gott!" Ursula said in exasperation. But she smiled, and that, Hanni decided, was a good thing.

[TWO]
Camp David, Maryland
8 August 1964

THE WORLD was far more interested in the Gulf of Tonkin Resolution passed by the Congress the day before (the *Washington Post* had already called it a "blank check to the President to do whatever he wanted in Indochina") than in the plight of a handful of Americans in a remote city in the middle of Africa.

Nor was the remote possibility of a small-scale American intervention in the Congo nearly as important as the immediate certainty of American intervention on a massive scale in Vietnam.

Consequently, when the President—having so far ignored what had happened in Stanleyville—turned the meeting he was presiding over toward the question of public relations, foreign and domestic, vis-à-vis possible American actions in Southeast Asia, Felter reasoned that his presence would be no longer required at the meeting. As quietly as he could, he closed his briefcase and walked toward the door.

"Where the hell are you going?" the President of the United States called out to him sharply and unpleasantly. "Goddamn it, Colonel, you can leave when I tell you you can. Who the hell do you think you are?"

Felter resumed his seat.

Felter's public humiliation pleased the Director of the United States Information Agency even more than it pleased the Director of the CIA and other high-ranking officials in the room.

The Director of the USIA, a holdover from the Kennedy Administration, was a friend and confidant of the Attorney General. Bobby Kennedy and he had once agreed that since every great man had to be permitted one enormous fault in judgment, Colonel Sanford T. Felter had to be Jack Kennedy's. His choice of Lyndon Baines Johnson as his vice president did not count, of course, since Johnson delivered Texas and a few other Southern states.

After President Kennedy's assassination, they had both been surprised when Felter was noticeably absent from the first Kennedy aides replaced. Johnson, for some odd reason, actually seemed to *like* him, even though he was in the habit of referring to Colonel Felter in terms that were insulting in several ways at once. When Johnson had learned that Felter's White House switchboard and Secret Service code name was "the Mouse," for example, he offered that he thought of him as "the Snip." And then, grinning with delight, he added that a snip was what fell to the floor after Jewish ritual circumcision.

But Johnson had kept Felter on, and it had quickly become apparent that he was treating Felter as Jack Kennedy had, with respect. This was bad enough. But worse, he shared confidences with him that he shared with no one else. No one knew what Felter was doing or where he would show up. Just that whatever he was doing was done for the President. And wherever he showed up, and whenever he asked for something, he was doing so with the authority of the President.

One of the theories advanced was that Johnson, who knew how his Attorney General and USIA Director loathed Felter, kept him on to remind them who was now the President.

It might be a little premature, the Director of the USIA decided, to interpret the President's humiliation of Felter as the first sign he was growing tired of him. But it was a possibility, and the Director of the USIA was pleased.

"Now I want to see Wheeler," the President said when he'd had enough of public relations. He aimed his finger at the Chairman of the Joint Chiefs of Staff, "and you, Earl," pointing at the Director of the USIA, "and you and you and you," indicating the Deputy Director of the CIA, the Secretary of State, and Colonel Sanford T. Felter. "The rest can go."

The President of the United States wanted to know what was going on in Stanleyville and who was doing what about it.

"The best information we have, Mr. President," the Deputy Director of the CIA said, "is that our people there are in no immediate physical danger—"

"What about the rescue mission?" the President asked impatiently, cutting him off.

"It was not feasible, Mr. President," Felter said.

"Mr. President," the Director of the USIA said, "I'm hearing this for the first time. What rescue mission?"

"Tell Earl, Felter," the President ordered.

"It was at one time contemplated attempting to evacuate consular personnel by helicopter, using assets already in the Congo—" Felter said.

"You're talking about the use of American military personnel?" the Director of the USIA interrupted incredulously.

"Shut up, Earl, and listen," the President said. "When we're finished, if you have any questions you can ask them." He turned to Felter. "Why wasn't it feasible?"

"One, we could not mount a force of sufficient strength to insure success," Felter said. "Two, even if we had gotten lucky and managed to get the consular personnel out, we almost certainly could not have gotten them all out. And three, I was advised that Olenga was very likely to retaliate against all Europeans—not only against any Americans still there—after a rescue attempt."

"Advised by who?"

Felter was obviously reluctant to answer the question.

"You mean he's still with them? And you're still in contact with him?"

"Yes, Sir," Felter said.

"May I ask who 'he' is?" the CIA Director asked.

"A Green Beret captain," the President said. "Apparently one hell of a man."

"It was my understanding," the Director of USIA said, "that whatever our options were in the Stanleyville situation, they did not include the use of United States military personnel."

"In other words," the President said to Felter, ignoring the Director, "nothing's going to happen right away?"

"Aside from what the CIA can do to help in the near term," Felter began, "and a plan I'd like to ask your permission—"

"It was my understanding," the Director of the USIA said doggedly, "that the question of the use of U.S. military personnel was pretty well decided. That there would be none, in other words, unless there is—"

"That's all, Earl," the President interrupted him. "You can run along."

There was an awkward silence as the Director of the USIA gathered his papers together, closed his attaché case, and walked out of the room.

[THREE]
Kamina Airfield
Katanga Province
Democratic Republic of the Congo
22 August 1964

THE AIR SIMBA Curtiss Commando, under charter to the Ministry of Transportation of the Democratic Republic of the Congo, made a rather steep approach to the runway, pulled up, and then dove at it again. Just in time, the pilot pulled back on the stick. The Commando was now in straight and level flight twenty feet off the runway. The pilot chopped the throttles and the aircraft settled so smoothly onto the runway that only the sudden rumble of the wheels announced that it had returned to earth.

Karl-Heinz Wagner, wearing the camouflage pattern coveralls and the pips of a captain of the Armée Nationale Congolaise, sat on the floor of the cabin, his back braced against the rear bulkhead. While the Commando was still slowing on its landing roll, as soon as he could get to his feet he went to the door and with an enormous shove forced it open. Air rushed into the cabin, warm, very humid, but fresh.

Karl-Heinz stood by the door, taking deep breaths.

The Commando had neither passenger seats nor provisions for either cabin pressurization or passenger oxygen. It had been a bumpy ride from a small airfield near Johannesburg. The Commando had not been able to climb above the regular afternoon low-altitude thunderstorms and the turbulence they caused. A dozen of the forty men aboard had been airsick. And worse.

The interior of the cabin smelled of vomit and feces. He himself had been very afraid that he was going to throw up. But he did think it behooved an officer, even an officer commanding scum of the earth like these, to avoid getting sick to his stomach. And he was just a little annoyed with Lieutenant Colonel Michael Hoare, who almost immediately after takeoff went into the cockpit and closed the door after him.

When the Commando was finally moved into its parking spot, there was a strong temptation to just jump off onto the ground. He could not do that, for two reasons: one, the cabin floor was too high off the ground to jump safely; and, two, an officer sees to his men before looking to his own personal comfort.

In English, and sharply, Captain Wagner ordered a sergeant to get the ladder in place. And then he ordered the Sergeant to debark first, to line the men up in the shade of the wing, and to keep them there.

Then he stood in the door and watched, his face expressionless, as the troops debarked.

A jeep drove up to the plane. It was a civilian jeep, Wagner noticed, painted olive drab to give it a military appearance. But it had thickly padded seats and a fold-down door in the back. He wondered if it would be otherwise identical to a military jeep; specifically whether the floor would be strong enough to hold a .50 caliber machine-gun mount.

Hoare came bustling down the cabin. He was wearing the pips of a major. Although he had been promoted to lieutenant colonel, the proper insignia had not been available in South Africa. Wagner's captaincy— his promotion from lieutenant—had been one of Lieutenant Colonel Hoare's first official acts.

"You're a good man to have around, Karl-Heinz," Hoare had told him the night before when the list of people on the first airlift (including Wagner) was announced. "You're a natural soldier."

Now Hoare spoke to him again. "Don't let them scatter all over," he said. "I'll go find out what's going on."

"Yes, Sir," Wagner said, and then saluted when Hoare drove off in the jeep.

When the last of the mercenaries had gone down the ladder from the cabin, Wagner climbed down it himself.

He looked at the men standing under the wing and wondered which of them had shit their pants. And what right now he was supposed to do about it.

Then he saw two men sitting on the ground, thumbing cartridges into magazines. He walked over to them.

"Anyone tell you to do that?" he asked levelly.

They looked up at him. Both seemed puzzled. One of them shook his head no.

"I am an officer," Karl-Heinz said. "When I or any other officer talks to you, you say, 'Yes, Sir' or 'No, Sir.' You don't shake your head."

They didn't like that.

"I asked you a question," Karl-Heinz said. "Did anyone tell you to load those magazines?"

Obviously, to judge by the look on their faces, no one had. And, just as obviously, they were deciding how to deal with the problem that had so pissed off the Captain.

Wagner was about to tell them to unload the magazines and not to charge them again until they were ordered to do so when one of the sergeants walked up behind one of them, put his boot in the center of his back, and shoved. The mercenary, a thin-faced South African with bad teeth, was sent sprawling on his face and stomach.

"You miserable sodding shit," the Sergeant said, raising his booted foot to the back of the other one. "You get to your sodding feet when an officer talks to you!"

The second mercenary scurried out of the way of the Sergeant's boot on all fours. The Sergeant ran after him, caught up with him, and applied his boot to his rear end. He went sprawling. Then he got to his feet and assumed what he believed to be the position of attention.

The first mercenary saw what the other had done, got to his feet, and stood to attention. He was now facing the runway. The second mercenary was ten feet away, facing the line of hangars.

The Sergeant went to the first mercenary, grabbed him by the arm, and dragged him into line with the first.

He put his hands on his hips and moved his face within inches of the first mercenary, then, spraying him with spittle, furiously announced; "The next sodding cartridge you load without being ordered, I will shove up your asshole!"

Then he stepped neatly in front of the second mercenary and glowered at him.

Karl-Heinz decided he would have a word with the Sergeant about kicking people, but this was not the time or place for it. "Sergeant," he said.

The Sergeant turned and stamped his foot in the British manner.

"*Sir!*"

"At the first opportunity, have those two men collect whatever soiled underwear there is and rinse it out."

"Sir!"

Karl-Heinz turned and faced the others. "No one is to load any weapon without specific orders. "I thought I had made that clear."

And then he saw the jeep. It was an American jeep, and Lieutenant Geoffrey Craig, wearing a flight suit, was at the wheel.

Geoff got out of the jeep and walked toward Karl-Heinz. There was neither a smile nor a sign of recognition on his face. Geoff saluted.

"Captain, may I see you a moment, please?"

Karl-Heinz returned the salute. "Carry on, Sergeant!"

"Sir!"

He followed Geoff to the rear of the airplane.

"Ursula and the baby are in Stanleyville," Geoff said.

"Ach, du lieber Gott!"

"So is Father Lunsford," Geoff said. "Father is now a captain in the Simbas."

"What about them?" Karl-Heinz asked, even as he realized that if there were bad news—worse news than that Ursula and the baby were in Stanleyville—he would have already been told.

"Father says they're all right," Goeff said. "The Simbas think they're Belgian, or at least not Americans."

"What the hell are they doing in Stanleyville?"

"Leopoldville was socked in," Geoff explained. "The UTA pilot decided to sit down in Stanleyville overnight. Hanni . . . Madame Portet?"

Karl-Heinz nodded.

"She wasn't going to spend the night in the Sabena guest house—"

"What's that?"

"Sort of a motel for stranded travelers," Geoff explained. "So she got off the airplane and went to the apartment Air Simba keeps downtown. The UTA pilot, the cocksucker, when he heard the Simbas were coming, took off without them."

"And nothing has been done to get them out?"

"You're it," Geoff said.

"That's all?"

"We wanted to go in with a couple of H-34s and the A-Teams, but they decided it was too risky."

"Who decided that?" Karl-Heinz asked, coldly angry.

"Felter made the call. But it was based on what Father Lunsford thought."

"I feel sick to my stomach," Karl-Heinz confessed.

"What they should have done was drop the 502nd in here," Geoff said.

The 82nd Airborne Division, at Fort Bragg, North Carolina, of which the 502nd Parachute Regiment was part, was charged with being the first U.S. Army unit to move into action. One regiment was always on standby, combat-loaded. The Air Force kept sufficient transports on immediate standby at the adjacent Pope Air Force Base to fly a regiment anywhere in the world.

"With what's happening in Vietnam," Karl-Heinz said, "it's probably a question of priorities. He may have to send the 82nd Airborne over there."

"And maybe the sonofabitch doesn't want to do anything that might make him lose the election," Geoff said.

Karl-Heinz shrugged. "What are you doing here?"

"Mostly standing around with my finger up my ass," Geoff said. "We try to keep an eye on the Simbas. Once a day, at night, I fly over there and try to talk to Father."

"How many people does he have with him?"

"He ran everybody else out," Geoff said. "The Simbas kill each other, especially if they get a little suspicious. Father is the only one who really speaks Jungle Bunny."

"They're here?" Karl-Heinz said.

Geoff nodded. "Some of them."

"Get to them, make sure nobody shows they know me," Karl-Heinz said.

"I'm way ahead of you. I was about to say the same thing to you."

"What do you mean?"

"You guys are going to be the point when you head for Albertville," Geoff said. "You will be accompanied by units of the Armée Nationale Congolaise."

Karl-Heinz nodded his understanding of that, but he was still confused.

"If you see familiar black faces in the ranks of your support forces," Geoff said, "don't smile and say 'Hi, there, Sergeant Portley, long time no see, how's the wife and kids?'"

"Portley's here? He's going with us?"

"Of course not. The participation of American personnel in any combat operation of the ANC is expressly forbidden."

"I don't understand," Karl-Heinz said.

At that moment an ANC corporal, a short, squat, very black man in battered, mostly unlaced boots, his web equipment hanging loosely over his mussed and sweat-soaked fatigues, came trotting across the airfield, carrying his FN assault rifle by the muzzle.

He was smiling broadly. When he reached Karl-Heinz and Geoff, he stopped, came to an absurd approximation of the position of "attention," and loosing a quick torrent of Swahili, saluted in the British manner with his palm outward.

Karl-Heinz returned the salute, a conditioned reflex reaction. *"Mein Gott!"* he said.

"What do you say, Dutch?" the ANC Corporal said. "Long time no see."

"I suppose you two think this is funny," Karl-Heinz said.

"Funny?" Sergeant First Class Edward C. Portley said. "Why funny? I'm just doing what I'm told. I was over there sunning my ass when some Limey honky wearing major's pips points his finger at me and says, in really *bad* French, by the way, 'You, there, Corporal, go out to the airplane and tell the Captain I wish to see him.'"

Geoff started to laugh, and it was contagious.

The mercenaries under the wing of the Commando looked at them curiously.

[FOUR]
Kamembe Airfield
Republic of Rwanda
28 August 1964

ENRICO DE LA SANTIAGO, wearing a gray cotton USAF tropical-climate flight suit, put his wallet, his gold bracelet (because his name was engraved on it), and everything else that could identify him into a manila envelope and then walked to a table behind which sat two men in civilian clothing.

"How about your watch?" one of the men asked.

"I forgot," de la Santiago said and unsnapped it from his wrist. The stainless-steel back of the Rolex was engraved *Enrico de la Santiago, con amor, Louise, 12/12/60.*

The man behind the table took it and put it into the manila envelope. Then he handed him a stainless-steel Omega chronometer. Enrico wound it several turns to start it and then pulled the stem out.

"Seven oh eight," the man behind the desk said, and Enrico set the time and pushed the stem in.

The second man went to de la Santiago and patted him down to make sure that there was not in any of the many zippered pockets of the flight suit a second wallet, or a photograph, or anything else that could identify him.

De la Santiago felt humiliated. He understood the rules and the reasons behind them, but it was still too much like a criminal being searched.

"Clean," the man, an American, said.

Enrico walked to the next table, where a cardboard tray was pushed to him. The tray held a heavy, sealed manila envelope in which there was supposed to be a thousand dollars' worth of gold Swiss francs and two thousand dollars in Belgian, French, and Swiss currency.

De la Santiago put the envelope in the lower left ankle pocket of the flight suit and closed the zipper. Then he took a Michelin road map— "Congo Belge 1:20,000"—and put that in the lower right ankle pocket of the flight suit.

Next, he picked up a Smith & Wesson .357 Magnum revolver, loaded it with the six cartridges lying in the cardboard tray, and slipped it into a shoulder holster. He was aware that he had become the obstruction in the pipeline. The other pilots, having given up all their personal property, were lining up behind him.

He put the shoulder holster on. There were a dozen other .357 cartridges in loops on the webbing that ran over his right shoulder. Finally he picked up the last item in the cardboard tray. It was a clipboard to which was clipped a plastic-covered aerial navigation chart and two grease pencils.

Then he stepped away from the table and went to the door. There was a white Chevrolet carryall waiting there, with the Air Simba winged lion painted on its doors. It was, he realized, the one he had ridden into Bukavu with Jack Portet the first time he had ever come to Kamembe, in the right seat of an Air Simba Commando.

He got in the front seat beside the driver and waited for the others to draw their equipment. When they were all inside, he turned on the seat.

"We won't make a production of this," he said. "I'll take off as soon as you all check in and fly down the river. Form up on me, in a line, not too close."

There was a murmured chorus of, *"Sí, Captain."*

He was no longer a captain. He was a civilian employee of a company called Supportaire, Inc., which allegedly had its home office in Nicaragua. But of the five pilots who would fly with him today, four had been in the Cuban Air Force, before Fidel, and remembered him from then.

The carryall drove down the parking ramp. When it reached the first T-28 it stopped and one of the pilots got out. Then it drove another hundred feet to the next T-28, where a second pilot got out, and so on down the line until it reached the last plane, which de la Santiago would fly.

There were three people at each aircraft. Two white men and an ANC officer in a flight suit. The white men, Americans, employees of Supportaire, Inc., were the crew chief and the armorer. The Congolese was officially the reason for the flight. He was to observe the Simbas on the ground. It was certainly within the sovereign rights of a nation to dispatch its officers to reconnoiter its own territory when that territory was in the hands of insurrectionists. Just as legal as Union Cavalry patrols reconnoitering Northern Virginia when it was under the control of General Lee of the insurrectionists.

And if that sovereign government wished to contract for the services of a civilian firm to facilitate the reconnoitering by flying the observer around, that was their legal right, too. And if the reconnoitering aircraft were fired upon, certainly an officer about the legal business of his sovereign government had the right to defend himself, even to strike back.

Six hardpoints had been added beneath the wings of the T-28s, a low-wing, single 1425hp piston-engine aircraft originally designed to serve as trainers for the U.S. Air Force and Navy. Each hardpoint could carry a bomb, or a cluster of rockets, or a machine-gun pod.

The T-28s on the Kamembe parking ramp were armed with bombs, rockets, and machine guns, although not all in the same way. There was a shortage of rockets. All had machine guns and bombs.

The Congolese Lieutenant who would fly with de la Santiago looked more than a little nervous, but he smiled and saluted and offered a polite *"Bonjour, M'sieu,"* as de la Santiago got out of the carryall.

He followed de la Santiago as he preflighted the airplane, looking over his shoulder as de la Santiago probed inside access ports and drained gas from the wing tanks, checking for water.

"Put a 'chute on him, will you please?" de la Santiago said to the crew chief as he picked his own chute up and shrugged into it.

Then he climbed on the wing root. And then, pushed from behind by the crew chief and hauled upward by de la Santiago, the Congolese Lieutenant struggled onto the wing and then into the front seat.

Enrico crossed himself, climbed in, and strapped himself in. The crew chief handed him a helmet, then strapped the Congolese officer in and handed him a helmet.

As soon as the crew chief was on the ground, de la Santiago called, "Clear," and started the engine.

As it was warming up, he checked with the other five pilots. They were all running and ready.

"Kamembe, Congo Hawk."

"Go."

"Ready for takeoff."

"How are you going to do it?"

The voice from the tower was obviously American and probably, de la Santiago thought, yet another employee of the oh so helpful Support-aire, Inc.

"Thirty-second intervals," de la Santiago said.

"Kamembe clears Congo Air Force Hawk flight as number one to take off on the active, at thirty-second intervals. There is no traffic in the immediate area. The winds are negligible. The altimeter is two niner eight fiver. The time is thirty-two past the hour."

"Hawk one taxiing to the active," de la Santiago said, releasing the brakes and nudging the throttle open. By the time he reached the threshold, everything was in the green. He stopped just long enough to close the canopy and to test the mags.

"Hawk one, rolling," he said to the microphone and pushed the throttle forward.

He broke ground and pulled the wheels up, went into a very shallow climb, due south, over the Ruzizi River, and waited for the others to catch up.

Hawk flight was headed for Albertville, via Uvira.

The Simba rebellion had begun in Albertville, on the western shore of Lake Tanganyika. Olenga's columns had moved northward along the shoreline and taken Uvira, which is near the northern end of Lake Tanganyika and then pushed on northward toward Bukavu at the southern tip of Lake Kivu and northwest to Stanleyville.

A line down the middle of Lake Tanganyika is the international border. At its lower end it's the border between the Republic of the Congo and Rwanda, and for the upper seventy-five miles, between the Republic of the Congo and Burundi, in what once had been German East Africa.

Bujumbura, the capital of Burundi, is almost in a straight line across the northern tip of Lake Tanganyika from Uvira. The Ruzizi River, which enters Lake Tanganyika at its extreme tip, is the international demarcation between the Republic of the Congo and Burundi for sixty miles farther northward. There, about twenty miles south of Bukavu, the Ruzizi River becomes the northern border of the Republic of Rwanda.

Olenga and his Simba army had failed to take Bukavu. Two things had happened. A remarkable ANC officer, Colonel Leonard Mulamba, was by coincidence in Bukavu. When he saw the situation deteriorating, he arranged for the ANC Commander to go to Leopoldville for "consultation" and assumed command himself.

Colonel Mulamba, who was short, stocky, and in his mid-thirties, put on a steel helmet and began his command by reminding his officers that the penalty for cowardice in the face of the enemy was death. He reminded them further that it was Simba practice to execute captured officers in the most unpleasant way they could dream up. That gave them, he said, two options: getting shot for cowardice by their own army or being beaten or slashed to death by the Simbas. Except, of course, for the third option, which was to stand and fight.

And then something useful happened. The Republic of Rwanda, learning that the Chinese (communist) Embassy in Bujumbura in adjacent Burundi was arming Rwandan insurgents and encouraging them to take over the Rwanda government, informed Joseph-Désiré Mobutu, Commander-in-Chief of the Congolese Armed Forces, that Kamembe Airfield, across the Ruzizi from Bukavu, was open to him for any purpose he desired.

The first planes into Kamembe had been T-28s, which, because of range limitations, had previously been unable to come to Colonel Mulamba's assistance. They struck at Olenga's Simbas and then landed at Kamembe. Their engines had barely time to cool before the first transport aircraft from Leopoldville and Kamina began to land, bearing fuel, troops, ammunition, rations, and even a couple of jeeps.

Inspired by both Colonel Mulamba's strong leadership and the sight of aircraft coming to their aid, the ANC chased Olenga's Simbas from Bukavu.

It was his first defeat. And it was now intended to hit him again while he was still reeling. Albertville was to be retaken, and then Uvira, and ultimately Stanleyville.

Hawk flight was part of that plan.

Ten minutes after breaking ground at Kamembe, Enrico de la Santiago looked over his shoulder to make sure that everybody was on his tail and then pushed the nose of the T-28 down and lowered his flaps. He flew down the road at 2500 feet until he saw a half dozen, maybe eight, trucks behind a crude barrier.

"Hawk leader," he said to his microphone, "two and I will take out those trucks. The rest maintain your positions."

He pushed the nose down again and flew toward the trucks.

"One bomb each," he said to the microphone.

"Roger," number two replied.

De la Santiago's 250-pound bomb landed in the middle of the trucks. The 250-pound bomb from the second T-28 missed the mark by at least a hundred yards. The pilot had been excited, Enrico de la Santiago thought, and dropped it early. It didn't matter. The trucks were destroyed.

He pulled the flaps up and climbed slowly back to 2500 feet.

"Three and four," he ordered. "Strafe targets of opportunity in Uvira . . . trucks if possible. Five and six, when we're past the city, you take the point and strafe, or bomb, if you think it's worth a bomb, anything that looks worthwhile. But save some ordnance for Albertville itself. And we'll come back the same way."

Hawk flight had taken off at 0732. They were back on the ground at Kamembe at 1005. All of their ordnance had been expended. De la Santiago estimated to the debriefing officer, to whom he had taken an instant dislike, that they had destroyed twenty-two vehicles, mostly trucks; had probably inflicted wounds on one hundred people; and that, when the flight had reached Uvira on the trip back without having encountered any previous targets worthy of that exotic ordnance, he had ordered the expenditure of the rockets on the Hotel Uvira.

"Christ, why did you do that? You know we're short of rockets."

"I presumed the senior officers of the force would establish themselves in the hotel."

"That was a bad choice," the debriefing officer said.

"Fuck you," de la Santiago said evenly and got up. "If you want to make on-the-spot decisions, get in the front seat."

Then he walked out. The Air Simba carryall took the pilots to the Hôtel Lac Kivu in Bukavu. They showered and then sat on the balcony off the dining room, drinking the very good local beer and throwing the empties off the balcony into the clear blue waters of the lake below.

By the time it was dark, they were a little drunk, and they talked about Camagüey, and Bayamo, and Cienfuegos, and Havana. De la Santiago noticed that one of them was gone and went looking for him. He found him around the side of the hotel, very drunk, leaning on the wall.

"Rico," he asked when he saw de la Santiago, "what do you think my Manuelo looks like now?"

"Like you, unfortunately," de la Santiago said.

"He's nine now," the mercenary pilot said. "No longer a baby."

"I know," de la Santiago said. "My oldest is twelve."

"Oh, my *God*!" the mercenary pilot said. "I *miss* them!

"Me, too," de la Santiago said. "Go to bed, Manuel. We're flying in the morning."

XIX

[ONE]
Near Albertville, Democratic Republic of the Congo
30 August 1964

CAPTAIN KARL-HEINZ WAGNER sat behind the wheel of his jeep, which was parked to one side of the road. A sergeant sat beside him and a private stood in the rear of the jeep, ready to fire the pedestal-mounted Browning .50 caliber air-cooled machine gun.

The rest of what the English-speaking mercenaries had begun to call "The Congo Foreign Legion" were lined up beside the road. The jeeps of small trucks were pulled to alternate sides of the road and separated by enough distance so that should it be necessary they could make a wide sweeping turn and head in the other direction.

They heard the sound of Lieutenant Colonel "Mad Mike" Hoare's jeep before they saw it coming back. Hoare had decided to make this reconnaissance himself, with only a sergeant to man the Browning in his jeep going along with him.

When he reached Karl-Heinz's jeep, Hoare stopped.

"Don't see a goddamn thing," he said, and then added: "Get out, Sergeant. And you please, Captain, come with me."

Karl-Heinz got out of his jeep and into Hoare's. He was not surprised at being asked to go off with Hoare. A commander often wishes to say things to his officers he doesn't want anyone else to hear.

Hoare, from time to time calling out softly to officers and noncoms, drove to the end of the assault element (that is to say, to the end of The Congo Foreign Legion's vehicles) and then continued down the road through and past the vehicles of the reinforced company of Armée Nationale Congolaise infantry.

Two hundred yards behind and out of sight of the last vehicle, he stopped the jeep in the middle of the road and got out. There was virtually no shoulder here; there was thick tropical growth within feet of both sides of the worn macadam two-lane road.

"We need to talk," Hoare said to Karl-Heinz.

Hoare was carrying a Sten 9mm submachine gun suspended from his shoulder by a web strap. Even though the strap was there, he had his hand on it. There was no way to tell whether he had his hand on it that way to keep it from slipping off his shoulder or because he thought he might shortly—and suddenly—have to use it.

And in that instant Karl-Heinz knew that Hoare was not going to discuss the attack on Albertville.

He got out of the jeep, leaving his FN assault rifle behind. He had a Browning 9mm automatic in a canvas holster hanging from his web belt, but there was no way he could get near it.

"That's far enough, Karl," Hoare said when Karl-Heinz was perhaps ten feet from him.

"I beg your pardon?" Karl-Heinz said, but he stopped in his tracks.

"You're a good officer, Karl," Hoare said. "I'm sure you're familiar with what von Clausewitz had to say about surprises—that a commander can't afford any."

"I'm not sure I know what you mean."

"From this moment on, Wagner," Hoare said, "no evasions. No playing around with words. We're about to get this show started and I don't have the time to toy with you."

Karl-Heinz nodded.

"There is an ANC corporal who is really an American Green Beret," Hoare said. "A technical sergeant, I believe. He seems to know you rather well. I want an explanation of that."

They locked eyes for a moment.

I cannot successfully lie to this man. More important, I do not want to.

"Sergeant Portley," Karl-Heinz said. "We served in Vietnam together."

"You told me—and somebody went to a good deal of trouble to make sure there were records to support it—that you had served in the East

German Army and had escaped over the Berlin Wall. You told me that, Karl, and I believed you."

"It's true, Mike," Karl-Heinz said.

"And now you're telling me you were a Green Beret in the American Army?"

"I am," Karl-Heinz said. "I mean, I am presently a Green Beret officer . . . a lieutenant."

"CIA? Is that it?"

"No. Not CIA. The only man the CIA had on you is the one you suspected and left behind."

"Then what?"

"I was sent to South Africa to keep an eye on you. I can't tell you more than that except that it was not by the CIA."

"For what purpose?"

"There is a man . . . at the highest levels—do I make that point?— who wanted someone with you who could give him an accurate assessment of your strengths and weaknesses and plans."

"That's espionage," Hoare said.

"That's intelligence. Neutral. Espionage is conducted by an enemy. This man is not an enemy."

"And you have been making reports on us?"

Karl-Heinz nodded.

"That's treason," Hoare said coldly.

"Same argument, Colonel," Karl-Heinz said. "I have not furnished information to your enemies."

"Can you give me one reason I should not end this academic discussion of who you are loyal to and why in what seems to me to be the only practical way?"

"My sister and nephew are in Stanleyville," Karl-Heinz said. "Under those circumstances you could reasonably presume my unquestioning loyalty until we take Stanleyville."

Hoare's surprise showed on his face, but he didn't respond.

"And you need me, Colonel. Most of your officers are a joke."

Hoare's eyes tightened.

"What are your sister—and your nephew, you said?—doing in Stanleyville?"

"A UTA flight to Leopoldville stranded them there."

Hoare exhaled audibly. "The bloody damned thing is that I want desperately to believe you."

"I have told you the truth, Colonel," Karl-Heinz said simply.

"You are a cold-blooded bastard, aren't you?" Hoare said, surprise and a touch of admiration in his voice. "You're not even afraid."

"I am *very* afraid," Karl-Heinz said. "Not so much of dying, but of drying before I can do something to help my sister and my nephew."

The two looked into each other's eyes for a moment.

And then Hoare shrugged. "I do need you," he said. "And I really would have hated to shoot you."

He put out his hand.

"Thank you," Karl-Heinz said, and then, formally: "I stand at your orders, Colonel."

"Friendlies coming through!" an obviously American voice called out from ten feet inside the thick bush. "Friendlies coming through!"

Mad Mike Hoare looked at Karl-Heinz Wagner, who was shaking his head and smiling.

Two black men in ANC uniforms crashed through the brush and onto the road, one of them a very small, fragile-appearing man wearing PFC stripes, the other "Corporal" Portley. They both carried FN 7mm assault rifles.

"I'm glad you and Dutch came to an agreement," Portley said. "You look like a pretty good officer, Colonel. I would have hated to blow you away."

Hoare looked as if he were going to say something and then changed his mind about saying what had popped into it.

"And you, I presume," he said to the very small, fragile-appearing PFC, "are also an American Green Beret sergeant?"

The small man saluted crisply. "Actually, Sir, I'm a first lieutenant. Williamson is my name, Colonel."

Thirty minutes later The Congo Foreign Legion, following a softening attack with rockets, bombs, and machine-gun fire from T-28 aircraft, marched on Albertville, essentially following the American tactic of reconnaissance by fire. They fired at everything that moved and at every place that might have housed a machine-gun position, or a rifleman, or a half-naked African armed with a spear. In an hour they had swept the city clean of Simbas. No prisoners were taken.

[TWO]
The Presidential Apartments
The White House
Washington, D.C.
2100 Hours 1 September 1964

WHEN THE DIRECTOR of the United States information Agency
was ushered into the Presidential sitting room, he tried but did not quite
manage to keep a look of annoyance and displeasure off his face—he saw
that he was not to have five minutes alone with the President of the
United States. Colonel Sanford T. Felter was in the room, sitting on the
edge of a armchair, talking on the telephone.

"Get him a cup of coffee," the President said to a white-jacketed
steward as he waved an impatient finger at the Director of the USIA.
Then he looked at him. "Be right with you, Earl," he said.

The implication was clear. Everything was on hold until Felter got off
the telephone.

"OK," Felter said, and hung up without saying goodbye. He looked
at the President and shook his head. The President shrugged, as if he
expected bad news.

"OK, Earl. What's up?"

"I appreciate your making time for me, Mr. President," the Director
of the USIA said. "I really thought it was necessary."

"I'm sure you did," the President said impatiently.

The Director of the USIA waited just long enough to be sure that
Felter was not going to leave.

"I'm sure, Mr. President," the USIA chief said, "that you are familiar
with the Leo cable concerning the missionary report that the rebels
intend to hold all Stanleyville Americans and Europeans hostage?"

The President nodded. The USIA chief handed him, nevertheless, a
copy of the cable, and then went on: "And with the one from the
Ambassador in Bujumbura, vis-à-vis the plea of the Catholic bishop?"

He handed a second cable to the President, who glanced at it quickly
and then handed both to Felter.

Felter glanced over them. He had seen both of them hours before.
The cable from the U.S. Embassy in Leopoldville simply passed on to
the State Department what had been reported to it by both (American)

Roman Catholic and Christian Missionary Alliance missionaries; that they had heard the rebel-controlled Radio Stanleyville announce that Europeans and Americans in Stanleyville would be held hostage until Moishe Tshombe's government stopped using mercenaries. Radio Stanleyville, referring to the mercenaries as *"Les Affreux,"* "The Horrible Ones," had gone on for nearly an hour about the criminal and uncivilized behavior of the mercenaries who had retaken Albertville.

The cable from the U.S. Embassy in Bujumbura, Burundi, relayed an appeal from the (Italian) Roman Catholic Bishop of Uvira addressed to the President of the United States. The Bishop said that following the bombing and strafing attack on Uvira, the "People's Liberation Army" had summarily executed two Italians. On behalf of himself, twelve priests, nine nuns, and six laymen, the Bishop pleaded with the President of the United States to call off all bombing.

"We've seen these, Earl," the President said. "So what's on your mind?"

"It has come to my attention, Mr. President," the USIA chief said, "that the Bishop—the Italian one—has sent a copy of his cable to the Vatican and to the Maryknoll religious community here. I don't know what the Vatican will do, of course, but I have it on very reliable authority that the Maryknoll priests plan to call a news conference, in which they will condemn all United States military intervention in the Congo."

"Let me tell you something, Earl," the President said. "Pay attention. There's two things going on in the Congo. One, which pisses me off mightily, is a bunch of jungle bunnies invading a U.S. Consulate and pissing on the American flag. I would love to do something about that. But I'm the President of the United States, and my name is Johnson, not Teddy Roosevelt; and this is now, not a long time ago; and I can't send the Marines—as much as I'd like to. . . . But understand me good, Earl. What the Maryknoll priests or the Vatican think is right or wrong has nothing to do with that decision. You understand all that?"

"Yes, of course, Mr. President," the Director of the USIA said. His lips were tight.

"The other thing that's going on in the Congo," the President said, "is that the Chinese communists, cheered on by the Soviets, are behind that lunatic Olenga. It's entirely likely that they'll misjudge me and go further than the President of the United States can let them go. If that happens, if it looks to me as if they stand a chance to take over the Congo, I'll do whatever I think is in the best interests of the United

States. By that I mean military intervention. And if the Maryknoll priests, or anybody else, don't like it, fuck 'em. If they want to run things, let them run for office. Right now *I* hold the office."

"I brought the issue up, Mr. President," the Director of the USIA said, "solely to inform you of a potentially difficult public-relations situation. I believe that is my duty."

"It is—and you do it well. But let me add to your burden, Earl. *I* have it on very reliable authority that until Felter managed to get it on hold—not stop it, just put it on hold—tomorrow's *Wall Street Journal, New York Times, Los Angeles Times,* plus of course the *Washington Post,* and every other major newspaper in the country, would have carried a full-page advertisement, signed by some of the most prominent people in the country. Under a banner headline reading "Shame!" it would have questioned this administration's handling of the Stanleyville Problem."

"I don't understand, Mr. President," the chief of USIA said.

"You ever heard of Craig, Powell, Kenyon and Dawes, Earl?"

"The investment bankers?"

The President nodded. "The Chairman of the Board is a man named Porter Craig. His daughter-in-law and his first and only grandchild—a baby boy—are in Stanleyville. I knew he was rich and powerful, Earl, but I was surprised to find how many prominent Democrats are more afraid of him than they are of me . . . and were willing to sign their names to his advertisement."

The announcement obviously greatly surprised the Director of the USIA.

"Did I understand you to say, Mr. President, that the advertisement will not run?"

"Felter's got it on hold, I said. I don't know how long that will last."

"How did you do that?" the Director of the USIA asked Felter, greatly surprised.

Felter looked at the President.

"Tell him," Johnson ordered.

"Mr. Porter Craig is close to an Army officer," Felter said carefully. "I managed to convince that officer that we are already doing everything that can be done, and that such an advertisement, at this time, would be counterproductive."

"Watch out, Earl," the President said. "I'm getting the idea that Felter's pretty good doing what you're supposed to do. Maybe he's really after your job."

"Mr. President," Felter asked, "may I show the Director the U Thant intercept?"

"Yeah, why not?" the President said after a moment's hesitation.

It was the first document classified Top Secret—Presidential Eyes Only that the head of the USIA had ever seen.

It reported that at 1705 Hours 30 September the Defense Intelligence Agency had intercepted and decrypted a message from the Swiss Foreign Ministry to the Swiss Ambassador to the United States. The Swiss Ambassador was directed to pass on to UN General Secretary U Thant a message from Lieutenant General Nicholas Olenga, Commander-in-Chief of the People's Army of Liberation in Stanleyville. In the message Olenga warned U Thant that he was holding five hundred hostages—"white men, women, and children"—against "any air raids by the Congolese government." He accused the UN, the International Red Cross, and the World Health Organization of an "imperialist plot."

"Well," the USIA chief said, "this will help of course. World opinion will go against him. In a public-relations sense, threatening women and children is not the thing to do."

"You can't use it," the President said. "Not until—if—U Thant releases it."

"I beg your pardon?"

"And I wouldn't take any heavy bets that he will ever release it," the President said. "He's had it since seven o'clock last night, and so far not a peep out of him. I think the sonofabitch agrees with your assessment that threatening children is stupid, and he wants to protect those bastards from their own stupidity."

"But Mr. President, we have it!" the USIA chief said.

"It was a tough call," the President said. "In the end I decided the price was too high. If we let that out, the Swiss will know we've broken their unbreakable code. Not only would that highly piss them off, but we wouldn't get to read any more of their mail for a while. Some of the Swiss mail is very interesting, Earl."

The telephone rang. The President pushed the flashing button and picked the instrument up. "Yeah?" he said, listened a moment. "OK. Delay him a couple of minutes and then send him up. McCone, too, when he gets here."

He replaced the phone.

"That's General Wheeler," the President said to Felter. "Do you want to see him?"

"No, Sir."

"OK," the President said. "Do what has to be done, Felter."

"Yes, Sir."

"Mr. President," the head of the USIA said. "How am I supposed to handle this?"

"Just keep pissing on the flaming embers, Earl. And keep your mouth shut about that U Thant intercept. So far, in the White House only you, me, and Felter have seen it."

[THREE]
Fort Bragg, North Carolina
1305 Hours 2 September 1964

THE COMMANDING GENERAL of the U.S. Army Special Warfare Center (ex officio, the senior Green Beret of the U.S. Army) and the Commanding Officer of the 7th Special Forces Group did not at the moment look either ferocious or even much like professional warriors.

Brigadier General Paul T. Hanrahan was wearing a pale-yellow, short-sleeved, knit-cotton shirt over aquamarine trousers. Colonel Edwin P. Mitchell was wearing an orange short-sleeved shirt over blue-and-yellow plaid trousers. They were wearing identical caps, blue-and-yellow plaid with a fuzzy yellow tassel. Their wives, separately and coincidentally, had bought the caps for them on sale in the PX.

When General Hanrahan told his wife that Ed Mitchell had an identical cap, she said she was surprised. Patricia Hanrahan said she personally thought it so ugly that no one else would buy one. It had, she pointed out, been marked down three times from $6.95 to ninety-nine cents. And she added that she had bought it as a joke, never thinking he would have the balls to actually wear it in public. It had not been a very satisfactory husband-wife confrontation.

And, of course, after that he had to wear it.

He wondered what Ed Mitchell thought of his cap. He had never asked.

General Hanrahan and Colonel Mitchell had a standing golf date for 1300 on Wednesdays. There was almost a military purpose to it. For one thing, with command came a lot of time sitting on your ass; and if nothing else golf provided the exercise of a long walk. And playing on Wednesday afternoons served two purposes: It broke the workweek exactly in half. And the course was not busy in the middle of the week. That kept him from competing for available weekend space with officers and soldiers who did not have the prerogative of commanding officers to take off when they damned well pleased. And finally, they always played alone, which allowed then to exchange confidences as they walked down the fairways that would have been difficult to discuss elsewhere. Hanrahan ran the school; Mitchell commanded the resident group. They usually had a lot to talk about.

And finally, since they played together, no one was privy to their scorecards. This removed the temptation of their juniors to mock them. It was a rare day indeed when either of them managed to get around in under ninety.

They had just moved from the first green to the second tee when a jeep came cutting across the grass toward them. Hanrahan glanced at it and saw it was festooned with antennae. His aide-de-camp was sitting beside the driver.

It drove up to them and the aide-de-camp jumped out and saluted. Hanrahan returned it.

"I don't think you're required to salute people wearing plaid hats with tassels," Hanrahan said. "But thank you anyway. What's up, Charley?"

"A Chief warrant officer named Finton called, Sir. Colonel Mitchell is to stand by at Pope from 1415. He is to have uniforms for five days."

"Who the hell is CWO Finton?" Ed Mitchell asked.

"Sandy Felter's gofer," Hanrahan said. "I gather this was in the nature of an order, Charley?"

"Yes, Sir. He said that if you, General, have any questions, Colonel Felter will answer them sometime later today when he has access to a scrambler phone."

"That's a little autocratic, isn't it?" Mitchell said.

Hanrahan looked at his watch. "You've got an hour and ten minutes, Ed," he said. "Is that going to be enough?"

"Yes, Sir."

They put their golf bags into the jeep. Colonel Mitchell and the aide-de-camp crowded uncomfortably into the back seat and General Hanrahan got in the front. The jeep returned in the direction it had come. As it moved across the course, a golf cart driven by an obviously annoyed master sergeant, the golf course manager, headed to intercept

it: *That goddamned jeep is leaving ruts all over my goddamned fairway!*
And then he saw who was in the front seat and turned away.

When Colonel Mitchell got to Base Operations at Pope Air Force Base
at 1355, there was an Air Force CT-39E, a small, twin-engine jet transport, waiting for him. An hour and fifteen minutes later it dropped him
off before Base Operations at McDill Air Force Base, Florida.

At 1525, two hours and twenty-five minutes from the moment he had
teed off at the Fort Bragg golf course, Colonel Mitchell entered the office
of the Commander-in-Chief, United States Strike Command.

The STRICOM J-2, Colonel Sanford T. Felter, Lieutenant Colonel
Craig W. Lowell, and a major whom Colonel Mitchell did not recognize
were on their knees, bent over a half-dozen maps which took up about
all the floor space there was between the furniture.

Colonel Ed Mitchell did not think, under the circumstances, that he
should salute.

"Good afternoon, General," he said.

General Matthew J. Evans, CINC STRICOM, who was supporting
himself on all fours, looked up.

"Hello, Ed," he said. "I understand we got you off the golf course."

"No problem, Sir."

"You heard about the Americans in Stanleyville, I suppose?"

"Yes, Sir."

"There is a possibility, repeat, *possibility*, that we may be authorized
to go get them," General Evans said. "Felter rates the chances at one in
three."

"Yes, Sir?"

"Get down on your knees with the rest of us, Ed, take a quick look,
and then tell us if you think you could get in there with two, three,
maybe four A-Teams and carry it off."

"Yes, Sir."

It was not the first time that Colonel Ed Mitchell had seen a map of
Stanleyville or considered how he would go about getting the U.S.
Consular staff out. He had given it a good deal of thought from the time he
had seen the first stories in the newspapers. But no one had asked him
whether he had thought about it and he did not volunteer the information.

He studied the maps for about ten minutes.

"Has anyone given this any previous study?" he asked.

"Not in specifics," General Evans said. "Off the top of your head, Ed,
please."

"I would night-drop three teams on the Stanleyville side of the Congo River, by moonlight if possible, if not then with a good radar vector," Mitchell said. "They would go downriver in rubber boats, infiltrate the consulate compound, secure it, and radio for extraction by H-34s orbiting out of sound. With a little bit of luck the infiltration of the consulate compound could be accomplished silently. If that were possible, then the first warning the Simbas would have that something was going on would be when the choppers started landing. In the worst possible scenario . . . fighting into the compound and then holding it . . . we would have the advantage of darkness. I don't want to sound esoteric, but if we had half a dozen infrared-scoped rifles, I don't think the Simbas would be too eager to attack in the dark."

"Why do I suspect, Ed," Craig Lowell asked, "that this has run through your mind before?"

"I've got two hot A-Teams just looking for honest employment, Lowell," Mitchell said.

"You're talking about landing upstream and floating downstream?" the J-2 asked.

"Yes, Sir."

"What about the Stanley Falls?" Lowell asked.

"What about them?" General Evans asked.

"Can you get over them? For that matter, where exactly are they?"

"Major?" General Evans asked.

"Sir," the Major said, visibly discomfited, "I just don't know."

"You're supposed to be the AIS," Felter said coldly—the Area Intelligence Specialist.

"No, Sir. I mean—I'm standing in for him," the Major stammered.

"I sent the AIS over there to work with Dills," General Evans said. "Major Ashe is just filling in. And he's done a good job, too."

"Sorry, Major," Felter said. "I didn't mean to jump on you. But, Jesus Christ, everybody in the world has heard of the Stanley Falls, and here we sit ready to jump on them, and apparently nobody knows exactly what or where they are!"

"Sandy, I've looked," Mitchell said. "I even looked in the goddamned *National Geographic*."

"We can have an answer—probably—from Leopoldville in twelve hours. Less, if you want to radio for it," the J-2 said.

"Or I can get the AIS back here in say thirty-six hours," General Evans said.

"I respectfully suggest, Sir," Felter said, "that the AIS is of more use where he is." Then he chuckled.

"What's funny?" General Evans said.

"I'm about to utter a military profundity," Felter said. "If you don't know what you're doing, ask a PFC."

The J-2, Colonel Ed Mitchell, and the AIS Major looked at him in confusion. Lieutenant Colonel Lowell and then General Evans chuckled.

Felter reached for one of the telephones on General Evans' desk. "Sergeant, this is Colonel Felter. Rig up a scrambler to CWO Finton in my office in Washington, will you, please?"

"Ed," Felter said, "while you're doing your planning, have a shot about infiltrating the Immoquateur Apartment Building . . ." He stopped and leaned forward and pointed it out on the map. "And picking up a half-dozen American dependents, either on your way in, your way out, or as a separate, concurrent operation."

"OK," Colonel Mitchell said. "What are dependents doing—"

He was interrupted by the intercom.

"Colonel Felter, the scrambler line is in, but Mr. Finton is not available. I have a Miss Dunne on the line."

Felter stood up and picked up the telephone.

"Mary Margaret, do you know where to find Finton?" he asked. She replied and then Felter said, "Well, get over there. Don't phone, go. And tell him I said, as priority one, to have him get PFC Portet on the first plane out of Berlin to Bragg. He is to report to Colonel Edwin Mitchell—that's right, two ells—at the 7th Special Forces Group. And then when you've done that, please call my wife and tell her there's no way I can get home before Sunday. Tell her I'm sorry, but something has come up and she'll just have to go to temple alone."

"Who is this PFC Port— What did you say?" Ed Mitchell asked.

"Portet," Lowell replied. "He's one of our more well traveled PFCs, Ed. More to the point, he knows Stanleyville."

"More to the point, Ed," Felter said, "his stepmother and half sister are in the Immoquateur Apartment."

"What's he doing in Berlin?" Mitchell asked.

"Sandy sent him there to hide him from the hand-wringers and other spineless types in the State Department, the JCS, and around the President," CINC STRICOM said.

[FOUR]
Fayetteville Municipal Airport
Fayetteville, North Carolina
4 September 1964

PFC JACK PORTET was tired. His uniform was not only mussed but soaked by the rain between the Piedmont airplane and the terminal. And he needed a shave. But first things first. He collected his dufflebag from the baggage carousel, threw it over his shoulder, and looked for a telephone.

"Seventh Group, Sergeant Major Oliver, Sir!"

"Sergeant, my name is Portet. PFC Portet. I was told to call this number."

"Where are you?"

"At the airport in Fayetteville."

"Hold on," the Sergeant Major said. And then, as if he had put his hand over the microphone, Jack could hear him go on: "Colonel, Portet's at the Fayetteville airport. What do I do now? They can't fly in this shit."

"Go in the coffee shop and wait," the Sergeant Major went on, his voice now clear. "You in uniform?"

"Yes."

"EUCOM patch? Berlin rope?"

Members of the Berlin garrison were part of the European Command and wore that shoulder insignia. In addition they wore from their right epaulet a red, black, and white fourragère, a woven, black, red, and white cord with a brass tip.

"Yes."

"Somebody will be there to fetch you in twenty minutes," the Sergeant Major said and hung up.

Jack started to bend over and pick up his duffle bag and then changed his mind. He counted the change in his pocket, then went and changed two dollars into quarters.

"First National Bank."

"Deposit two dollars and forty cents, please."

"Miss Marjorie Bellmon, please."

Two eons and a century and a half later:

"Marjorie Bellmon." There was no immediate reply. "Hello?"

"Hi."

"Jack!"

"Hi."

"Honey, where are you?"

"In the airport at Fayetteville, North Carolina."

"What are you doing there?"

"I don't know," he said. "I can make some interesting guesses."

"How long have been in the States?"

"About five hours," he said. "I'm waiting for somebody to pick me up."

"You don't know who? Or you can't tell me?"

"They gave me the phone number of some colonel—Mitchell—and my orders read '7th SFG,' whatever the hell that means."

"Seventh Special Forces Group," she said. "That'd be Colonel Ed Mitchell. He's a friend of Daddy's and of Uncle Sandy's."

"I wonder why that doesn't surprise me. Anyway, you didn't hear it from me. And for God's sake don't tell your father."

She giggled.

"How's the car?"

"Not 'How are you?' Just how's the car?"

"What did you do, run it into something?"

"You can go to hell, Jack Portet!"

"I love you," he said. "Was that what you were fishing for?"

"Absolutely."

"And now I wait, with bated breath, for a reply in kind."

"I can't do that, for the obvious reason."

"I don't care if anybody knows," he said. "You do, I guess."

"I love you," she said.

"Much better."

"When can you come here?"

"Don't hold your breath," Jack said. "As soon as I find out something I'll call you back."

"But you are going to be there a while?"

"Honey, I don't know. I feel like a shuttlecock."

"As soon as you know *anything*, you call me."

"If I ever get close to a phone again, I'll call anyway," Jack said. "You want to say it again?"

"I don't think that's possible under the circumstances."

"Well, we now know who feels strongest about who, don't we?"

"Deposit one dollar and thirty cents for an additional three minutes, please."

"I don't have it," Jack said.

"I love you, Jack," Marjorie said.

The line went dead.

He hung up the phone and replayed the sound of her voice in his ears for a moment, and then picked up his duffle bag and went looking for the coffee shop. He ordered a cup of coffee and a doughnut, and then saw a newspaper in a rack by the cash register. The word CONGO in a headline halfway down the page caught his eye and he got up and bought the paper.

The full headline was: UN'S U THANT REPORTS AMERICANS IN CONGO CONSIDERED REBEL HOSTAGES.

Twenty minutes later Jack was so deep in thought that he didn't see the man in camouflage fatigues approaching until he had slid into a chair at the table.

"Portet?"

"Yeah."

"Finish your coffee," the man said. And only then did Jack see that he wore the bars of a captain on his collar points.

Jack looked at him. "I didn't see the bars," he said.

"No sweat," the Captain said. He put out his hand. "My name is Stacey."

Jack shook his hand. "What's going on? Am I allowed to ask?"

"First you finish your coffee," Captain Stacey said. "And then you put this on and we walk out of here and get in my truck."

He pushed a green beret across the table.

"What the hell is that? I'm not a Green Beret!"

"The first and great commandment around here, Portet, is that you do what you're told. *Then* you can ask questions."

Jack looked at him and saw that he was serious. He shrugged and put the green beret on.

"Very good," Captain Stacey said. "And to complete my response to your interrogatory, PFC Portet, after we get in my truck, we will drive to the boonies where my associates and I are making plans to get your stepmother and stepsister back where they belong."

Jack looked at him and saw that the Captain was dead serious about that, too.

"Really?" he asked.

Captain Stacey nodded.

XX

[ONE]
Leopoldville, Democratic Republic of the Congo
6 September 1964

URGENT
FROM US EMBASSY LEOPOLDVILLE DEM REPCONGO
TO SECSTATE WASH DC
STANLEYVILLE SITUATION UPDATE AS OF 2400 ZULU
5 SEPTEMBER 1964
INTELSOURCE RATING ONE PAREN 1 PAREN REPORTS CON-
SULGEN STANLEYVILLE AND STAFF REMAIN CONFINED MILI-
TARY PRISON CAMP KETELE STANLEYVILLE. SUBJECTED TO
VERBAL AND PHYSICAL ABUSE. SOURCE BELIEVES THEIR
LIVES ARE IN DANGER BUT HAS NO REPEAT NO EVIDENCE TO
SUPPORT.
SAMESOURCE REPORTS NO REPEAT NO EVIDENCE OF CHICOM
SUPPLY OF OLENGA EXCEPT POSSIBILITY SMALL ARMS AND
FUEL, ALL UNTRACEABLE.
SAMESOURCE REPORTS THAT AT 0900 5 SEPTEMBER STANLEY-
VILLE TIME, AT CEREMONIES AT LUMUMBA MONUMENT,
OLENGA PROCLAIMED QUOTE PEOPLE'S REPUBLIC OF CONGO
ENDQUOTE WITH CHRISTOPHE GBENYE AS PRESIDENT AND
GASTON EMILE SOUMILAUT AS MINISTER OF DEFENSE.

SAMESOURCE BELIEVES POWER REMAINS WITH OLENGA. USAMBASSADOR CONCURS.

SAMESOURCE INSISTS FOLLOWING BE RELAYED VERBATIM UNSPECIFIED ADDRESSEE WASHINGTON QUOTE IN VIEW APPARENT INABILITY FURNISH US MILITARY ASSISTANCE RESPECTFULLY REQUEST DISPATCH PEACE CORPS VOLUNTEERS TEACH PUBLIC SANITATION AS PROTOCOL OFFICERS DID NOT BOTHER TO WASH BLOOD FROM MASSACRE OF HUNDREDS FROM LUMUMBA MONUMENT PRIOR PROCLAMATION OF PEOPLE'S REPUBLIC OF CONGO THUS CREATING UNHEALTHY ENVIRONMENT FLIES MAGGOTS ETCETERA ENDQUOTE

SAMESOURCE UNDENIABLY SHOWING SIGNS OF STRESS DUE TO LENGTH AND NATURE OF ASSIGNMENT. REPLACEMENT IMPOSSIBLE AT THIS TIME. SUGGEST ACKNOWLEDGMENT OF SAMESOURCE MESSAGE INDICATING RECEIPT AT HIGHEST ECHELON.

DANNELLY DEPUTY CHIEF OF MISSION

★★★★★★★★★★★★★

URGENT
FROM WHITE HOUSE WASHINGTON
TO US EMBASSY LEOPOLDVILLE DEM REPCONGO
PERSONAL ATTENTION US AMBASSADOR
REFERENCE YOUR 5 SEPTEMBER STANLEYVILLE UPDATE
BY DIRECTION OF THE PRESIDENT RELAY FOLLOWING FIRST OPPORTUNITY QUOTE TEX STUDYING YOUR PEACECORPS SUGGESTION REGARDS SMALL JEWISH SOLDIER UNQUOTE
FELTER COLONEL GSC USA COUNSELOR TO THE PRESIDENT

[TWO]
The U.S. Army Special Warfare Center
Fort Bragg, North Carolina
0745 Hours 12 September 1964

"Gᴇɴᴇʀᴀʟ Hᴀɴʀᴀʜᴀɴ's quarters."

"Mrs. Hanrahan?"

"Yes, it is."

"Mrs. Hanrahan, this is Marjorie Bellmon. Bob Bellmon's daughter?"

"Oh, yes. Hello, Marjorie. It's nice to hear your voice. How's your family?"

"Just fine, thank you. Is General Hanrahan there? Could I speak to him, please?"

"Oh, I'm sorry, Marjorie, he's not. Is there anything I can do? Can I give him a message?"

"No, ma'am," Marjorie said, and then: "Daddy asked me to give him something personally while I was here."

"Oh, you're here?"

"Yes, ma'am."

"I expect him for lunch," Patricia Hanrahan said. "Why don't you come over here and have lunch with us? I'm sure he'd love to see you, too."

"I would love to, but I'm just leaving. Is there any way—"

"He's at the office," Patricia Hanrahan said. "I'd send you over there, but I don't think he'll have time to see you."

"Well, then, I'll just drop it by your quarters before I leave. Thank you, ma'am."

"Marjorie—" Patricia Hanrahan said, but by then Marjorie had hung up.

Marjorie left the pay station in the lobby of the Main Officer's Club and went out and got in the Jaguar.

Since I have already proven how skilled a liar and how devious a human being I am, I might as well see just how far I can get before I get stopped.

She drove to Smoke Bomb Hill and parked Jack's Jaguar outside the headquarters building of the U.S. Army Center for Special Warfare in a space reserved for official visitors.

Then she walked to the door. It was locked. She knocked on it. A sergeant first class, obviously the duty NCO, opened the door a crack. He looked at her—approvingly, she decided—and then at the red Jaguar in the parking lot.

"Ma'am, we're closed for the weekend," he said.

"I'm here to see General Hanrahan."

"Ma'am . . ."

"Mrs. Hanrahan said that when he takes a break, you're to tell him I'm here. My name is Bellmon."

He looked at her dubiously but finally concluded that as devious as the bastards might be, he didn't think the Russians would be clever enough to send a well-stacked broad like this one, driving a red Jaguar, to penetrate the headquarters of the Center for Special Warfare.

"I don't know how long he's going to be in there," the Sergeant said as he opened the door for her.

"Thank you," Marjorie said.

She had to wait twenty minutes, during which the Sergeant offered her a cup of coffee and a doughnut. And she gratefully accepted; the last thing she'd had to eat was at three, when she'd stopped for gas.

She chatted with the Sergeant and told him the truth, but not the whole truth. She told him that she was an Army brat, and that her father was stationed at Fort Rucker.

And then a door opened down a corridor and the Sergeant jumped up from his desk. "Wait here please, ma'am," he said and went down the corridor.

A minute later General Red Hanrahan appeared in fatigues.

"Here she is, Sir," the Sergeant announced.

"Hello, Marjorie," General Hanrahan said. "What's going on?"

"I want to see Jack Portet," Marjorie said. "I'm sorry to bother you, General, but I was over at 7th Group, and they said they never heard of him."

General Hanrahan did not reply.

"I know he's here," Marjorie said firmly.

"Sergeant," General Hanrahan said after a moment, "would you go in there and ask Sergeant Portet to come out here, please?"

Sergeant Portet?

Jack appeared a minute later. He was in fatigues and jump boots, and there were sergeant's chevrons on the sleeve.

"This young lady wishes to see you, Sergeant," General Hanrahan said. "I've been wondering how she knew you were here."

Jack looked at General Hanrahan and then at Marjorie.

"What the hell are you doing here?" he asked.

"I wanted to be with you," Marjorie said simply.

"Marjorie, does your father know Jack is here?" General Hanrahan asked.

"No, Sir."

"Does he know *you're* here?"

"No, Sir."

"How did you get here?" Jack asked.

"I drove your car," Marjorie said.

"Sergeant," General Hanrahan said to the noncom on duty, "you and I will walk down the corridor for exactly five minutes, following which Miss Bellmon is going to go over to my quarters. . . . You will telephone Mrs. Hanrahan and tell her she's coming and say that I asked her to entertain Miss Bellmon until I get there. Until Sergeant Portet and I get there."

"Yes, Sir," the duty NCO said.

They walked away. Jack and Marjorie heard General Hanrahan say one more thing to the Sergeant: "Never get in the way of true love, Sergeant. It's that irresistible force you're always hearing about."

Then Jack put his arms around her.

[THREE]
Quarters #5
Fort Bragg, North Carolina
12 September 1964

P ATRICIA HANRAHAN was upset and annoyed when Marjorie told her what had really happened, but she couldn't stay that way. She had known Marjorie since she was a little girl, and she was touched by Marjorie's determination to be with her boyfriend, come hell or high water.

And after Marjorie delivered a long litany of the virtues and all-around charm of Jack Portet, she was interested to see him for himself.

General Hanrahan and Sergeant Portet arrived at half past eleven.

"I have a little speech to make," Red Hanrahan said, "following which you can feed us. Whatever direction the conversation takes, it will not get into the subject of what Jack is doing here. Or that he's even here at all."

"All right," Patricia Hanrahan said.

"I understand," Marjorie said.

Hanrahan looked at Jack appraisingly. "You're bigger than me," he said. "But I think you're about the size of Son Number One. Would you like to get out of the fatigues and into blue jeans?"

"Yes, Sir," Jack said.

"Come on, then. And then we'll have a beer. I think we've earned it."

Patricia Hanrahan served lunch in the kitchen—hamburgers, which the men cooked themselves, and french fried potatoes which Marjorie peeled and sliced and then fried.

"When did you make sergeant?" Marjorie asked. "Or is that a question I'm not supposed to ask?"

"I'll answer it anyway," General Hanrahan said. "He's working with some of my men. Unless he wore a green beret he would stick out like a sore thumb. And since fully qualified Green Berets are all at least sergeants, I told him to put on sergeant's stripes, too."

Jack looked at Marjorie and shrugged. "I am still a poor but honest PFC."

There was a quick knock at the kitchen door and a tall, chic woman stepped into the kitchen.

"Oh, I'm sorry," she said. "I didn't know you had a guest, Patricia. I didn't see a car."

Jack thought she had an accent.

"Don't be silly, Jane," Patricia Hanrahan said. "Come in and say hello to Marjorie Bellmon . . . you know Marjorie, don't you?"

"You are Barbara's daughter?" the woman said. Barbara came out Bar-Bar-Uh, and Jack was now convinced the woman was French.

"Yes, ma'am."

"I don't know you, but when your little brother was here with the cadets last summer, we had him to supper. You are here with your mama?"

"No, ma'am," Marjorie said.

"Jack," Patricia Hanrahan said, "this is Mrs. Jane Rowan. General Rowan commands Bragg. Jane, this is Jack Portet. He's Marjorie's friend."

"Fiancé," Marjorie corrected her quickly.

"I am so happy to know you!" Mrs. Rowan said.

Jack took the chance. "*Je suis enchanté*, Madame," he said.

"Oh, you speak French!" Mrs. Rowan said, obviously pleased. "And you heard my accent?"

"*Oui, Madame.*"

"Yours is not Parisian," Mrs. Rowan said. "Not even French, I think. Belgian?"

"Belgian," Jack said in French. "My father is Belgian; I went to college in Brussels."

"More than Belgian," Mrs. Rowan said. "Let me show you how clever I am. You have been in the Congo. Yes?"

"Yes," Jack said and looked at General Hanrahan. "My father lives in Leopoldville."

"I knew it!" Mrs. Rowan said triumphantly. "I could hear it. I know Leo, but not very well. I was in the Congo for six years, but in Stanleyville. My father was the French Consul in Stanleyville. Stanleyville is like a second home."

"I'll even bet you know where the Stanley Falls are," Jack said with a strange look on his face.

"Of course I know! What kind of a question is that? We lived right by the falls, just down the street from the American Consulate. I am sick at heart when I hear what is going on there. I know every rock, every tree . . ."

She stopped, an angry look on her face. General Hanrahan and Jack Portet had begun to chuckle, and their efforts to restrain it failed. They started laughing out loud.

"Red!" Patricia Hanrahan said, shocked.

"I am the butt of a joke I do not understand," Mrs. Rowan said coldly.

"Forgive me, Jane," General Hanrahan said. "We were not laughing at you. And we know what's going on in Stanleyville is no joke. Jack, especially. His stepmother and half sister are in the Immoquateur Apartments."

"Then what?" she said, not mollified.

"They flew Jack here from Berlin," General Hanrahan said—"here goes security out the window—because they couldn't find anyone else in the whole U.S. Army who knew anything about Stanleyville."

"So you have permission to go get those poor people out of there?" Mrs. Rowan asked.

"I didn't say that, Jane," Hanrahan said.

"You didn't have to," she countered.

Hanrahan stood up and walked to a wall-mounted telephone. He dialed a number. "This is General Hanrahan. I want a scrambled line on immediate standby to the White House switchboard in case I need it. And while you're setting it up, put me through—my code name is the Greek—to the Mouse, via the White House switchboard."

Felter came on the line almost immediately.

"Sandy, General Rowan's wife, Jane, lived for six years in Stanleyville. I'd like to pick her brains," Hanrahan said. "How much can I clear her for? She's already guessed what's going on. She identified Portet's accent as Belgian-Congo French."

He turned from the telephone.

"Jane, you have just been granted a Top Secret—Eagle clearance. Do you understand what that means?"

"Red," Mrs. Rowan said, indignantly, "I have been in the Army almost as long as Patricia. What do you want me to do?"

"You better call the General and tell him that whatever the two of you had planned for the weekend is off," Hanrahan said.

[FOUR]
The Holiday Inn Motel
Fayetteville, North Carolina
1545 Hours 12 September 1964

"IF YOU'RE SERIOUS about making an honest woman of me," Marjorie Bellmon said to Jack Portet, "maybe you better start doing something about it."

Jack let flow a torrent of French.

"What did that mean?" Marjorie asked.

"An old Belgian proverb," Jack said. "'Afterward, a man wants to go to sleep; a woman wants to get married.'"

"You bastard!" Marjorie said and grabbed his male appendage.

"I'm willing to discuss the issue, of course."

She laughed and put her face in his neck.

"Why the sudden interest in marriage?" he asked, running his fingers down the small of her back.

"I'm an old-fashioned girl," Marjorie said. "I am embarrassed when my parents' friends know where and how I'm spending the afternoon."

"That's the only reason?"

"Because I want to share my life with you and bear your babies," she said. "Because when I'm not with you, I'm dead inside."

"OK, I'm sold," he said. "You've talked me into it."

"I'll pull it off," she said.

"You better not, it's the only one I have."

"I told my father if you came back, I was going to marry you," Marjorie said. "I think my mother already knew how I feel."

"You do have a one-track mind, don't you?"

"I didn't mean back like this," Marjorie said. "I meant back for good."

"Huh?"

"When are they . . . when are you going over there?"

"I don't think I am," he said. "Actually, I'm pretty sure of it. They don't want me along."

"Why not?"

"These guys are pros," Jack said. "They're nice to me—they're really good guys, I like them—but they can't quite hide that they think of me as a civilian in uniform, which of course is true."

"Jack, the Green Berets are not ten feet tall," Marjorie said. "Uncle Sandy and Craig Lowell and Geoff Craig, they're all Green Berets."

"Then you underestimate all of them."

"You're really impressed, aren't you?" she asked, genuinely surprised. She raised herself on her elbows and looked down at him.

"What they're going to do, Marjorie," Jack said, "is fly several hundred miles at night without ground-navigation aids, jump out of an airplane at ten thousand feet, and hope they're over a wide spot in the Congo. From the moment they jump, they can forget having the U.S. government behind them. They're going in black."

"I don't know what that means."

"No identification. No uniforms. Not even U.S. Army weapons. If they get caught, they expect to be killed. And once they're on the ground—more accurately, in the water—and presuming they don't attract the attention of a crocodile, they will inflate their rubber boats, hope the outboard engines start—they're muffled, and they are a *bitch* to start—and then go upstream to infiltrate—all twenty-four of them, presuming all twenty-four get as far as the inflate-boats phase—a town full of several thousand Simbas. They will then attempt to snatch the consular personnel, and if it doesn't look absolutely suicidal, Ursula, the baby, and my family, and then hold off several thousand Simbas until a couple of H-34s can find them and land and then take off again. Am I impressed? You bet your ass I'm impressed. I don't think I'd have the balls to go in with them if they'd have me."

"You're sure they won't take you?"

"If you were them, would you want me along?"

She didn't reply. She lowered herself onto his body and held him tightly.

Please God, don't let them change their minds and take him along.

[FIVE]
Leopoldville, Democratic Republic of the Congo
19 September 1964

URGENT
FROM US EMBASSY LEOPOLDVILLE DEM REPCONGO
TO SECSTATE WASH DC
STANLEYVILLE SITUATION UPDATE AS OF 2400 ZULU
18 SEPTEMBER 1964
INTELSOURCE RATING THREE PAREN 3 PAREN REPORTS CONGOLESE MILITARY FORCE IDENTIFIED AS QUOTE FIVE SLASH ONE COMMANDO ENDQUOTE CONSISTING OF ONE COMPANY OF 100 PLUS KATANGESE ANC TROOPS AND FORTY TWO MERCENARIES RECAPTURED LISALA APPROX THREE HUNDRED PAREN 300 PAREN MILES DOWNSTREAM FROM STANLEYVILLE 17 SEPTEMBER.
FIVE SLASH ONE COMMANDO BY LIEUTENANT GARRY WILSON, TWENTY-FIVE YEAROLD BRITSUBJECT, EX-SANDHURST AND ROYAL ARMY CYPRUS. SAMESOURCE REPORTS SIMBA CASUALTIES 160 PLUS CONFIRMED DEAD. WOUNDED ESTIMATED 300 PLUS. GOVT FORCE CASUALTIES ONE REPEAT ONE WOUNDED.

SAMESOURCE REPORTS DISPROPORTIONATE SIMBA CASU-
ALTIES CAUSED BY SORCERERS ACCOMPANYING SIMBAS WHO
WAVE PALM BRANCHES AND CONVINCE SIMBAS THEY ARE
IMMUNE TO BULLETS.

SAMESOURCE REPORTS FIVE SLASH ONE COMMANDO LIBER-
ATED BUMBA APPROXIMATELY 250 MILES DOWNRIVER
STANLEYVILLE AT 1240 BUMBA TIME 18 SEPTEMBER.

SAMESOURCE REPORTS FOURTEEN PAREN 14 PAREN EURO-
PEANS IN BUMBA SCHEDULED FOR 1300 EXECUTION. LIBER-
ATED PERSONNEL INCLUDE NO REPEAT NO AMERICAN
NATIONALS. USAMBASSADOR AUTHORIZED TRANSPORT BY
US HELICOPTERS TO LEO.

CONGOINTELSOURCE RATING ONE PAREN 1 PAREN REPORTS
OLENGA PREPARING FOR SECOND ASSAULT ON BUKAVU AND
BELIEVES ATTACK WILL OCCUR WITH TWENTY FOUR TO
THIRTY SIX HOURS.

THERE HAS BEEN NO REPEAT NO CONTACT IN THREE AT-
TEMPTS WITH INTELSOURCE STANLEYVILLE. ATTEMPTS
CONTINUING.

DANNELLY DEPUTY CHIEF OF MISSION

[SIX]
The Hôtel du Lac
Bukavu, Democratic Republic of the Congo
20 September 1964

COLONEL LEONARD MULAMBA had not requested reinforce-
ment with a platoon of mercenaries. But there had been a radio message
from General Joseph-Désiré Mobutu's headquarters (as opposed to from
Mobutu himself) in Leopoldville informing him that a platoon was being
air-lifted to him.

There was a line between really needing mercenaries—which was
tantamount to needing white men—to provide the ANC with a little
backbone (which inarguably it sometimes desperately needed) and hav-

ing white troops dominate an operation, thus convincing the ANC that
they were nearly worthless by themselves.

He was not yet sure that the time had come when he was going to need
mercenaries, even with Olenga ten miles or so out of town.

Colonel Mulamba did not think much of Olenga, and certainly not as
"Lieutenant General" Olenga, or indeed as any kind of officer at all. You
don't get to be any kind of an officer in any kind of an army by announcing you are a lieutenant, or a colonel, or a lieutenant general, and
outfitting yourself in a stolen uniform. And he refused to permit his
officers to refer to Olenga as "General Olenga." If they didn't wish to
refer to him by his last name, they were under orders to refer to him as
"the rebel leader."

Colonel Mulamba didn't like the term "Simba" either, as applied to
the forces he was facing. He admired lions, and he didn't consider his
opposition lionlike. The lion was a noble beast who did not kill for
pleasure. Colonel Mulamba had thus made it known that he didn't want
to hear the term Simba in his presence unless it applied to a four-legged
beast of the jungle. Or of course to the very decent Bukavuian Pilsener
beer.

He was informed by telephone at his headquarters (which he had
established in the Hôtel du Lac) in Bukavu when the C-46 bearing the
mercenaries he hadn't asked for landed across the Ruzizi River at the
Kamembe airfield. He was somewhat surprised to hear that there were
half a dozen ANC soldiers with the mercenaries. He ordered that they be
brought by truck to the Hôtel du Lac.

When he heard the sound of truck gears clashing, he rose up from his
desk and looked out the window down to the street. An officer, apparently the commanding officer, got out of the truck cab. He stood with his
hands on his hips as a sergeant (who acted English, Mulamba decided)
off-loaded the troops from the rear and lined them up.

The officer and the Sergeant at least looked like soldiers, Colonel
Mulamba decided. Their uniforms were cleaned and pressed. Their
trousers were tucked neatly inside their boots, and they were cleanly
shaven. Some of the mercenaries looked like rabble, which was not
surprising, but they were obviously in fear of the officer and the Sergeant.

The ANC troops who got off the truck looked like rabble. He wondered what in the hell their purpose was. He was further confused when
three of them were ordered into line with the white soldiers, and the

other three followed (*shuffled* after, Mulamba thought unpleasantly) the officer into the lobby of the Hôtel du Lac.

By the time his administrative sergeant knocked at his door to report that a mercenary captain wished to see him, Colonel Mulamba had had time to seat himself at his desk and open a manila file.

The mercenary officer marched into Mulamba's office, stopped three feet from his desk, came to attention, and saluted.

"Captain Wagner and a detachment of Katangese Special Gendarmerie reporting to the Bukavu area commander as ordered, Sir."

Colonel Mulamba returned the salute, but did not put the Captain at rest. At some time, rather obviously, this mercenary had been a soldier. Possibly even an officer.

"I did not ask for your services, Captain," Mulamba said after a while.

Captain Wagner did not reply.

"What good do you think you can do me?"

"We are at your disposal for any service you may desire, Sir."

"Are you?"

"Several of us have some experience in situations like this, Sir."

"When you were in Katanga, you mean?"

"When we were in Vietnam," Wagner said.

"You were in the U.S. Army?"

"Sir, may we go off the record?"

"All right," Mulamba said.

"Williamson," Wagner called. "Bring them in!"

Three black men in ANC uniforms marched into the room and came to attention. The smallest of them, a PFC, saluted.

"Lieutenant Williamson and a detail of two reporting as ordered, Sir."

Mulamba returned the salute and then smiled. "If I were a suspicious man, I would suspect that these three are some of those American Green Berets who are reported to be missing from the air base at Kamina."

"Sir, if I may, I think they'll turn up sooner or later, having somehow become lost in this enormous country," Wagner said.

"That wouldn't surprise me at all, Captain," Colonel Mulamba said. He looked at Williamson. "Why are you a PFC?"

"The only uniform I could find to fit, Sir, I bought from a PFC."

"And, tell me . . . Williamson, you said?"

"Yes, Sir."

"How do you think you may be of service here?"

"May I approach the Colonel's map, Sir?"

Mulamba nodded.

Williamson went to the map and started pointing. "On our way here, Sir, we conducted as much of an aerial observation as we could from the aircraft. It seems to me the Simba—"

"Don't refer to these criminals by using that word!"

"Sorry, Sir," Williamson said. "It seems to me, Colonel," he went on, "that the most logical route on which the insurgents can advance is this way."

The presentation lasted three minutes. The true test of an intelligent man is the degree to which he agrees with you, and Lieutenant Williamson's suggestions about how to blunt Olenga's attack—by attacking them from high ground nine miles from Bukavu—could have been taken from Colonel Leonard Mulamba's personal notebook.

"There are three major positions," Mulamba said. "They are supposed to have been prepared by now. Whether they have been or not remains to be seen. With your permission, Captain Wagner, I would like to send these gentlemen out there to see that they are."

"My men are at your orders, Colonel," Wagner said.

Mulamba called for his administrative officer and told him to procure officer's insignia for the three black Green Berets.

"These gentlemen will be considered members of my personal staff and presumed to be acting on my orders," he said. "Go with the Major please, gentlemen, he'll take care of you."

When they were gone he looked at Wagner.

"There is an unfortunate story going around, Captain," he said, "that the foreign volunteers think they have a license to loot. How do you feel about that?"

"I don't like it, but I don't see how I can stop it without shooting half the mercenaries." Karl-Heinz considered his reply and then added: "Three-quarters of them."

Colonel Mulamba's response surprised Wagner.

"That would indicate that you are neither a liar nor a fool. I will now entertain your suggestions vis-à-vis the employment of those who have so nobly rushed to the aid of my country in its hour of distress. An employment, it is to be hoped, that would keep them at some distance from the temptation to help themselves to other people's property."

Fifteen minutes later Mulamba and Wagner had agreed that the white mercenaries would be used as a reserve blocking force, stationed six miles from Bukavu. And when Olenga's assault was turned, they would be the lead element of the counterattacking force.

[SEVEN]
23 September 1964

URGENT
FROM US EMBASSY LEOPOLDVILLE DEM REPCONGO
TO SECSTATE WASH DC
STANLEYVILLE SITUATION UPDATE AS OF 2400 ZULU
22 SEPTEMBER 1964
INTELSOURCE RATING ONE PAREN 1 PAREN REPORTS ASSAULT ON BUKAVU BY ESTIMATED 4000 SIMBAS UNDER PERSONAL COMMAND OLENGA TURNED BY ANC UNDER COMMAND COLONEL LEONARD MULAMBA MORNING 22 SEPTEMBER BEFORE SIMBA FORCE REACHED BUKAVU. SAMESOURCE REPORTS OLENGA FORCES SUFFERED SEVERE REPEAT SEVERE LOSSES PERSONNEL AND MATERIEL. ANC LOSSES NEGLIGIBLE. SAMESOURCE REPORTS CAPTURE OF SMALL QUANTITIES SMALL ARMS AND AMMUNITION MANUFACTURED BY CHICOM, CZECHOSLOVAKIA AND PAREN AMMO ONLY PAREN EASTGERMANY. SAMESOURCE REPORTS AMMO BEARS MAY AND JUNE 1964 HEADSTAMPS. MATERIEL EN ROUTE LEOPOLDVILLE.
CONTACT REESTABLISHED INTELSOURCE RATING ONE PAREN 1 PAREN STANLEYVILLE.
SAMESOURCE REPORTS STANLEYVILLE NEWSPAPER PAREN LE MARTYR PAREN CARRIED 21 SEPTEMBER STORY PARTIALLY FOLLOWING: QUOTE THE PRESIDENT OF THE PEOPLE'S REPUBLIC OF THE CONGO INFORMED THE PUBLIC THAT MR. PAUL CARLSON A MAJOR OF AMERICAN NATIONALITY WAS CAPTURED 20 SEPTEMBER DURING BATTLE OF YAKOMA. MR CARLSON IS IN GOOD HEALTH. A MILITARY TRIBUNAL WILL STUDY HIS DOSSIER BEFORE HE APPEARS IN FRONT OF A COURT OF JUSTICE. ENDQUOTE.

SAMESOURCE REPORTS ENGLISH SPEAKING WHITE MALE AP-
PROXIMATELY THIRTY-FOUR YEARS OF AGE TRANSPORTED
BOUND HAND AND FOOT TO CENTRAL PRISON STANLEYVILLE
BY TRUCK 21 SEPTEMBER. INDIVIDUAL SHOWS SIGNS OF PHYS-
ICAL ABUSE. ATTEMPTS TO MAKE CONTACT SO FAR UNSUC-
CESSFUL.

USEMBASSY BELIEVES CARLSON IS ALMOST CERTAINLY PAUL
EARLE CARLSON MD PAREN SURGEON PAREN THIRTY-SIX
YEAR OLD USNATIONAL BORN CULVER CITY CALIFORNIA. DR
CARLSON OPERATED MEDICAL CLINIC IN WASOLA PAREN
SMALL CITY IN NORTHERN CONGO NEAR BORDER CENTRAL
AFRICAN REPUBLIC PAREN CLINIC SPONSORED BY EVAN-
GELICAL COVENANT CHURCH OF CALIFORNIA. CARLSON AC-
COMPANIED IN WASOLA BY WIFE LOIS AND CHILDREN WAYNE
PAREN NINE PAREN AND LYNETTE PAREN TWO PAREN. FAM-
ILY WHEREABOUTS UNKNOWN BUT NOT REPEAT NOT BE-
LIEVED TO BE IN STANLEYVILLE. DR CARLSON HAD NO
REPEAT NO OFFICIAL RELATIONSHIP OF ANY KIND WITH ANY
US GOVERNMENT AGENCY IN REPCONGO. LIEUTENANT
COLONEL MICHAEL HOARE OF KATANGESE SPECIAL GENDAR-
MERIE HAS ADVISED USAMBASSADOR VIA GENERAL MOBUTU
THAT HE HAS NEVER HAD ANY CONTACT OF ANY KIND WITH
DR CARLSON AND THAT CARLSON HAS HAD NO REPEAT NO
CONNECTION OF ANY KIND WITH ANY MILITARY FORCES UN-
DER HIS CONTROL.

STANLEYVILLE INTELSOURCE FURTHER REPORTS GBENYE
GAVE 21 SEPTEMBER SPEECH IN WHICH HE SAID QUOTE
THOUSANDS OF AMERICAN TROOPS ENDQUOTE ARE IN-
VOLVED IN QUOTE BATTLE OF BUKAVU ENDQUOTE.
SAMESOURCE BELIEVES OLENGA DEFEAT AT BUKAVU WILL
DANGEROUSLY RAISE TENSIONS IN STANLEYVILLE. AMBAS-
SADOR CONCURS.

DANNELLY DEPUTY CHIEF OF MISSION.

[EIGHT]
Golden Hawk Compound
Camp Mackall Military Reservation, North Carolina
23 September 1964

Dᴜʀɪɴɢ Wᴀʀ II, Camp Mackall had been a division training camp. As quickly as possible, the Army had thrown up on a cost-plus-basis frame barracks buildings, mess halls, theaters, a hospital, and all the other housing and facilities necessary to house fifteen thousand men while they were being trained to function as a United States infantry division.

Colonel Ed Mitchell, Commanding Officer of the 7th Special Forces Group, once heard which division—had there been more than one?—had trained at Mackall, but he promptly forgot what he had been told. But he thought of it now, as General Red Hanrahan's ancient H-19 Sikorsky flew him and his Sergeant Major low over Mackall's pine trees to Golden Hawk Compound.

There was nothing left of the War II installations except concrete pads here and there where once barracks furnaces had rested, some battered roads, and a sewage system that was cheaper to leave than tear down. The frame buildings were all gone. It was hard even to make out where they had been.

Mackall was a "dormant U.S. military reservation, under the supervision of the Commanding General, Fort Bragg, and available, if needed, as a maneuver ground."

It was also where, quietly, the U.S. Army Center for Special Warfare trained Green Berets—the campus of the John Wayne School for Boys. It was where the Green Berets learned to eat snakes, make fire by rubbing sticks together, and blow things up. There were a few rough buildings set up, kitchens, showers, that sort of thing. But these were pretty rudimentary.

There was also room—where no one else could see—to erect mockups of areas they might find themselves operating. Mockups, for example, of a villa near a river from which twenty-seven Berets were going to extract nine members of the Foreign Service of the United States from illegal detention by indigenous forces in rebellion against their government.

Mitchell had radioed ahead, so they knew he was coming. And when the H-19 fluttered to the ground they were all there. They were in dyed-black fatigues, their heads wrapped with cloth, their faces darkened with greasepaint. They were armed with a wide assortment of weapons, none of them issued by the United States government. And they were probably the best soldiers in anybody's army in the world, Colonel Ed Mitchell thought as he climbed out of the chopper and told them to stand at ease.

"I'll get right to the point," he said. "It's on hold. Permanent hold. I have orders to stand down."

"Shit!" someone said.

"What the fuck!" someone else said.

"It has been decided at the highest level of government," Colonel Mitchell said, "that in the present circumstances Golden Hawk would exacerbate the situation, even if successful."

"What 'present circumstances,' Colonel?"

"The ANC seems to be getting its act together," Colonel Mitchell said. "They have recaptured four cities from the Simbas. A major Simba attack on Bukavu, their second attempt, has been turned with severe losses to the Simbas."

"They still got our people, don't they?"

"Permission has been granted for a plane under charter to the International Red Cross to fly to Stanleyville," Colonel Mitchell said. "It is hoped that it will bring out not only our diplomatic personnel but all United States nationals in the area."

"That's right, first you let the cocksuckers piss all over you and then you say 'thank you' when they're willing to sell you a towel to wipe your face."

"That will be quite enough, Lieutenant," Colonel Ed Mitchell said. He quite agreed with the lieutenant, a very large, bulletheaded black man who had been an All-American tackle at Notre Dame. But it was neither the time nor place to do so publicly. "We're soldiers—we do what we're told."

He fixed the Lieutenant with an icy stare until the man came to attention and said, "Yes, Sir."

"At this very moment," Mitchell went on, "under the chairmanship of Jomo Kenyatta, Premier of Kenya, representatives of ten African nations are meeting in Nairobi. They constitute The Congo Reconciliation Commission, and it is hoped they will be able to negotiate a peaceful solution to the situation."

Three people said "Bullshit!" but Colonel Mitchell did not appear to have heard them.

"It is recognized," Mitchell went on, "again at the highest levels of our government, that efforts to reach a peaceful solution might not be successful. Therefore, Golden Hawk is not scratched, just put on hold. No equipment will be turned in; everyone remains assigned to Golden Hawk. But training is suspended. General Hanrahan's sending a bus out here carrying some people to watch the store while you people take a seventy-two hour pass. Check in with Group when that's over."

He turned to his Sergeant Major.

"You got anything, Sergeant Major?"

"I shouldn't have to say this, but keep your mouths shut," the Sergeant Major said. He turned to Mitchell. "That's all, Sir."

"You guys have done a good job," Mitchell said. "I know it, and General Hanrahan knows it. That's all I have."

"'Ten-hut!" the Sergeant Major barked, then, "Dismissed."

"Captain Stacey," Colonel Mitchell said, "I'd like to see you and Sergeant Portet for a minute, please."

He walked to the far side of the H-19 with his Sergeant Major at his heels. Captain Stacey and Portet followed him, both looking a little uneasy.

Like the others, Jack Portet was wearing dyed-black fatigues and a head cloth, and his face was covered with greasepaint.

"I'm surprised to see you dressed up like that, PFC Portet," Colonel Mitchell said, "since I thought I made it pretty clear you were here solely to fill in the blanks in the intelligence summary."

"Sir," Captain Stacey said, "I told Portet to suit up. I thought he would blend in better if he looked like one of us."

"And that's why he made the last three night jumps, right? To blend in better?"

"Sir," Stacey said, uncomfortable but sure of the righteousness of his position, "Portet speaks the languages. He knows the terrain. And he was jump qualified when he came here."

"But not free-fall qualified, right?" Colonel Mitchell said, looking at Jack Portet. "You did the minimum five static-line jumps at Benning and got your wings of silver, but that's all, am I correct?"

"Yes, Sir," Jack said.

"Let me guess," Colonel Mitchell said. "At the last minute, Captain Stacey was going to come to me and say he'd like to have you along— because you speak the languages and know the terrain. And I would agree that you would be useful, but I would say that your going along was obviously impossible, because you weren't free-fall-qualified or a qualified Green Beret, period. Whereupon Captain Stacey would say that he'd found time in his busy schedule to give you a little on-the-job training, that in fact you'd been free-fall jumping at night right along with the big boys. And *they* had had found time in *their* busy schedules not only to qualify you with the weaponry but teach you to make fire by rubbing sticks together. And in fact he considered you fully qualified. Is that about the scenario you had in mind, Captain Stacey?"

Captain Stacey came to attention.

"Yes, Sir," he said. "That's about it, Sir."

"And what had you planned to say to me if PFC Portet had turned up dead? Or something minor, like breaking his leg? Did you even consider the possibility of how embarrassing it would have been for me to get on the telephone and call Colonel Felter and say, 'Colonel, you know that Congo expert you sent me? Well, one of my A-Team leaders went bananas and jumped him at night, and he now has a fifty-foot pine tree up his ass. Dead, you see. Sorry 'bout that'?"

"I accept full responsibility, Sir," Captain Stacey said.

Colonel Mitchell glowered icily at him for a full thirty seconds.

"The question is of course now moot," Mitchell finally said, "since you're probably not going. The question is what we do with PFC Portet. When I spoke with Colonel Felter, and he told me the hand-wringers and pansies had won, I asked him what about Portet. And he said that he wants him here at Bragg and that I should find something useful for him to do. Any suggestions, Captain Stacey?"

"No, Sir."

"Captain Stacey's usually active imagination has apparently stalled, Sergeant Major. Does that surprise you?"

"Yes, Sir, it does."

"How's that, Sergeant Major?"

"Well, I would have thought, Sir, that the Captain would have suggested that we run PFC Portet through the basic course, Sir. I mean, now that he's sort of already had the advanced course, Sir."

"How does that strike you, Captain Stacey?" Mitchell asked. "For that matter, how does it strike you, PFC Portet?"

"Could we do that?" Stacey asked. "Would the school stand still for it?"

"I have reason to believe that General Hanrahan would suggest to the Deputy Commandant that under the circumstances an exception could be made for PFC Portet," Mitchell said. "If for no other reason than that his starting the basic course would legalize those sergeant's stripes he's been wearing." He turned to Portet. "What about it, son? Do you want to cut off those stripes and have the Sergeant Major find you a broom or a mop or would you like to come back out here next Monday and join one of the basic classes?"

"I think I'd like to come back out here, Sir," Jack said. "Thank you."

"Between now and Monday morning, Stacey," Colonel Mitchell said, "I expect you to have a quiet word with the cadre. They can make him eat all the snakes they want, but he is *not*, repeat *not*, to make any more night jumps. I really don't want to have to tell Felter that he's in the base hospital in a cast. There is still a chance, slight, but a chance, that Golden Hawk will go. If it does, I want Sergeant Portet to go with it."

XXI

[ONE]
Stanleyville, Democratic Republic of the Congo
24 September 1964

THE GROUND FLOOR of the Immoquateur Apartments held half a dozen shops. For no apparent reason three of them had been spared and were open for business. The others had been looted, their plate-glass windows shattered, and patriotic signs (including one reading KIL! ALL! AMNERICAN! MERSANAYS!) painted on their walls.

Access to the apartments on the upper floors of the building was by two passenger elevators in a small and narrow lobby in the left of the building, and by a service elevator at the end of a corridor running from the end of the lobby to the Congo River side of the building. The design had taken into account the belief held by many Congolese that if anything of value is left unattended, the previous owner no longer has use for it.

In the Good Old Days there had been a guard armed with a billy club at both passenger and service elevators. Their function had been to ensure that any Congolese seeking to board an elevator had business in the building.

There were still two elevator guards in the Immoquateur, but they were now armed with FN 7mm assault rifles, and they were both on duty at the passenger elevators, since the service elevator was no longer functioning. The elevator-maintenance crew of the Stanleyville branch of Otis S.A. du Congo were not available. They had been apprehended trying to make their way out of Stanleyville in an Otis truck. Soon afterward they had been taken to the Lumumba Monument, where a summary court had found them guilty of treason to the People's Republic of the Congo. They had been executed on the spot, mercifully by small-arms fire. After being left in front of the Lumumba Monument overnight, *pour encourager les autres*, their bodies had been taken to Congo River and thrown in.

There were more crocodiles in the river these days, and closer to the city, than there had been in many years.

Guard duty at the Immoquateur Apartments was a desirable duty. The guards could count upon a generous tip from the Europeans living there every time they entered or left the elevator.

A Simba officer, a captain, came down the exposed aggregate concrete sidewalk on the Immoquateur and entered the lobby. An FN 7mm rifle hung from his shoulder, and one hand firmly grasping the grip of a dress sword, the other was grasping even more firmly the neck of a bottle of Johnnie Walker Red Label Scotch, from which he had obviously been taking much sustenance.

The guards told him that by order of Lieutenant General Olenga himself, the Immoquateur was off limits to everyone except those on official business. The Simba Captain said that he had official business. The guards said that if he had business, then he must have a pass and could they see it.

The Captain produced an official-looking document which both guards studied carefully and in turn, blissfully unaware that they were holding it upside down. Then the senior of them saluted and pushed the elevator button, causing the door to slide open.

The Captain got in the elevator and pushed the buttons for floors two, four, six, and eight. The elevator stopped obediently at each floor. He rode to the eighth floor, got out, went to the fire stairs, and climbed to the top floor, the tenth.

There was no doorknob on the stair side of the doors. Once they had closed, there was no way to open them from the stair side. The building had been designed so that someone entering the fire stairs on one floor could not exit on another; it was necessary to go all the way to the ground floor.

The Captain took a thin, oddly shaped flat piece of brass (it had been a 7mm cartridge case) from the pocket of his filthy white dress shirt and slipped it between the tenth-floor door and the door frame. He felt the spring-loaded part of the door lock slide out of the way.

Then he drew his dress saber (according to engraving on the blade, it had once belonged to a student at the Ecole Polytechnique in Paris) and slipped it into the opening between the door and the door frame, intending to use it as a lever to pry the door open.

The tip of the saber snapped off.

He tried slipping the sharpened edge of the blade into the opening. It fitted, but whenever he tried to twist it, it slipped out.

He considered his predicament a moment and then picked up the saber with both hands and struck the door as hard as he could. The first blow dented the door; the second blow dented it more; the third blow snapped the saber blade off six inches from the handle.

And the noise sounded like he was inside a drum.

He took the FN 7mm assault rifle from his shoulder, snapped off the safety, and made sure the lever was on single shot. Then he held the rifle close to the door and fired. The noise was deafening, and there was a spray of parts of the bullet, some of which richocheted off the steel stairs and concrete walls and struck his legs and arms.

But there was now an inch and a half cut in the steel of the door. The Captain picked up the flattened cartridge case and put it back in the door lockwork. After that he put what was left of the saber blade into the hole in the door. When he pulled on it, the door opened enough for him to get his fingers on the edge and then pull it all the way open.

He went into the tenth-floor corridor and stationed himself around a corner where he could if necessary quickly train the FN on anybody getting out of the elevator. The elevator floor-indicator was working. The elevator went to the second floor and stayed there for several minutes, then went to the third floor and stayed there.

There was time, he decided. What they were doing was investigating the sound of the gunshot floor by floor, very cautiously and very carefully.

He went down the corridor and knocked on the door of an apartment. There was no answer so he knocked again. When there was no answer after the third knock, he slipped the piece of flattened brass into the lock and pulled the door open.

He went inside, closed the door, and turned around.

Bile rose in his throat.

A huge black woman, a large butcher knife in one hand, a bone-handled carving knife in the other, was advancing at him, stalking him, obviously about to attack.

"*Je suis ami*," he said. "Jesus H. Christ, lady—wait a minute!"

"Mary Magdalene!" a female voice called. "*Attends!*"

The black woman didn't lower the knives, but she stopped her careful advance.

"Madame Portet?" the Captain asked.

"Who are you?"

"My name is Lunsford, ma'am," he said, and then Ursula stepped into a doorway with her baby in her arms. A blonde girl stood behind her, looking at him with wide, frightened, eyes.

"Mrs. Craig, do you remember me? I'm Captain Lunsford. I'm a buddy of Geoff's. We were together in 'Nam."

Ursula couldn't speak. Tears ran down her face. But she nodded.

She looked awful, Lunsford thought. Her hair was parted in the middle, then drawn tightly over her head and pulled together with a rubber band. Her face was white and her eyes looked sunken. He wondered if she had been raped. There had been a lot of rape. It was forbidden by Olenga, and the punishment was death. The result was that a lot of Simbas had been shot, either on the spot or ceremoniously before the Lumumba Monument. But it hadn't stopped the raping.

"You want to tell her to put those knives down?" Father Lunsford said.

Hanni gestured to Mary Magdalene and told her in Swahili that he was a friend, an American officer, who had come to help.

Mary Magdalene looked at him suspiciously. Lunsford smiled at her. She did not return it.

"Are you all all right?" Lunsford said.

"We're managing," Hanni said.

"Have you got food for the baby?"

"Condensed milk," Ursula said. "And Mary Magdalene has been able to get bananas and fruit. He's all right."

"What about you?" Lunsford said.

"There was some food in the freezer here," Hanni said, "but when the electricity was off for three days, it spoiled. Mary Magdalene goes out every day and buys what she can. Fish and chicken. We have some canned vegetables left. We're managing."

"Ma'am," Lunsford said very gently, "that really wasn't what I was asking. I've got some penicillin and some other antibiotics. And if you need anything else, I probably can arrange to have Geoff air-drop it."

"We haven't been . . . molested," Hanni said. "If that's what you're asking."

"How's Geoff?" Ursula asked. "Where is he?"

"At Kamina," Lunsford said. "He or Pappy Hodges fly over—or near here—every day. He's all right."

"What are you doing here?" Hanni Portet asked.

"There's a Red Cross plane at the airport," Lunsford said. "There's a chance we can get you out of here. There's risk involved. I'll tell you what I can do and leave it up to you."

He told them he would commandeer a truck in the morning—he'd found three he thought he could get, and a couple of Simbas—and come to the Immoquateur and pick them up and take them to the airport. The Red Cross was negotiating with Soumialot. He didn't know what would happen, but there just might be a chance, as a goodwill gesture, that Soumialot would let the Red Cross fill the plane with women and children.

"What about Mary Magdalene?" Hanni Portet asked.

"Who?"

Hanni inclined her head toward Mary Magdalene.

"No," he said. "No way. That sonofabitch won't let any Congolese go."

"Then you will take Ursula and the baby and my daughter," Hanni said. "I will stay here."

"I've got no advice to give," Father Lunsford said.

"I am Belgian," Hanni said. "I have, anyway, a Belgian passport. They know who my husband is. Some man who said he was the Minister of Aviation has already called here and said he hopes to have a long and profitable relationship with Air Simba. I'll be all right."

"I don't want to go without you," Jeanine Portet said.

"You help Ursula with Jiffy," Hanni said. "Mary Magdalene and I can take care of ourselves."

"Mama!"

"You settle between you who's going and who's staying," Father Lunsford said. "I have to get out of here. When the time is right—and I don't know when that will be—I'll be outside in back with a truck. I'll blow the horn: 'Shave and a haircut, two bits.' Whoever is coming, come quickly down the fire stairs. I'll meet you on the ground floor."

"All right," Hanni said. "We'll be ready."

"Have you got any whiskey? Gin? Anything?" Father Lunsford asked.

"There's the bar," Hanni said, giving him a strange look.

Father took two bottles and headed for the door.

"You speak English?" he asked Mary Magdalene.

"I speak English."

"I'm glad you're on our side, honey," Lunsford said, and then went through the door.

He went to the elevator and pushed the call button.

After a long minute he heard the elevator rising.

When the door opened, the Simba guards had their FNs pointing at him. They were obviously afraid.

Lunsford smiled broadly. He extended one of the bottles of Scotch.

"Who did you shoot?" one of the guards asked.

"I didn't shoot anybody," Lunsford said. "I thought that was you."

The guard took the bottle of Johnnie Walker, removed the cap, and took a pull.

Then Lunsford got on the elevator and rode down to the lobby. He shook hands ceremoniously with each of the guards and staggered out of the building.

Whatever discussion there was between Hanni and Ursula and Jeanine about whether or not to try to make it to the airport, and about who was to go and who was to stay, was a waste of breath.

At first light the Red Cross plane took off from Stanleyville, crossed over the Immoquateur Apartments, and headed for Bujumbura, Burundi. It carried no one out that it had not flown in.

President Christophe Gbenye had decided that it was not in the best interests of his government to permit any Europeans whatsoever to leave Stanleyville. In the interest of peace, he told the International Red Cross, it was clearly necessary for his government to hold hostages.

[TWO]
Washington, D.C.
26 September 1964

BULLETIN
AP WASH 926-14
    WASHINGTON, DC—SEP 26—THE WHITE HOUSE HAS AN-
NOUNCED THAT PRESIDENT LYNDON B. JOHNSON WILL NOT
RECEIVE THE DELEGATION FROM THE CONGO RECONCILIA-
TION COMMISSION WHICH IS SCHEDULED TO LAND IN NEW
YORK SOMETIME THIS AFTERNOON. THE OFFICIAL REASON
GIVEN IS THAT THE PRESIDENT CANNOT MAKE ROOM FOR
THEM IN HIS SCHEDULE.
    IT HAS BEEN REPORTED THAT THE DELEGATION, MADE UP
OF REPRESENTATIVES OF FIVE AFRICAN NATIONS, INTENDED
TO PRESENT TO THE PRESIDENT THE DEMANDS OF THE RE-
CENTLY CONCLUDED COMMISSION MEETING IN NAIROBI,
KENYA, AND THAT THOSE DEMANDS INCLUDED A DEMAND
THAT JOHNSON ORDER THE COMPLETE WITHDRAWAL OF
ALL US MILITARY PERSONNEL IN THE CONGO, AS WELL AS
THE WITHDRAWAL OF ALL MILITARY EQUIPMENT, IN PAR-
TICULAR AIRCRAFT, WHICH THE UNITED STATES HAS
LOANED TO THE GOVERNMENT OF MOISE TSHOMBE IN
LEOPOLDVILLE.

[THREE]
The White House
Washington, D.C.
4 October 1964

"MY EYES HURT, Felter," the President of the United States
said. "Read it to me."

"There has been an intercept of a message from Stanleyville to Olenga, Mr. President," Felter said. "The message is from the People's Army Commander in Stanleyville to the Commander-in-Chief, which almost certainly means Olenga, who is in Paulis, about two hundred fifty miles from Stanleyville."

"What does it say?" the President asked impatiently.

"He requests, I now quote, 'permission to kill all Americans who are held in the liberated zone,' unquote."

"That's new," the President said. "That just come in?"

"No, Sir. It came in 2 October at 1755 Zulu—about one o'clock Washington time."

"Why haven't I seen it before now?"

"For the same reasons I feel it reliable, the Congo Working Group felt the intercept unreliable," Felter said. "Presumably they didn't want to waste your time with it."

The Congo Working Group was an interagency working group with members representing the State Department, the CIA, the USIA, and the Joint Chiefs of Staff. It was charged with responsibility for the "Congo Situation."

"Goddamn it, Felter," the President sighed. "I'm tired and in no mood for word games. Why didn't they think it was reliable?"

"The intercept was made by a teen-aged boy, an amateur radio operator, in Leopoldville."

"Hardly the most reliable source, wouldn't you agree?"

"Ordinarily," Felter said. "But this is a very bright kid. His father is one of the assistant military attachés."

"And you believe it reliable?"

"Yes, Sir."

"There's been no answer from Olenga that we know about?"

"No, Sir."

"Then it's possible even if the intercept was for real that the kid heard what he said he heard—in other words that whoever sent it was off base—and Olenga is ignoring him?"

"That's possible, Mr. President."

"Thank you for coming to see me, Colonel."

[FOUR]
5 October 1964

URGENT
FROM US EMBASSY LEOPOLDVILLE DEM REPCONGO
TO SECSTATE WASH DC
SPECIAL STANLEYVILLE SITUATION UPDATE 1300 ZULU
5 OCTOBER 1964
FOLLOWING IS EXTRACT OF TRANSLATION OF FRENCH LAN-
GUAGE BROADCAST BY GASTON SOUMAILOT, REPORTED TO
BE MINISTER OF DEFENSE IN REBEL GOVERNMENT OVER RA-
DIO STANLEYVILLE 1200 ZULU TODAY
QUOTE I INFORM THE AMERICAN GOVERNMENT THAT I CAN
SAFEGUARD PEACE AND ALSO THE PROPERTY OF CONGOLESE
AND FOREIGNERS. I AM VERY SURPRISED THAT THE AMER-
ICANS ARE CONTINUING TO KILL WOMEN AND CHILDREN
AND ALSO PATIENTS IN HOSPITALS. IF THE AMERCIANS DO
NOT STOP DROPPING BOMBS ON TOWNS ALREADY LIBERATED
THEN THEIR BROTHERS WHO ARE KILLING PEOPLE WILL BE
KILLED WHEN FOUND IN THESE TOWNS.
QUOTECONTINUES I HAVE NEVER KILLED AMERICANS AND I
DO NOT LIKE TO KILL, BUT IF THIS BOMBING GOES ON WE
WILL BE COMPELLED TO TAKE ACTION AGAINST THESE
AMERICANS IN THE CONGO.
QUOTECONTINUES IF THEY CONTINUE KILLING MEN,
WOMEN, AND CHILDREN THEN I INFORM THEM THAT IF ONE
CONGOLESE IS KILLED, HE WILL BE BURIED IN HIS GRAVE
TOGETHER WITH TWELVE AMERICANS ENDQUOTE
TRANSLATION VERIFIED BY TWO QUALIFIED LINGUISTS.
USAMBASSADOR BELIEVES SPEAKER WAS IN FACT
SOUMIALOT. TAPE RECORDING OF BROADCAST IN TODAYS
DIPLOMATIC POUCH. COURIER ABOARD UTA FLIGHT 404
CONNECTING BRUSSELS SABENA 600 TO NEWYORK ETA 1650 6
OCTOBER.
DANNELLY DEPUTY CHIEF OF MISSION.

[FIVE]
The White House
Washington, D.C.
8 October 1964

" **I** SORT OF THOUGHT you would be in to see me, Felter," the President of the United States said.

"Sir?"

"Earl was just in here to summarize the feeling of the Congo Working Group for me. They seem to feel that the situation in the Congo is becoming manageable. Did you see this?"

He handed Felter a yellow radioteletype printout.

URGENT
FROM US EMBASSY LEOPOLDVILLE DEM REPCONGO
TO SECSTATE WASH DC
STANLEYVILLE SITUATION UPDATE AS OF 2400 ZULU
7 OCTOBER 1964
INTELSOURCE RATING ONE PAREN 1 PAREN REPORTS CON-
GOLESE MILITARY FORCE INCLUDING 40 KATANGESE SPECIAL
GENDARMERIE UNDER CAPTAIN K. WAGNER LIBERATED
UVIRA NORTHERN TIP OF LAKE TANGANYIKA AS OF 1430
ZULU 7 OCTOBER. REBEL FORCES SUFFERED SEVERE REPEAT
SEVERE PERSONNEL, TRANSPORT, AND MATERIEL LOSSES.
SAMESOURCE QUOTES WAGNER AS SAYING REBEL FORCES IN
UVIRA IN PROCESS PREPARING RECEIPT LARGE QUANTITIES
OF ARMS AND MATERIEL FROM BURUNDI. WAGNER DOES
NOT BELIEVE LIBERATION OF UVIRA IN AND OF ITSELF WILL
HALT SUPPLY OF REBEL FORCES FROM CHICOM AND OTHERS
IN BURUNDI.
USEMBASSY BELIEVES WAGNER TO BE SOUTHAFRICAN NA-
TIONAL FORMERLY OFFICER IN EASTGERMAN ARMY. HE IS
KNOWN TO HAVE BEEN INVOLVED IN SUCCESSFUL DEFENSE
OF BUKAVU.
DANNELLY DEPUTY CHIEF OF MISSION.

"Yes, Sir, I've seen it."

"I thought McCone was going to shit a brick when he read that the Ambassador was using an East German mercenary as a source for his intelligence. I was tempted to tell him who he really is."

"Did you, Sir?"

"No. I felt a little dishonest. But if I had told him, the State Department would have found out, and sure as Christ made little apples, one of those bastards would convince himself it should be leaked. Jesus, what the newspapers would do with that if they latched on to it!"

"Yes, Sir, I agree."

"But what if something goes wrong and they capture Wagner? And show him off to the press?"

"The Simbas are not taking prisoners, Mr. President."

"But *if* they *did*? If I were Wagner, and they caught me, I'd damn sure tell them anything they wanted to hear. What makes you think this guy's so reliable?"

"You can never be absolutely sure of anything, Mr. President, but I don't think that Lieutenant Wagner, or any of the others, would permit themselves to fall into enemy hands."

The President looked at him thoughtfully. "You're pretty goddamned unemotional about that, aren't you?"

"These are all pretty special people, Mr. President," Felter said. "They understand what is involved. And being very cold-blooded about it, I think they would all decide that being a Simba prisoner was the worst possible scenario and take whatever action was necessary to keep that from happening."

The President grunted. "Save the last round for themselves? Like a John Wayne cowboys and Indians movie? Why do they do it, Felter?"

"There is an element of adventure, Sir. And probably what they call peer-group pressure. But I happen to believe that they believe in what they're doing. Using your John Wayne analogy, they see themselves as standing between the Indians and the wagon train."

"I'm not sure I could do something like that," the President said.

". . ." Felter stopped saying whatever his open mouth was about to say.

"Say what you were going to say, Colonel."

"I was about to say, Mr. President, that I think you could."

The President looked intently at Felter for a moment. "Didn't you ever hear that you can't bullshit a bullshitter, Felter?"

"I have something else, Mr. President."

"I'm afraid to ask what."

Felter reached in his pocket and handed the President a single sheet of white typewriter paper, folded in thirds—

The following was intercepted at 2120 Zulu 7 October. It originated in Kindu and was a voice transmission in the Swahili language. The message was recorded off the air and our translation confirmed by a Belgian priest fluent in Swahili.

Attention—this is a message from Lieutenant General Olenga, Commander-in-Chief of the Army of Liberation, to His Excellency President Christophe Gbenye, His Excellency Minister of Defense Gaston Emile Soumailot, and Colonel Opepe.

[repeated three times]

I give you official order. If NATO aircraft bomb and kill Congolese civilian population, please kill one foreigner for each Congolese of your region. Only chance which remains for us is to die with foreigners inhabiting liberated zones. If no bombing, please treat foreigners as honored guests in accordance with Bantu custom. Give them food and drink.

[repeated three times]

The entire message, with minor variations, is being repeated at approximately thirty-minute intervals.

The President raised his eyes from the sheet of typewriter paper and looked at Felter. "What's out of place here?" he asked. "What's different?"

"Sir?"

"I got it," he said. "Why isn't this stamped Top Secret—Presidential? Why is it on a regular piece of paper? This didn't come from the DIA did it? *Where did you get it, Felter?*"

"I have an intercept team in the Congo, Sir," Felter said. "It came from them. I'm sure the DIA will have it shortly and get it to you."

"Explain that," the President ordered. "Where the hell did you get your own intercept team?"

"There are several tactical ASA intercept teams attached to STRICOM, Sir," Felter said. "General Evans loaned me one of them."

The ASA's—or Army Security Agency's—original (and basic) function is the interception of enemy battlefield communications.

"What you're telling me is that there is civil war between the Congo Working Group and you and STRICOM to the point where one of you keeps the other in the dark?"

"I wouldn't put it quite that way, Sir. . . ."

"How *would* you put it, Colonel?" the President asked, coldly sarcastic.

Felter did not reply.

"Get out of here, Felter. I want some time to think before I get this latest bit of information through the proper channels."

[SIX]
Kongolo, Democratic Republic of the Congo
0600 1 November 1964

KONGOLO IS on the left bank of the Lualaba River, some 470 miles south of Stanleyville, where the Lualaba becomes the Congo River.

The senior military officer of the Democratic Republic of the Congo present in Kongolo was a Belgian, Commandant (Captain) Albert Liégeois, who was on loan to the Leopoldville government. He was small, soft-spoken, and old (forty-eight) by American standards for his rank. But he was strong-willed, and he had been a soldier since his youth, working his way up from the ranks.

Liégeois had swapped his Belgian captain's insignia for that of an ANC colonel after Michael Hoare showed up wearing the pips of an ANC lieutenant colonel.

Albert Liégeois was the officer commanding, and he wanted there to be absolutely no question about that. He had been charged with the recapture of Stanleyville and the liberation of the population (including the 1600 plus Europeans), as rapidly as humanly possible.

He was operating under a great handicap. In the interests of maintaining peace, both the United States and Belgium (90 percent of the Europeans in Stanleyville and elsewhere in rebel-occupied territory were Belgian nationals) had declined to open the doors of their military warehouses to Liégeois. His arms and equipment were what could be gathered together from ANC stocks already in the Congo and from stocks left behind by the UN Peace-keeping Force.

The original plan called for a force made up of 300 mercenaries and

1800 Congolese, transported in two hundred vehicles behind an "armored force."

He had been provided with fifty vehicles, 500 Katangese soldiers, and Michael Hoare had brought with him 120 mercenaries, of whom 100 spoke English, and of whom perhaps 35 had bona fide previous military service.

For the spearhead of a column which was to fight its way through 470 miles of Simba-occupied jungle, he had four armored vehicles, all of which had been left behind by the UN Peace-keeping Force. Three of these were Swedish armored cars, manufactured by Scania-Vabis. They were ungainly and heavy (eight tons) and both underpowered and thinly armored. And they could not be relied upon to turn either .30 caliber or 7mm rifle bullets. They were armed with three Browning .30 caliber machine guns, a dual mount in front and a single machine gun firing toward the rear. The fourth armored vehicle was an ex-Royal British Royal Army Ferret reconnaissance car, armed with one .30 caliber Browning machine gun.

Liégeois organized these assets into something he called Lima-One. His name began with an L, and the Belgian military phonetic code for L is Lima. And One because this was the first task force under his command.

Liégeois' fifty vehicles—most of them ordinary (as opposed to military, multiwheel-drive vehicles) two-ton trucks, but including some pickup trucks and even some jeeps—could carry only so many people. It was decided that all of Hoare's mercenaries would go in these. And when space for them was set aside, there was room for only 150 Congolese soldiers.

It was necessary for Lima-One to take with it its own fuel, food, water, ammunition, and spare parts. And Colonel Liégeois agreed with Lieutenant Colonel Hoare that although it was hazardous to load fuel and ammunition and troops on the same truck, it would have been more hazardous to the mission to risk losing a truckful of gasoline cans or ammunition all at once to a lucky shot by the Simbas.

It had been made quite clear to Liégeois that he could not expect resupply by air (or for that matter in any other way) during his operation, and there was no chance at all that he would be able to replenish his supplies of anything from captured enemy stocks.

So ammunition, parts, gasoline (in five-gallon tin containers—not Jerry cans), food, water, and personnel were divided among the vehicles. And Lima-One waited for permission to set out to recapture Stanleyville and other places in between.

Liégeois had supposed that permission would be automatic once he reported that he was ready to move out. But it hadn't come right away. One of Hoare's captains, a one-time officer in the East German Army, offered the theory that permission to move was waiting for the Presidential elections in the United States. He theorized that once they were over, permission would come.

Permission came at 0500 1 November. The former East German officer claimed that did not disprove his theory. It would take forty-eight hours, at least, for news of what they were doing in Kongolo to appear on American television or in American newspapers. That would be election morning at the earliest, too late to affect the outcome of the election.

At 0600 Lima-One moved out, with the Ferret in the lead. The Ferret was driven by a Congolese, visibly proud of his responsibility. Its .30 caliber Browning was manned by a French mercenary.

Lima-One crossed the Mulongoie River, a tributary of the Lualaba, shortly after noon. The bridge there had been destroyed by the Simbas, but Liégeois had thought of that and had dispatched two Belgian noncoms and a platoon of the Congolese, who were to remain behind to build a temporary bridge immediately after he had radioed Leopoldville that Lima-One was ready.

The heat was brutal, and the chemically purified water carried along tasted bad. And the troops, both Congolese and mercenary, were not well disciplined. Every time the convoy stopped near running water, the troops drank it. By nightfall diarrhea was common.

On 2 November, Lima-One reached and captured without resistance Gaston Emile Soumialot's hometown, Samba. It had been stripped of everything of value and deserted. They spent the night there, and in the morning, moved out again. There was a delay at the Lufubu River, another tributary of the Lualaba. The Simbas had tried but failed to destroy their bridge. But they did manage to blow up the approaches to it.

Liégeois ordered the construction of a ferry, on which the vehicles were floated across the river. He sent a small truck back to Kongolo with orders to send the Belgian noncoms to repair the bridge approaches.

That day in the United States, Lyndon Baines Johnson, who had acceded to the Presidency on the assassination of John F. Kennedy, was elected to that office in his own right.

Lima-One encountered its first resistance the next afternoon, 4 November, at the outskirts of Kibombo. Simba riflemen hidden here and there in the jungle brought the column under fire. The Scania-Vabis armored cars and the Ferret returned the fire and the Simbas fled.

Captain Wagner, who was operating from a jeep equipped with a .50 caliber Browning on a pedestal mount, ordered one of the Scania-Vabis reconnaissance cars (by now, perhaps inevitably, known as "the Sons of Bitches) to take the point. He followed it in his jeep. Two hundred yards down the road they found a grievously wounded Belgian sprawled in the road. He had been shot in the head with a shotgun; much of his face had been blown away.

Wagner sent his jeep back for a medic, then, motioning his driver to follow him, moved farther down the road. He came to a European house, on the veranda of which sat three elderly European men in rocking chairs. They did not respond to Wagner's hail, and when he got closer he saw that they were all dead. They had been shot in the chest and stomach with shotguns, one of them at least five times.

He returned to where he had found the wounded man. By then medics in a pickup truck and his jeep were at the site. He radioed to Colonel Liégeois, reporting what else he had found. Liégeois responded that he was coming up.

The man in the road was beyond help, but the morphine the medics gave him to ease his pain brought him around. When it became apparent that he was trying to say something, Colonel Liégeois and Captain Wagner were summoned.

He told them the Simbas were holding a total of seventy-five Europeans in Kindu, approximately seventy miles to the north. And he said he had heard Olengo himself vow to kill them.

Wagner was ordered to prepare to move out for Kindu immediately. The rest of Lima-One would follow as soon as they had secured Kimombo. The wounded man died before Wagner's force, headed by the Ferret and one of the Sons of Bitches, had formed up.

Shortly after dark, Wagner's column, running as fast as the Son of a Bitch could manage, turned a curve and found itself facing a Simba armored car. It was a Chevrolet stake truck to which the Simbas had welded steel plates, and on which they had mounted a Browning .50 caliber machine gun.

As the Son of a Bitch and Wagner's jeep slid to a stop and began to turn, the Ferret raced past them, its .30 caliber Browning blazing. The fire wiped out the Simba crew and did enough damage to make the truck unusable.

The machine gun was added to Lima-One's stock. Wagner examined the weapon and the ammunition. The ammunition was headstamped FA 50, which meant that it had been made at the U.S. Army Frankfurt Arsenal in 1950. It could have been ex-Belgian stock, or for that matter ex-Chicom. In the early days of the Korean War, the Chinese had captured vast quantities of United States armament from the U.S. Army.

If there was one "armored car," it was reasonable to presume there would be others. Wagner's column now moved much more slowly through the night. They were sniped at, and there were two failed attempts to ambush the column. Just after dawn the balance of Lima-One caught up with them.

It was midafternoon before Lima-One was in position outside Kindu and prepared to strike.

At 2:40, local time, six B-26K bombers appeared and made several passes, strafing and rocketing known or suspected Simba positions. Lima-One attacked before the B-26Ks were out of sight, under orders from Colonel Liégeois to drive straight through town to the river and then turn and mop up.

The Simbas took the truck-borne force under fire, but they were no match for the automatic weapons and the machine guns of Lima-One. After several ferocious firefights, the Simbas broke and ran for the river. Two hundred and fifty Simbas managed to board the ferry and other boats and to push off into the Lualaba before the mercenaries arrived.

But the mercenaries arrived in time to take the ferry and the other boats under machine-gun fire. They raked the boats until all the Simbas were dead.

Wagner, charged with locating Europeans, found a total of 125. Twenty-four of them were white men, Belgians and Greeks, who were wearing only their undershorts. The Simbas had selected them for immediate execution to coincide with the arrival of Lima-One. They had been ordered to strip (their clothing would be of use to the Simbas) and were being led to the rear yard of a house for the actual execution when the B-26Ks made their first strafing run. When a rocket landed near their captors and designated executioners, they fled.

Wagner found the Kindu monument to Patrice Lumumba. The pavement around the monument was cracked and fire-blackened, and Wagner sent Sergeant (Brevet Captain, Katangese Special Gendarmerie)

Edward C. Portley, whose Swahili was pretty good, to find out what had been burned there.

"They were saving their ammo to use on you honkies, Dutch," Portley, visibly shaken, reported a few minutes later. "So when they wanted to put their own people down, they brought them here, made 'em kneel, and poured gas on 'em."

"Blow it up, Portley," Wagner ordered.

"The guy I talked to said they did that to eight hundred people."

"Blow it up, Ed," Wagner repeated.

"Maybe we ought to find a photographer and take pictures of it and send them to those candy-asses in the State Department."

"Ed, all it would show would be some buckled pavement," Wagner said. "Nobody would believe what it was. Blow it up."

There was the sound of aircraft engines. They searched the sky and finally located the source. Two Curtiss Commandos.

"I thought we weren't going to get resupplied," Portley said.

"Liégeois's been radioing everybody he can think of," Wagner reported. "Maybe they're finally going to get off the dime."

"Sure," Portley said bitterly. "Two lousy C-46s. You know how fucking far we are from Stanleyville?"

He is pretty close to being hysterical, Wagner realized.

"You know how long, at this rate, it's going to take us to get there?" Portley went on furiously. "You know, I suppose, that Geoff Craig's wife and baby are in Stanleyville? You are a cold-blooded sonofabitch, aren't you? Don't you really give a shit?"

"Geoff Craig's wife is my sister," Wagner said quietly.

"Jesus Christ."

"Would you please blow this fucking monument up?"

"Dutch, I'm sorry. I didn't know."

"Do a good job," Wagner said. "Don't just knock it down. Blow it up."

"You got it, Dutch."

XXII

[ONE]
2301 Kildar Street
Alexandria, Virginia
7 November 1964

WHEN THE DOOR CHIMES sounded, Colonel Sanford T. Felter was sitting before the television set in his living room watching the NBC Evening News. He could not, if his life depended on it, report what he had just seen. He had other things on his mind. He had turned the television on because Sharon Felter probably would not try to cheer him up while he was watching the news.

"You want me to get that?" she called from the kitchen.

"No," he said, rising from the chair almost as a reflex action. Then, realizing how abrupt he had been, he added: "I was already up anyway, honey."

He pulled the door open.

"Good evening, Sir," Lieutenant Colonel Craig W. Lowell said. "I'm working my way through college selling magazines and the lady next door suggested you know how to read."

"Hello, Craig," Felter said and immediately raised his voice. "Sharon!"

Felter saw one of the White House motor pool Oldsmobiles parked at the curb.

"You flew Evans up?" Felter asked.

Lowell nodded.

"Craig!" Sharon Felter called happily and ran across the room to him. She hugged him quickly. "What brings you here?"

"They threw me out of the White House too," he said, "and I figured I could mooch a meal here."

"*Too?*" Sharon asked, looking at her husband.

"Not actually *thrown out*," Lowell said, "but it was made plain that I was as welcome as a hooker in church."

"How'd you get the car?" Felter asked.

There was a procedure, invariably scrupulously followed, for authorized personnel to avail themselves of cars in the White House fleet. There was a man in charge of the fleet. You or your secretary called him, gave him the destination, and if your name was on the proper list and a car was available, he would schedule a car for your use. Lowell was not on any White House list, and Felter's curiosity was aroused.

"I walked outside, walked up to it, and told the driver to take me to Colonel S. T. Felter," Lowell said. "He said, 'Yes, Sir' and opened the door for me and here I am."

Felter shook his head. There was no doubt in his mind that Lowell had accurately described what had happened. He had—had had since he was second lieutenant—an aura of authority about him. When he told people to do things, they simply didn't question his authority.

"You probably will get the driver in trouble," Felter said.

"I didn't hold a gun on him."

"I don't understand," Sharon said.

"It's not important," Felter said.

"What did he mean about getting thrown out of the White House, too?" Sharon asked.

"They are having a meeting to which we were not invited," Lowell explained. "My orders were to keep myself available. I had my choice between waiting in the chauffeurs and errand boys' lounge or coming here. I figured no matter what happens, Sandy would be among the first to know."

"And what if Evans sends for you?" Felter said.

"Why would he do that?"

"In case there were questions about—"

"Dragon Rouge?" Lowell asked. "Impossible. *I* wrote Dragon Rouge. When I write an OPLAN, as you should know by now, there simply aren't any ambiguous areas."

"God!" Felter said in exasperation.

"They aren't debating *how,* Sandy," Lowell said, now seriously. "They are debating *if.*"

"'Dragon Rouge'?" Sharon quoted. "Red Dragon? Can I ask—"

"No," Felter said.

"It's the operations plan to drop Belgian paratroopers on Stanleyville," Lowell said.

"Goddamn it, Craig!" Felter snapped. "Doesn't security mean a thing to you?"

"He obviously suspects you're an enemy agent, Sharon," Lowell said. "For my part I consider you absolutely trustworthy."

"You really push things, Craig," Felter said. "I really don't understand you sometimes."

"You'll have to forgive me, Colonel," Lowell said, a little irritated now. "But you will recall that I have kin in Stanleyville. We should have executed Dragon Rouge long before this. It may be too late now."

Felter didn't reply.

Lowell warmed to his subject.

"There is a new twist to military operations, Sharon. First, having concluded that some military action is necessary, they tell the military to plan an operation. And then, when the OPLAN is all done and all the services are agreed that this is the way to do it, then they have a meeting. First they decide all over again whether or not they really want to do it. Most of the time they decide it isn't really necessary after all. But if they decide it should be executed, then every sonofabitch and his brother gets a chance to play soldier. They 'modify' the OPLAN. You can't really consider yourself a bureaucrat of importance unless you have made a major modification to a plan drawn up by military professionals—"

"I think I better get you a drink," Sharon said. "I understand how you feel, Craig. And I'm sorry for you."

"Running off at the mouth isn't going to change things, Craig," Felter said.

"If I can't run off at the mouth at you, who then?" Lowell asked reasonably.

"I know what Craig drinks," Sharon said. "That really awful-tasting Scotch. Do you want something, Sandy?"

"Give me the same, please," Felter said.

There was surprise on his wife's face.

"Make his a weak one, Sharon," Lowell called to her. "It's liable to be a long night, and you know what happens when he gets a snootful. He sings bawdy songs and makes passes at strange women."

She laughed.

There was a buzzing sound.

"That's *that* phone," Sharon said.

"They have just found out they have a missing car," Felter said. "They haven't had time to decide on tea or coffee yet, much less anything more important."

Then he started up the stairs quickly, taking them two at a time. A few minutes later, just as Sharon was handing Craig Lowell a drink, he came back down the stairs, slowly this time. There was a troubled look on his face.

"Aw, come on, they can't be that pissed off about a lousy car," Lowell said.

"That was the President," Felter said. "All he said was, 'Colonel Felter, this is the President. Execute Operation Dragon Rouge.'"

[TWO]
Camp McCall U.S. Government Reservation,
North Carolina
8 November 1964

T HE WOULD-BE Green Berets had been parachuted into remote corners of the Camp McCall reservation, given a few rations, a compass, and a map, and told that their graduation depended on their being able to make their way from where they were to point A on their maps within seventy-two hours and without being discovered.

They had been involved in this exercise for nearly sixty-five hours, and the Major in charge of their training told Captain Stacey and Lieutenant Foster that he really had no idea where they would be.

"They have a radio," he explained, "radios, plural, in case somebody gets hurt or something. And they are supposed to report in once a day. But the clever ones—and this group includes some clever ones—generally figure out that if they go on the radio, we can fix their location by triangulation and bag them. So their radios malfunction. Get the picture?"

"May I make a suggestion, Sir?" Lieutenant Foster asked.

"Shoot," Captain Stacey said.

"Get a helicopter with a PA system and fly back and forth calling his name and telling him to let off a flare."

"They would probably figure that was a trick, too," the Major said.

"The alternative to giving that a try is calling General Hanrahan on the radio and telling him you have no idea where these guys are," Captain Stacey said.

"Or waiting another seven hours until their time is up."

"We don't have another seven hours," Captain Stacey said.

The discussion was interrupted by the cacophony of simulated war: the sputter of blank cartridges, the puff of smoke grenades, and the astonishingly lifelike—and thus terrifying—sound of simulators artillery (incoming whistle, momentary pause, and then deafening explosion) going off.

"Our pigeons," the Major said, "are apparently returning to the roost."

"Foster, go get him, will you please?" Captain Stacey said.

The enormous bulletheaded former Notre Dame All-American walked with a quick grace to the door of the shed and stepped out into the darkness.

"Portet!" he called in a booming voice. "Yo, Jack!"

"I'd just love to know what's going on," the Major said.

"I bet you would," Captain Stacey said.

"And you're not going to tell me, are you?"

"No," Stacey said, smiling. "I'm not."

"Then 'No, Sir, I'm not.'"

"No, Sir, I'm not."

"Prick."

"I respectfully suggest the Major has been out here eating snakes too long," Stacey said, "without adequate sexual release. There is obviously something Freudian in what you just said."

The door opened and Portet walked in. He was filthy. His face and hands were scratched and marked with insect bites. His uniform was soaking wet and he looked exhausted. He looked at Stacey curiously.

He's going to look like hell in civilian clothes, Stacey thought. *But that can't be helped.*

"Well, if it isn't Prince Charming," he said.

"Sergeant," the Major said, "I have been ordered to turn you over to these officers."

"Now what?" Jack said. He was too tired to be polite.

"I hope you didn't have heavy plans for the weekend," Stacey said. Portet's eyes lit up.

"Don't ask, Jack," Stacey said quickly. And then, as if it was all a joke: "Just come along quietly. Lieutenant Foster will read your Miranda rights to you in the car."

[THREE]
The Hotel Continental
3, Rue Castiglione
Paris, France
10 November 1964

THE HOTEL CONTINENTAL sits on the corner of the Rue Castiglione (which runs from the Place Vendôme—where the Ritz Hotel is located—to the Tuileries Gardens) and the Rue de Rivoli (which runs along the Tuileries Gardens from the Place de la Concorde).

It is an old and elegant hotel, with something of a military history. General of the Armies John J. Pershing lived there during World War I. And in World War II Hitler's last message to Paris before its liberation, *"Brennt Paris?"* (Is Paris burning?) was addressed to General von Choltitz, who lived in the Continental. Von Choltitz there decided to ignore his Führer's order to reduce Paris to rubble, aware that the penalty for doing so was death.

Tonight, the hotel was full of senior military officers in their most colorful dress uniforms. It was the birthday of the United States Marine Corps and the occasion was being marked with the traditional Marine Corps Ball. The senior Marine present in Paris (a major general attached to the United States European Command at Camp des Loges just outside Paris) and his lady had issued invitations not only to all Marine officers in the area, but to all the general, flag, and field-grade officers assigned to EUCOM regardless of service, and to a list (prepared for him by the U.S. Embassy protocol officer) of foreign officers, including all the military attachés of the friendly embassies. The Deputy Commandant of the Royal Marines and his lady had flown in from London for the occasion, and the band of the United States Seventh Army had been shipped in by train from Heidelberg to provide the music.

The invitation specified dress uniform. The unofficial word went out from the office of the full general commanding EUCOM that he expected to see his officers there, and in dress uniform. No rented dinner jackets, no class A's with white shirts and black bow ties. *Dress uniform,* and in the case of general and flag officers, dress mess uniform.

There was some grumbling of course. Goddamned Marines. And *dress mess?* In dress mess you looked like a goddamned pansy tenor in a Sigmund Romberg operetta. But there were also those who privately were pleased. The Marines always threw a good party, and since you had to lay out all the goddamned money to buy the sonofabitch, you might as well get some wear out of it. And besides, there weren't all that many opportunities to do so.

Brigadier General and Mrs. Harris McCord, USAF, arrived at the Hotel Continental shortly after ten P.M. General McCord personally thought whoever had designed the full-dress uniform for general officers of the USAF had gone a little overboard. But at the same time he thought, *What the hell, why let the Marines and the Army and the Navy have all the sartorial glory?*

He checked his cap and his cape, and Mrs. McCord her brand-new silver fox stole, and then he stood on the parquet floor outside the ladies' room while she touched up her hair and face. Then she came out and took his arm, and walked to the Grand Ball Room and handed over their invitation to a Marine buck sergeant in dress blues. He glanced at it and then boomed, "Brigadier General and Mrs. Harris McCord, United States Air Force!"

Then they went down the reception line and shook the hands of the United States Ambassador, the EUCOM Commander, the senior Marine in the area, the senior sailor, and the senior Air Force officer.

General McCord did not get the expected "Good evening, Harry" from the senior Air Force officer.

The senior Air Force officer said quietly, "Harry, I don't know what the hell it's all about, but we got an operational immediate that a courier is en route with orders. I'm probably going to need you. Hang loose. And don't go anywhere but here and home."

The weather was bad and the courier's flight was delayed, so he didn't land at Orly until half past four the next morning. It wasn't until half past five the next morning that EUCOM had its orders. A few minutes later Brigadier General McCord had his.

TOP SECRET

Duplication Forbidden

For Distribution By Officer Courier Only

THE JOINT CHIEFS OF STAFF WASHINGTON D.C.

8 November 1964

Commanding General, United States Strike Command

Commanding General, European Command

Commanding General, United States Air Force, Europe

Commanding General, Seventh United States Army

1. By Direction of the President; by Command of His Royal Highness, the King of the Belgians; and at the request of the government of the Democratic Republic of the Congo, a Joint Belgian-American Operation, OPERATION DRAGON ROUGE, will take whatever military action is necessary to effect the rescue of American, Belgian, and other European nationals currently being held hostage in Stanleyville, Democratic Republic of the Congo, by forces in rebellion against the legal and duly constituted government of the Democratic Republic of the Congo.

2. By Direction of the President, Sanford T. Felter, Counselor to the President (Colonel, General Staff Corps, USA) is designated Action Officer, and will be presumed, in connection with military matters, to be speaking with the authority of the Joint Chiefs of Staff.

3. OPERATION DRAGON ROUGE is assigned an AAAA-1 Priority with regard to the requisitioning of personnel, equipment, and other U.S. military assets.

4. Addressees will on receipt of this directive immediately dispatch an officer in the grade of colonel or higher to the United States Embassy, Brussels, Belgium, where they will make themselves available to Colonel Felter or such officers as he may designate to represent him.

FOR THE CHAIRMAN, THE JOINT CHIEFS OF STAFF

Forbes T. Wilis
Brigadier General, USMC
Executive Officer, JCS

TOP SECRET

By then, weather had really turned to shit and flying was out of the question. It was necessary for General McCord to drive to Brussels. He arrived there in a freezing rain shortly after noon.

[FOUR]
Brussels, Belgium
1320 Hours 11 November 1964

BRIGADIER GENERAL HARRIS MCCORD thought he had yet another proof—if one were needed—that life is full of little ironies. Sixteen hours before—in anticipation of having a nip or two, tripping the light fantastic with his wife, and perhaps having a romantic breakfast at dawn in one of the quaint old restaurants before the Sacré-Coeur church in Montmartre—he had been wearing a military uniform, complete to real medals (rather than ribbons) and more silver embellishments than a Christmas tree. A warrior dressed up to party.

Now that he was about to engage in what promised to be a really hairy exercise, he was wearing a somewhat baggy tweed jacket and well-worn flannel slacks. Just before he had left Paris, he had been told to wear civilian clothing. What he had on was all that had come back from the dry cleaners.

In a none-too-fancy conference room in the U.S. Embassy were five peers, most of whom he knew at least by sight, all in civilian clothing, and all waiting for Colonel Sanford T. Felter and his staff. The whole damned continent had been socked in, and Felter's plane had had to sit down in Scotland to wait for Brussels to clear to bare minimums.

He had heard of Felter, of course, but he had never seen him in person.

He was not very impressed when Felter walked into the room. He was small and slight and in a baggy gray suit.

"Sorry to keep you waiting, gentlemen," Felter said. He threw a heavy briefcase on the table, then took a key from his pocket and unlocked the padlock which he had chained—more accurately steel-cabled—to his wrist.

Five men in civilian clothing had followed him into the room, and Felter impatiently gestured for them to find seats. McCord looked closely as Felter worked the combination lock on the briefcase. He had something in his lapel buttonhole that represented some medal. McCord didn't know what one it was, however. Medals came in a box that contained the medal itself, the ribbon representing the medal, and a pin intended for the buttonhole. Whatever it was called, Felter was wearing one, and McCord studied it until he was sure what it was.

It was the Distinguished Service Cross, the nation's second-highest award for valor. McCord had heard (and he almost completely accepted) the military folklore that winners of the DSC were people entitled to the Medal of Honor who had somewhere along the line pissed off somebody important.

The DSC, McCord decided, not only proved that he was a bona fide hero, but that he was clever. With a DSC in your lapel you didn't have to prove to anybody that you were a warrior, even if you were a little Jew who looked like a middle-level bureaucrat.

"Colonel Bradeen I know," Felter said, flashing half a smile at a tall, stocky, barrel-chested man McCord knew to be an armor colonel on the 7th Army staff.

"How are you, Sandy?" Colonel Bradeen said.

"My name is McCord, Colonel," General McCord said, and went to Felter and offered his hand.

"I'm glad you were available, General," Felter said.

As the others introduced themselves to Felter, McCord considered that. Felter knew who he was, and there was an implication that he had asked for him by name. That was flattering unless you were rank conscious and thought that general officers should pick colonels rather than the other way around.

"For those who don't know him," Felter said, "this is Colonel Joseph Pellman, USMC, of JCS."

Who, General McCord thought, *has obviously been sent by JCS to keep an eye on Felter. The brass on JCS must have really shit a brick when "by direction of the President" Felter was put in charge.*

"I think the best way to handle this, gentlemen," Felter said, "is to give you a quick sketch of what's going on in the Congo, specifically in Stanleyville, and then to tell you what we intend to try to do to set it right.

"There are sixteen hundred people—Europeans, white people—in Stanleyville. A four-column relief force—in other words, four different columns—under the overall command of Colonel Frederick Van der Waele of the Belgian Army has been charged with suppressing the rebellion, which includes, of course, the recapture of Stanleyville.

"There have been some successes, as you probably know from your own sources, but Van der Waele probably will not be able to make it to Stanleyville before the end of the month.

"That poses two problems. The first is the rebels' announced intention to kill the hostages—a threat we consider bona fide—before Van der Waele can get to them. The second is that we have hard intelligence that since 20 October unmarked Ilyushin-18 turboprop aircraft—at least two and probably as many as four—have been flying arms and ammunition from Algeria into the Arau air base in northern Uganda on a regular basis. Should they decide to do so, it would be easy for them to move the arms and ammunition to Olenga's forces. The possibility of their doing so, it is believed, increases as Van der Waele's mercenaries and ANC troops approach Stanleyville.

"The President has decided, in consultation with the Belgian Premier Spaak, that the first priority is to keep those sixteen hundred people alive. The Belgians have made available the First Parachutist Battalion of their Paracommando Regiment. I'm familiar with it. The First Battalion was trained by the British Special Air Service people in War Two, and they pride themselves now on being just as good. The regiment is commanded by Colonel Charles Laurent, who is a fine officer and who I suspect will lead the First Battalion himself.

"They will be carried to Stanleyville in USAF aircraft, where, after the airfield is softened up with some B-26s, they will make a parachute landing and seize the airport. Part of the force will remain at the airport to make the airport is ready to receive the C-130s, and the balance will enter Stanleyville, find the Europeans, and bring them to the airport. They will be loaded aboard the C-130s and then everybody leaves. No attempt will be made to hold Stanleyville. I don't want any questions right now. I just wanted to give the rough idea.

"These gentlemen," Felter went on, turning to indicate them, "are Lieutenant Colonel Lowell, Captain Stacey, Lieutenant Foster, and Sergeant Portet. They're Green Berets. Colonel Lowell is on the STRICOM staff and wrote Dragon Rouge. Captain Stacey and the others have been practicing a somewhat smaller operation intended for Stanleyville, now called off. But they know the town and rebel dispositions and the probable location of the Europeans. And I brought them along to share their expertise."

Lowell, General McCord thought, looked like a bright guy, though not much like what he expected Green Berets to look like. Stacey, General McCord decided, looked like a typical young captain, a hard charger, tough mean and lean. The black guy looked as if he could chew railroad spikes and spit tacks. The Sergeant . . . there was something wrong with the Sergeant. His face was scratched and blotchy and swollen. He could hardly see out of his eyes. And whatever was wrong with his face was also wrong with his hands.

"As soon as we wind it up here, Colonel Lowell will be available to explain any questions you might have about the OPLAN for Dragon Rouge. Stacey and Foster are going to liaise with the Belgians," Felter said. "Sergeant Portet, General McCord, I'm more or less going to give to you. He's a former airlines pilot with extensive experience in the Congo, including of course, Kamina and Stanleyville. And equally important, because he was involved in getting the B-26Ks to the Congo, he knows most of the Cubans Dick Fulbright hired to fly them."

"Glad to have all the help I can get," McCord said.

I wonder if he caught whatever it is is wrong with his face and hands in the Congo? I wonder if it's contagious?

"From Seventh Army, Jim," Felter said to Colonel Bradeen, "I want stocks of whatever the paracommandos may not have. I understand they're in good shape, but I want supplies ready if I need them. Get on that right away. As soon as I know where and when to take them, I'll let you know. But I want the stuff already on trucks when I call for it."

"You'll have it," Bradeen said.

"Today is Armistice Day," Felter said. "So that the press would not get suspicious of activity at the War Ministry on a holiday, I have scheduled the first staff conference for tomorrow morning at eight. It's at 8, Rue de la Loi, in downtown Brussels. Civilian clothing. I feel obliged to say this: If word of this gets out, it will mean the massacre of civilians. And there are people here in Brussels watching to see what if anything the Belgians are going to do."

He looked around the room. "I have rough OPLANS here. Study them overnight, take what action—in your case, General McCord, that probably will mean making sure we have the necessary aircraft available, and without calling attention to it—you know will be necessary, and be prepared to offer fixes for what is wrong with the OPLAN tomorrow morning. That will be all for now, gentlemen. Thank you. But keep yourselves available."

Felter and three of the Green Berets started to leave the room. Lowell opened a well-stuffed briefcase. Felter caught the Sergeant's attention and nodded toward General McCord. The Sergeant walked over to General McCord.

"Colonel Felter said I am to make myself useful, Sir." Jack Portet said.

McCord resisted the temptation to offer his hand.

"You've been into Stanleyville, Sergeant?"

"Yes, Sir."

"Purely as a matter of idle curiosity, I've looked at the Jepp charts," General McCord said. "I know we can get 130s in there."

"Yes, Sir, easily. I've seen them there."

"But I should have looked closer," McCord said. "How many will it take at once?"

Portet's swollen face wrinkled in thought. "No more than six at once, Sir. To be safe, I would say no more than five."

Then, as if he were no longer able to resist an awful temptation, he put his hand up and scratched at the open blotches his face. With a hand that was similarly disfigured with suppurating sores.

"What's wrong with your face, son?" General McCord asked. "And your hand?"

"It's nothing, Sir. A little rash."

"A little rash, my ass. How long has it been that way?"

"It started on the plane from the States, Sir. It's some kind of an allergy probably. Nothing to worry about."

"Where were you in States? Bragg?"

"Yes, Sir."

"Come with me, Sergeant," McCord said.

He had seen the Military Attaché's office on the way to the conference room, and he led Jack there.

There was a captain on duty, who glanced up and was not very impressed with what he saw. Two messy Americans in mussed clothing, one of them with what looked like a terminal case of scabies on his face.

"Yes?" he asked.

"I'm General McCord," McCord said, which caused the Captain to come to his feet and to stand to attention.

"Yes, Sir!"

"Would you be good enough to get me the Commanding Officer of the nearest U.S. military medical facility on the telephone, please?"

"General," Jack said, "I'll be all right. I don't want to get put in a hospital now."

"I expected as much from a Green Beret," McCord said. "But I would be very surprised if they'll let you get on the airplane, much less jump on Stanleyville. It looks to me as if the whole purpose of the Belgians is to keep Americans out of it."

"My stepmother and my sister are in Stanleyville, General. I'm going in."

McCord looked at him. Before he could frame a reply, the Captain handed him a telephone.

"Colonel Aspen, Sir."

"Colonel, this is General McCord. This may sound a little odd. But I want you to dispatch, immediately, one of your best medical officers. I am in the U.S. Embassy and I have a young sergeant with me who, if my diagnosis is correct, has been rolling around in poison oak." There was a pause. "No, Colonel, he cannot come there. I don't want to argue about this. I expect to see either you or one of your doctors here within twenty minutes."

He hung up the phone and turned to smile at Jack.

"They give you a shot," he said. "It clears it up in a couple of hours. I had it in survival school in Utah a couple of years ago."

"Thank you very much, Sir."

"Don't get your hopes up about anything else, Sergeant," General McCord said. "I know they won't let you go."

"Yes, Sir," Jack said.

[FIVE]
Leopoldville, Democratic Republic of the Congo
15 November 1964

URGENT
FROM US EMBASSY LEOPOLDVILLE DEM REPCONGO

TO SECSTATE WASH DC

STANLEYVILLE SITUATION UPDATE AS OF 2400 ZULU
14 NOVEMBER 1964

FRENCH LANGUAGE 1800 ZULU BROADCAST OVER RADIO STANLEYVILLE SAID MAJOR REPEAT MAJOR PAUL CARLSON HAS BEEN SENTENCED TO DEATH BY WAR CRIMES TRIBUNAL. BROADCAST SAID CARLSON HAD BEEN DEFENDED QUOTE BY CONGOLESE OFFICERS OF HIS OWN CHOOSING ENDQUOTE

FOLLOWING FULL TEXT TRANSLATION STATEMENT FRONT PAGE LE MARTYR NEWSPAPER STANLEYVILLE 13 NOVEMBER 1964 SIGNED GBENYE QUOTE WE HOLD IN OUR CLAWS MORE THAN THREE HUNDRED AMERICANS AND MORE THAN EIGHT HUNDRED BELGIANS WHO ARE KEPT UNDER SURVEILLANCE AND IN SECURE PLACES. AT THE SLIGHTEST BOMBARDMENT OF OUR REGION OR OF OUR REVOLUTIONARY CAPITAL, WE SHALL BE FORCED TO MASSACRE THEM.

QUOTE CONTINUES ALL AMERICANS AND BELGIANS LIVING UNDER OUR PROTECTION HAVE WRITTEN AND SIGNED THEIR LAST WILL. WE SHALL SEND THESE DOCUMENTS SHORTLY TO THEIR RESPECTIVE DESTINATIONS. THE SECURITY OF THESE INDIVIDUALS IS SUBJECT TO THE RETREAT FROM THE CONGO OF THE BELGIANS AND AMERICANS WHO MASSACRE OUR PEOPLE CONTINUOUSLY.

QUOTE CONTINUES WE SHALL MAKE FETISHES WITH THE HEARTS OF THE AMERICANS AND WE SHALL DRESS OURSELVES IN THE SKINS OF THE BELGIANS AND THE AMERICANS ENDQUOTE

THERE HAS BEEN NO REPEAT NO CONTACT WITH INTELSOURCE

STANLEYVILLE IN FORTY EIGHT HOURS.

DANNELLY DEPUTY CHIEF OF MISSION

[SIX]
Washington, D.C.
16 November 1964

URGENT
FROM SECSTATE WASH DC
USAMBASSADOR NAIROBI KENYA
IMMEDIATELY SEEK AUDIENCE WITH JOMO KENYATTA
AND RELAY FOLLOWING:
DEAR MR. PRIME MINISTER:
BOTH PERSONALLY AND ON BEHALF OF THE AMERICAN PEO-
PLE I IMPLORE YOU TO USE YOUR GREAT PERSONAL INFLU-
ENCE THROUGHOUT AFRICA TO SPARE THE LIFE OF DR. PAUL
CARLSON.
THE US GOVERNMENT DECLARES UNEQUIVOCALLY THAT DR.
CARLSON IS NOT IN ANY WAY CONNECTED WITH THE US
MILITARY AND HAS BEEN ENGAGED ONLY IN HIS ACTIVITIES
AS A MEDICAL MISSIONARY. DR. CARLSON IS A MAN OF PEACE
WHO HAS SERVED THE CONGOLESE PEOPLE WITH DEDICA-
TION FOR YEARS.
HIS EXECUTION ON PATENTLY FALSE CHARGES WOULD BE AN
OUTRAGEOUS VIOLATION OF INTERNATIONAL LAW AND OF
ACCEPTED STANDARDS OF HUMANITARIAN CONDUCT.
END MESSAGE.
SECSTATE CONSIDERS DELIVERY OF THIS MESSAGE
AT EARLIEST POSSIBLE TIME ABSOLUTELY ESSENTIAL.

[SEVEN]
Kleine-Brogel Air Base, Belgium
2225 Hours 16 November 1964

BRIGADIER GENERAL HARRIS MCCORD had asked for permission to go along. But it had been denied.

But the pilot of Chalk One was a friend of his, and he was not able to resist going to the flight deck and standing between the seats and chewing the fat a little as they waited for The Word.

The Word came.

"Chalk One."

"Chalk One, go."

"The Word is go, repeat go."

"Chalk One understands go," the Colonel said, and made a wind-it-up motion with his index finger.

"Clear!" the copilot shouted out the window.

"Good luck, Don," General McCord said.

"Thank you, General," the pilot said.

Three of the C-130's engines were turning by the time General McCord walked down the passenger compartment to the open door, past the rows of red-bereted Belgian paratroopers.

And then he stopped and looked very closely at one of the paratroopers. "I see your skin has cleared up."

"Yes, Sir, thank you, Sir."

General McCord nodded to the Belgian paratrooper and then exited the aircraft.

"Kleine-Brogel, Chalk One taxiing to the active."

"Kleine-Brogel clears Chalk One as number one to take off."

"Roger, understand number one."

Chalk One turned onto the threshold. Without stopping it turned onto the runway.

"Chalk One rolling," the copilot said to the microphone.

Seven minutes later, having followed Chalk One at thirty-second intervals, the remaining fourteen C-130Es of Dragon Rouge were airborne. They climbed to twenty thousand feet and headed for Morón de la Frontera, an air base in Spain, where they landed, took on fuel, and immediately took off again, this time headed for a small speck of volcanic matter in the Atlantic Ocean known as Ascension Island.

XXIII

[ONE]
Gene-Gene, Democratic Republic of the Congo
0530 25 November 1964

CAPTAIN KARL-HEINZ WAGNER of the Katangese Special Gendarmerie was more than a little worried that Colonel Hoare would know that the men in the jeeps were not drinking coconut juice from the coconuts they had in their hands.

Hoare's sometimes violent temper flared when he found the men drinking when an operation was scheduled.

And Karl-Heinz Wagner wondered whether his decision—to play dumb and blind—was proper behavior for him as an officer. He had rationalized his decision. They didn't have that much to drink. And as soon as they got under way, the brutal heat would burn the alcohol from their bodies. If he raised hell about it, not only would there be bitter resentment (and they were already drunk, and a nasty confrontation was likely), but Colonel Hoare would probably be curious about the uproar and then there would be hell to pay.

Or is it that I am just so damned tired that I no longer give a damn?

Hoare came walking down the line of vehicles. When he reached Wagner's jeep, Karl-Heinz started to get out. Hoare motioned to him to stay where he was. He walked up to him.

"I notice that the men have taken to coconut milk," Hoare said. He let

Wagner stew for a moment and then went on: "I think you and I had better wait until we get to Stanleyville, don't you?"

"Yes, Sir."

"Get it moving, Wagner."

Karl-Heinz made a wind-it up gesture to his jeep driver and then stood up in the jeep, resting on the .50 caliber Browning until he saw that all of his vehicles had their engines turning.

"OK, Ed," he said. "Move it out."

"We're supposed to be sixty miles from Stanleyville," Portley said. "And the last twenty miles are supposed to be paved. Do you think that's so?"

"I would be very pleasantly surprised," Wagner said.

[TWO]
Stanleyville, Republic of the Congo
0600 25 November 1964

A s a tradition, the men of the First Battalion, the Paracommando Regiment, Royal Belgian Army, continued to use the English-language jump commands the battalion had learned in England in World War II.

"*Out*board sticks, stand *up!*"

The two outside files of men inside Chalk One stood up and folded up their nylon and aluminum pole seats back against the fuselage wall.

"*In*board sticks, stand *up!*"

The two inside files rose to their feet and folded their seats.

"Hook *up!*"

Everybody fastened the hook at the end of his static line to a steel cable.

"Check static *lines*! Check equip*ment!*"

Everybody tugged at his own static line to make sure it was securely hooked to the cable and then checked the harness and other equipment of the man standing in front, that is to say, in the lines which now faced rear and led to the exit doors on either side of the aircraft.

Now the jumpmaster switched to French: *"Une minute!"* and then back to English: *"Stand* in the *door!"*

Chalk One was down to seven hundred feet or so and all dirtied up: flaps down, throttles retarded, close (at 125mph) to stall speed.

"Go!"

Jack Portet was the sixth man in the portside stick.

He felt the slight tug of the static line almost immediately after exiting the aircraft, and a moment later felt his main chute slithering out of the case. And then the canopy filled and he had a sensation of being jerked upward.

There was not enough time to orient himself beyond seeing the airfield beneath and slightly to the left of him, and to pick out the white Immoquateur building downtown, before the ground seemed to suddenly rush up at him. He knew where he was now. He landed on the tee of the third hole of the Stanleyville Golf Course. He landed on his feet, but when he started to pull on the lines to dump a little air from the nearly emptied canopy, there was a sudden gust of air and the canopy filled and pulled him off his feet.

He hit the quick release and was out of the harness a moment later. He rolled over and saw that the sky was full of chutes from Chalk Two and Chalk Three.

And then there were peculiar whistling noises, and peculiar cracking noises, and after a moment Jack realized that he was under fire.

And there didn't seem to be anybody to shoot back at.

And then, all of a sudden, there was.

There were Simbas firing from the control tower, of all places.

He dropped to the ground, worked the action of the FN assault rifle, and took aim at the tower. Which, as he lined his sights up, promptly disappeared in a cloud of dust. In a moment he had the explanation for that. Two paratroopers had gotten their machine guns in action.

Jack got to his feet and ran toward a trio of Belgian officers. When there was transportation—either something captured here or else the jeeps or the odd-looking three-wheelers which the C-130s were supposed to land—the officers would get first crack at it. And he wanted to be there when it arrived. He had to get to the Immoquateur and he needed wheels to do that.

A sergeant drove up in a white pickup with a Mobil Oil Pegasus painted on its doors.

One of the Belgian officers looked around and then pointed to Jack.

"That one—*l'américain*—knows the town. Put half a dozen men in the back and make a reconnaissance by fire."

And then he made his little joke:

"You better hope you get killed, because *le grand noir* was looking for you and couldn't find you." He paused and looked hard at the other man. *Le grand noir*—the Big Black—was of course Lieutenant Foster. "He said he was going to kill you if he found you in Belgium, and if you managed to come along, he would pull your legs and arms off, one by one, if you came through this."

Jack smiled and climbed on the running board of the Mobil Oil pickup, holding the FN in one hand.

But he was suddenly very frightened. Not of fighting, or even of dying, but of what he was liable to find when he got to the Immoquateur.

They first encountered resistance three hundred yards down the road, just past the Sabena guest house. A Simba wrapped in an animal skin, with a pistol in one hand and a sword in the other, charged at them down the middle of the road. Behind him came three others armed with FN assault rifles. They were firing them on full automatic.

The pickup truck screeched to a halt. Jack went onto his belly, his rifle to his shoulder. As he found a target, he was baffled to see that the Simba's weapon was firing straight up into the air. There was a short burst of 7mm fire over his head. The Simba with the sword stopped in midstride and then crumpled to his knees. Before he fell over, a torrent of blood gushed from his mouth.

The Simbas with him stopped and looked at the fallen man in absolute surprise. Then they stopped shooting and started to back up. There was another burst of the fire from the pickup, this time from several weapons. Two of the three Simbas fell down, one of them backward. The remaining Simba, the one in Jack's sights, dropped his rifle and ran away with great loping strides. There was another burst of fire from the truck, no more than four rounds from a paratrooper's assault rifle. The Simba took two more steps and then fell on his face to the left.

Jack scrambled to his knees and turned to look for the truck. It was already moving. He jumped onto the running board as it came past, almost losing his balance as the driver swerved, unsuccessfully, to avoid running over the Simba who had led the charge with a sword.

There was a furious horn bleating behind them, and the pickup pulled off the shoulder of the road. A jeep raced past them, the gunner of the pedestal-mounted .30 caliber Browning machine gun firing it in short bursts at targets Jack could not see.

The pickup swerved back onto the paved surface, almost throwing Jack off.

There was the sound of a great many weapons being fired, but none of the fire seemed directed at them. They reached the first houses. There were more Simbas in sight now, but none of them were attacking. They were in the alleys between the houses and in the streets behind them.

The jeep that had raced past them was no longer in sight, but Jack could still hear the peculiar sound of the Browning firing in short bursts.

The Mobil Oil pickup truck came to an intersection and stopped. Jack looked at the driver.

"You're supposed to be the fucking expert," the driver said to him. "Where do we go?"

"Right," Jack ordered without really thinking about it. The Immoquateur was to the right.

The pickup jerked into motion.

Fifty yards down the road they came across the first Europeans. Three of them, mother, father, and a twelve- or thirteen-year-old boy, were sprawled dead in pools of blood in the road. They'd obviously been shot as they had tried to run.

Jack felt nausea rise in his throat, but managed to hold it down.

Ahead, over the roofs of the pleasant, pastel-painted villas, he saw the white bulk of the Immoquateur.

Then there was fire directed at them.

The pickup screeched to a stop in the middle of the street. Jack felt himself going, tried valiantly to stop himself, and then, bouncing off the fender, fell onto the pavement on his face.

He felt his eyes water, and then they lost focus.

Jesus Christ! I've been shot!

He shook his head, then put his hand to his face. There was something warm on it.

Blood! I've been shot in the face!

He sat up. Someone rushed up to him. Indistinctly, he made out one of the paratroopers leaning over him, felt his fingers on his face.

And then the sonofabitch laughed.

"You're all right," he said. "All you've got is a bloody nose."

He slapped Jack on the back and ran ahead of him.

Jack's eyes came back in focus. He looked at his lap and saw blood dripping into it.

He looked around and saw his assault rifle on the street six feet from where he was sitting. He scurried on his knees to it, picked it up, fired a burst in the air to make sure it was still functioning, and then looked around again, this time at the Immoquateur. There were bodies on the lawn between the street and the shops on the ground floor. Simba and European. He got to his feet and ran toward the Immoquateur.

[THREE]

JACK RECOGNIZED one of the bodies on the lawn before the Immoquateur. It was the Stanleyville station manager of the Congo River Steamship Company. He had met him when they had shipped in a truck. The man had been shot in the neck, probably with a shotgun, from the size of the wound. The stout, gray-haired woman lying beside him with an inch-wide hole in her forehead was almost certainly his wife.

Jack ran into the building itself. There were two dead Simbas in the narrow elevator corridor. One of them had most of his head blown away. The other had taken a burst in the chest as he came out of the elevator. It had literally blown a hole through his body. Parts of his ribs—or his spine, some kind of bone anyhow—were sticking at awkward angles out his back.

He was lying in the open elevator door. The door of the elevator had tried to close on his body. When the door encountered the body, it reopened and then tried to close again. It had been cycling like that since the man fell there.

Jack laid his FN assault rifle against the wall, put his hands on the dead man's neck, and dragged him free. The elevator door closed, a melodious chime bonged, and the elevator started up.

"Shit!"

Jack went to the call button for the other elevator and pushed it. It did not illuminate. He ran farther down the corridor and pushed the service elevator call button. It lit up, but there was no sound of elevator machinery. He went back to wait for the first elevator.

One of the Belgian paratroopers from the pickup truck came into the corridor. He was in a crouch with his rifle ready.

"The Sergeant said you are to come back to the truck," he said.

"Fuck him—my mother's upstairs."

The paratrooper ran back out of the building. The elevator indicator showed that it was on the ninth floor. Then it started to come down.

The paratrooper came running back into the building. Jack wondered if he was going to give him any trouble.

"I got a radio," he said. "They are leaving us."

Jack felt something warm on his hand, looked down, and saw blood.

The elevator mechanism chimed pleasantly and the door opened. Jack stepped over the dead Simba. The Belgian paratrooper followed him inside and crossed himself as Jack pushed the floor button.

The door closed and the elevator started to rise.

It stopped at the fourth floor.

A Simba in parts of a Belgian officer's uniform did not have time to raise his pistol before a burst from Jack's assault rifle smashed into his midsection.

The noise in the closed confines of the elevator was painful and dazzling. Jack's ears rang enough for him to doubt whether he'd be able to hear anything but the loudest of sounds for a long time. The paratrooper with Jack jumped in a crouch into the corridor and let loose a burst down the corridor. It was empty.

The Simba he had shot had backed into the corridor wall and then slid to the floor, leaving a foot-wide track of blood down the wall. Jack thought he saw life leave the Simba's eyes.

He took the Simba's pistol, a World War II–era Luger, from the Simba's hand, stuffed it in the chest pocket of his tunic, and then backed back into the elevator. The paratrooper backed into it after him. The chime sounded melodiously again, the doors closed, and the elevator started up again.

When the door opened they were on the tenth floor. There was no one there.

Neither Jack nor the paratrooper moved.

The chime sounded again and the door closed.

Jack reached out with the muzzle of his FN and rapped the rubber edge of the door. The door started to open again.

Copying what the paratrooper had done on the fourth floor, Jack jumped in a crouch into the corridor. But the corridor was empty.

Jack ran to the door of the Air Simba apartment. There were bullet holes in it, and it was battered as if someone had tried to bash his way in. He put his hand on the doorknob. It was locked.

He banged on it with his fist.

"Hanni!" he shouted. *"Hanni, c'est moi! C'est Jacques!"*

There was no answer.

He raised the butt of the FN and smashed at the door in the area of the knob. The butt snapped off behind the trigger assembly.

He felt tears well up in his eyes. He pulled the trigger to see if it would still work, and there was another painful roar of sound, and a cloud of cement dust as the bullets struck the ceiling.

He raised his boot and kicked at the door beside the knob with all his might. There was a splintering sound and the lock mechanism tore free.

Jack kicked it again and it flew open. The Belgian paratrooper rushed into the apartment in his now-familiar crouching stance.

There was not the expected burst of fire.

Jack ran into the room.

Hanni was standing in front of the bedroom door, white-faced.

"Bonjour, Madame," the Belgian paratrooper said.

Hanni saw Jack.

"Oh, my *God*! It *is* you! I thought I was losing my mind!"

"Hanni!" Jack croaked.

The bedroom door opened. Jeanine appeared.

"Jacques!" she screamed.

And there was somebody with her. Black. Wearing an animal skin.

"Don't shoot!" Hanni screamed. "He's a friend!"

"Jacques, don't!" Jeanine said when Jack trained what was left of the FN at him.

"Who the hell is he?"

"Captain George Washington Lunsford," the man in the animal skin said. "United States Army, at your service, Sir."

He walked into the room with his hands above his shoulders.

"Jacques, for God's sake," Hanni said, "he saved our lives. Put the gun down."

Jack saw Ursula Craig holding the baby in her arms in the bedroom. Beside her, a large knife in each hand, was Mary Magdalene. Jack went to the bedroom. Mary Magdalene dropped the knives and enveloped him in her massive arms. As her huge body heaved with sobs, and tears ran down her cheeks, she repeated over and over, *"Mon petit Jacques . . . mon petit Jacques."*

"I hate to break that up," Lunsford said, "but there are savages all over the building and I'd feel a lot more comfortable if I had my rifle."

Jack freed himself.

"You OK, Ursula?"

"I am now," she said.

Jack turned to Lunsford.

"Captain, I don't know what you're doing here, but I'm grateful."

"He knew what the Simbas would do once they saw the paratroopers," Hanni said. "He came to protect us."

"If I go get my rifle," Lunsford said, nodding at the Belgian paratrooper, "does he know what's going on, or—"

"*Je suis à votre service, mon capitaine,*" the paratrooper said, coming to attention, and then added proudly, "I speak good the English."

Lunsford went into the bedroom and came back with his rifle. "That radio work?"

"*Oui, mon capitaine,*" the Belgian said.

"Then you get on it and tell somebody important where we are, and to come fetch us."

"*Oui, mon capitaine.*"

"You close the door," Lunsford ordered Jack. "We'll put the ladies back in the bedroom until the cavalry gets here."

"Yes, Sir," Jack said.

[FOUR]
Stanleyville International Airfield
Stanleyville, Democratic Republic of the Congo
1100 Hours 25 November 1964

THE FIRST FOUR VEHICLES of what Operation Dragon Rouge referred to as Van der Waele Column One made contact according to the schedule with Belgian forces at 1100.

They were four armed jeeps. Captain Karl-Heinz Wagner, of the Katangese Special Gendarmerie, was in command. According to Dragon Rouge, when they approached the outskirts of Stanleyville near the airfield, they fired three green signal rockets and waited until the Belgians fired two orange rockets before proceeding.

There is always a shock when driving to Stanleyville through the jungle. The virgin jungle suddenly gives way to civilization. Today the shock was even greater. Just as they left the jungle, a C-130 flashed over their heads on takeoff, so low that they could feel the vibration of the engine, and then a moment later smell the fumes of the not completely burned JP-4 fuel. And before they were halfway down the length of the runway, there was another C-130 on it, this one landing with an awesome roar as the pilot reversed the pitch of his props for braking.

The airfield held as many of the large transports as it possibly could. Captain Karl-Heinz Wagner saw the Belgian paratroopers had set up a perimeter defense of the airfield. He also saw a U.S. Army L-23, a glistening VIP transport dwarfed by the C-130s, parked across the runway from the terminal building, and he wondered what the hell that was doing there.

The command post, he decided, would probably be set up in the airport terminal building, so he headed there. His orders were to report to the Belgian paratrooper commander, Colonel Laurent, and inform him that the head of the column was thirty to forty-five minutes behind him. And then to prepare for Van der Waele's forces to relieve the paratroopers.

As he neared the terminal building, he saw paratroopers loading body bags aboard one of the C-130s which had shut down only two of its engines. And there was a bunch of Europeans standing at the rear of the airplane, waiting for the bodies to be loaded.

He signaled to his driver to pull up beside a Belgian major.

"What's happened?" Wagner demanded.

"About what?"

"How many were killed?"

"We don't know yet," the Major said. "When we first landed, the bastards lined up all the whites they could find and made a human shield out of them. They were marching them toward the airfield when we showed up. Then they opened up on them."

There would be no point, Karl-Heinz decided, strangely calm, in asking the Major if he had a casualty list. Even if there was a preliminary one, it would not be complete.

"Command post in the terminal?" he asked.

The Major nodded. Karl-Heinz motioned for his driver to move on.

Colonel Laurent had his command post set up in the Sabena station manager's office.

"Sir, Captain Wagner—I'm the lead element of Column One," Wagner said, saluting.

Colonel Laurent, who looked exhausted, casually returned the salute.

"The column is about half an hour behind me, Sir," Wagner said.

"You have another officer with you, Captain Wagner?"

"Yes, Sir."

"Turn over to him. You have five minutes."

"Sir?"

Colonel Laurent made a come-here gesture with his hand to a man standing just outside the office. He was wearing a U.S. Army tropical-regions flight suit without insignia, and there was a Model 1911A1 Colt pistol in an Army holster hanging from a web belt around his waist. When he came close, Colonel Laurent said, "This is Wagner, Major."

"You're Karl-Heinz Wagner?" the man asked.

Wagner nodded.

"Glad to see you made it," the man said. "I've been sent to fetch you. Get your gear."

"Who are you?"

"My name is Hodges."

"Fetch me where? Who are you?"

"You want to get your gear? I'll tell you on the way," Pappy Hodges said.

"Fuck you," Karl-Heinz said. "I'm not going anywhere with you."

"You know what DP means, Lieutenant?"

"No," Wagner snapped. "I don't!"

"It means Direction of the President. I've got a DP TWX that says I am to locate you and get you out of here."

"My sister and nephew are here," Wagner flared.

"Oh, shit, I'm sorry," Pappy Hodges said. "I don't know what the fuck's the matter with me. I should have told you first thing. Ursula and the baby and the Portets were on the first plane to Leopoldville out of here. They're all right. Geoff Craig is with them."

"They're all right?" Karl-Heinz Wagner asked very softly.

"They're all right," Pappy repeated. "You know the Portet boy?"

Karl-Heinz shook his head no.

"He's got a busted nose," Pappy said. "He fell off a truck. They evacuated him, too."

"I can't go to Leo?" Karl-Heinz asked.

"You've got five minutes to turn over."

"What about Colonel Hoare?"

"Hey, Wagner, you're in the U.S. Army, not the Katangese Gendarmerie. You get a DP, Lieutenant, you say Yes, Sir and you do it."

Wagner looked at him.

"Yes, Sir," he said after a moment.

"We're in that L-23 across the runway," Hodges said. "I don't want to have to come looking for you. Five minutes, Lieutenant."

The left engine of the L-23 was already turning over when Karl-Heinz ran across the runway to it. He jumped up on the wingroot and climbed in. Pappy Hodges leaned over him to make sure the door was properly closed and then started to taxi across the grass to the end of the runway.

A hand touched Karl-Heinz's shoulder. He turned and found a bottle of Johnnie Walker Black Label being thrust at him.

"Here you go, you fucking Kraut," Captain George Washington Lunsford said. "A little liquid courage for the flight."

Father Lunsford looked awful. He was wearing a flight jacket that had Geoff Craig's wings and first lieutenant's bars on it. And he was obviously quite drunk.

"What's up, Father?" Karl-Heinz asked.

"Well, I don't suppose there will be flags flying and bands playing, but we're going home, pal. Back to the land of the Big PX. And about fucking time, too."

Karl-Heinz took the bottle from him and took a healthy pull.

Pappy Hodges turned the L-23 onto the runway and without slowing pushed the throttles to the firewall.

"If we're going home, why aren't we going to Leo?" Karl-Heinz asked when they were airborne.

"Because there's a President Special Missions jet waiting for you at Kamina."

[FIVE]
Quarters #1, The U.S. Army Aviation Center
Fort Rucker, Alabama
1 December 1964

MAJOR GENERAL ROBERT F. BELLMON walked into his living room. His daughter, Marjorie, was sitting before the television but not seeing anything.

"How goes it, honey?" he asked.

"Did you find out anything for me?"

"No. I told you I have no need to know, and I know better than to ask. If something had happened to Jack, we would have heard. Sandy would have got word to us."

"No news is good news, right?" she said sarcastically. He chose to let it pass.

"If I had to make a guess," he said, "Jack is probably on Ascension Island. That's as far as they would let him go. And the planes didn't return that way. So he's out there waiting for transportation."

He handed her the *New York Times* and the *Atlanta Constitution*. "I asked somebody to get these for me. For you. They'll have more in them than that goddamned *Dothan Eagle*."

The same picture was on the front page of both newspapers, over the caption: *Bloody-Bandaged, Battle-Weary Belgian Paratrooper Tenderly Comforts Rescued Girl in Stanleyville.*

Marjorie glanced at the picture and started reading the story.

"They killed that doctor," General Bellmon said.

"What?" Marjorie asked, and looked up at him.

"I said, they killed that doctor—the missionary. Carlson? It's in there. Just shot him down in cold blood as the parachutists were taking the town."

"Oh, my *God*!" Marjorie wailed.

General Bellmon looked at his daughter in surprise.

"What?"

"Look at that!" she said, thrusting the *Constitution* at him.

"What am I looking at?"

"That's no Belgian paratrooper," Marjorie said, tears running down her face. "That's my Jack! I can tell by his eyes! And that little girl is his sister. I've seen pictures of her. Oh, my God, he's been shot in the face!"

General Bellmon examined the photograph carefully.

"I'll be damned," he said. "I think that's Jack, all right." Then he raised his voice. "Barbara! Come take a look at this!"

Second Lieutenant Robert F. Bellmon looked at the photograph after his mother and then informed his sister that he had been shown a film at West Point demonstrating what miracles of reconstructive surgery were now possible.

Marjorie, her mother saw, was about to respond when the telephone rang.

"Bobby, answer that," Barbara Bellmon ordered very quickly.

"Your brother gets his tact from his father," Barbara said to Marjorie. "But Bobby's right, honey, they can work miracles."

"Hey, Marg!" Second Lieutenant Bellmon called.

"Now what?" Marjorie snapped.

"We got a collect call from Sergeant Jack Portet at Pope Air Force Base, North Carolina. You want to pay for it?"